"THERE'S A FRESH NEW VOICE IN PARANORMAL AND THAT VOICE BELONGS TO AUTHOR CHLOE NEILL."
—Romance Novel TV

Praise for Chloe Neill's
Chicagoland Vampires Novels

Hard Bitten

"Delivers enough action, plot twists, and fights to satisfy the most jaded urban fantasy reader." —Monsters and Critics

"A fast and exciting read." —Fresh Fiction

"A descriptive, imaginative, and striking world . . . rich with real-world problems as well as otherworldly creatures . . . roughly fantastic from beginning to end, with one of the best endings in urban fantasy history." —*Romantic Times*

Twice Bitten

"The pages turn fast enough to satisfy vampire and romance fans alike." —*Booklist*

"Neill continues to hit the sweet spot with her blend of high-stakes drama, romantic entanglements, and a touch of humor . . . certain to whet readers' appetites for more in this entertaining series!" —*Romantic Times* (4½ stars)

Friday Night Bites

"Wonderfully entertaining and impossible to set down." —Darque Reviews

"First-rate fun!" —*Romantic Times*

continued . . .

"A REFRESHING TAKE ON URBAN FANTASY."
—*Publishers Weekly*

Some Girls Bite

"Neill creates a strong-minded, sharp-witted heroine who will appeal to fans of Charlaine Harris's Sookie Stackhouse series and Laurell K. Hamilton's Anita Blake."   —*Library Journal*

"Chloe Neill owes me a good night's sleep. With her wonderfully compelling reluctant vampire heroine and her careful world building, I was drawn into *Some Girls Bite* from page one and kept reading far into the night."
          —*USA Today* bestselling author Julie Kenner

"Smart, sexy, and delightful. A must read."
          —Candace Havens, author of *Dragons Prefer Blondes*

"A fun cast of quirky characters and smoking-hot sexual tension . . . a stunning combination."
          —Tate Hallaway, author of *Honeymoon of the Dead*

"Packed with complex subplots, embittered family members, and politics, this is an excellent first installment to what should be an outstanding series in a crowded field."   —*Monsters and Critics*

"There's a new talent in town, and . . . she's here to stay. . . . An indomitable and funny heroine . . . truly excellent."
          —*Romantic Times*

"Engaging, well executed, and populated with characters you can't help but love."   —*Darque Reviews*

A CHICAGOLAND VAMPIRES NOVEL

BITING
COLD

CHLOE NEILL

NAL NEW AMERICAN LIBRARY

NEW AMERICAN LIBRARY
Published by New American Library,
a division of Penguin Group (USA) Inc.,
375 Hudson Street, New York, New York 10014, USA
Penguin Group (Canada), 90 Eglinton Avenue East, Suite 700, Toronto,
Ontario M4P 2Y3, Canada (a division of Pearson Penguin Canada Inc.)
Penguin Books Ltd., 80 Strand, London WC2R 0RL, England
Penguin Ireland, 25 St. Stephen's Green, Dublin 2,
Ireland (a division of Penguin Books Ltd.)
Penguin Group (Australia), 250 Camberwell Road, Camberwell,
Victoria 3124, Australia (a division of Pearson Australia Group Pty. Ltd.)
Penguin Books India Pvt. Ltd., 11 Community Centre,
Panchsheel Park, New Delhi - 110 017, India
Penguin Group (NZ), 67 Apollo Drive, Rosedale, Auckland 0632,
New Zealand (a division of Pearson New Zealand Ltd.)
Penguin Books (South Africa) (Pty.) Ltd., 24 Sturdee Avenue,
Rosebank, Johannesburg 2196, South Africa

Penguin Books Ltd., Registered Offices:
80 Strand, London WC2R 0RL, England

First published by New American Library,
a division of Penguin Group (USA) Inc.

First Printing, August 2012
1   3   5   7   9   10   8   6   4   2

REGISTERED TRADEMARK—MARCA REGISTRADA

LIBRARY OF CONGRESS CATALOGING-IN-PUBLICATION DATA:
Neill, Chloe.
Biting cold: a Chicagoland vampires novel/Chloe Neill.
p.   cm.
ISBN 978-0-451-23701-9
1. Merit (Fictitious character: Neill)—Fiction. 2. Vampires—Fiction. 3. Chicago (Ill.)—
Fiction. I. Title.
PS3614.E4432B58 2012
813'.6—dc23   2012013109

Set in Caslon 540
Printed in the United States of America

PUBLISHER'S NOTE

This is a work of fiction. Names, characters, places, and incidents either are the product of the
author's imagination or are used fictitiously, and any resemblance to actual persons, living or
dead, business establishments, events, or locales is entirely coincidental.

The publisher does not have any control over and does not assume any responsibility for
author or third-party Web sites or their content.

"Love is a familiar; Love is a devil.
There is no evil angel but Love."
—*William Shakespeare*

BITING COLD

CHAPTER ONE

ON THE ROAD AGAIN

Late November
Central Iowa

It shone like a beacon. More than a thousand feet of skyscraper, the lights at the top of its antennas blinking through the darkness that blanketed the city. The Willis Tower, one of the tallest buildings in the world, was nestled in downtown Chicago, surrounded by glass and steel and the waters of the Chicago River and Lake Michigan. Its bulk was a reminder of where we'd come from . . . and where we were going.

We'd left Hyde Park, our home turf, and were heading west across the plains toward Nebraska and the *Maleficium*, an ancient book of magic that my (former?) best friend, Mallory, was evidently intent on stealing.

My nerves on edge, I tightened my grip on the steering wheel of my companion's sleek Mercedes convertible.

That companion, Ethan Sullivan, smiled at me from the passenger seat. "You needn't look so morose, Sentinel. Nor should you keep looking at the postcard of the city you've taped to the dashboard."

"I know," I said, sitting up a little straighter and scanning the freeway before us. We were somewhere in the cornfields of Iowa, about halfway between Chicago and Omaha. It was November and the corn was gone, but the acres of wind turbines arced in the darkness above us.

"It's just weird to be leaving," I said. "I haven't really been out of Chicago since I became a vampire."

"I think you'll find life as a vampire is fairly similar regardless of the location. It's really only the food that's different."

"What do you think they have in Nebraska? Corn?"

"And steak, I imagine. And probably most everything else. Although your Mallocakes may be hard to find."

"That's why I packed a box in my duffel bag."

He burst out laughing like I'd told the funniest joke he'd ever heard, but I'd told the absolute truth. Mallocakes were a favorite dessert—chocolate cakes filled with marshmallow cream—and they were exceedingly hard to find. I'd brought some along just in case.

Regardless of my culinary choices, we were on our way, so I smiled and worked on adjusting to the fact that Ethan, the once and future Master of Chicago's Cadogan House, was sitting in the seat beside me. Less than twenty-four hours ago, he'd been completely and utterly deceased. And now, by a trick of ill-intentioned magic, he was back.

I was still pretty dumbfounded. Thrilled? Sure. Shocked? Absolutely. But mostly dumbfounded.

Ethan chuckled. "And are you aware you keep looking over here like you're nervous I'm going to disappear?"

"It's because you're devastatingly handsome."

He grinned slyly. "I wasn't questioning your good taste."

I rolled my eyes. "Mallory brought you back from *ashes*," I reminded him. "If something like that is possible, there's not much in the world that's impossible."

She'd raised Ethan from ashes to make him a magical familiar . . . and to release an ancient evil that had been locked away in a book by sorcerers who thought they were doing the world a favor. They had been, at least until Mallory decided releasing the evil would fix her weird sensitivity to the locked-away dark magic.

Fortunately, her spell had been interrupted, so she hadn't actually managed to set the evil free or make Ethan a familiar. We assumed that was why she'd escaped her bonds and was chasing down the *Maleficium*—she wanted another try.

Familiar or not, Ethan was back again: tall, blond, fanged, and handsome.

"How do you feel?" I asked.

"Fine," he said. "Unnerved that you keep staring at me, and pissed that Mallory has interrupted what should be a very long and involved reunion between me and my House and my vampires." He paused and looked over at me, his green eyes fire bright. "*All* of my vampires."

My cheeks burned crimson, and I quickly turned my gaze on the road again, although my mind was decidedly elsewhere. "I'll keep that in mind."

"As well you should."

"What, exactly, are we going to do if we find Mallory?"

"*When* we find her," he corrected. "She wants the *Maleficium*, and it's in Nebraska. There's little doubt our paths will cross. As for the what . . . I'm not entirely sure. Do you think she'd be amenable to bribery?"

"I'm aware of only one thing she wants," I said. "And she has a head start, which means she'll probably get there before we do."

"Assuming she manages to evade the Order," Ethan said. "Which seems pretty likely."

The Order was the union of sorcerers that had been overseeing Mallory in rehab and was responsible for keeping the *Maleficium* safe. All around, they'd done an embarrassingly bad job of both.

"That's funny, Sullivan. Especially for someone who's been alive for barely twenty-four hours."

"Don't let my youthful good looks confuse you. I now have two lifetimes of experience."

I made a sarcastic sound but said a silent thank-you. I'd grieved for Ethan, and it was glorious—all the more for being so unexpected—to have him back again.

Unfortunately, my gratitude was matched by the icy gnawing in my stomach. He was here, but Mallory was out there, inviting an ancient leviathan back into our world.

"What's wrong?" he asked.

"I can't shake the Mallory funk. I'm furious with her, mad at myself for missing the fact that she was the one trying to destroy Chicago, and irritated that instead of celebrating your return, we have to play supernatural babysitters for a woman who should know better."

I rued the day Mallory had learned she had magic; things had gone downhill for her—and by extension, her friends and family—since then. But she'd been my friend for a long time. She'd jumped to my defense the first day we'd met, when a thug tried to snatch my backpack on the El, and it was her shoulder I'd cried on when Ethan made me a vampire. I couldn't abandon her now, even as much as I might have wanted to.

"We're on our way to find her. I'm not sure what else we can do.

And I agree that you should be basking in my glory . . . especially since I took a stake through the heart to save your life."

I couldn't help but grin. "And it didn't even take you twenty-four hours to remind me."

"One uses the tools at one's disposal, Sentinel."

There was a twinkle in his eye, even as the telltale line of worry appeared between his eyebrows.

"Do you have any idea where we're actually supposed to go when we get to Nebraska? Where the silo is? It's a big state."

"I don't," he said. "I'd planned to give Catcher time to get his bearings and then ask for details."

Catcher was Mallory's boyfriend. He'd been employed by my grandfather, Chicago's supernatural Ombudsman until Diane Kowalcyzk, the city's new mayor, stripped him of the title. Like Mallory, Catcher was a sorcerer, but he'd been on the outs with the Order much longer than she had.

My cell phone rang, a herald of news, good or bad.

Ethan glanced at it, then propped it up on the dashboard between us. "I guess he's ready to talk."

"Ethan, Merit," Catcher said in greeting. His voice was gravelly, his tone even lower than usual. He wasn't one for displays of emotion, but Mallory's disappearance had to be wearing on him.

"How are you doing?" I asked.

"The woman I'd planned to spend the rest of my life with is trying her best to open Pandora's box, and damn the consequences. I have had better days. And weeks."

I winced sympathetically. "So fill us in. What do we know?"

"She was staying at a facility not far from O'Hare," Catcher said. "There were armed guards to keep an eye on her and medical staff to make sure she was stable."

"I thought the Order didn't have operations in Chicago?" Ethan asked.

"Baumgartner claims it's not an Order facility. Just an inpatient medical facility where he has friends," Catcher said. Baumgartner was the head of the Order. From the sound of Catcher's voice, he wasn't buying Baumgartner's excuse.

"So what happened?" Ethan asked.

"She slept for a while, woke up, and started talking about her addiction. She seemed self-aware, remorseful, so they removed her restraints for a med exam."

"That's when she attacked the guard?" Ethan asked.

"Yeah. Turns out, she wasn't groggy. The guard's still in the hospital, but I understand they're releasing him today."

"Where did she go?" I asked.

"Transit authority security cameras have a record of her," Catcher said. "She caught the El and then took the train to Aurora. She was spotted at a truck stop, catching a ride on an eighteen-wheeler headed to Des Moines. The trail ran cold in Iowa. She hasn't popped up again since."

Catcher had been the one to put a stop to Mallory's familiar spell by knocking her out. Pity he hadn't knocked her out a little harder.

"So she's probably headed toward Nebraska," I guessed. "But how did she know to go there? How did she know the Order would send the *Maleficium* there instead of to a new guardian?"

"Simon told her about the silo," Catcher said. "And he and Baumgartner visited and talked about the book being transported when she was supposedly asleep."

"That's two more strikes against Simon," I said.

"Yep," Catcher said. "He'd be out of the Order if Baumgartner wasn't afraid of him. Too much knowledge, too little common sense. If he's still a member, Baumgartner still has some authority."

"Tough position to be in," Ethan mused. "Any thoughts on our strategy?"

"First step is to get closer," he said. "You'll want to head toward Elliott, Nebraska. It's about five miles northwest of Omaha. The Order's archivist lives in a farmhouse outside the silo. I'll send directions."

"The archivist?" I asked.

"The recorder of Order history."

"And will he be the only sorcerer guarding the book?" Ethan asked.

"*Her* name is Paige Martin. She's the only sorcerer at the farmstead; she's also the only sorceress in Nebraska. The *Maleficium* isn't always kept there. Since it travels, there's no need for a full contingent. I've asked them to reconsider letting me go," Catcher quietly added. "I want to be there if things go bad. If worse comes to worst. But they're afraid I can't be objective."

We were all quiet for a moment, probably all imagining just how bad things might go, and the possibilities that we couldn't save Mallory . . . or that she wouldn't want to be saved.

"But they'll allow this archivist to be there?" Ethan asked.

"She doesn't know Mallory," Catcher said, "and she's part of the Order. They think she can handle herself."

And they probably thought they could handle her, too. Just like they could handle Simon, Mallory, and Catcher, before he was kicked out. The Order had an awful track record for managing its employees.

"You'd think they could spare one or two more soldiers to stop a problem they created in the first place," Ethan mused.

"Unfortunately," Catcher said, "this isn't the world's only

magical crisis, and there aren't many sorcerers to go around. They're assigned as they're available."

I'd been taught as Sentinel to make do with what I had, but that didn't mean I had to like a bad set of odds, or the thought of similar crises around the world.

"We'll chart a course for Elliott," Ethan said. "Mallory got a head start, so it seems unlikely we'll reach the book before she does. You might warn the archivist, if you haven't already."

"She knows. And there's something else." Catcher cleared his throat nervously. At the sound, Ethan shifted uncomfortably in his seat.

"It's possible you and Mallory aren't the only ones on the road. Seth Tate was released this morning."

I swore under my breath. Seth Tate was the former mayor of Chicago, deposed after we'd discovered he'd been running a drug ring.

Tate was also a supernatural with an old, unfamiliar magic, one that had lifted the hairs on my neck more than once. Unfortunately, we knew nothing else about his powers.

"'This morning' was hours ago," Ethan said. "Why are we just learning this?"

"Because we're just learning it. We aren't employees anymore, so Kowalcyzk didn't feel the urge to fill us in. Our new mayor has decided Tate was framed, in part because one of the individuals allegedly killed at his residence was spotted outside Cadogan House earlier tonight."

"That would be you," I whispered to Ethan.

"And no thanks to Tate," Ethan said. "Do we think he's looking for the *Maleficium*, too?"

"We don't know for sure," Catcher said. "He was pardoned by Kowalcyzk, so the CPD didn't feel they had the authority to follow him, even if they had the resources. And we're short staffed today."

"Short staffed?" I wondered. There were three unofficial Om-buddies, as I liked to call them, in addition to my grandfather: Catcher; computer wizard Jeff Christopher; and the admin, Marjo-rie. None seemed like the type to miss work.

"Jeff called in today. Said he had some things to take care of. Which is only fair since he's not an employee and isn't actually paid to be here."

Logical, sure, but it still seemed weird. Jeff was uncommonly reliable, and he was usually planted in front of his very large computer. Of course, if he'd needed our help, he wouldn't have been shy about asking for it.

"We can't be sure he's looking for the book," I said, "but I wouldn't be surprised to find him in the middle of the action. After all, he was the one who told me about the *Maleficium*." He'd been clearly intrigued by the magic, and it wasn't hard to imagine he'd cash in on an opportunity to grab it. It was too bad I hadn't brought along my worry wood, a token of magic from my grandfather that gave me protection from Tate's more subtle forms of magic.

"No argument there," Catcher said.

"In the unlikely event Tate causes problems in Chicago, you can call Malik," Ethan said. "He can rally the rest of the Cadogan guards."

Malik was the official Master of Cadogan House, Ethan's sec-ond until he'd been killed and still in charge until Ethan was offi-cially Invested as Master again.

"You can also call Jonah," I offered, but the offer was met with silence. Jonah was captain of the guards of Chicago's Grey House, and he'd been my substitute partner while Ethan had been gone. Although neither Catcher nor Ethan knew it, Jonah was also my official partner in the Red Guard, a secret organization dedicated to keeping an eye on the vampire Masters and the Greenwich Pre-sidium, the British council that ruled us.

"We'll cross that bridge when we come to it," Catcher said. "For now, I need to wrap this up. I'll call you if I learn anything else."

We said our good-byes, and Ethan switched off the phone.

"He seems to be holding up," Ethan said.

"He doesn't have much of a choice. He loves her, or I assume he still does, and she's out there head over heels in danger, and he can't do a damn thing about it. For the second time."

"How did he fail to see what she was doing the first time around?" Ethan wondered. "They were living together."

Mallory had set Chicago ablaze in her attempt to make Ethan a familiar. She'd made the magic in the basement of the Wicker Park brownstone she and Catcher shared.

"I think part of it was denial. He didn't want to believe she was capable of the mess she put the city through. And she was studying for exams—and taking them, apparently—the entire time. If Simon didn't suspect anything, why should Catcher?"

"Simon again?"

"Unfortunately. And that's not the end of it. Catcher thought she and Simon were having an affair. Not a romantic one, maybe, but they were becoming too close for his comfort. He was afraid she was going to take Simon's side—the Order's side—against Catcher."

"Love does strange things to a man," Ethan said, his voice suddenly distracted. He tapped a finger on the dashboard. "There's something in the road there. A dog?"

I squinted at the freeway ahead, trying to ferret out what Ethan had spotted. After a moment, I saw it—a dark mass on the centerline a quarter mile ahead. It wasn't moving. It also definitely wasn't a dog.

Two arms, two legs, six foot tall, and standing in the middle of the road. It was a person.

"Ethan," I called out in warning, my first thought that the figure was McKetrick, a Chicago-based vampire hater who'd guessed our route and was ready to launch an attack against the car.

The sudden punch of peppery magic that filled the car—and the cloying scent of sugar and lemons that accompanied it—proved this was a magical problem . . . and a problem I knew all too well.

A cold sweat trickled down my back. "It's not an animal. It's Tate."

We didn't have time to decide whether to fight or take flight. Before I could speed up or change course, the car began to slow.

Tate had somehow managed to take control of it.

I wrenched the wheel, but it made no difference. We were heading right for him.

Fear and anticipation tightened my chest, my heart fluttering like a frightened bird beneath my ribs. I had no idea what Tate was capable of, or even what he really was. Well, other than an asshat.

We slowed to a stop in the middle of the westbound lanes, straddling the centerline. Fortunately, it was late and we were in the middle of Iowa; there wasn't another car in sight. Since Tate had rendered the car useless and there was no point in wasting gas, I turned off the ignition but left the headlights on.

He stood in the beam in jeans and a black T-shirt, his hair ruffled into dark waves. There was a glint of gold around his neck, and I knew instantly what it was. Every Cadogan vampire wore a small gold disk on a chain, a kind of vampire dog tag, that identified their name and position. I'd bargained mine away to Tate in exchange for information about the *Maleficium*.

Ethan had given me the medal, and although I'd gotten a replacement, I didn't like to see Tate wearing it.

"I'm open to any suggestions you might have, Sentinel," Ethan said, eyes fixed on Tate.

Unfortunately, our sharp and sleek Japanese swords were in the trunk, and I doubted Tate was going to give us time to grab them.

"We face him," I said. "And in case we need to make a run for it, leave your door open." Knowing Ethan could maneuver the Mercedes more effectively than me, I handed him the keys, sucked in a breath, and opened the door.

CHAPTER TWO

HE'S A MAGIC MAN

We stepped outside at the same time, two vampires facing down a magical mystery man on a dark Iowa night. It wasn't exactly how I preferred to spend an evening, but what other option did I have?

Tate's eyes darted to Ethan, widening in surprise. "I didn't expect to see you here."

"As you orchestrated my death, no, I imagine you didn't."

Tate rolled his eyes. "I orchestrated nothing."

"You set the wheels in motion," Ethan said. "You put Merit in a room with a drugged vampire who hated her. You had to know I'd look for her and that Celina would react. Since it was her stake that hit me, I think 'orchestrated' is rather accurate."

"We'll have to agree to disagree, Sullivan." Tate smiled drowsily at me. "Lovely to see you again, Ballerina."

I'd danced when I was younger, and Tate had filed that information away. "I can't say the feeling is mutual."

"Oh, come now. What's a little reunion between friends?"

"You aren't a friend," I said, and I wasn't in the mood for a re-union. "How did you get Mayor Kowalcyzk to release you?"

"Easily, as it turns out. There's no evidence against me."

That was a lie. They'd found Tate's fingerprints on the drugs, and his favorite minion, a guy named Paulie, had spilled the rest of the details to the Chicago Police Department.

"Did you tell her your arrest was part of a supernatural con-spiracy?" I asked. "Woo her with your tales of oppression by vam-pires?"

"I've found Diane to be a woman who appreciates a reasonable argument."

"Diane Kowalcyzk couldn't pick a reasonable argument out of a lineup," I countered. "What do you want?"

"What do you think I want?" he asked. "I want the book."

Ethan crossed his arms. "Why?"

"Because our girl made it sound so interesting." His smile was oily. "Didn't you?"

"I'm not your girl, and I didn't tell you about the *Maleficium*."

"So my memory isn't perfect. But I can only assume you en-joyed our visits, or you wouldn't have visited me twice."

Beside me, Ethan growled possessively.

"Quit baiting him," I demanded. "I visited you to get informa-tion, which is the only thing I want now. Why do you want the *Maleficium*?"

"I told you already," Tate nonchalantly said. "I told you when we sat together in my prison of human making, when I advised you the division of evil and good was unnatural, that 'evil' was a human construct. Holding it captive in the *Maleficium* is unnatural. I have an opportunity to right that wrong, to release it. And I don't plan to let that chance pass me by."

There was an intent gleam in his eyes and a shock of chilling magic in the air. There was little doubt he didn't plan to let us stand in his way.

"We don't have it," Ethan told him.

"Given the direction you're traveling, that's obvious. But I also assume you're on your way to retrieve it, perhaps before Ms. Carmichael does something drastic?"

A sickening feeling blossomed in my stomach. "Stay away from her."

"You know that's not possible. Not when we're all racing for the same prize. And besides, she might come in handy."

I felt the rising tide of magic lift further as my own fury contributed to the swell. "Stay. Away. From her," I gritted out, "or you will answer to me."

Tate rolled his eyes. "I could finish you in a minute." Then he looked at me askance, which was even more frightening. Like he was studying me. "I bet it hurts, doesn't it, to feel like your best friend has betrayed you? She isn't so unlike your father in that respect, is she?"

Tate had told me—only moments before Ethan's death—that my father had offered Ethan money to make me a vampire. But that hadn't been the entire truth.

"Ethan didn't take the money, and you know it."

"But he knew, didn't he? Ethan knew your father was asking around, and he did nothing."

"You are a son of a bitch," Ethan said. Before I could stop him, he strode forward, struck out with a mean right hook, and punched Seth Tate in the mouth.

"Ethan!" I screamed out, equal parts horrified that he'd just punched someone in the face . . . and proud he'd done it. Ethan *punched* him. Maybe it wasn't a great decision under the circumstances, but that didn't mean Tate didn't deserve it and I didn't enjoy it.

Tate's head snapped back, but he didn't otherwise move except to raise his knuckles to the lip Ethan had split. He glanced down at the blood there before slowly lifting his gaze to Ethan. Magic poured across us as Tate's anger rose.

"You'll regret that, Sullivan."

Ethan's lip curled, and his gaze narrowed. "Only that I didn't have a chance to do it sooner. Consider it a down payment on what you're owed for arranging the deaths of two Master vampires and putting a third vampire through two months of hell."

Tate shifted his gaze to me. "At least I was able to keep company with you, Ballerina, in his absence."

Another burst of magic pulsed from Ethan's direction, and he bared his teeth maliciously. I put a hand flat against Ethan's chest to keep him from rushing Tate again.

"Stop it," I gritted out.

They growled at each other like animals.

"If you think you can land another punch," Tate said, "I invite you to try."

"I won't have to try," Ethan gritted out, taking a step forward. But before he could lash out again, I wrapped an arm around him and hauled him back.

"Ethan! We have enough trouble right now."

Tate was already in rare form; the last thing we needed was for Ethan to rile him up further—or for Ethan to get riled up any further.

Ethan freed himself from my arms, then straightened his shirt.

The pause didn't diminish Tate's indignation. His magic deepened and strengthened. A thick fog began to seep across the freeway toward us, covering the ground like rolling smoke. It took me a second to realize this wasn't just fog. Filaments of bright blue shot through it, each spark punctuating the air with a sharp, irritating tingle.

Ethan's gaze didn't waver. "We won't let you destroy the world."

"No one is going to destroy the world. If anything, it will be made better—stronger—by a return to the natural order and the rule of natural laws. To that which existed *before*."

The air warmed, and the wind began to swirl around us. Tate stared at me, his body frozen, the energy still growing. Small blue sparks hopped across the fog, like electricity beginning to build toward something big.

This wasn't weather. It was *magic*.

Goose bumps peppered my arms, and I glanced back over my shoulder. Behind us, the fog of magic began to rise, one foot at a time, into a shimmering wall of sparks. My hair stood on end.

I looked back at Tate, whose arms were crossed as he glared at me. He stared back at me with unconcealed malice.

"What are you going to do?" I asked.

"What needs to be done. What *must* be done. You seek to interrupt that which should happen—and should have happened long ago. The emptying of the *Maleficium*. Sorcerers split magic asunder, Merit, and it's time to bring the pieces back together. I won't allow you to stop that. I cannot allow you to stop it."

Whoever Tate had been before—reformer, politician, romancer of women—he'd changed. He meant to stop us, whatever it took.

"Get in the car, Merit."

My gaze was glued to Tate's, so it took a moment for my brain to register what Ethan was saying. I looked back at him. "What?"

"Get in the car. *Now*." Ethan still had the keys, so he pushed me toward the passenger side as he ran for the driver's.

We both yanked open the doors and hustled inside, and he started the car and punched the accelerator, zooming around Tate and farther away from the wall of magic behind us. Whatever Tate's origin, he must have been pouring his power into the magical cloud; I assumed that was the only reason he wasn't controlling the car again.

I yanked on my seat belt as the speedometer climbed. Sixty miles an hour. Seventy. Eighty. We were gaining speed, but when I turned around to check the back window, the wall—now shimmering with blue filaments—was moving ever closer. It was gaining speed even faster than we did, its acceleration exponentially faster than ours.

And that wasn't even the worst part. It was *growing*.

It spread left to right across the median and both strips of the freeway, and it didn't spare anything it touched. The asphalt buckled and split like crushed-up crackers, chunks of debris flying through the air. Trees split and fell with thunderous cracks. A reflective green mileage sign folded in half as if made of construction paper instead of construction-grade steel.

And the distance between us and the wall of destruction kept shrinking.

"It's going to catch us," I yelled out over the howling wind.

"We'll make it," Ethan said, knuckles white on the wheel as he worked to keep the car on the road. Another sign flew past us, barely missing the Mercedes and skittering across the road and into a field on the other side.

The back of the car began to rattle as the wall grew closer, and the world outside went white as fog and mist surrounded us.

"Oh, God," I muttered, grabbing the door handle with one hand and the shoulder strap of my seat belt with the other. Immortal or not, life felt suddenly fragile.

The wheel jerked to the right, and Ethan swore out a curse as he tried to maintain control. "I can't hold it, Merit. Brace yourself."

He'd only gotten out the words when we ran out of time. It felt like we'd been nailed from behind by a locomotive—in this case, a

completely impossible, out-of-nowhere magical storm of a locomotive driven by a would-be book thief with no apparent qualms
about killing those who got in his way.

The back of the car lifted and sent us into a spin, passenger
side first, toward the road's shoulder—and the guardrail that separated the car from the shallow ditch below.

"Guardrail!" I yelled out.

"I'm trying!" Ethan yelled out. He pulled the wheel back to
the left, but his effort was for naught. Winds swirling around us,
the car made a complete circle as it skidded across the road.

We hit the metal guardrail with a head-thudding jolt, but not
even steel could stop the momentum of a Mercedes pushed along
by magic. The car screeched along the rail with all the subtlety of
nails on a chalkboard, before another burst of wind or magic or
both tipped the driver's side into the air.

I screamed. Ethan grabbed my hand, and over we went, the car
rolling sideways over the guardrail and down the hill, somersault-
ing into the gulley that separated the road from the neighboring
land.

Our fall couldn't have taken more than three or four seconds,
but I remembered a lifetime, from childhood with my parents to
college to the night Ethan made me a vampire, and from his death
to his rebirth. . . . Had I gotten him back again only to lose him
again at Tate's hand?

With a final bounce, we landed upside down in the gulley.

The car rocked ominously on its hood, the metal creaking, both
of us hanging from our seat belts.

There was a moment of silence, followed by the hiss of steam
from the engine and the slow squeak of a spinning tire.

"Merit, are you okay?" His voice was frantic. He put a hand on
my face, pushing my hair back, checking my eyes.

It took me a moment to answer. I was alive but completely dis-oriented. I waited until the roaring in my ears subsided and I could feel the parts of my body again. There was an ache in my side and scrapes along my arms, but everything seemed to be in place.

"I'm okay," I finally said. "But I really hate that guy."

He closed his eyes in obvious relief, but blood from a cut on his forehead seeped into his eye.

"The feeling is entirely mutual," he said. "I'm going to get out; then I'll come help you. Stay there."

I wasn't in much of a position to argue.

Ethan braced himself and unclipped his seat belt, then scam-pered out. A second later, his hand appeared at my window. I un-clipped my belt, and he helped me climb out of the car and onto the ground, then wrapped me in his arms.

"Thank God," he said. "I thought that might be the end of both of us."

I nodded and put my head on his shoulder. The grass was wet, and mud seeped through the knees of my jeans, but I was grateful to be on solid ground again. I sat there for a moment, waiting for my stomach and head to stop spinning. But my panic only swirled faster. Tate apparently wanted us dead. What if he was still up there?

"We have to get out of here," I told Ethan. "He could come back."

Ethan wiped the blood from his head and cast a glance up toward the road, body tensed like an animal scouting his territory. "I don't feel any magic. I think he's gone."

"Why go to the trouble of pushing us off the road without checking to make sure he'd really done us in?"

"He's in a hurry to get to the book," Ethan said. "Maybe he only wanted to get there before we did."

He offered me a hand. I stood up and looked back at the car, covering my mouth with a hand. Ethan's car—his beautiful, sleek Mercedes—was a wreck. It lay upside down in the ditch, two of its wheels still turning impotently. It was undeniably totaled.

"Oh, Ethan. Your *car* . . ."

"Just thank God it's November and we had the top on," he said. "We'd be in a world of trouble otherwise. Come here. Let's see if we can get our things out of the trunk."

The trunk had popped halfway open in the fall, so we maneuvered and tugged until we could wedge our bags and swords out of it.

"You didn't hear me," he suddenly said.

"Didn't hear what?"

"Before he threw us off the road, I called you. You didn't hear me?"

I shook my head. Vampires had the ability to communicate telepathically, that power usually, but not always, limited to Masters and the vampires they'd made. Ethan and I had talked silently since he'd officially Commended me into Cadogan House as its Sentinel.

"I didn't hear you," I said. "Maybe that's a side effect of your coming back? Because Mallory's spell got interrupted?"

"Perhaps," he said.

We'd only just pulled our swords out when a shout echoed down from the road. We looked up. A woman in a fluffy down coat waved at us. "I saw that twister throw you off the road. Came out of nowhere, didn't it? Are you okay? Do you need help?"

"We're fine," Ethan said, not correcting her about the twister comment, but casting one final glance back at his former pride and joy. "But I think we're going to need a ride."

Her name was Audrey McLarety. She was a retired legal secretary from Omaha with a brood of four children and thirteen grandchildren scattered across Iowa, Nebraska, and South Dakota. All the grandchildren were in soccer, dance class, or peewee baseball, and Audrey was on her way back to town after watching a dance recital for three of the girls near Des Moines. Late as it was, it hadn't occurred to her to spend the night with her children afterward.

"They have their families to attend to," she said, "and I have mine." She meant her husband, Howard, and their four terriers.

As much as we appreciated the ride, Audrey was a talker.

We drove toward Omaha through pitch-black darkness, past more empty fields and the occasional factory, its lights and steam pulsing across the flat plains like a sleeping monster of metal and concrete.

As we neared the city, the horizon began to grow orange from the glow of streetlights. Fortunately, Audrey had grown up near Elliott and agreed to drive us all the way to the farmhouse. Doubly fortunate, actually, because the sun would be rising soon, and we needed a place to bed down.

We crossed the Missouri River and drove north through Omaha's compact downtown, passing a pedestrian-heavy plaza with a lot of old brick buildings and a hilly string of skyscrapers before popping back into a residential neighborhood. Older houses and fast-food joints eventually gave way to flat fields and farmland, and we ended up on a long, bone white stretch of gravel road.

The road was long and straight, and it divided fields now stripped of their crops as winter approached. Dust rose in our wake, and in the darkness I couldn't see much behind us. That made me nervous. Tate could be hiding there, waiting for us. Ready to strike again, ready to throw us off the road—and on his second try, we might not be so lucky. And we'd have dragged an innocent human into it.

We passed farms that all followed the same form—a main

house and a few outbuildings behind a wall of trees, which I assumed was protection against the wind. The houses glowed under the shine of bright floodlights, and I wondered how their inhabitants slept with the glare . . . or how they slept at all. Something about the idea of sleeping under the flood of a spotlight in the middle of an otherwise dark plain made me nervous. I'd feel too vulnerable, like I was on display.

After fifteen minutes of driving, we reached the address Catcher had given us, large steel numbers hammered into a post that stood sentinel at the end of a long gravel driveway. A farmhouse much like the others sat at the end of it, a few hundred yards back from the road, glowing under its security light. Its wooden clapboards were dark red, and it was accessorized with white awnings and wooden gingerbread in the corners of the small front porch. It had a pitched roof, with one gable over a large picture window. I had a *Little House on the Prairie*–esque image of a girl in a gingham dress sitting behind that glass, spending long winter days staring out at endless winter snow.

Audrey pulled to a stop, and we grabbed our swords and bags, offered prolific thank-yous, and watched the cloud of dust whisk her back toward Omaha.

"She'll be fine," Ethan said.

I nodded, and we walked down the driveway, the world silent except for our footsteps and an owl that hooted from the windbreak. I had a sudden mental image of great, black wings swooping down to pluck me up off the driveway and deposit me in the hayloft of an ancient barn. I shivered and walked a little faster.

"Not much of a farm girl?"

"I don't mind being in the country. And I love woods—lots of places to hide."

"It appeals to the predator in you?"

"Precisely. But out here, I don't know. It's a weird mix of being isolated and completely on display. It's not my bag. Give me a high-rise in the city, please."

"Even with parking permits?"

I smiled. "And the 90 bumper-to-bumper during rush hour." I looked around. Beyond the halo of the floodlight, the world was dark, and I wondered what might be hunkering around out there. Watching.

Waiting.

The owl hooted again, sending goose bumps up my arms. "This place gives me the creeps. Let's get inside."

"I don't think owls feed on vampires, Sentinel."

"I'm not in the mood to take chances," I said. "And we're not long for sunrise." I gave Ethan a gentle push toward the house. "Let's go in, sunshine."

CHAPTER THREE

AN ORDERLY HOME

The worn wooden porch steps creaked as we took them, and the doorbell sounded with a long, old-fashioned chime.

A moment later, a woman opened the door in a pale silk robe she'd pulled tight around her chest. It looked old-fashioned, something a woman might have worn in the 1950s. Her hair was a tousled bob of brilliant red waves, and her eyes were shockingly green—emeralds against her alabaster skin. In a word, she was gorgeous.

Still muddy and bruised from the rollover, I felt mousy and awkward.

She gave me, then Ethan, an appraising look. "Can I help you?" she asked, but then filled in the blank. "You're the vampires."

"I'm Ethan Sullivan," he said, "and this is Merit."

"I'm Paige," she said. "Please, come in." The required invitation offered, Paige turned and padded down the hallway in bare feet, the door open behind her.

I glanced at Ethan, intent on letting him go first, but his gaze was on the woman disappearing down the hallway.

"Ethan Sullivan," I said, jealousy fluttering in my chest.

"I'm not looking at her, Sentinel," he admonished with a wink, "although I'm not blind." He pointed at the hallway.

My cheeks warming, I looked back again. The walls were filled with vertical stacks of books, one beside another, packed so tightly together there was scarcely room between them. And these weren't just discount-table paperbacks. These were the old-school, leather-bound type—the kind you might see in the house of an Order archivist . . . or on the basement table of a rebellious sorceress. As much as I loved books, that made me nervous to step into a space full of magical tomes.

I followed Ethan to the sitting room at the end of the hall. It was small but comfortable, with vintage fabrics and cottagey decor. A small fireplace put the smell of woodsmoke in the air, which mingled with the scents of ancient paper and fragrant tea.

Paige curled up on a couch and picked up a teacup from a small end table. "Sorry I'm a bit of a mess. *She* hasn't shown up yet, and I wanted a few minutes of peace and quiet. Have a seat," she said, pointing at a facing couch with a delicate teacup and saucer dotted with small pink flowers. "Would you like some tea?"

"No, thank you," Ethan said. We took seats on the couch, bags and swords at our feet.

"You have a lot of books," he said.

"I'm an archivist," she said. "It's what I do."

"Read?" I asked.

"Learn and catalogue," she said. "I compile the history of what came before, and I record the history as it happens. And, frankly, I have a lot of time to read out here."

"This isn't quite the frontier," Ethan said.

"For humans, no. But magically? It's basically a vacuum. Isolated, both from magic makers and supernatural populations. That makes it a great place to house the *Maleficium*, when it's our turn to keep it, but not much else."

"Is it here?" Ethan asked.

"Safe and sound in the silo," she said. "So, officially, welcome to the repository for the *Maleficium*. At least for now. When they found out Mallory escaped again, they started making arrangements for a new location."

"Shouldn't they have picked it up by now?" I wondered.

She smirked. "You're assuming they're eager to carry it around. That is not the case. Baumgartner's having to call in substantial favors just to get potential transporters to consider it. Too much risk. When someone finally volunteers, it will be a blind drop to protect their identity. Or supposedly." Paige narrowed her gaze at Ethan. "The Order wasn't thrilled when it was taken from Cadogan House. We all expected it would be safe there."

"At the risk of being insensitive to your concerns," Ethan said, "I was dead when the book was stolen. And it was stolen by one of your own, not a vampire. Who then tried to make me into her familiar."

She tilted her head. "You don't much look like anyone's familiar."

"I'm not, so far as we can tell. Her spell was interrupted before she finished it."

But not before the skies were roiling and Midway Plaisance was aflame, I thought.

Paige scanned him with magical interest. "She got just far enough to bring you back, but not quite far enough to make you a slathering minion. Good for you. On the other hand, that really doesn't say much for Simon."

"Not that I disagree with the sentiment," I said, "but how so?"

Paige shrugged. "She tried to create a familiar, and Simon

didn't notice. That's complicated magic. A lot of bits and pieces. Ingredients, mechanisms, props, and, in this case, the *Maleficium*. Before Baumgartner told me about that part of it, I was going to give Simon the benefit of the doubt about missing what she was doing, but . . ."

"Now not so much?" Ethan finished.

Paige shrugged. "A little spell, a minor charm, a sorceress only has to say a few words. Those bits of magic are more akin to sleight of hand than true enchantments. They're all but illusions, and they don't take long—or much—to manage. It wouldn't have surprised me if Simon had missed those. But making a familiar? That's the real deal. Complicated, picky, and heavy-duty. There would have been signs, not just in her workspace, but on her."

"Working black magic chaps her hands," I said.

"Signs," Paige said with a nod. "And Simon's less of a sorcerer for failing to notice them . . . and failing to stop her."

"And Catcher?" Ethan wondered.

Paige's expression shuttered. "He's not a member of the Order, so it's not my place to discuss him."

She deferred, but the narrowing of her gaze and acerbic breeze of magic said plenty enough: It had been an all-around bad week for Chicago sorcerers. It made me feel better that vampires weren't, for once, the ones causing the problems.

Paige looked at me. "I understand you were friends with Mallory. Has she made any contact with you?"

She said we "were" friends, like Mallory and I had gotten a divorce and gone our separate ways. That thought didn't exactly sit well.

I shook my head. "No contact. Last time I saw her, she was being taken away by the Order."

"And now she wants another shot at the *Maleficium*," Ethan said. "She failed to achieve her goal, and she wants to try again."

"She was trying to put dark and light magic back together," I explained. "Good and evil. Her magic makes her uncomfortable—physically ill—and she thinks releasing the evil in the *Maleficium* will make her feel better. From what I understand, the familiar spell was her means to that end. She thought by working dark magic, she'd tilt the balance of good and evil in the world, and that imbalance would force the evil out of the *Maleficium*."

Paige winced. "That's an ungainly method. It might have gotten the job done, had she been able to finish the spell, but it's not exactly elegant. A spell that awkward is the mark of a young sorceress. Inexperienced," she added. "Do we know if she took books or supplies or anything before she left?"

Ethan shook his head. "We don't know, but it doesn't sound like she stopped for anything. She just left."

"Maybe she had a backup plan ready," Paige suggested, "or she's confident enough that she thinks she can come up with one on the fly."

"So where is she now, do you think?" Ethan asked Paige.

"Nearby and planning, I imagine," Paige said. "If she's still using the same method, she's debating which spell to use and trying to figure out a way to break in here, best me, and be off with the *Maleficium*."

"You're very nonchalant about the fact that a sorceress is planning to come to break in, best you, and be off with the *Maleficium*," Ethan said.

Paige sipped her tea for a moment, as if carefully choosing her words. "I know you're friends of hers, and that she's a big magical deal in Chicago . . ."

"I assume there's a 'but' on its way?" Ethan asked.

"*But*," Paige said, "while Mallory definitely has some mojo, she's really just small change."

"She tried to destroy Chicago," Ethan said, a curious tilt to his head.

"By using the ashes of a powerful Master vampire. That's not exactly like she'd willed the destruction herself, is it?" Paige shrugged. "I'm sure the light show was big, but that's precisely why you want a familiar who has a lot of power—so that you can use their power to beef up yours.

"Look," Paige said. "I'm not trying to be rude, and I'm not trying to make light of the chaos Chicago was facing. But I'm a magical realist, and I don't play favorites. Controlling the universe isn't about pretty lights and colors and irritating humans. It's about *controlling the universe*. And if we're going by the book, what she did barely ranks at all."

"Any thoughts about what spell she might attempt this time?" Ethan asked.

Paige shook her head. "I honestly don't know. I've never actually read the *Maleficium*. Not for lack of curiosity on my part, but it's part of the oath I have to take to serve here. No peeking equals no temptation."

"A sound policy," Ethan flatly said. "Pity no one advised Mallory."

"Could she try another familiar spell?" Paige asked.

Ethan shook his head. "That seems unlikely. The only other vampire ashes in Chicago were Celina's. Suffice it to say they are no longer in Chicago."

Paige nodded. "She could always go the familiar route with something—or someone—else. Beyond that, there are millions of spells in the world, all of them somewhere on the scale between good and evil. She could pick any number of spells on the evil end of that spectrum."

"Speaking of evil," Ethan said, "Mallory isn't the only one who's after the *Maleficium*."

Ethan filled Paige in on our pit stop with Tate and his own goal of unleashing evil. By the time he was done, Paige had abandoned her teacup and was leaning back on the couch, arms crossed, gaze glued to Ethan.

"And this Tate is what kind of creature, exactly?"

"We were hoping you might know," I said.

Frowning, she rose from the couch, moved to the hallway of books, and began to scan the spines. "Unfortunately, there are lots of options, and we don't have enough information to do a fair diagnosis. Demigod? Djinn? Fairy?" She pulled out one book, flipped through it, then slid it back onto its shelf. "Maybe an incubus?"

"I don't know about the others," I said, "but he's not a fairy."

"We work with them," Ethan explained, as mercenary fairies guarded the gates of Cadogan House. But that's not what I'd meant.

"I've also met Claudia, the queen."

Paige's eyes widened. "You met the queen of the fairies?"

I nodded, thinking of the tall, curvaceous, strawberry blond woman. "During Ethan's unfortunate demise. We were looking for the cause of the sky turning red. They're known as the sky masters, so we paid them a visit. They gave us a little information, I nearly bit one of them, and yadda yadda yadda, we learned they had nothing to do with the color change."

"You can't yadda yadda yadda nearly biting a fairy," Paige said.

"You can if the fairy queen baits you into it by shedding fairy blood. Tip for the future: Fairy blood is rather alluring for vampires."

"Noted," Paige said, selecting another book and bringing it back to the couch.

"While we're on the subject of Tate," I said, "I think... something about him has changed recently."

"How do you mean?" Paige asked.

"He's not the man he used to be. For years he was campaigning for antipoverty measures and pushing his 'Tate for a New Chicago' agenda, and all of a sudden he's flipping drugs to vampires?" I shook my head. "That seems odd."

"He's an actor," Ethan pointed out. "And a magical one. The entirety of it was an act."

"For ten years?"

"Ten years could barely be a drop of time for him, for all we know. And he did destroy my car, you'll recall. I'm not exactly feeling friendly toward Seth Tate right now."

"I know. And I'm not, either. If it wasn't for him, you and Celina . . ."

Tightness clutched at my chest at the memory of that look in Ethan's eyes—just as the stake hit him, and just before he disappeared. "Anyway, I'm not suddenly a Tate fan. I just think there was a transition."

Silence, until Paige slapped the book closed and placed it on the floor again. "Enough with the doom and gloom. The sun's nearly up, and I know you need to avoid that. How about I show you to your rooms, and tomorrow night we can take a look at the silo?"

"Is it a good idea for all of us to sleep?" I wondered. Tate and Mallory didn't seem like the types to hunt for the *Maleficium* in broad daylight, but who knew?

"I'll set the house alarms," she said. "They'll alert us if there's magic in the vicinity. Well, they're supposed to." She cast a wary glance at the front door. "Maybe I'll just turn on the regular alarm, too."

"I don't suppose you have any blood?" Ethan asked. "Our stock was in the car, and it didn't survive the trip."

My appetite suddenly perked up.

Paige nodded. "I thought you might need it, especially if things got complicated with Mallory. I'll grab some."

We picked up our bags and swords, then waited for Paige to emerge from the kitchen with a tray of old-fashioned glass tumblers. "This way," she said.

We followed her to the staircase, then to the second floor and a long, straight hallway of rooms.

"The farm's original owners had six children," Paige explained. "The master bedroom is downstairs, and there are six bedrooms up here. You can take your pick." She cast an appraising glance at Ethan. "Unless you're single and interested in sharing the bedroom downstairs?"

"As thoughtful as that offer is," Ethan said, "I must decline. Merit would undoubtedly take another of my lives."

"Disappointing," Paige said. "I've always wondered about vampires. And the biting."

"Every word is true," Ethan cannily said.

Pity I couldn't talk to him silently right now. I might have a few words about his flirting with Paige Martin. Instead, I settled for an arch look that had him grinning back at me. Both the look and his grin made me feel better.

Paige gave us the tray and said her good nights, then disappeared down the stairs, leaving me and Ethan alone again.

The house's six bedrooms were remarkably similar, and it looked like they hadn't changed much since the 1940s. Each held a cast-iron bed, a nightstand, and a bureau. Pale floral wallpaper adorned the walls. The floors were well-worn hardwood, and the bed linens were old-fashioned chenille spreads. They looked like the types of rooms in which children would have hidden old baseball cards and Cracker Jack toys in the backs of the bureau drawers or under the mattresses.

Each room had a single window covered by a heavy velvet curtain. I guessed Paige hadn't wanted to encourage snoopy neighbors.

"Do you have a room preference?" I asked Ethan.

"Whichever you prefer," he said, "since I'll be staying with you."

There was no equivocation in his voice. No question, no request for permission. It was a statement, an announcement of something he meant to do. Something he *would* do.

"Of course you will," I said. "It would be rude to muss two of her bedrooms. We might as well bunk up and save her the trouble."

Ethan rolled his eyes. "That isn't exactly the reasoning I had in mind."

"Oh, I know," I said, walking back to the first bedroom. "But if I don't keep a check on your ego, you'll become insufferable."

He made a sarcastic, but pleased, grunt.

Figuring it made sense to pick the easy exit, I opted for the bedroom closest to the stairs and dropped my bag on the side of the bed closest to the door. I was the Sentinel, after all, and still responsible for my Master's safety.

Without hesitation, Ethan dropped his bag by the bed, then grabbed the glasses of blood from the tray. He handed me a glass, and we drank them dry in seconds, thirsty from hunger and our bodies' healing the scrapes and bruises we'd gotten in the crash.

The necessities addressed, Ethan closed the bedroom door and locked it. When he turned around to face me again, his eyes had silvered—the sign of vampire arousal, emotional or otherwise.

Desire spilled into the room, rising above the scents of blood and leather and the well-oiled steel of our swords.

"We have unfinished business, you and I."

My lips parted. "Unfinished business?" I asked, but there was no mistaking the look in his eyes—or the earnest intent.

An eyebrow popped up, challenging me to argue, but I wasn't about to do that. He'd been gone for two months, and I figured the universe owed me one . . . even when his phone rang audibly from the pocket of his pants.

Ethan's lip curled, but he managed not to look at it.

For a moment, we stood there in silence, staring at each other, desire curling between us like the forks of an invisible fire.

"It could be Catcher," I said, not thrilled about the interruption—but equally unthrilled at the proposition that Mallory was floating around outside the farmhouse and we were ignoring the warning.

With obvious resignation, he pulled the phone from his pocket and checked the screen. "It's Malik. I apparently missed some calls."

I did a quick calculation. "It's nearly sunrise here, which means it's already dawn there. He stayed up—past sunrise—to get you the message. You should take it."

He frowned, clearly torn by duty and desire. Since he'd normally have answered the phone immediately, I took that as a compliment.

At least I could ease the agony of the choice. "Take the call," I told him. "I'm not going anywhere."

He pointed at me. "This isn't over," he said, and answered the phone. This time, he didn't switch it over to speakerphone. As a vampire—and a predator with keen senses—it wouldn't have been difficult for me to ferret out their conversation. But I respected his decision and didn't pry. Besides, as soon as the call was over, he'd probably tell me everything anyway.

I grabbed pajamas and a toothbrush from my bag and disappeared into the small bathroom adjacent to the bedroom.

I probably should have checked a mirror sooner. My dark bangs were matted together, and my high ponytail barely contained a mess of tangles. Dried blood dotted a now-healed scrape above my eyebrow, and dirt still streaked my cheeks. I looked worse for wear, and certainly not like the object of anyone's desire.

Towels and washcloths were folded on a small table on the other side of the room. I wet a cloth and scrubbed my face clean, then pulled the elastic from my hair and brushed it until it gleamed. The bathroom's claw-foot tub had been fitted with a showerhead and wraparound curtain, and I quickly scoured away the rest of the grime from our trip into the Ditch That Ate Ethan's Mercedes.

When I was clean and pajama clad, I walked back into the bedroom, eager for another try at the reunion we'd begun before.

But the second I stepped into the room, I knew it wasn't meant to be. Ethan was still on the phone, and the needle sting of magic in the air foretold that Malik's news hadn't been good. He murmured quietly for a few more minutes, then put the phone away again.

"Give me the bad news first," I requested.

"It seems Malik's 'fuck you' to the receiver did not go over well."

Concerned that Cadogan House was causing problems in Chicago and beyond, the Greenwich Presidium had assigned a receiver, a piece of work named Franklin Cabot, to temporarily take over the House after Ethan's death. He'd implemented awful rules during his blessedly brief tenure, including limits on our ability to meet together and drink blood. Not exactly popular restrictions for vampires who were basically living in a fraternity house.

When Ethan had returned, he and Malik unceremoniously kicked Cabot to the curb.

"How unwell did it go?"

"No decisions have been made yet, but Darius has called a *shofet*. It's an emergency meeting where the GP discusses matters of urgency."

Darius West was head of the Greenwich Presidium. His rank was so high that even Ethan referred to him as "sire."

"Like a rebellious American House that doesn't seem to respect their authority?" I asked.

"Like that," Ethan said, but didn't elaborate. I began to work over mental scenarios about Cadogan's vampires being cast out into the night. Along with the more dire problems, I'd have to find an apartment. In Chicago, in winter. That would not make me happy.

"Exactly how serious is this?"

"Serious enough." Ethan frowned and rubbed his temples.

"Are you okay?"

He smiled a little. "Just a bit of a headache. It will pass."

The atmosphere in the room had changed, from unfulfilled desire to political and magical anticipation. The sun chose that moment to breach the horizon; I couldn't see it through the draperies, but the sudden weight on my eyelids was telling enough.

"It seems certain things are not meant to be," Ethan said.

I nodded, unable to do much more. Vampires slept during the day, not just because direct exposure to sunlight would kill us, but because the rising of the sun pulled us into unconsciousness. We could fight the exhaustion, but it was a hard and losing battle. We'd succumb eventually.

He seemed to understand my hesitation.

"We both have other things, other people, on our minds," he

said. "There will be plenty of time for the remainder when we have addressed this particular crisis."

"And if we can't?"

"We will," he said. "Because I will goddamned see you naked under much more auspicious circumstances before the year is up."

I couldn't help but laugh at that.

Ethan took his turn to freshen up, then emerged from the bathroom in pajama bottoms that didn't leave much of his body to the imagination. His Cadogan medal hung just above the scar that puckered his chest—the mark he bore from taking Celina's stake.

Too soon for my preference, he flipped off the light, and we climbed onto the hard, creaky mattress. Ethan wasted no time in pulling my body against his.

I relished the feeling, the glory, of having him there. Of his warmth, his scent, his energy, his *everything*.

"We can do nothing to stop the rising of the sun," he said. "So let us rest, and we will fight the good fight tomorrow." He pressed me back tighter against him, and his arm snaked around my waist.

Reflexively, I shivered.

"Are you cold?"

"It's a habit. I used to have trouble falling asleep."

"Before the sun?"

"Before the sun," I agreed. "I'd be exhausted, but my mind would race with all the things I needed to do, papers I needed to grade, other nonsense. And so, I developed a little trick."

"Shivering?"

"Imagining. I would hunker down into my blankets and close my eyes, and I would imagine it was wintertime and a storm was raging outside. Freezing temperatures. Chilling wind. Howling blizzard."

"Not exactly a comforting scenario."

"It wasn't the blizzard that was comforting. It was the idea of being safe and warm inside."

"And it worked?"

"I always fell asleep eventually."

Ethan chuckled. "Then tell me your story, Sentinel. Lull me to sleep."

I smiled and closed my eyes. "We're off the coast of Alaska, on a freighter in the Bering Sea. It's late summer, and the air is turning colder. The seas are calm, but there's a brisk wind."

Ethan shivered a bit and stretched against me. Closer to me.

"We're in a stateroom. Nothing plush, but there's a thick, soft mattress. We lie together, the wind whistling outside, the waves beneath us. We close our eyes, and as the world goes quiet, and the snow begins to fall, we fall asleep."

"A nice story," Ethan quietly said. "But I have a tale to weave, as well. Imagine a roaring fire in the dark depths of a Chicago winter. Imagine the warmth of the fire against your skin—"

"I'll probably be wearing flannel pajamas," I teased, but Ethan wasn't fazed. He leaned in, his lips at my ear.

"You'll be wearing nothing but your Cadogan medal and a smile, Sentinel."

"Is that a prediction?"

"It's a promise."

And with the possibility of that promise foremost in my mind, I let my body rest and drifted off to sleep.

✦ ✤✦✤ ✦

CHAPTER FOUR

INTO THE DEEP

When I awoke, the bed was empty, the sheets cool. For a horrible moment I thought I'd dreamt he was back, that his return had been a cruel figment of my imagination.

But the bedroom door opened, and Ethan walked inside, a coffee mug in one hand and small basket in the other. He looked at me and smiled. "You slept in."

"I didn't know vampires could do that." I crossed my legs and pulled my hair back from my face. "I must have needed the rest."

"Your bruises are gone, but you look pale."

I made my confession. "I don't think I slept very well. I'm still afraid to let you out of my sight."

"Because I might disappear?"

I nodded.

"There's no valor in disappearing," Ethan said. "Really, the stake was only worth it for the points it got me. For saving your life twice," he added, in case I hadn't remembered that he'd made me a vampire *and* jumped in front of a stake to save me. As if either was something I could easily forget.

I rolled my eyes. "I'm giving you one week to use the stake against me, and then you're done."

He smiled smugly. "It won't take me one week, Sentinel."

I didn't bother to ask what he was trying to accomplish.

"But for now there's business at hand, and I prefer to have you undistracted when the time comes."

His eyes flashed silver before falling back to emerald green again. A bolt of desire shot through my body, raising goose bumps on my arms and magic in the air.

Ethan and I were both strung taut, our physical reunion clearly on both our minds, but pushed to the back of our agendas because of, as he'd put it, the business at hand.

Mallory's business.

When this was all said and done—and God granted that it would be—I was going to kick her ass for interrupting my time with him, even if I did owe her for bringing him back in the first place.

Ethan sat down on the edge of the bed and handed over the mug—which was filled to the brim with warm blood—and the basket. My stomach growled ominously, and I didn't waste any time sipping the blood while Ethan picked through the contents of his duffel bag.

When the mug was empty, I peeked into the basket. There were four muffins inside: poppy seed; blueberry; one filled with chunks of fruit, nuts, and carrots; and a chocolate version studded with chunks of white and dark chocolate.

It was an easy choice.

"Paige bakes?" I wondered, plucking the chocolate muffin from the basket. It was even *warm*.

"The *Maleficium* is usually settled somewhere else," Ethan said. "And, to paraphrase her, there are only so many Order meeting minutes she can transcribe. She apparently has the time. Is it good?"

He glanced back at me, and I was already licking the chocolate from my fingers. "I'll take that as a yes. You don't mess around."

"Not when there's chocolate at stake." I winced. "Sorry. I probably should wipe that phrase out of my vocabulary."

"Don't change on my account," he chuckled, then grabbed the blueberry muffin.

"You know, feeding me isn't part of your job. I'm perfectly capable of managing my own meals."

He arched a very dubious eyebrow.

"I *am*," I stressed.

"Not to the degree necessary to keep you healthy and able to handle matters like these. Before this is said and done, I wager you'll need every ounce of your strength and every bit of moxie in that stubborn head of yours. Ensuring you're well fed makes that more likely, and it makes my life easier."

I wanted to argue with him but found that I couldn't. Sure, it was irritating that he'd taken my measure and found a flaw. I didn't want him aware that I *had* flaws, much less pointing them out. But it was also comforting. Instead of adding the issue to his mental "red flags" column, he'd figured out a way to cope with it.

What a strange and awesome thing.

He finished his own muffin, then glanced back at me. "What?"

"Nothing," I said, reaching for muffin number two.

When the blood and muffins were gone, we prepared for the possibility of battle. There was no knowing, of course, whether Mallory or Tate would pick tonight or tomorrow or a week from now to seek out the *Maleficium*, but they both seemed impatient enough to force the issue sooner rather than later.

I checked the blade of my katana, ensuring the steel was clean and ready for action, then climbed into my battle-worthy leather pants, a thin, long-sleeved shirt against the chill, and my leather jacket. The leathers were, ironically, gifts from Mallory for my last birthday. It seemed appropriate and sad that I was donning them to take arms against her again tonight.

When I was ready, I watched Ethan dress—jeans and a leather jacket covering his long, lean form—and recalled my current to-do list:

1. Stop and secure Mallory.
2. Stop and secure Tate.
3. Get the hell back to Chicago.
4. See Ethan naked under more auspicious circumstances.
5. Repeat, ad infinitum.

Tasks four and five were, like Ethan, alluring. But for now, we had a sorceress and a something else to deal with, so I belted on my katana. Thinking we were ready to head downstairs, I put a hand on the doorknob, but Ethan stopped me.

"Merit."

I looked back, eyebrows lifted in question.

He moved forward, as swift as a cat, stopped mere inches from me, and stared down at me with hooded emerald eyes. Even in jeans and a jacket, he was so handsome, this blond warrior, with ferocity in his eyes and a sword at his side.

"You'll be careful."

"About what?"

"About this mission."

"As careful as possible," I promised. My tone was lighthearted, but that wasn't enough for him. He put a hand on my arm. "And if she's a threat to you?"

I looked up at him, my heart suddenly pounding.

"She may be a threat," Ethan said. "Mallory has attempted, and likely will attempt again, magic that has no purpose but to harm others, including you."

The fierceness in his eyes made my stomach clench with nerves. The protectiveness was thrilling, but I was afraid it boded poorly for Mal.

"If it comes down to you or her . . ."

I was silent for a moment. "What?"

He didn't finish the sentence; he didn't need to. He was warning me, apologizing for what he might do to Mallory if—*when*—she popped into our lives again. But I didn't want to have this conversation.

"She's my best friend. She's practically my sister."

"And she's put you down with her magic. She tried to destroy the third-biggest city in the country, and she tried to turn me into her servant because she thinks she has the right to unleash evil on the world."

I swallowed down fear and a fierce bolt of sudden anger at Mallory, and I made myself face him. "I can't let you hurt her, Ethan."

His gaze went fierce, and he lifted my chin with his finger and thumb. "I know you love her. I have no doubt of it. But if it comes down to a choice between you and her, my choice is already made."

"Ethan—"

"No," he said, crystalline green eyes boring into me. "*You* are my choice. I told you before—you are mine, by blood and bone. I won't let her come between that, no matter how sick she is."

Maybe seeing the panic in my eyes, his expression softened. "I don't wish it," he said. "I don't want it to come to that. But the decision is made. It is and will be."

"We're not doing this to punish her," I reminded him. "This is a rescue mission. We find her, and we bring her home, safe and sound. All three of us, safe and sound. She brought you back to me, Ethan. I can't forgive her for what she's done, but I can't forget that, either."

He wrapped himself around me, his mouth on mine so suddenly it took my breath away. Then he captured my face with his hands and kissed me with an insistence that left no room for question, or doubt, about who I was to him.

We began as enemies, Ethan and I. He saved my life but was unwilling to accept me for who I was—or I, him.

We grew as colleagues but fought our attraction to each other. And when I was ready to give in to his advances, he let fear lead him away.

He gave his life for me, and I finally admitted the depth of my feelings for him.

And by a miracle—a miracle by a blue-haired girl intent on destroying the world around us—he was back again . . . and she was still the obstacle between us.

Paige's voice echoed up the stairs. "Ready if you are!"

Ethan stepped back and rubbed a hand across his jaw. "We should get downstairs."

I nodded back at him, unsure how to begin again.

Worry heavy in my heart, we met Paige on the first floor. She looked ready for work in heavy pants, black boots, and a short plaid coat with a matching cap and earflaps, her red curls gleaming beneath it. She might have been out here alone, but this girl was serious about her job.

We followed her outside into the crisp fall air. It was a lovely night for late November, the chill in the air just cool enough to be refreshing instead of toe numbing. Paige led us around the farmhouse and into the field behind it, where the grass was short and yellowed. The moon shone high and white in the sky.

"So, Paige," I said, "if you're the only one here, how do you keep an eye on everything?"

"I have friends. The prairie may be empty of sorcerers, but it's not empty of sups. I also have potions. You've heard of Sleepytime tea? I've invented the opposite—a magical pick-me-up. I call it Wakeytime tea. It gives me the energy to keep an eye out."

"That's what you were drinking earlier?"

"No. That really was Sleepytime tea. I took the day off since you were here, too. It made me feel better to have someone else in the house, even if you were unconscious. It was the first time I've slept in days."

I was impressed that she looked so good on so little sleep. I'd have looked like a plague victim on a bad hair day. "You look fantastic."

"Not all of us are vampires with ageless skin. We do what we can. Sometimes we do it with magic."

Paige led us down a well-trodden path across a small pasture and through the gap in a split-log fence. The next field was furrowed, the remains of yellowed cornstalks stumpy along the ground.

"You grow corn here?" Ethan asked.

"Keeping up appearances," Paige said. "There's the entrance to the silo." In the middle of the field, which had to be three hundred yards across, sat a small cube of concrete. "The missile bay doors are hidden under the topsoil."

"The Order definitely picked a hard-to-reach location," Ethan said.

"The armed forces picked it first. We're in the middle of the country," Paige said. "It was a great place for missile defense, if you want maximum protection from the enemy."

We crunched across the frozen ground to the silo entrance, which didn't appear to be more than a concrete box with a utility door. Paige unlocked and opened it, revealing a small metal platform.

"Climb aboard," Paige said, pulling off her cap and revealing a tangle of red curls. "The bunker is thirty-two feet down. The platform's on a scissor lift, so it will take us to the bottom."

The "platform" consisted of a plank of corrugated metal—the kind you could see straight through—and a few strips of railing. Below us was only darkness.

Paige joined me and Ethan, then punched a red button on a giant metal box that hung from one side of the railing. Slowly, and with a metallic *screech*, we began the descent.

I wasn't much for dark, confined spaces. I could feel my chest tightening as claustrophobia took hold. The dim light that glowed beneath us didn't do much to diminish the lingering sense of doom.

After a few seconds, we hit the bottom floor. The platform stopped with a jerk, revealing the end of a long concrete hallway.

"Basement," Paige said, "ladies' accessories and hosiery."

We followed her off the lift and into the hallway, which was cold and silent but for the steady hum of machinery we couldn't see. The air was warm but smelled musty, like the same air had been recycled since the silo had been built. The walls were the glossy, pale green of hospitals and antiquated DMV offices, and they were broken intermittently by more closed utility doors.

Paige pointed at them in turn as we walked to the other end of the hall. "These are all living quarters. When the silo was operational, it was staffed twenty-four hours a day, seven days a week. There were at least two men here at all times—and they were always guys back then."

"Heaven forbid the ladies should accidentally launch a PMS-driven missile," I snarked.

"Precisely," Paige dryly agreed. "We're strong enough to birth children but hardly trustworthy when national security's on the line."

"Is the missile still stored here?" Ethan asked.

"No. It was removed when the silo was decommissioned. But the tube remains. And that's what's helpful for us."

The hallway ended in a giant sliding concrete door. Paige pushed it sideways along its tracks.

"This is the silo," she quietly said, and led us inside.

The room was enormous, a concrete circle with cavernous holes in the middle of the floor. Panels with thousands of small, sharp-cornered buttons lined consoles along the walls beside brightly colored warnings not to touch the buttons without authorization.

I had to curl my fingers into fists to keep from pressing them just to see what might happen.

And the gaping concrete hole where a missile had once stood? Big enough that I had trouble wrapping my mind around the scale of it. I stood at the railing that bound the gap and looked down. The shaft was well lit, and it was lined with steel supports I assumed would have supported the missile.

"The silo itself is one hundred and three feet tall," Paige said, her voice echoing in the vastness of the room.

"And we're roughly thirty feet down," Ethan said, "which means there's seventy more feet of hole below us."

"Correct. The concrete is three feet thick on all sides. Quite impenetrable."

"It boggles the mind," Ethan said, staring down into the abyss.

She pointed to a metal staircase across the room. "There are floors above and below. They hold tanks and more operational controls."

"And the *Maleficium?*"

She walked to the railing and pointed down into the silo. "It's at the very bottom on a pedestal, ironically or otherwise. You can just see it."

I looked down. Sure enough, I could see its red leather cover. It didn't glow or vibrate or give off a weird vibe. It just sat there, minding its own business, holding within it the power to destroy a city and a friendship.

"It's the most secure point in the facility—six concrete doors to get through, assuming you could find your way down there. This place is a maze."

Difficult to maneuver unless you could fly straight down the silo and nab it. Thank God sorcerers didn't actually use broomsticks, although the thought of Mallory in pointy black witch's shoes riding a push broom did a lot to perk up my mood.

"You've done a masterful job making it difficult to get to," Ethan said.

"It's not just to keep people out," she said. "It's to keep the evil in. The world used to be a much harsher place. The sorcerers who created the *Maleficium* thought they were creatively solving a problem—lock evil away and everything's just hunky-dory. As it turns out, a magical book is pretty porous."

"Evil seepage?" I wondered.

"Yep," Paige said. "The mechanism isn't perfect. It's just the best mechanism we have, though, so it's worth protecting."

"Point made," Ethan said.

My stomach picked that moment to rumble impolitely. In the cavernous space of a missile silo, it wasn't exactly a quiet sound.

Ethan shook his head. Paige smiled. "Let's head back upstairs, and I'll start getting a real meal together. You two can explore the property a bit, get the lay of the land. It's a big acreage—a square mile in all, and it's bounded by the roads on all four sides, so if you reach gravel, you've gone too far."

Ethan nodded. "Thank you. Having a feel for the place might come in handy."

Undoubtedly, I thought. The question was, when?

The platform carried us to the surface again. Paige made her good-byes, pulled on her cap, and relocked the door as we stepped outside. The wind had picked up and the air was brisker. I zipped up my jacket.

Paige walked back toward the house, a lonely silhouette in the dark emptiness.

"I wonder if she's being punished—sent out here all alone by the Order," I said. "They have a history of punishing their members." Or in Catcher's case, kicking them out altogether.

Ethan put his hands on his hips and scanned the empty field. "Like this is an island of misfit witches?"

"Something like that, yeah."

"Paige seems to take her job seriously. She doesn't seem like the punished type. Unfortunately, even if she was faking it, I'm not sure we'd know. I'm beginning to doubt there's a single sorcerer or sorceress in existence capable of telling the entire truth about anything."

"Bitter much?"

"With good cause," he said. "Catcher was in denial. Simon was an idiot. Mallory is addicted to something that has the potential to destroy her, and Paige has been stationed out here alone. Neither the Order nor its representatives inspire confidence at the moment."

He gestured toward a line of trees on the other side of the field.

"There's not a lot of visibility over there, and I find that makes me uncomfortable. Let's take a look."

As we walked toward the stand of trees, the sound of moving water grew louder, and the crunch of spent cornstalks gave way to the crunch of dead leaves.

The trees, maybe fifty yards deep on each side, lined a small, rocky creek that flowed into the distance. The trees were old and gnarled, their crabby black branches reaching for the moon-bright sky.

Winter was steps away, and if the sudden biting cold was any sign, it wasn't going to be a nice one. The air had become frosty enough to suck the air from your lungs and bring tears to your eyes.

"It's getting colder," I said.

Ethan nodded. He took my hand, and we followed the stream for a bit in the quiet dark, then crossed through the trees to the edge of another field. This one was bounded by a fence and held a scattering of cows.

"I think I prefer woods to empty fields," I said. "Trees seem safer somehow."

"I suppose," Ethan said quietly. He dropped my hand and rubbed his temples.

"Another headache?"

He nodded, then took my hand again. We made it only a few more steps before he wrenched his hand from mine and began scrubbing his hands across his arms.

"Christ almighty," he swore.

"Ethan?" I tentatively asked. He was obviously in pain, but I had no idea how to help. And when he looked at me, there was fear in his eyes that made my blood run cold.

"Is it Tate again?"

He shook his head.

"Is it the accident? Did you hit your head?"

He reached out for a nearby tree, bracing his arm against it. "You told me Mallory said her need for the dark magic was uncomfortable. An irritation."

I nodded, fear squeezing my chest tight.

"I think I feel that itch beneath my skin."

My eyes widened. "You can sense what she's feeling?"

He squeezed his eyes shut and balled his fists on his forehead like he was holding back a scream. "It's infuriating. Like fire beneath my skin. Like things are wrong."

"When did it start?"

"Just now. This is the first time . . . this has happened."

But was it? Ethan's rebirth hadn't been unicorns and rainbows at first. He'd managed to walk through smoke and fire back to me, only to collapse a few minutes later.

"On the midway, you collapsed. You fell down right after she resurrected you."

"I don't remember that," he said.

I thought back to that moment, looking for some fact that might link what had happened then and what he was feeling now. "You walked across the grass. Jonah saw you first."

"Where was Mallory?"

"She was unconscious. Catcher had knocked her out." She'd passed out, and then he had, too. I worked to keep my voice steady. "Do you think you're connected to her somehow?"

He shook his head. "I don't know. Had the familiar spell been completed, I certainly would have been. But she didn't manage to finish it."

"Maybe what she did finish was enough," I said, and the fears began to pummel my brain. *Please*, I silently prayed, *please don't let her turn him into a zombie.*

He squeezed his eyes shut and grunted, his face contorted. "It hurts. If this is what she's feeling, I get it. I understand the pain."

I felt a sudden sympathy for her—not for what she'd done, but for the demons she'd had to fight along the way. They didn't excuse her behavior, but if this was what she was feeling, they certainly explained it a little: better to destroy the world than to let it drive you completely crazy.

"But you wouldn't harm others to be rid of it," I quietly reminded him. "Why are you feeling it now? Can you tell if she's upset? Angry?"

He opened his eyes, his face still tight with pain. "Maybe. I don't know. But I think she's nearby."

I put a hand on the pommel of my sword and opened myself to any hints of magic in the air. But there was nothing. If she was nearby, I couldn't tell. "Do you know where?"

Ethan shook his head. I could tell he was struggling to maintain his composure, but I wasn't about to give up on him or let him succumb to whatever was overcoming Mallory. And I realized that if he couldn't overcome it—a vampire with four hundred years of experience in dealing with magic—how could we possibly ask her to?

I tipped his chin up so that he was forced to look at me. And then I recalled all the speeches he'd ever given me, and all the motivational things he'd ever said, and the fact that he'd never let me quit or stop when something big was on the line.

"Ethan Sullivan. You are four hundred years old, killed and resurrected twice. You are stronger than she is. Fight back. Do not let a self-centered sorceress bring you to your knees."

He tried to look away, but I held his chin tight, red welts

appearing beneath my fingers. I'd been a vampire for less than a year, but I was a strong one. Might as well show it off for a good cause.

It worked: When his gaze found mine again, there was fury there. His eyes had changed from emerald green to molten silver, and he clearly wasn't pleased with my attempt at an intervention.

"Watch your tone, Sentinel."

Mimicking him perfectly, I arched a single eyebrow. "You watch your tone, Sullivan. You will not allow a child to make you weak. She is no vampire. She is no predator. She is a *witch*."

There was a rumble deep in his throat. He was getting pissed, so I knew I was on the right track. It was just a matter of making him remember what he was.

"You are a vampire," I repeated. "A predator among predators. A creature of deep nights and full moons. But you have learned to survive in an urban environment. You have learned to block out the sensations you don't need. Mallory is one of those sensations. The feelings aren't yours—they're hers. So suck it up, and block them out."

He shivered as he fought for control, trying desperately to separate what he felt from what she felt.

I saw the moment Ethan's control kicked in—his eyes flashed back to green shards of ice.

"Thank you," he quietly said, unusually still with the effort of keeping her angst in check.

"You're welcome."

We looked at each other for a moment, and something passed between us. Something new. For months, I'd been comforted by others, and now I was comforting him . . . at least until a sharp pain radiated from my shin.

"Ow!" I yelped, instinctively looking down—and staring in shock.

There, at my feet, tapping his foot impatiently, stood a brightly uniformed . . . Well, he looked like a garden gnome. White cap. Stumpy shoes. Long beard. Red pants and green shirt. Just like the kind you'd see in someone's backyard. Except for the sulking. Which he was clearly doing.

"If you two are done with all the lovey-dovey crap," he said, "can we get down to business?"

"Well," Ethan said, eyebrow arched at the man at our feet. "I did not expect that."

CHAPTER FIVE

GNOME SWEET GNOME

I could hardly form words. "Are you—you're a—"

"Gnome, yes. Clearly. *Obviously*." He sighed with obvious irritation. "Let's go."

"Go where, exactly?" Ethan asked.

The gnome rolled his eyes and dropped his shoulders dramatically. "You're here to help take care of the witch. We're here to help take care of the witch. And the witch is clearly brewing something up, so we need to take our positions and prepare to kick her ass."

Okay, the gnome had a potty mouth. Which was an odd juxtaposition.

"Wait," Ethan said, holding up a hand. "Paige made you to help her guard the book?"

His lip curled in anger, the gnome tottered forward and kicked Ethan in the shin.

Ethan spewed out a curse, but he had it coming.

"No one *made* me, bloodsucker. I am what I am. We help Paige only because we don't want the world to go completely crazy just because some stuck-up Chicago sorceress can't mind her own business. I don't especially like sorceresses; they don't get me. Much like vampires." Then he muttered something under his breath about vampires and arrogance and our being "basically really big mosquitoes."

"Okay," I said, "let's all calm down." I looked down at the gnome. "I'm sorry for the confusion. We weren't aware you were working with Paige. And we didn't catch your name?"

One eye squinted closed, he looked me over, gauging my trustworthiness. "My name is Todd."

Not the type of name I would have expected for a gnome, but fine all the same. "Todd, I'm Merit, and this is Ethan."

"Nice to meet you. Now that we're all buddy-buddy, we should probably deal with that."

"With what?" Ethan asked.

Todd pointed across the pasture. The scattering of clouds above the field had turned blue, and they were swirling with a speed that wasn't natural.

I'd once joked with Jonah that we'd find the source of the city's magical drama when we found the giant sucking tornado that marked the spot. I must have been right.

"Is she controlling the weather now?" I wondered aloud.

"It's not a real tornado," Todd said. "It's magic."

Visible magic, just like Tate could do, which did not make me feel any better.

Ethan winced, squeezing his hands closed as, I assumed, he battled Mallory back mentally.

"You okay?" I asked him.

"I'll manage," he said, but as a harsh, magical wind that smelled of smoke and sulfur began to pour across the land, I wasn't exactly confident he was going to stay that way.

I looked down at our new ally. "What's the plan, Todd?"

Todd adjusted his small, conical hat. "We stop this. There are more of us than there are of her."

His confidence was surprising . . . and not entirely believable. I couldn't imagine the three of us were going to be much of a match against a woman who had the power to move heaven and earth.

"Three to one aren't great odds," I said.

Todd laughed mirthlessly. "No, but they aren't the correct odds, either. Guys?"

The forest floor erupted into a carpet of gnomes. They emerged from open splits in nearby trees and what looked like burrows in the ground, and spilled out around us, probably a hundred in all, all in the same primary-colored uniforms and white caps, long beards extending nearly to their belts.

The ground looked like the overstock aisle at a garden accessory store.

Todd put his fingers between his lips and made an ear-shattering whistle. Like troops before a flag, they gathered to attention.

"The witch is nearly here," he said, "and we know what she's going for."

The gnomes nodded in agreement, and there were whispers of "the book" across the sea of them.

"Across the woods and stream is the door to the silo," Todd said. "She must not reach it or the book. She must not cross the stream. We cannot allow it, or for the evil to fly across the land again."

Todd pointed at a gnome who was wearing a particularly garish pair of plaid pants. "Keith, take the left flank. Mort, take your crew down the right. Frank will cross the stream and keep an eye on the rear, and I'll lead my crew head-on."

Those orders given, Todd began discussing specific strategies with his troops. It was an amazing thing to behold, and I was ashamed I'd doubted him and assumed he was any less of a soldier because of his stature. He ordered his troops around with the aplomb of a seasoned general and the adeptness of an expert tactician.

Unfortunately, not even Todd was entirely sure what Mallory would do—and I wasn't, either. I knew she could work a spell, and I knew she could throw orbs of magic that hurt like hell when they made contact. (I'd had orb-avoidance training with Catcher.) We all knew what she wanted, and we knew she was intent on doing whatever it took to get it, regardless of how many people she hurt along the way.

When the gnomes began to take their positions, I looked to Todd. "What do you want us to do?"

"What can you do?" He didn't sound confident he'd be impressed by my answer.

I tapped the pommel of my sword. "We're both good with steel. Also, I know her. I could help with distraction."

"How so?"

I looked around. "If the goal is keeping her on this side of the trees, maybe I can distract her so your troops can surround her? It might help your flanks get better position."

"That's not a horrible idea," Todd said, but Ethan wasn't impressed.

"You will not use yourself as bait," he gritted out.

I hadn't thought about it in those terms, but he probably wasn't too far off base. And I knew he meant it protectively, but my safety was secondary. Our first—and only—priority was keeping Mallory away from the *Maleficium*.

I faced Ethan. "I still stand Sentinel of Cadogan House," I reminded him. "I'll do what it takes to keep you safe."

"Merit—"

"Ethan," I quietly, but sternly, interrupted. "*I* have to do this, and you know it. I can't stand around and let other people fight this battle for me. I have more honor than that. You wouldn't have let me stand Sentinel otherwise." But was it honorable? I was helping set up my best friend for an ambush. Sure, I wanted to throttle her and scream at her, but I didn't want her hurt.

"How exactly are you going to stop her?" I asked Todd.

"We're gnomes," he said. "Skilled warriors."

"Could you not kill her? Please?"

Todd blinked at me, that simple action showing me exactly how stupid he thought that was. "We're gnomes, not humans." He cast a telling glance at the sword at my side. "Our goal is to keep her out of the silo, not put her in the ground. If we best her, she'll have no choice but to submit to us. It's a rule of civilized combat."

It might be a rule of civilized combat, but I seriously doubted Mallory had taken any classes in that.

Our roles decided, Todd joined his company of troops, and they began to take their positions. Their departure left Ethan and me alone. It took a moment of courage before I could look back at him. I hadn't exactly given him a chance to speak his piece.

It went pretty much as poorly as I'd expected. His eyes were glassy green, and magic rolled off his body like an angry tide.

I knew he wasn't angry at me, not really. He was afraid. Afraid that I'd be injured, or that I'd sacrifice myself to save Mallory. I couldn't eliminate his fear, and I couldn't prevent the violence that would likely come to pass, but maybe I could remind him that he'd prepared me for it.

"You know, you're the one who trained me to stand Sentinel. To be a warrior. At some point, you have to trust that I was paying attention." My tone was lighthearted, and it was precisely the wrong course.

He grabbed my arm—hard. And in his eyes was a sudden storm of fear and anger. "You will not sacrifice yourself because of her."

I could all but see his temper rise. Was this about Mallory? The overflow of her magic?

My arm ached beneath his fingers. "I don't have any intention of doing that," I assured him, wiggling my arm to free myself. But he wouldn't budge. His fingers tightened.

"Distract her if you must, but let them bring her down. This isn't your fight. It's hers, and she has enough to answer for without adding your name to the rolls."

"I'll be careful," I promised. "Now relax and let go of my arm. You're hurting me."

His eyes widened, and he froze, then pulled his hand back and stared at me, horror in his eyes. "My God, I'm sorry. I'm so sorry."

I rubbed my arm absently.

He looked at me and opened his mouth to speak, but it was too late for more words.

"The eagle has landed," called out one of the gnomes.

It was like something from *The Wizard of Oz*. Out of the swirling clouds dropped a giant glowing orb as large as a compact car. It rotated and split open in a flash of light, and just like a good witch, Mallory stepped into the Midwest.

But there were no coiffed curls or magic wand or glittering gown in this story. In fact, I barely recognized her. She looked awful, and an awful lot like an addict in the throes of a bad craving. I'm not sure what the Order had done or what she'd been through since she left, but she seemed to look even worse than she had the last time I'd seen her. Thinner and sadder. Her hair, once blue, had lost its color and luster. It now hung blond and limp at her shoulders. There were dark circles under her eyes, and her cheeks looked gaunt.

But her appearance didn't faze the gnomes. It took only a second for them to launch their attack. As the cows scattered to the other side of the pasture, they revealed long wooden bows and began showering Mallory with a spray of feathered arrows.

I winced on her behalf but shouldn't have wasted the effort. She might not have looked her best, but the girl had undeniable skills. She threw out a volley of magical sparks that incinerated the arrows on contact. The air glowed like the Fourth of July . . . if it had commemorated a battle against a self-interested witch.

I glanced behind us. Where was Paige? All things considered, this was really her fight. She should have been out there by now, fighting back with the magic that we didn't have.

Another unit of gnomes stepped forward, springing a net of vines hidden in the dirt beneath Mallory's feet. She was pulled up and into its grasp, but she quickly recovered and blasted the net into a thousand tiny wicks. The net collapsed and dropped her to the ground again with a thump.

She looked pissed.

I had been surprised by Mallory's appearance, but that emotion paled in comparison to the shock I felt at what she did next. Without any warning to the gnomes, and without any apparent hint of remorse, she threw out an orb of magic that whipped the gnomes back like rag dolls. They hit the ground, obviously unconscious, if not worse.

And she didn't stop with one. She threw orb after orb until she'd cleared a twenty-foot circle around her.

It was time to go for broke. I looked at Ethan, who nodded. With swords in our hands, we stepped out of the trees and prepared to do battle.

"Mallory Carmichael!" I called out. "Stop this right now!"

She rolled her eyes with the arrogance of a self-absorbed, sadistic teenager. "Walk away, Merit, or bring me the *Maleficium* and we can all leave together like one big happy family. I know you don't want anyone to get hurt."

She was right, but it wasn't as if giving her the book would actually save lives. She'd already thrown aside a dozen gnomes like they were nothing more than scattered leaves.

On the other hand, if she wanted me to bring the *Maleficium* to her, maybe she wasn't entirely sure where it was. We could work with that. I stalled, giving the gnomes time to regroup a bit.

"We've talked about this before," I said. "Releasing evil isn't going to fix you. You've put supernaturals and humans in danger, wreaked havoc across Chicago, and you're AWOL from the Order. Give this up so we can all go back to our lives."

"You know I can't do that," she said, and that's when I could see it—the regret in her eyes. She knew what she was doing was wrong, but she was doing it anyway. Doing it despite the damage she'd caused and would keep causing.

"This book won't help anything," I pleaded with her. "It will only make things worse."

"Really? It helped you. You got Ethan back."

She was simultaneously right and wrong. "I'm glad he's back, but you didn't do that for me, and you didn't do it for him. You used him to get what you want—and you used me to get his ashes out of the House. If he thought destroying the city was the cost of bringing him back, even he wouldn't have paid that price."

"Don't be dramatic."

"I shouldn't be dramatic? I'm not the one who landed in Nebraska to steal something that doesn't belong to her."

"Do you have any idea what I'm going through? What I'm feeling right now? It hurts, Merit! Physically. Mentally. Emotionally. The only thing that will make it better is balancing the magic in the world."

I could see the pain etched into her face. And as she faced her pain, Ethan screamed out and fell to his knees, clutching his head.

They were connected. Tied together, somehow, as a result of her magic, and there was nothing I could do to stop it. My heart skipped a beat, watching him there in pain and knowing I was helpless to intervene. But I could be brave and face her down, and so I stepped forward.

"This ends now, Mallory." I stepped forward, katana at the ready. "You'll get the *Maleficium* over my dead body."

She looked back at Ethan, and I thought for a second I'd finally gotten through to her, that she was actually considering the consequences and implications of her actions.

But I was doubly wrong. She hadn't been looking at Ethan . . . she'd been looking at Keith, the gnome of the horrendous plaid pants.

She rolled together another ball of magic, then pitched it at him. He screamed out as the shock of magic hit, but then froze for a moment.

As we all watched in horror, we realized Mallory hadn't meant to kill or even stun him.

She meant to *change* him.

Keith began to stretch and expand. His shoulders widened, and his arms grew into tree limbs. His torso tripled, and his legs lengthened until his head rose over us to horrific proportions, from a smiling two-foot-tall gnome to a twenty-foot-tall lumbering beast. He looked down at me and grinned menacingly through domino-sized teeth, and it wasn't a pleasant smile.

Mal hadn't just made him larger; she'd made him meaner.

"Oh, that is just wrong," I muttered.

I swallowed down fear, took a defensive stance, and held up my sword, preparing for battle.

Keith stumbled toward me, hands extended as if he meant to swipe me up off the ground. The gnomes might have been spritely in their original size, but stretched and expanded like Silly Putty, he lumbered about. Of course, he was throwing a lot more weight around.

I felt miserable about striking back at him; it wasn't his fault Mallory had turned him into a monster. So I tried other tactics. It didn't take much effort to run around and avoid him. Although I'm sure the sight was comical—sword-bearing vampire being chased around a cornfield by a twenty-foot-tall garden gnome—I hoped I might be able to wear him out before he could do any real damage.

Todd was a little more optimistic.

"Keith, stop this!" Todd ran in front of him, arms waving. "Snap out of it, man. This girl is on your side. You don't want to hurt her."

I instantly forgave Todd for the kick on the shin. But if there was any bit of Keith that remembered Todd or anything else of life before Mallory, I couldn't see it. His eyes—oversized and shaded by his giant white cap—were empty. Not just dazed, but completely void of emotion or recollection or any intellect at all.

Poor Keith.

And goddamn Mallory.

Even if we brought her back from the brink, I'm not sure I could ever forget, or forgive, what she was willing to do to get what she wanted. But that problem assumed we would survive to bring her back, so first things first . . .

Keith swiped at Todd, knocking him off his feet. I held my breath, but he sat up a moment later and signaled the gnomes. They launched another attack, this time on one of their own.

While I helped Todd stand again, the gnomes peppered Keith with rocks and their few remaining arrows, but Keith was big enough to ignore the few pricks that made it through. He howled out when an arrow caught him in the shin, yanking it out and tossing it to the ground, and then stomping around to try to catch the gnome who'd gotten the lucky shot.

The battlefield silenced for a moment, and Todd's eyes went cold. He looked up at me.

"He is gone," Todd said. "Perhaps if we knocked him out, magic could be worked?"

I didn't waste time arguing. I ran toward the middle of the field, where Keith was throwing clumps of dirt—and probably some chunks that weren't actually dirt—at the gnomes around him.

"Keith!" I called out, facing him with sword extended.

He looked back, then stomped toward me.

"I'm sorry," I murmured, and when he swung down a meaty hand to knock me off my feet, I slashed out with the katana.

I caught the back of his hand. Blood splashed the ground, and Keith yelped in pain, a horrible sound that probably woke the few remaining farmers who hadn't already been awakened by the giant garden gnome tromping around their neighbor's land.

I paused for a moment at the sight of blood, afraid I'd be overtaken by the need to drink. But there was nothing remotely palatable about the smell of it. It smelled of dirt—not dirty, but damp and mineral. Not an altogether bad scent, but nothing I wanted to drink.

Not that Keith would have given me the opportunity to do so. Monstrous teeth bared, he wrenched in the other direction. I hit the ground to avoid the swing of his palm, but I wasn't far enough to avoid the swing of his fingers. They hit me like tree logs, tossing me ten feet across the field. I landed facedown with a bounce that echoed through my body and radiated pain through my limbs.

There was no time to rest. The earth shook as Keith moved closer. I winced at the stabbing pain in my ribs—another rib broken, I guessed—and slowly got to my feet.

A bundle of gnomes came again to my defense, but they were soon out of weapons. Keith tossed them away like irritating gnats, then turned his gaze on me again.

He bounded toward me. Ignoring the pain in my side, I two-handed my katana and drove it into his foot. He howled with pain. When he bent over to clutch at his injury, I pulled my sword away and ran through his legs.

Before he could get his bearings, and before I had time to think better of it, I jumped onto his back and scrambled upward. My weight distracted him from the pain, and he stretched and twisted back and forth, trying to throw me off.

It was like the world's strangest amusement ride . . . but all good things must come to an end.

My broken rib hardening my heart against the violence, I climbed to his shoulders, adjusted my sword, and thrust the butt-end of the sword handle into the pressure point behind his ear. *Hard.*

Keith froze, then began to fall toward the earth. I jumped away to safety, rolling across the ground while he hit the earth like a fallen tree.

The night was silent for a moment.

I brushed hair from my face and stood up again, looking around until I found Mallory. She stood nearby, her expression suddenly horrified, her gaze on the giant gnome on the ground. He was out cold.

I wiped the mud from my katana on my pants and walked toward her, stopping ten feet away.

"Any more minions you want to create, or are you ready to face me on your own?"

When she didn't answer, I moved closer.

"It's me and you," I said, only inches away. "Are you ready for that? Are you willing to kill me to get what you want?" I rotated the sword in my hand, hoping I might intimidate her at least enough to let her guard down.

"I'm not afraid of you."

"That's funny, because I'm afraid of you. I'm afraid of who you've become and who you're going to be if you finish this the way you want to. I'm afraid you'll never come back from it."

"I'm not afraid," she repeated, but there was clearly fear in her eyes. As much as she wanted the *Maleficium*—as much as she believed she needed it—she was scared.

Good. Maybe the Order had managed to talk a little sense into her in those few hours before her escape.

Thinking I was making progress, I kept pushing. "Look at what you've done. You've hurt people, Mallory, for a spell you think is going to make your life better. But if that was true, wouldn't the sorcerers have done it by now?"

"They don't understand."

"Then make them understand. But with words, not by turning our lives upside down."

No response.

"Please," I quietly said. "Just come home with me. You can see Catcher and talk to the Order. We can try to get you back on track.

I know it will be hard, but you can do it. I know you. I know who you are and what's in your heart."

Silence. And for a moment, I thought I had her. I thought I might have convinced her to give up her misguided quest for peace of mind and go back with me to Chicago.

But it wasn't to be. She suddenly looked up, like a deer scenting a predator in the woods, then looked at me.

"This isn't over," she said, then disappeared in blue light of her own making.

CHAPTER SIX

SWORDPLAY

The world was quiet again.

"Where did she go?" Todd asked. His hat was dirty and rumpled, and his clothes were torn and filthy. He'd had a hard night.

"I'm not entirely sure." I glanced around, momentarily panicked that I wasn't sure where Ethan had gone. He was rising from the ground at the edge of the trees, a couple of gnomes assisting him. But he still winced at the apparent pain, and his steps were labored as he joined us.

"Are you all right?"

"Headache," he said. "And still dizzy."

"Is she still nearby?"

He closed his eyes and nodded.

"So you're definitely connected to her?"

He opened his eyes again. "Emotionally, I think. I feel her anger, her stress. Her addiction." He looked at me with apology in his eyes. "Her frustrations."

I think he meant to apologize for grabbing me, but we could have that conversation later. "If she's still here, where is she?"

"She didn't make it through the trees," Todd said. "So she couldn't have gotten into the silo."

"And Paige?" Ethan wondered. "Where is she?"

"And how did she miss the fight?" I quietly wondered.

But that question answered itself as soon as I'd asked it. I closed my eyes . . . and smelled the faint aromas of lemon and sugar.

"What is it, Sentinel?"

"Tate is here." My heart began to pound in anticipation.

"How do you know?"

"He has a scent—lemon and sugar." I felt stupid suggesting it—what supernatural creature smelled like sugar cookies?—but there was no denying the scent, or whom it signaled.

Ethan didn't seem to think it strange. "If he's here, and you already know it, why doesn't Paige?"

"I think we need to get back to the house," I said, and I started running, with Ethan following me.

We'd gone far enough in exploring the property that we'd ended up on the other side of the house and silo, and I nearly tripped crossing uneven ground that wasn't familiar. I vaulted two fences, my heart pounding, before the back of the house appeared on the horizon again. I ran around to the front door, which stood wide open, the foyer floor littered with books, their pages open and fluttering gently in the breeze.

Ethan stepped behind me and swore softly.

"Paige?" I called out, treading carefully down the hallway. The living room was empty and dark, as was the kitchen. I kept walking, then peeked into the room I assumed was the master bedroom. It was empty, the bed neatly made, the light off.

"Paige!" I called out again, but the house was silent, and there wasn't even a hint of magic in the air. Nothing but the lingering, cloying scent of lemon and sugar.

"She isn't here," I said.

"I don't suppose we need to ask where she's gone," he said.

I didn't think so, either. "The silo," I said. "They want the *Maleficium*, and that's where it is." And I feared that wasn't the worst of it. Mallory had disappeared just before I caught Tate's signature scent on the wind—but she'd been nowhere near the silo or the *Maleficium*. And we'd been so busy handling her that we hadn't had time to think about Paige or Tate . . . or the entrance to the silo.

Could Mallory and Tate have been working together?

I looked at Ethan. "I think Mallory may have been a distraction."

"A distraction?"

"Tate and Mallory both want the book. Mallory knows it's in the silo, and a little Internet research would have shown her where the door was. If finding it was that easy, why did she pop up so far away from it?"

"She was a distraction," Ethan said. "She was there to draw us away while Tate found Paige and forced her to show them where in the silo the book was. But why would Tate and Mallory work together? How would they even have found each other?"

"I don't know," I said. "But why not work together? Mallory wants the book, they both want the evil to be released, and there are more of us than there are of them. They both have magic, but so does Paige, and they couldn't have known what kind of security would be waiting for them."

I walked back to the front door and glanced outside, but there was no other sign anything was amiss. The farm looked like a farm at the edge of winter, waiting for snow to fall, and snow to clear, and seed to be planted again.

"The silo?" he asked.

I nodded. "Let's go."

We walked quietly to the field that held the missile silo, eyes peeled for any sign of them. As we neared it, the scents grew stronger, like a cookie factory had opened up shop down the road.

The concrete box looked the same as it had when we'd left it. The door was closed, and there weren't any supernatural lights or sounds that suggested Tate and Mallory were throwing evil around.

Hope blossomed; maybe we weren't too late.

"They're here."

We turned and found Todd behind us, a new patch of crimson on his shoulder.

"Are you all right?"

"I'll heal," he said. "They went in. I took an orb to the shoulder."

"Paige?" I asked.

"Paige, the other witch, and the dark one."

Tate, with his head of dark hair, must have been the dark one.

"While we were fighting Mallory," Ethan said, "Tate was nabbing Paige and waiting for Mallory to finish us off."

Maybe Paige had been right. With every action she took, Mallory was sliding closer to friendship in the past tense.

"Thank you for your diligence," I told Todd. "And thank you for your help earlier."

He nodded. "We are done with this fight for now. We'll go to ground. We'll regroup. It's the way of our people."

When he looked up again, he looked pissed. "End this tonight."

"That's our every intention," Ethan promised, holding out a

hand. "My apologies again for my behavior earlier. My comments were shortsighted and naive. We are better for having met you, and we are honored that we shared a field of battle."

Todd hesitated for a moment, then took Ethan's hand. "Good luck," he said, then disappeared across the field. The night was quiet again, stars speeding by overhead.

"I'd feel a lot better if they were going down there with us," I said.

It took Ethan long enough to answer that I looked over at him. His eyes were squeezed closed, his forehead pinched.

I put a hand on his arm. "Where is she?"

"Nearby," he said, rubbing his temples. "I can feel her fretting. But this is different from earlier."

"She's probably preparing to use dark magic again—the real deal. Are you going to be okay?"

"I'll be fine. Let's get this over with."

The snap in his voice convinced me not to push the issue. He was a big boy. If he wanted help from me, he could ask for it.

Carefully, swords drawn, we opened the door to the silo. It was dark even in comparison to the black night outside, and my eyes hadn't yet adjusted. I walked carefully forward.

But not carefully enough.

"Stop!" Ethan called out, wrapping an arm around me before I vaulted into the darkness below.

The elevator was gone.

Ethan wrenched me back just as the momentum would have taken me over the edge. An uncontrolled fall into the depths wouldn't have ended comfortably.

"Jesus," Ethan said, settling me back from the edge, his hands shaking with nerves.

"I guess they took the lift," I said, glancing down over the edge. "How are we going to get down there?"

"It's thirty feet," Ethan said. "I can jump it, but you don't have the experience."

"That's not entirely true."

Ethan slowly looked at me.

"While you were gone, I learned how to jump. Well, how to fall, anyway. Jonah taught me."

"Ah" was all Ethan said. But he looked at me for a moment, an expression of mild curiosity on his face.

"He helped me while you were . . . gone," I explained, not that he'd asked for an explanation.

"I'm not jealous, Sentinel."

"Okay."

"I have no need of jealousy."

I was equally amused and aroused by the bravado. This was Ethan in the fast lane, hugging the curves instead of constantly riding the political brakes.

"Back to the point," I recommended. "Whoever goes first could send the platform back up?"

"Too noisy. We'll need to be quiet once we're down there. Between them, they probably already know we're on our way, but there's no sense in announcing it." He looked at me. "You're sure you can do it?"

I wouldn't deny that this jump, as all others, scared me, but I didn't think he needed to hear that now, and my fear certainly wasn't a very good reason not to do it. If I avoided everything I was afraid of, I'd never leave the House.

"I'll go first," he said, and before I could agree, he'd disappeared, leaving a *whoosh* of air in his wake. Two seconds later, I heard his feet hit the ground.

My eyes were finally accustomed to the darkness, and I glanced over the edge. Ethan signaled a thumbs-up. When he'd cleared the way for me, I resheathed my sword, took a breath, and took a step.

The worst part about jumping as a vampire—and really the only bad part—was that first step. It was as unpleasant for vampires as it was for humans—that sickening lurch of the stomach, the sudden sensation of falling, and the fear you wouldn't survive the jump.

But then everything changed.

The world slowed down as if to keep up with you. Dozens of feet became a single graceful step, and as long as you kept your knees soft, the landing didn't pose a problem at all.

I landed in a superheroine crouch, one leg bent, the other extended, a hand on the ground and the other on the pommel of my sword. I looked up at Ethan through my bangs.

His eyes blazed fiercely with pride.

"You can do it," he whispered.

I stood up and adjusted the belt of my katana and the hem of my jacket. "Did you doubt me?"

"I didn't doubt," he said. "I . . . had reserved judgment."

I humphed but let it go. God willing, there'd be plenty of time for me to harass him later.

We peeked into the hallway that led away from the elevator shaft. The lights were on, and there was no sign of Tate, Mallory, or Paige.

I glanced over at Ethan, my vampire-proximity alarm. He was wincing against what I assumed was another Mallory-spawned headache, but he was still on his feet.

"Do you think Paige led them directly to the book?" I wondered.

"Depends on the state she left in. And we won't know that until we see her."

"Strategy?"

Ethan looked around. "If they want the book, they'll have to get to the bottom of the silo. But I want a look before we attack them head-on. Let's check the launch room. We can check the hole and figure out where they are. Radio silence from here on out. You remember your signals?"

I nodded. Luc had taught the Cadogan House guards a series of hand gestures we could use to signal one another during missions. They'd come in handy before and would definitely be handy now, when we were trying to hide our presence from a former mayor and testy witch. Assuming they didn't already know we were coming, which seemed unlikely.

Swords drawn, we moved down the hallway. Ethan skirted the right side, and I skirted the left a bit behind him. We listened at each door we passed, trying to detect sound, but there was no sign of it, even with vampire senses in full operation.

It probably didn't help that the place was loaded with concrete to protect the missile from attack. I wasn't really sure how that would affect the loosing of an ancient evil, but I had a sense we'd soon be finding out.

We'd nearly reached the giant sliding door to the silo room when I spotted a glistening drop of crimson on the floor. The droplet was small, but the smell of fresh blood was undeniably pungent.

I crouched down and dabbed it with a fingertip, then sniffed it delicately. Definitely blood, and spicy with magic. Whether Paige or Mallory I couldn't tell, but that really wasn't important. One of our sorceresses had shed blood.

I stood up again and wiped my hand on my pants, then gestured toward the sliding door. Ethan pointed me toward the handle, then took point at the door, sword at the ready. When he nodded, I pulled.

The door slid open, and Ethan slid inside. I followed. The room was empty and mostly dark. But the silo glowed from below, the spot where the *Maleficium* had been located.

Ethan motioned me forward. Swallowing down a burst of fear that tightened my chest, I crept to the silo and peeked down.

For the second time in a matter of weeks, the *Maleficium* was gone.

But the drama had only just started. The building suddenly shook with a pulse of magic that screamed through the building. If we weren't too late already, we were going to be in a minute.

I didn't waste any time.

"Merit!" Ethan yelled, but I was already in the air and on my way into the missile shaft. I landed in a crouch on the pedestal the *Maleficium* had once rested on.

In front of me, in a large circular room, were the enemies I'd sought. Mallory was hunched over the *Maleficium*, which was open on the ground. Tate stood between me and Mallory, and Paige lay injured on the ground beside him, bloody and unconscious. She wasn't wearing her jacket or cap; Tate must have conned—or dragged—her out of the house.

"Hello, Ballerina," Tate said.

Tonight he wore a dark suit over a dark shirt and tie. Death in a beautiful package, except that he, too, looked exhausted—worn out and gaunt, and not any better than Mallory did. Perhaps he wasn't immune to the effects of black magic, either.

"I suppose I could say I'm pleased you survived your trip, although that would probably sound hypocritical."

I heard footfalls behind me and knew Ethan had landed in the shaft.

"And him as well," Tate flatly said. "But that would just be dishonest."

"Move away from the book," I told them, crouching a bit and readying for action.

"You know I'm not going to do that."

Another pulse of magic lit through the room, the book its obvious origin point. The floor and walls shook with it.

I'd be damned if I was going to end up crushed beneath the concrete and steel of a forty-year-old missile silo in Nebraska.

"Ethan," I said, "I'm going low."

"Then I've got high," he said, stepping forward, sword outstretched.

I stepped back, then ran full speed toward Tate. His eyes widened as I moved, but Ethan distracted him with a slash of his sword.

I dropped to my knees and let the momentum push me along the slick, painted concrete floor to Mallory's spot on the other side of the room.

I popped back up again, leaving Ethan to deal with Tate, and pointed my sword at her.

"This is the last time I will tell you this, witch. Back off!"

She looked up from the *Maleficium*, her fingers bloody and hovering over the text, nothing but pain in her eyes.

I might have been able to talk her out of anger or fear or exhaustion, but pain was its own kind of demon, and I wasn't sure talking would have any effect.

I heard the crack of flesh and bone and glanced back at Ethan. He'd gone the old-fashioned route and attempted to give Tate another right hook across the jaw, probably as a thank-you for the damage to his Mercedes.

But this time, Tate knew the shot was coming, and he was fast enough to avoid it. He'd put out a hand to catch Ethan's fist, and held him there for a moment, Ethan's eyes wild.

"I'd have thought my prior warnings would have had some effect."

"I'm a slow learner."

"I suppose wisdom doesn't come with age, eh?" With barely a brush of Tate's hand, Ethan flew across the room and landed against a steel support column.

The column buckled and Ethan hit the ground.

"Ethan!" My heart skipped a beat in the split second before he looked up at Tate. Blood ran down the side of his face from a gash on his head, and it took him much longer than usual to stand up again, but he did stand up.

I started forward to go to him, but his eyes widened.

"Behind you!" he called out.

I looked back. Mallory had gathered together a ball of magic that now glowed between her hands. The bluish light reflected unflatteringly up and across her face, like a flashlight held beneath the chin of a schoolchild. And then, as if I were a stranger—a threat instead of a longtime friend—she pitched that magic directly at me.

My first instinct was to duck. After all, I'd taken an orb or two and the sparks from a dozen others when I hadn't been fast enough in training. I assumed those had contained only low-grade magic, but they still hurt, leaving ugly burns that took a few days to fade, even on a quick-healing vampire.

Honestly, that instinct kicked in pretty quickly, and I dodged and wove around two or three orbs that shattered against the walls behind me.

But as I dodged, I also wondered . . .

Catcher hadn't let me use my sword during magical dodgeball. I'd assumed he hadn't wanted to risk damaging my antique katana. But what if the issue wasn't damage to the sword—but damage to the orb?

That possibility was, I thought, worth a little experiment. And so, instead of continuing to avoid Mallory's magic, I decided to stare it down.

I gripped the handle of my sword in both hands and raised the sword in front of me . . . just like a bat.

Going, I thought to myself.

Mallory slung the orb into the air like a major league pitch, its flight straight and true and aimed for my heart. I wiggled my fingers around the handle . . . and when the moment was right, I swung.

Going.

The vibration of pure magic and magical steel—steel I had tempered with my own vampiric blood all those moons ago—nearly wrenched off my arm. But I kept my fingers tight around the leather and ray-skin handle . . . and watched the orb shatter into a million blue sparks.

"Gone," I murmured, watching the fireworks until the sparks dissipated, then sliding my gaze back to Mallory, eyebrow arched in a perfect imitation of Ethan. "Got anything else?"

She apparently took my sarcasm as a challenge. One orb after another flew in my direction, each one spicier—more magically potent—than the last. She worked with the effort—teeth gritted, forehead damp even in the November chill.

And she made me work, too. I pulled out every move and maneuver I'd ever practiced, or seen Catcher or Ethan execute, or watched on Wrigley Field. I slashed forward, backward, and from both sides. I flipped backward to avoid a pale blue orb, then flew to the floor to avoid a shot aimed at my head.

It missed me by more than it should have. Mallory was getting tired.

Normally, she'd have been smart enough to think through her

actions, to plan a couple of steps ahead. But tonight, if she was already tired, maybe I could bait her one more time.

I stood up again and crooked a finger in her direction, as Ethan had done so many times for me. "You want me? Come and get me."

She bared her teeth, then began to spin her fingers and pull together another ball of magic from the ether.

I opened my arms. "You think you can hit me, witch? Right in the chest?"

She wound up and threw her pitch.

I let every vampire sensibility loose—sight, sound, taste, smell. The world exploded into sensations, but events around me seemed to slow down because of it. I watched the orb of blue light inch toward me; in slow motion, its surface was a pitted swirl of energy, and it sought out a landing spot, a home.

I fully intended to give it one.

Before she could reload or move out of the way, I pulled up my sword—not to bat the orb into a thousand pieces . . . but to reflect it. I held the katana directly in front of me, the cutting edge to the side, and the mirrorlike steel toward Mallory.

The orb hit the blade with enough force to rattle the steel. But tempered and honed, it did its job. The orb bounced right off and flew back toward Mallory. Slower on the return trip, but its direction true. It hit her square in the chest and sent her flying across the room. She hit the wall and then the floor, thudding down with a bounce that probably broke a few of her ribs, too.

At least she couldn't hurt anyone else, or herself, for a little while. One bad guy down . . . Now back to the other one.

And the other one was engaged in his own fierce battle. Tate, who could manipulate a car right off the road with magic, had apparently wanted a different kind of challenge. He'd produced a sword of his own, a gigantic two-handed blade with complicated engravings that caught the light as it shifted. A katana was intended to slice; this thing looked like it was intended to pummel.

Ethan had his sword, and there was no denying he was good at wielding it. But Tate was a man with an agenda, and he wouldn't be deterred. The smile on his face reminded me of a cat playing with a mouse just before the final snap of its jaws. Tate had every intention of finishing the fight—and finishing Ethan—but wanted to play with his food a bit first. Ethan's jacket was ripped from several cuts already.

"Ow."

I glanced at the other side of the room. Paige was sitting up, a hand to her bleeding head.

I rushed to her, hoping she could find a way to stop all of this, and went down on my knees beside her. "Are you okay?"

"He made me follow him out, then made me tell him where the book was." Her lip trembled, tears hovering at the edge of her lashes.

"It's okay. We all knew this was coming. He and Ethan are fighting. Is there anything you can do? Can you knock Tate out or something?"

She shook her head, tears falling down her cheeks, an ugly bruise beginning to surface on one. "He did something to me. I couldn't stop him from coming here or making me tell him where it was."

It sounded like a violation by magic, a kind of psychic extortion used by Tate to get to the book. As if he needed any more reasons for me to detest him.

Chunks of concrete flew past us as Tate's sword nipped a bit of the wall. Mallory was out, Tate was occupied, and Paige was injured. If she couldn't use her magic, maybe I could at least get her out of the room to keep her out of any more danger—or to keep Tate from using her for anything else.

"Do you think you can walk?"

She shrugged. "I don't know. Maybe."

I put an arm beneath her and helped her to her feet. But that plan didn't last long.

"Merit!" Paige said. "Mallory! The book!"

I looked back. Mallory had awoken and was stretched full out on the floor of the vault, one hand stretched over the book, her lips moving as she continued her incantation.

The sounds of the scuffle stopped as Tate turned toward the sound of the ancient words. Ethan took advantage of the distraction and thrust his katana down.

The strike should have sliced Tate open from throat to stomach, but Tate put up a hand, and Ethan flew back against the wall again.

My heart nearly stopped again, but Ethan groaned and rolled over. Unfortunately, my relief was dwarfed by my shock at Tate's power and the violence he threw around so casually. *What was he?*

Undeterred by the violence around her, Mallory continued her chanting, words that were chunky and rhythmic like Latin, but with thicker consonants and a twist that sounded almost Russian.

With Ethan handled, Tate vaulted a table and reached out to grab the book.

"Mallory, stop!" I called out, but I was too late.

Tate stretched for the book, and just as his fingers made contact with its red leather cover, Mallory screamed out an incantation. "*Adnum malentium!*"

A thunderous clap split the air, the energy pushing Mallory back . . . but not Tate.

The *Maleficium* exploded into a burst of bright blue light that wrapped around Tate's hand, still on the book, and up his arm like a snaking vine. Within seconds he was enveloped in light. Mallory had done something, finished something, and the *Maleficium* was reacting.

The light glowed around him like a visible aura, and for a moment he smiled, as if he'd achieved some part of his plan.

But his elation didn't last long. The light around him began to shake, and the outline of his body along with it. He wobbled and quivered inside the cloud of light, and his expression grew pained. He opened his mouth to scream out, but no sound escaped the light, just the dull throbbing of the magic.

Within seconds, his vibrating form began to lurch up and down, and then his body began to widen. It didn't grow bigger—it stretched horizontally as he howled out his displeasure.

The shield of magic grew as he did, and I scampered back to avoid the edge of it.

Suddenly, like a string of DNA dividing, double-wide Tate began to cleave in two. The split started at his head, and in sputtering stops and starts. Flashes lit the room like a sun-powered strobe, and then it was over.

A loud crack of magic crossed the room, and the lights in the silo flickered once, then twice.

When the room was calm again, Seth Tate stood in the middle of the room, sweating and rumpled.

And beside him stood another Seth Tate.

It took seconds for my mind to actually start working again—and even then I hadn't managed to wrap my mind around what I'd seen.

Seth Tate, former mayor of Chicago, had become *two* Seth Tates.

The Tates looked at their hands and then each other, and then both pushed out their chests. They screamed out—a sound wholly inhuman and ear-burstingly loud.

I hit the concrete on my knees, covering my ears against the sound. The entire structure vibrated, and I'd have sworn the concrete and steel warped from the energy they put out.

For a moment, there was silence.

And then they both shot upward, straight up the shaft of the missile silo. I ran beneath the opening and watched them ascend—twenty feet, forty feet, sixty feet, eighty feet—and then the metal doors of the missile bay burst open, sending a shower of dirt and roots and cornstalks into the silo. The Tates disappeared through the opening and into the night, supernatural missiles of unknown proportions.

The dirt cleared, and lights shone down through the hole in the sky. And all was quiet again on the midwestern front.

✦─◄❈►─✦

CHAPTER SEVEN

THE GAMBLER

"Wat the hell just happened?" Ethan asked, but given the silence that followed his answer, no one had any idea.

We stared up through the silo, as if the answer to our questions was somehow written in the Cold War–era walls.

"He split into two," Ethan said, glancing back at Paige. "How is that possible?"

She grimaced and hobbled over to the table, where he leaned against it. "I have no idea."

We looked back at the *Maleficium*, which still sat on the floor beside Mallory. It had been reduced to little more than a book-shaped chunk of charcoal. A few hints of yellowed pages were visible, but mostly the book was a cinder that seemed like it might blow away if someone breathed too heavily on it.

But if the *Maleficium*—the vessel—was destroyed, what had happened to all that it contained? "Paige, what about the dark magic? The evil?"

She shook her head. "I'm not really—"

"It's gone."

Mallory's voice was quiet, and there was a melancholic thread of surprise in it.

We all looked at her. She was on the ground, still on her knees, staring at her hands. They were still chapped and raw, and they shook like she was an addict in withdrawal. She wrapped her arms around herself and stared into the distance, maybe ruing the fact that things hadn't turned out the way she'd intended.

"Gone?" Ethan asked.

Slowly, she turned her gaze on him. "It was in the book, and the book is gone. So it's gone, too."

"How do you know?" I asked, but I realized I didn't need her answer.

It was clear in her face.

Mallory didn't look any better than she had before all this had started. She looked just as strung out. Just as tired.

She'd tried one more fix of black magic, and it hadn't worked. And now there was no more magic to try.

She had officially reached rock bottom.

"She knows the magic is gone because she doesn't feel any different," I said. "Because she worked another spell, and she triggered the *Maleficium*, but it didn't cure her. And now the book is gone, so it's too late. There won't be any more *Maleficium*-inspired black magic, right?"

Mallory looked up, and she must have caught the anger in my eyes. She looked away, tears spilling over her lashes. I wasn't sure that emotion was remorse, but maybe—sooner rather than later—she'd own up to the consequences she'd been so quick to ignore earlier.

"Then, what happened with Tate?" Ethan asked.

I thought back to what we'd seen and what had happened seconds before he'd split in half. "He touched the book. If Mallory worked the spell but no other evil escaped, could it have, I don't know, funneled into Tate?" I looked at Mallory. "Is that possible?"

"I don't know," she pathetically whispered.

Ethan wasn't moved. "You don't know? You don't *know*? You just decided to unleash all the evil in the world from an ancient book, but you didn't know about the possible outcomes? Stupid, foolish girl."

"Ethan," I quietly said.

"No, Merit, she needs to hear this." He crouched before her, that new fire in his eyes and a thoroughly chilling expression on his face. "She didn't care to consider the consequences of her actions before. Perhaps now she will."

Mallory didn't answer him; she just sat on the floor, staring back at him with wide and horrified eyes, as if suddenly and fully aware of her own fallibility.

All that work, all that research, all those spells—pointless. *Fruitless.* She'd gambled everything—her friends, her skills, her lover—and she'd lost it all for the sake of something she thought was a sure bet. But the cards had been stacked against her, and the house always won.

I put a hand on Ethan's shoulder, and he rose and put a hand on my cheek. I think he meant not to apologize, but to comfort me for the things that would come, for whatever would happen with Mallory.

"We need to know what just happened," Paige quietly said, and I could practically hear the magical gears clicking along in her head. "We need to know what he is—what they are. We need to understand it."

It was natural she'd want to know. She was the Order's archivist, and I had to assume she'd be writing all this down. But writing the history could wait.

"Right now," I said, "we need to know what they are and what they're going to do next. There's no telling the kind of damage they can do together." One Tate had been bad enough. "Let's get out of here."

I helped Mallory to her feet. She didn't speak and wouldn't make eye contact with me. But she allowed me to help her toward the door.

Ethan did the same for Paige, and our motley crew hobbled back down the hallway and onto the elevator platform. Up we went, back into the world.

We stepped outside to the sharp, acrid scent of smoke.

At the edge of the field, the farmhouse was ablaze, red-orange flames licking the sky.

Had Tate—the two of them—done this? Was it a final act of vengeance? Seth had sworn to me and Ethan that he wouldn't let us stop him. Maybe the two of them had decided they needed to punish us for our interference.

Paige muffled a sob with a hand, horror in her eyes as she stared at her home. And then she started running. For an injured sorceress, she moved pretty well.

I handed Mallory over to Ethan. "I'll get her."

"Be careful." He nodded, and I took off across the field. It was colder now, and the ground seemed to have hardened since we'd gone into the silo. It was like running on an upside-down egg carton—small, uneven hills and valleys that made it impossible to plan your steps.

It nearly didn't surprise me when I stumbled and the ground came up to meet me. I stopped myself with my hands but scraped them up pretty good. Hoping no one had seen me fall in the darkness, I climbed back to my feet, wincing as a bolt of pain radiated through my right ankle.

But there was no time to wait for healing. Paige was moving ever closer to the house, and in her mental state, I didn't trust her to stay safe.

I muttered out a curse just to make myself feel better and ran-limped forward as well as I could. I vaulted the fence and was immediately assaulted by the heat from the blaze. Acrid smoke poured from the house, and fire poured from the windows. Paige, her arm crooked around her face, was edging toward the front door.

"Paige!" I called out, but she didn't stop. She didn't even glance back. Of course, she may not have heard me. The fire roared like a jet engine, wood cracking and splitting as bits of the farmhouse's interior fell.

I wasn't a big fan of fire. I'd burned myself on an errant bottle rocket as a child, and the thought of moving closer to a raging inferno wasn't exactly comfortable. But I was immortal; she was not. There was only one thing to do.

I pulled the neck of my shirt over my mouth into a make-do mask and moved forward.

The smoke and ash thickened the nearer I moved to the house, and it became nearly impossible to breathe. The air was scalding hot, searing my lungs with every intake of breath. But I kept walking.

"Paige!" I shouted, as something large fell somewhere nearby. "Don't get any closer."

She coughed loudly. "I need my books!" But she stopped within a few feet of the front door and lifted her arms. Even through the energy of the fire, I could feel the buzz of magic. She must have shaken off Tate's magic and could work her own again.

"At least she didn't go inside," I murmured, and watched as one book, then another, then another, flew from the doorway of the house to safety outside.

She must not have had the power to save the house, but at least she could save a few of her most prized possessions.

My relief didn't last long. When another crack split the air, I looked up. Flames licked the small portico over the front door, and one corner tilted dangerously low.

Suddenly the portico began to drop.

I didn't stop to think. I ignored the shooting pain in my ankle and propelled myself forward through pain and smoke and the fingertips of fire that I would have sworn reached out through the window to snag me.

She didn't see me coming and realized I was there only when I used my body and momentum to push her out of the way. We flew through the air, hitting the ground a few feet away just as the portico crashed to the ground, covering the spot where Paige had stood with a blazing mass of wood—and completely blocking the door.

"Good God," she said, chest heaving as she looked from me to the blaze and back again. "Thank you. I could have been killed."

Still on the ground, I swatted at a spark on the arm of my jacket. "Least I could do. Sorceresses were having a bad-enough night."

When another burst of sparks flew through the window, I climbed to my feet again, then held out a hand to Paige. "We're too close."

She let me help her to her feet, her face dark with soot, and we limped back to the pile of books she'd managed to save. Six volumes, their covers singed and dusted with ash.

"All my books," she said. "All my writings, completely gone."

"Did you save anything useful?"

She picked up a book and dusted off the cover. "Each book is just one bit of the whole collection. Six books? That's not even a start."

Paige hugged the book to her chest. There in the dark, the raging fire reflecting off her vibrantly red hair, she looked like a creature from a Grimm fairy tale.

We both looked up at the sound of footsteps. Ethan, an arm around Mallory, moved toward us.

Paige didn't waste any time. "You did this." She bounded forward, intending to pummel Mallory, but I wrapped an arm around her waist and held her back.

"She did this!" Paige screamed, red hair flying about her face as she struggled in my arms. "This is all her fault. All of it! You think we don't all feel the imbalance? We do! That's how we know right from wrong, Mallory. That's how we know it! It's not a punishment; it's part of our *gift*. You use it. You learn from it. You don't let it drive you to destroy the world!"

"Paige, stop it! This isn't going to help." I worked to maintain my grip, but her arms reached out for Mallory, who seemed completely oblivious to the conversation.

"She should have to pay for what she's done!"

"She will pay," Ethan said. "But her punishment is not for you to decide."

"It should be mine. Look what she did!"

"Paige," I said, "that's exactly what Mallory tried to do—control things she shouldn't have controlled. She shouldn't have done it, and you shouldn't do it, either."

Paige shook her head, but after a moment she stopped squirming, so I let her go.

"Everything I owned was there. Everything. All my stuff. All my *clothes*." She swallowed thickly. "I don't have anywhere else to go."

Our clothes, too, and everything else in our duffels. Thank God we'd taken our swords with us. The heat of a house fire might not have had much impact on finely tempered steel, but I'd rather not test that theory firsthand.

"If you want to return with us to Chicago, you can stay at the House until you make other arrangements," Ethan said. "We'll also need to get Mallory back safely. We've seen her before in magical handcuffs. Perhaps . . . ?"

Paige nodded and wiped her eyes and, with a bare flick of her finger and thumb, whipped out a fierce bite of magic that pulled Mallory's hands together like they'd been zip-tied.

Mallory just let it happen. No argument. No squirming. I couldn't help but wonder: Was this the beginning of her contrition or another chance for her to fake remorse until she could escape again?

"Those will keep her for a little while," Paige said, pulling a cell phone from her pocket. "And I'll call Baumgartner. He can decide where to put her. Maybe in the same place they held her before, but with a little more security this time."

At the sound of boots on dirt, we looked up. Dark figures approached from the other side of the house.

"Tate?" Paige asked.

I opened my senses and caught the sharp, wild scent of animal. A bit of the tension left my shoulders. Our odds were evening a bit.

"No," I said, shaking my head. "Shifters."

Specifically, Gabriel Keene, brawny and tawny haired, with golden eyes that seemed to look right through you. He was the head of the Apex of the North American Central Pack of shifters. And beside him, a pack mate: tall and lanky Jeff Christopher, my grandfather's employee. Or former employee, anyway.

They both wore jeans and thick leather jackets, and I guessed their motorcycles were parked nearby.

"What are you doing here?" I exclaimed.

"Is that any way to greet an old friend, Kitten?"

Gabe was right. I jumped forward and hugged him. He laughed and patted my back. "That's enough. Sullivan here will get jealous."

I stepped back, then gave Jeff a little wave. He blushed.

"Sullivan assures me he won't get jealous," I said.

But Gabriel's smile faded when he looked at Ethan. As if not quite sure what he was seeing, Gabe gave him a good, long once-over.

By the look in Gabriel's eyes and the tingle of magic around him, this was something heavy, weighty. Gabe hadn't seen Ethan since he'd returned, and it seemed clear that Gabe was evaluating who Ethan was—whether he was still vampire, whether he was still good, whether he was still Ethan. Whether the magic had tainted him, changed him into something else, or damaged him irreparably.

"The sorceress did a number," Gabriel finally said.

Ethan held out a hand for Gabriel, but Gabriel ignored it and wrapped Ethan in a bear hug that nearly lifted him off the ground.

"And that's but one of the weird things I've seen tonight," I muttered.

"It's good to see both of you," Ethan said. "What brings you to Nebraska?"

"They're the escorts for the *Maleficium*," Paige said. "They dropped it off before Mallory escaped."

I pointed a finger at Jeff. "That explains why you weren't at work yesterday. You were on your way out here with the book."

He shrugged his narrow shoulders with impressive machismo. "A man's gotta do what a man's gotta do."

"After much begging, we're here to retrieve it again," Gabriel said. But he cast a dark glance back at the burning farmhouse. "But something tells me we might be changing our plans."

"The *Maleficium* has been destroyed," I said, and Gabriel's eyes went wide with horror. "And it seems the evil it contained was destroyed along with it. Or most of it."

"Most of it?" Jeff asked.

"Seth Tate touched the book just as Mallory finished the spell," Ethan said. "He split into two."

Gabriel blinked. "I don't understand."

"One Tate became two Tates," I confirmed.

"The book burned to a crisp, and they propelled themselves through the missile shaft." Ethan looked back at the farmhouse. "We came outside to discover the house on fire."

"What is he?" Gabriel asked, and I think he meant it rhetorically. Even if he didn't, it wasn't as if we could answer.

"That's the million-dollar question," I said. "Whatever they are, one or both of them set Paige's house on fire. It's not hard to imagine they've headed back to Chicago to make more trouble. We need to get home."

"Actually, there's trouble at home, too," Jeff said.

"Oh?" I asked.

"Four cops beat the holy hell out of a couple of vamps and two humans they were hanging out with."

"Were they from a House?"

"Rogues," he said. "The cops say the vamps attacked them. The vamps say they were hanging out near a bodega with the humans and the cops jumped them for no reason, shouting obscenities about vamps and humans mixing together. Pretty clear things have gone a little downhill in the CPD since your grandfather left."

"Racism is alive and well in the twenty-first century," I ruefully said.

"When the mayor tells the city vampires are the enemy," Ethan said, "such violence isn't surprising."

"And having to register with the city isn't going to help us," I said. That was one more thing I needed to add to my to-do list. "There won't be any way to blend in when we have to carry papers that show our identity."

"Sad but true," Jeff agreed.

"What are you going to do with her?"

We all looked at Mallory.

"She's going back to Chicago with us," Ethan said. "After that, it's up to the Order."

"They didn't do so well with her the last time. Not even twenty-four hours before allowing her to escape."

"No," Ethan agreed, "they did not."

Gabriel looked at Jeff. "Could you excuse us for a moment?"

When Ethan waved a hand collegially, Gabriel led Jeff a few feet away. Heads together, they began to whisper.

"What's that about?" I quietly asked.

"I'm not entirely sure," Ethan said, but there was no denying the curiosity in his voice.

After a moment, they walked back toward us. "We'll take her," Gabe said.

Stunned silence filled the air.

"You'll take her where?" Ethan asked.

"We'll take custody of her. The Order didn't manage her before. You know I'm not one to get involved in politics, but I'd also really prefer that the city not burn down around us, since we've decided to stay in it."

Ethan looked completely befuddled. "I'm sorry, but I'm having trouble wrapping my mind around this. Where would you take her?"

"We have a place" was all Gabe said. "And you'd be welcome to visit her at your convenience. Catcher, too," he said, looking at Mallory. "She wouldn't dare try that bullshit she pulled on the Order with us."

He gave her an ugly, pointed stare that should have scared the shit out of her. It scared me a little, and I wasn't even the one in trouble.

"She'll need caretakers," Ethan said. "She believes she's ill—that she has a magical imbalance that necessitated what she's done."

Gabriel's lip curled. "She doesn't need to be coddled. She has acted like a criminal without remorse. If she were one of mine, the problem would have solved itself."

Gabriel had been betrayed by his youngest brother, Adam, and we hadn't heard from Adam since. "She won't work magic around us. We can arrange that fairly easily. As it is, she doesn't need excuses. She needs to get her shit together."

"And you can help her do that?"

"No," Gabriel said, eyes narrowed at Mallory. "No one can *help* her. She either does it or she doesn't. That's the choice we'll give her."

So he was taking the tough-love approach. It certainly didn't sound easy, but nothing else had worked. The Order put her in a medical facility—gave her around-the-clock care and treatment—and look where that got us.

"I'll want to check on her," Paige said to Gabriel, apparently willing to let them have the burden of watching her.

He nodded. "I understand decisions will need to be made about her long-term status. She has amends to make. Many amends, to friends and family." Gabriel looked up at me. "I'm going to give her the chance to do that. Success or failure is up to her."

"It's a lot of responsibility," Ethan said.

Gabriel nodded. "And I'm not looking for new responsibilities. I've got a wife and a son and problems of my own. But if I can help address this now, I won't have to worry about it later. Besides," he said, turning his golden eyes on me, "you've helped us before. I still owe you one."

Gabriel had made a prophecy about me and my future with, or without, Ethan. It had something to do with a favor I was going to do for him, but of course he hadn't given away any details about that.

Ethan glanced at Mallory. "Are you sure you can make it back to Chicago without her causing trouble?"

Gabriel chuckled. "There's always a solution to that problem." He walked over to Mallory and crouched down before her.

"How are you doing?"

She looked up to respond to him, but before she could speak he put a hand on her cheek and tapped it gently. When her head went limp on her shoulders, Gabriel stood up again. "And that takes care of that."

"Is she okay?" I asked.

"She's fine. Just a careful touch. It's like holding a shark upside down—it calms them. A handy little technique for putting out errant sorceresses. Gives us a good four or five hours before she wakes up again. And when she does wake up, we can have a nice chat."

I gave him a flat look. "You couldn't have done that three days ago?"

Gabe shrugged. "No one asked me to."

And that was a succinct lesson in using all available assets during a crisis.

"How will you get her back to Chicago?" Ethan asked.

"Sidecar," Jeff said, thumbing his hand back toward the driveway.

"You have a sidecar?" I held up a hand. "Wait. Let me restate that. You rode to Nebraska in a sidecar?"

Adorable as Jeff was, I couldn't get the image of him riding excitedly in an old-fashioned sidecar—brown locks waving in the wind, as happy as a puppy—out of my mind.

"I drove my own rig," he said. "The sidecar was for the book. And now it's for the girl who destroyed the book."

We all looked at her again, limp on the ground, plans for her future being decided around her and without her permission, because she'd given up her right to object.

The low roar of a fire truck sounded in the distance. It must have taken the neighbors a while to realize that anything was amiss. That meant it was time for us to make our exit. The Order could clean up the rest of this mess.

"How will you get back?" Gabriel asked.

"I have a truck," Paige said. "Fortunately, the keys are inside it."

"Then, if you can give us a ride to the airport, we can take the jet," Ethan said.

I stared at him. "I'm sorry—the jet?"

"The House has a jet," Ethan said. "Well, the House leases a jet on occasion. And I'd say this is an appropriate occasion."

"Were you going to mention we had a jet before we spent eight hours driving to Nebraska and destroyed your Mercedes in the process?"

He looked up and arched an eyebrow at me. "If I'd done that, we wouldn't have had all those hours together, Sentinel."

That might have been an unintended benefit, but he wouldn't have delayed us with a car ride if a faster alternative had been so easily available. "Couldn't find a pilot on such short notice?" I asked.

"Perhaps. But don't ruin the illusion."

I rolled my eyes.

"We'll get her settled and introduce her to the rules," Gabriel said, "and then you can say hello. It'll give you a chance to check out her situation. Although I'm fairly certain you'll approve; you've already met the caretaker I have in mind."

I didn't have a good reason to object to that offer, so I nodded. "By the way, there's a strip along I-29 that's probably going to require a detour."

Gabriel frowned. "It was clear on the way down."

"That was pre-Tate."

Gabriel sighed, and I looked at Ethan. "By all means," I said, "let's take the jet."

CHAPTER EIGHT

HOME IS WHERE THE SHOWER IS

I took the passenger seat, and Paige drove us in a beat-up extended-cab pickup truck with FARM TRUCK license plates to a private hangar at Omaha's airport. Ethan was in the backseat with our swords and Paige's pile of cherished books.

To call the mood somber was an understatement. Mallory had proven again that she was willing to hurt others to rid herself of pain. It wasn't exactly a cause for celebration. But at least the *Maleficium* was gone.

We were mostly silent, probably all ruminating on what we'd seen—and what was to come. I was especially worried about Ethan. He was connected to Mallory in a way that was causing him physical pain. If a new sorceress could bring a four-centuries-old vampire to his knees because she was feeling agitated, what else could she do? It wasn't a question I was comfortable considering, and Ethan couldn't have felt any better about it.

Paige broke the ominous silence. "And I suggested she was a novice. The gnomes came because I asked them to, because I promised them she was all smoke and mirrors and very little skill. They were hurt because of me in a fight they didn't want to wage in the first place."

The regret on her face was clear. I didn't relish the fact that she'd been wrong, or that the gnomes had suffered because of it, but at least she was willing to reconsider her choices. Mallory still hadn't come around to that point yet.

"Because of Mallory," I clarified.

"Does it matter?" Paige asked. I'm not sure she meant me to answer it, so I changed the subject.

"Todd said they'd go back to ground," I said.

She nodded. "They live in underground networks. They're incredibly industrious, and the tunnels keep the soil aerated. You ever wondered why the midwestern states are so big on agriculture? It's not the dirt," she said. "It's who's *under* the dirt."

Ethan rubbed his temples. That small action was enough to make the panic flare in my chest.

"What is it?" I asked. "Is she free again?"

"Just a headache," he said, smiling apologetically. "I think she's still unconscious. She's certainly still drained, and I can feel it. But it's lessening since we're headed in opposite directions, at least until we get to the airport."

"You can sense her?" Paige asked, brow furrowed with concern.

"They have some kind of connection," I explained. "It started after she brought him back, but destroying the *Maleficium* apparently didn't stop it."

I met his gaze in the rearview mirror. "We'll figure it out."

"We'd better," he said.

His link to Mallory was a liability, not just for his safety, but for Cadogan. Until that link was severed, he'd never regain control of the House. I'd hoped finishing Mallory's work with the *Maleficium* might do the trick. Since it hadn't, I might have to rely on her for answers. That idea didn't thrill me.

"It's not surprising she's tired given the amount of magic she threw out tonight," Paige said. "Controlling the universe is generally a subtle thing. Powerful, but subtle. Her magic is definitely not subtle. It's very disco magic. Flashy, but expensive to the aura."

It was expensive in every possible way: her livelihood, her friends, her family, her karma. No one trusted her, and for pretty good reason.

"You know what I need?" I asked.

"A chocolate fountain?" Ethan suggested. "A complete paper set of the *Encyclopedia Britannica*? A lifetime supply of grilled meat?"

"I like all those ideas, but I was thinking a magical spray I can use on Mallory to wash the crazy off her."

"Like Lysol for evil?" Paige asked.

"Something like that, yeah."

Ruminating on that impossibility, we fell silent again. I heard the occasional clicking of Ethan's phone in the backseat, and I took the opportunity to update Jonah on our progress and the shifters' intervention with Mallory.

His text message in response encapsulated the problem: WHAT ARE WE GOING TO DO WITH TWO TATES?

I wished I had an answer to that.

Just as promised, the jet was sleek and white. It was parked in the middle of the tarmac, where a set of stairs unfolded to the ground.

We waited in a small lobby while the plane was prepared, and then headed outside when they called our names. Paige ascended the stairs first. I followed, and Ethan brought up the rear.

"Good God," I said, glancing around the fuselage. "This is definitely the way to travel."

The cabin was divided into two sections—the first held rows of chairs much like a normal plane, and the second held a conversational area with a couch and flat-screen television. All the surfaces were clad in buttery leather or gleaming wood, and the carpet was a thick, lush taupe.

"Not bad, hmm?" Ethan asked, taking a seat and buckling his seat belt with a *click*. Paige sat in a chair behind us, the stack of books in her lap.

I took the seat beside Ethan, and the steward immediately closed the door. As soon as the door was secured, we were moving.

"Very efficient," I said.

Ethan nodded. "The faster we're on our way, the faster we're home."

"And we move from one bit of drama to another."

The steward, a tidily dressed woman in a white shirt and navy skirt, brought us glasses of orange juice. "Beverage?" she asked.

I thanked her and took one. I was starving.

"Also, if you'd turn off all electrical devices, please," she said, then disappeared behind us.

Ethan pulled his cell phone from his pocket to turn it off but stared down at the screen. Whatever he saw there, it wasn't good.

"Bad news?" I asked, not that there was much guesswork needed given the expression on this face.

He turned off his phone and slid it back into his pocket, his expression carefully neutral. "The *shofet* has met. Whatever their conclusion, Darius is on his way to Chicago to announce it."

My stomach twisted. If Darius was traveling across the ocean to make some kind of GP pronouncement, the news couldn't be good.

"That's disconcerting," I said.

Ethan nodded. "I'm sure Darius will have choice words about their decision."

"Darius always has choice words. And I get the sense he likes to hear himself talk."

"Most men in power do, I find."

The steward walked back to the front of the plane. Ethan signaled her, and she nodded back.

As the plane ascended sharply into the air, the smell of roasting meat filled the cabin. My stomach grumbled, and loudly.

Ethan chuckled. "Hungry much?"

"When am I not?" I grumpily asked. "I suppose they're bringing you dinner?"

"That wouldn't be a very wise move when I know you'd pounce on a meal before I could get at it."

The steward appeared at my side, presented me with a silver-domed plate, and then whipped off the dome.

The sight and smell of sizzling steak made my mouth instantaneously water. And beside it, a tidy pile of bright green broccoli, a scoop of garlic-permeated mashed potatoes, and a Thermos of blood. As I stared down at it, she delivered a similar plate to Paige.

"Oh, sweet God," I said appreciatively, my eyes all but eating the food.

"Omaha's finest," Ethan said with a smile. "For a good night's work."

The man procured steak to reward me. Say what you might about Ethan Sullivan, but he knew just how to butter me up. On the other hand, I wasn't convinced I'd done anything right. "When we arrived here, we had one Tate and one book. We now have two Tates and zero books."

"The book is a move in the right direction."

"And the Tates?"

There was fear in his eyes. "If you have a preferred god, Sentinel, I suggest you start praying. And soon."

I couldn't fault the ride on a multimillion-dollar jet. It was even smoother than a hundred-thousand-dollar Mercedes, and a helluva lot faster.

We flew out across the dark waters of Lake Michigan before landing at O'Hare, my delightful meat coma giving way to relief as the steward unlocked the door and we prepared to descend the stairs.

The weather was miserable—the ground wet from earlier rain, the air cold and damp. Not exactly a warm greeting from my hometown, but that didn't make me any less glad to step down onto the tarmac. It was good to be home, even though the trip was short and there was no doubt we'd find just as much drama in Illinois as we had in Nebraska.

Hopefully, this time, it would be *our* kind of drama.

A sleek, silver sedan with a grill like a wide grin was waiting for us a few steps away from the plane. A guy in a Windbreaker and khakis stood beside the car, a set of keys in hand.

"Is that an Aston Martin?" Paige asked.

I slid Ethan a glance, but his gaze was already caressing the car's lines and curves.

"You'll recall my car was quite totaled," he said, without taking his eyes off his new ride.

"And how much did it cost to have this nice gentleman bring a new ride to you at the airport?"

"A drop in the bucket compared to the overall cost, Sentinel."

"I'll bet."

He checked his watch. "Gabriel won't have made it back to

Nebraska, even as fast as they likely drove." He looked at me. "We can go to the House. You can shower and get changed, and we can get Paige settled."

"A shower sounds glorious," I agreed.

"For me, too," Paige said.

Ethan held out a hand toward the car. "In that case, ladies, let's be on our way."

There was no faulting *that* ride, either. On the way, in the smooth comfort of Ethan's new Aston Martin, I texted Jonah again to let him know more GP trouble was brewing. I didn't know what the *shofet* had decided, but it didn't portend anything good that they were coming here to announce it. That was just the kind of thing the Red Guard needed to be prepared for.

It also didn't surprise me that Darius wanted a look at Ethan, to assure himself that Ethan was the vampire who'd earned the Masterdom of the House. There were only twelve vampire Houses in the United States. That meant Ethan had, relatively speaking, a good bit of power. I'd have wanted a look at the reincarnated vamp, too. But I didn't think it wise to voice that particular opinion to Ethan.

We drove to Hyde Park, where the pale stone of Cadogan House emerged from darkness. It was a large, three-story mansion with features from another time—an arched entrance, a turret, and a widow's walk around the roof. The grounds were even larger than the House and offered a bit of the gated outdoors for itchy vampires who needed fresh air and space from vampire drama.

The sidewalk in front of the House was peppered with protestors; they'd become a fixture over the past few months, and Mallory's recent shenanigans certainly hadn't helped. They were citizens of all ages and genders and ethnicities, but the hatred in their hand-painted signs was similar: GO HOME, VAMPS. NO VAMPS IN ILLINOIS. WINDY CITY, NOT VAMPIRE CITY. What they lacked in creativity, they made up in good old-fashioned discrimination.

They sat in lawn chairs, bundled up against the cold, many eating dinners like they'd pulled up to a drive-in movie instead of a vampire hate fest.

Normally, I'd have squeezed my car into a spot on the street and faced them all down as I strode into the House, but Ethan had a coveted basement parking spot. No snow, no parking permits, no dibs. Just a few steps to the stairs, and a few stairs to the lush first floor . . . and a few backward glances from a Master vampire clearly smitten with his new purchase.

"She'll probably still be here when you come back," I reminded him.

He huffed but still gave the sedan one last look. "She is a beauty."

"She is a *car*," Paige reminded him.

"And he is a man," I said, pointing her toward the door. "Let's not dig too deeply into it."

We took the stairs, and I couldn't fight the relief of feeling like I was home again. Which was pretty weird, since I was returning to a vampire frat house I hadn't even lived in for a year.

Tonight, the House smelled like cinnamon, and much to my surprise, the interior had been decorated for the holidays. Malik had been busy while we were gone. Fragrant garland hung from doorways, mantels, and the railing of the wooden staircase that led upstairs. Sugared fruit and sparkling candleholders stood on tables and bookcases, and silver bowls of old-fashioned ribbon candy sat on side tables.

It would be a Cadogan House Christmas—and it made a nice change from the swaths of black fabric that had wrapped the

House while we were in mourning. The House deserved it. Grieving was exhausting, and two months of mourning took a physical and emotional toll.

A few of the House's ninety or so live-in vampires, all dressed in traditional black, were busy in the foyer. They nodded and waved as we passed, which didn't make me nearly as uncomfortable as it once would have. I'd become part of the House, of the family of Novitiates who lived there.

"Ladies, I'm going to leave you here," Ethan said. "I believe I could use a bit of a cleanup myself." He gestured toward the foyer, where Helen, the House's new vampire liaison, waited. "Paige, Helen will get you a room key and some basic necessities. Merit, drop by later so we can talk about next steps."

I nodded and did my duty, escorting Paige to meet Helen.

"Merit," Helen said, "lovely to see you again. And you must be Paige."

She probably wasn't thrilled to see me again, since we hadn't exactly hit it off the first time we'd met, but she was all politeness today. Helen handed Paige a laminated Cadogan House guest pass on a lanyard and a key on a Cadogan House key ring.

We were all about the branding.

"You'll be staying in the guest suite," Helen said, then smiled at me. "Perhaps you could show her the way?"

"Of course. Where is it?"

"Third floor, three doors down from Ethan's. There's a star on the door."

I nodded. "I'll find it."

Helen looked at Paige. "There are some clothes upstairs and, as Ethan noted, 'necessities' for you until you have a chance to get your own things."

Paige looked relieved. "I don't even have a toothbrush. Thank you."

"Of course." With that, Helen smiled and marched back through the House.

We walked upstairs to the third floor and then down the quiet hallway past half the House's bedrooms; the rest were on the second floor. Each of the ninety-ish vampires who lived in the House (of three hundred total House members) had his or her own room. They were all small and dormlike: hardwood floors, simple furniture, small bathroom. Each room was just large enough to afford the vampire a place to sleep and a little privacy at the end of the night.

Near the end of the long hallway, three doors down from Ethan's, was the star-marked guest room, which looked from the outside like the dressing room of a television guest host.

"This must be it," I said.

Paige unlocked the door and stepped inside. I also peeked inside to get a look. It was a nice suite—a little bigger than our dorm rooms, but a lot smaller than Ethan's three-room apartment. The decor was neutral, like a midrange business-class hotel. This was definitely a place for guests—to keep them comfy for a little while, but not so comfy that they overstayed their welcome.

Paige put her books on the bed and glanced back at me. "I'm going to clean up. And I might rest a little bit. I'm pretty exhausted, and I have a lot of Order business in front of me."

"Of course. When Gabriel calls, I'd like to go see Mallory. I can let you know."

"That would be great. I'll want to get a sense of where she is so I can tell the Order."

I nodded. "If you need anything before then, feel free to call Helen."

We said polite good-byes, and I closed the door behind me and nearly ran back to the stairs, where hot-water oblivion awaited. I wanted a long, steamy, environmentally irresponsible shower that wrinkled my skin and fogged the bathroom mirror.

My room was on the second floor of the House. One floor up from the main, one floor down from Ethan's apartments. In another time, I'd appreciated having space between us.

A note was tacked to the bulletin board on the front of my door. It was from Lindsey, my best girlfriend in the House.

Girl! I hope you did lots of nasty with Our Dear Sullivan and made us all proud. Please bring him back in a good mood. And eager to give us all raises. We need shoes. Hearts, Lindsey.

Unfortunately, there was decidedly no "nasty," and I doubted Ethan was in a better mood—not when he was returning to political spite and double the number of enemies he'd had when he left.

When the door was locked behind me, I peeled off my leather jacket and filthy clothes and climbed into the shower.

It was even better than I'd imagined. I scrubbed the soot from my face and let the heat push the remaining pain from my presumptively broken rib and twisted ankle and the green-purple bruise on my arm where Ethan had grabbed me. There was no doubt they were healing, but the residual aches hadn't yet gone away.

When I was pink and clean, I climbed out again and dried my hair. I returned to my basic fall uniform—jeans, boots, a snug long-sleeved T-shirt, and my leather jacket.

Since Paige was resting, I took the time to check my e-mail and the news of the world, then gave my sword a wipe-down with rice paper and oil. A good thing, too—it was filthy. Catcher would not have been impressed that I'd carried it back from Nebraska without cleaning it. Hygiene, sword or otherwise, took an unfortunate backseat in a crisis.

When we were both clean again, I made a trip across the hall to the second floor's small kitchenette.

There'd been an unfortunate lack of deliciousness in the House when Franklin Cabot, the receiver, had been here; he was a fan of green and organic. I was a fan of cellophane wrapped and seriously processed. Now that Cabot was gone, sugar was back in play. The kitchen was stocked with treats, including Mallocakes and bags of blood from Blood4You, our delivery service.

I nuked a bag for a few seconds, poked in a straw, and drained it dry. Even steak only went so far. I drank another pint just to be on the safe side, and because I was being mature, I skipped the Mallocakes for a granola bar that I ate while reading flyers posted to a newly hung bulletin board in the kitchen.

Unfortunately, they weren't exactly cheery. There were instructions for registering with the city and an article about the attack on the vampires and humans Jeff had mentioned.

If no news was good news, was all news bad news?

My stomach (temporarily) sated and Paige (temporarily) out of service, I decided to check on Lindsey. I wasn't sure she'd be in her room in the middle of the night, but since I hadn't seen her since before we left for Nebraska, I figured it was worth the time to knock.

There was silence for a moment, and I almost turned to walk away.

Oh, if only I'd walked away.

I heard a bout of giggling, and then the door opened. Lindsey stood in the doorway, blond hair in all directions, wearing only a sheet and, of course, her Cadogan medal.

And behind her, on her small bed, was Luc. He was also wrapped mostly in a blanket, except for the tooled leather cowboy boots on his feet. He waved collegially, as if I hadn't just interrupted him midcoitus.

"I am . . . clearly interrupting . . . something," I said, taking a step away from the door. "And I don't want to keep doing that, so I am going to just go on about my business."

Lindsey pressed her lips together, then slipped out the door and into the hallway, closing the door behind her. "You good?"

"Me? Oh, sure. I'm—I'm great. I'm just going to go . . . find something else to do."

"Didn't want to see your other boss half-naked, did you?" she asked.

"Or wearing cowboy boots," I agreed. "But I'm glad to see you're getting along so well."

"I'm doing what I can for House solidarity."

"I can see that. Okay. You two have fun. Find me . . . when you're dressed."

Without waiting for her reply, I walked down the hallway again.

"Home sweet home," I murmured.

＋—◄═◆═►—＋

CHAPTER NINE

THE CABBAGE CURE

Ethan may not have been officially Master of the House, but that hadn't stopped him from reclaiming his old office on the first floor. It was big, with a handsome desk, a seating area, and a giant conference table. He sat behind the desk, dressed in a button-up white shirt, his hair pulled back at the nape of his neck. He stared down at a spread of papers, a single lock of golden hair falling across his brow.

He was so handsome. So strong—the epitome of the alpha male. Smart. Strategic and stubborn, often to his detriment. And although I'd spent plenty of time trying, it was pointless to deny the attraction between us. Which was equally strong and stubborn.

I watched him work for a minute—the long fingers and steady gaze, the quirk of an eyebrow when he read a passage he apparently didn't like.

This was hardly the time to have lascivious thoughts about my boss, but if not now, when? The world was not perfect, and the timing probably would never be.

I walked in, made sure we were alone, and shut the door. He

looked up at the sound and watched me stride toward him, then rose from his seat with alarm in his expression.

"What is it?"

I didn't waste time with explanations or pretensions. I wrapped my arms around him and pressed my face into the slick warm cotton of his shirt.

He stroked my hair. "You're all right?"

I nodded. "I'm just really glad to be home."

He pulled back and looked down at me, and the comfort turned into a kiss, inviting and full of promise. He splayed his hands against my back, his fingers hot to the touch, and used teeth and tongue to remind me that I'd come home into his arms again.

He slid his hands down my arms . . . and I instinctively flinched as his fingers made contact with the bruise he'd made.

Ethan pulled back and stared down at me, a new anxiety in his eyes.

Without another word, he returned to his seat, leaving me standing there awkwardly, my stomach doing somersaults.

"What just happened?"

He wouldn't meet my eyes. He looked down at the papers on his desk and kept his eyes there, shuffling through them like they held the world's precious secrets.

"Ethan."

"Merit, I have work to do."

"Don't you think we should talk about this?"

He didn't answer, but his gaze shifted to my arm, the one he'd grabbed. The one he'd bruised. "I hurt you."

"I'm fine. It's *nothing*."

"Did I leave a mark?"

I let my silence answer, and he swore under his breath. After a moment of twisting nerves, he looked up at me again.

"You didn't hurt me," I insisted.

"I bruised you. You flinched."

"You're a vampire and you're strong. It happens."

"Not to me it doesn't." He wet his lips and looked away. "Paige is settled?"

I had no idea what to say, so I answered the question. "She's in the guest suite."

He nodded. Just a single nod before focusing on his papers again.

"Ethan," I began, but I wasn't sure how to finish.

He looked up. "Merit, Darius is on his way. I really need to prepare."

He seemed earnest, and I didn't have any reason to doubt that he wanted to be ready for his meeting with Darius . . . but that didn't ease the low ache in my stomach.

I'd just made it back to the main staircase when Catcher texted me: GABRIEL IS READY.

Stunned, I checked my watch. We'd been home for only a few hours. I guess shifters weren't keen on speed limits, and it wouldn't have surprised me to learn he'd used a little of his own magic to speed up the trip, particularly given his cargo.

Catcher provided an address, so I assumed I was supposed to meet him there. Well, *we* were supposed to meet him there. Paige actually seemed like she had a level head on her shoulders, and she surpassed Simon in common sense by a large margin. That made her the better of the two potential Order representatives who undoubtedly wanted to check in on Mallory. The choice was clear.

I grabbed my sword and dropped by the guest suite to let Paige know we were ready to go. She was in trendy clothes this time: skinny jeans, a long cardigan, and furry boots.

"Helen did good," I said. "With the clothes, I mean."

She looked down at her ensemble. "I was pleasantly surprised. Vamps seem to wear a lot of black. I was afraid she'd put me in head-to-toe waiter wear." She seemed to remember I was wearing black, too, and winced a little. "No offense."

"None taken. Black is the House uniform." I gestured toward the stairs. Paige fell into step beside me and we headed back down to the second floor.

"Color is the new black."

"Not according to Ethan Sullivan."

"So where are we going exactly?"

I glanced down at the address Catcher had given me . . . and smiled a little. If we were going where I thought, Gabriel had been right about my knowing Mallory's caretaker.

"Someplace familiar" was all I said.

We drove into a neighborhood in the western part of the city known as Ukrainian Village. It was a working-class neighborhood with churches and food and people from the old country, and it was home to the unofficial Chicago headquarters of the North American Central Pack, a bar called Little Red.

That's precisely where we were headed.

The bar was on the corner of a strip of run-down buildings. Shifters tended to favor substance over style . . . and hearty Eastern European food over delicate snacks. We hadn't even parked the car when I could begin to smell the tangy, meaty goodness.

I pulled into a spot at the end of a line of diagonally parked motorcycles. Shifters also preferred bikes to cars and prided themselves on the leather and chrome of their usually custom rides.

"They're holding her in a bar?" Paige asked.

"I'm not entirely sure. But it's the Pack's bar, so we'll see."

We got out of the car and skirted the bikes for the sidewalk. Out of respect, I left my sword in the car. Cadogan House vamps had a delicate alliance with the NAC, and I had no interest in screwing that up, especially since they were doing us a favor by keeping Mallory safer and more secure than the Order had been able to.

Catcher pulled up on the other side of my car in his hipster sedan. He popped out of the driver's seat, looking completely exhausted, his eyes red, his cheeks gaunt. He was another casualty of her obsession with the *Maleficium*. He'd probably spent more than a few sleepless nights lately worrying about Mallory and wondering what he might have done to prevent the trauma.

We stopped on the sidewalk. "Jeff gave me the basics," Catcher said, "but I want to hear it from you, because it makes no sense to me."

"If he told you the *Maleficium* was destroyed, and in the process Tate split into two, he was telling the truth. It was as simple and insane as it sounds."

Paige stepped beside us.

"Catcher, this is Paige, who I believe you've heard of. The Tates burned down her house and her entire research library."

"I'm sorry to hear that."

Paige didn't seem impressed with the apology.

Eager to change the subject, I nodded toward the bar. "Did Gabriel say anything about what she's doing here?"

He shook his head. "Not a thing, which doesn't thrill me. I'm not happy about what she's done, but I also don't want her mistreated. I'm here to make sure she's okay."

"If you don't like it," Paige suddenly burst out, "you'll have nothing to say about it. You neither observed her nor stopped her, which is exactly what the Order predicted would happen. You want to know why you were prohibited from coming back to Chicago? For exactly this reason. The prophecy was made—that if you came back to Chicago, things would go bad. You ignored the Order's requests, and now you've fulfilled that prophecy. And look where that's gotten us."

Awkward silence descended.

We'd been told Catcher had been kicked out of the Order because he'd wanted an HQ in Chicago, but the Order was being too stubborn to let him do it. I guessed we hadn't gotten the entire truth. But it also seemed unlikely we were going to get the truth outside a bar in Ukrainian Village, so I pressed on.

"Let's just get this show on the road," I said, and started walking toward the door.

Guitar-heavy music accompanied the smells of food that spilled onto the sidewalk and announced to the world that the bar's patrons were serious about their food, their drink, and their rock.

We walked inside, a bell on the door announcing our existence, but no one paid us any mind. The bar was lined with tables in front of a giant picture window. Members of the NAC nursed drinks and chatted quietly, completely ignoring our trespass into their territory.

They must have known we were coming, because shifters were rarely so nonchalant about intruders in their homes, alliances or not.

"You. Come. Sit."

We looked over at the long wooden bar that lined the other side of the room. A heavy woman stood behind it, her formerly bleached blond hair now a vibrant shade of crimson. This was Berna, Little Red's resident den mother and barmaid.

I walked over to the bar. "Hi, Berna."

She immediately scowled at me. "Still too thin. You eat?" she asked, her voice thick with an Eastern European accent.

"I eat constantly," I promised.

She shook her head and muttered something under her breath. Then she pounded a fist on the bar and stared at all of us. "You will eat now."

I sat down. Paige was smart enough to do the same.

"Where's Mallory?" Catcher asked.

"She is not ready yet. You sit; you eat."

"She's my girlfriend," Catcher said, as if that information would be enough to change Berna's mind.

He was incorrect.

The entire bar went silent, and a fog of prickly magic crossed the room. Catcher may have been a friend of Jeff's and a friend of mine, but he wasn't one of them. He wasn't a shifter, and he wasn't a known ally. He was the boyfriend of the woman who'd unleashed evil on the city and brought them another round of trouble they hadn't asked for.

But Berna didn't need the glares of the shifters at tables around the room to enforce her will. She put a hand on the bar and leaned over it, her bosoms nearly touching the counter as she stared Catcher down.

"You sit. You eat," she said.

Catcher slid onto the stool beside mine while Berna, a victorious smile on her face, disappeared behind the red leather door that led to the back of the bar.

"Good choice," I said.

Catcher rubbed his hands over his face. "I don't want food," he said. "I want this to be over."

"I get that," I whispered back. "But I think part of this exercise is giving up control. Mallory did what she wanted without regard for others; look where that got us. The Pack is intervening, giving her a chance they don't owe her and she arguably doesn't deserve. You're letting them do the heavy lifting; let them make the rules, too."

Catcher made a sarcastic sound, but he didn't walk out. I called that my own victory.

Berna and a shifter helper I didn't recognize brought out plates of food that she set down in front of each of us. Cabbage rolls, by the look of them, which were a particular specialty. While we unrolled paper-wrapped silverware, she poured an unmarked glass bottle of wine into three short cups, then passed those out as well.

"I hope no one's a vegetarian," I said, wasting no time digging into the heady, spicy meat and cabbage. There were few things that took the edge off stress like a good, hearty meal, and I thanked the gods—Ukrainian or otherwise—that I could eat what I wanted with impunity. Sometimes, it didn't suck to be a vampire.

We ate quietly and with purpose while Berna watched behind the bar. She alternated between checking the amount of food on our plates and the status of the soap opera on the small, fuzzy, black-and-white television behind the bar. I didn't know the show or the characters, but a doctor and a nurse were having an affair over the comatose body of, I think, the doctor's stricken wife.

When we'd cleaned our plates—Berna allowed no other option—she cleared them away, then made a low whistle.

After a moment, Gabriel walked through the red leather door. He beckoned us to follow him into the bar's shabby back room, where three other shifters in leather jackets sat around an old vinyl-topped table, cards in their hands and glasses of liquor within easy reach.

I gave them respectful nods and was pleased when they nodded back. Catcher, wisely, kept his mouth shut.

We followed Gabriel through another door into a part of the bar I hadn't seen—the kitchen, which smelled strongly of disinfectant, meat, and well-cooked cabbage.

A few more footsteps put us in the doorway of the back room, where a petite woman in jeans, a T-shirt, and a hairnet stood in front of an industrial sink, scouring food from dishes with a giant sprayer.

Each time something surprised me, I was pretty sure it was the last surprising thing I'd see for a while. And it never, ever was.

The girl with the sprayer? One Mallory Delancey Carmichael.

"Mallory," Gabriel said.

She turned off the sprayer and looked over at him, crimson rising in her cheeks when she realized whom he'd brought into what was apparently her new abode.

She hung the sprayer over a hook on the wall and dried her hands on her pants. Her thin T-shirt was nearly soaked through, and her hands were raw and chapped. That was probably less from the water than from the magic she'd just done.

"Hi," she said meekly.

Cool air flowed in from a screen door at the other end of the room. In front of it stood a beefy shifter in an NAC jacket, a large automatic weapon in his hands. I guessed they weren't taking any chances on another escape.

"You're okay?" Catcher asked.

She nodded, gnawing on her bottom lip. "All things considered." She wouldn't make eye contact with me, so we stood there in silence for a moment.

"Why don't we let them catch up?" Gabriel asked. "Mallory has more work to do before the night's over, and she can finish while she talks to Catcher."

Given the height of the stack of dishes she hadn't yet cleared, she had a good bit of work to go. I wondered if Berna had seconds.

"Good idea," I said, turning around, then motioning Paige to follow me. We walked back into the back room, the table now empty of booze and card players.

"Have a seat," Gabriel said.

I did as I was told. "That guy has a big gun," I noted.

"She caused big trouble."

I couldn't argue with that. "Is this her punishment? Doing dishes?"

"It's not my job to punish her," Gabriel said. "And, frankly, there aren't enough dishes in my lifetime or yours. But that's not the point. The task is irrelevant. The *doing* is what matters. You know what my number one problem is with the Order?"

A dozen snarky answers popped to mind—*They beat you in soft-ball? No official T-shirts? Cheap booze at Order/Pack mixers?*—but I managed to keep them to myself. Paige, wisely, did, too.

"They have monumental power, and for the most part, they use it to serve themselves."

"That's not entirely true—" Paige interrupted, but Gabriel wasn't asking for a discussion and stifled her with a glance.

"I know you imagine yourselves to be problem solvers. But you created the very problems you seek to solve; that doesn't make you philanthropists. It just makes you narcissistic."

"The Packs wanted to decamp to Alaska to avoid involvement in all supernatural problems," I pointed out. "How is that any better?"

"Because we aren't out there pretending to be holier-than-thou sorcerers with answers to all the world's problems."

Paige looked down at the tabletop. That wasn't an admission

the Order had problems, but it was better than the denial everyone else seemed to be wrapped up in.

"Do you have a long-term plan?" I wondered.

"Survival is her long-term plan," he said. "Surviving in *our
environment*—no coddling, no magic, no respect that isn't earned."

That made sense to me. On its face, it was more suited for an
unruly teenager than for a sorceress with a black-magic problem,
but whatever worked.

Twenty minutes later, Catcher came back through the door. He
and Gabriel shared quiet words, and after that, a handshake that I
thought boded well for the state of supernatural relations.

"She's all yours," Catcher said. "She just went upstairs for a
break."

Gabriel nodded. "She gets fifteen minutes after every two-
hour shift when she's on manual labor. It's a very fair system."

Was it weird that the shifters had a system for situations like
this? Nevertheless, I looked at Gabriel. "I'd like to talk to Mallory
if that's okay?"

"Your call, Kitten."

"In that case," I said to Catcher, "I think Paige will need a ride
somewhere."

She rose and nodded, too. "I need to talk to Baumgartner. It's
probably not a bad idea if you do, too."

Catcher nodded, then glanced warily back at the door behind
which Mallory had been at work.

"Go home," I told him. "She's safe here, and you look like you
could use some rest."

"If I weren't exhausted, I'd tear you down from the insult."

"You are exhausted, so I'll pretend you made a sarcastic retort."
I put a hand on his arm. "Seriously. Go take a nap."

He nodded, then led Paige out of the room.

"You sure you're ready for her?" Gabriel asked.

I blew out a breath. "I think the better question is whether she's ready for me."

After Gabe offered directions, I found Mallory in a small bedroom at the top of a narrow staircase at the back of the kitchen.

There wasn't much to the room. A twin-sized bed. A small table. The walls were hung with old-fashioned wallpaper bearing cartoonish strawberries.

Mallory sat on the edge of the bed, staring down at the chapped hands in her lap.

She looked up at me and blew a wisp of lank blond hair from her face. "What are you doing up here?"

"I wanted to check on you."

Silence descended. I'd imagined my reunion with Mallory would be awkward, and I'd been right. "Awkward" was a gentle word for the thousand unspoken words that hung between us. But she was the one who had explaining to do, so I walked inside and shut the door. I sat down on the hardwood floor cross-legged and, in the awkward silence, took a look at my nails. They didn't look great, but I had fought a mutant gnome, a sorceress, and a Tate.

"How are you feeling?" I finally asked.

She laughed mirthlessly and wiped the tears from her cheeks. "The same. Bad. Stupid. I felt wrong, Merit. Deep in my bones, I felt wrong. I still do."

"I know."

She looked back at me. "I wasn't trying to hurt anyone."

"That you weren't trying to do it doesn't mean you aren't responsible for it."

She nodded.

"You could be dead right now, Mallory. We all could be. As it is, Paige's house burned down and the *Maleficium* is toast. Tate is twice the man he used to be, and we have no idea where he is or how to stop him."

"I know," she said. "I know."

"How did you and Tate hook up?"

"I knew the book was in the silo, but I didn't know how to get in there."

So much for my Internet research theory.

"I watched the farm, thinking you'd show up and get into the silo. That's where he found me. He said we could help each other."

"You'd be the distraction, and he'd get Paige to show him the book?"

She nodded. "I'm sorry. I know that's not enough, but I'm sorry."

"Do you understand how much danger you've put the city in? How much danger you put vampires in? When shit goes bad, Mallory, they blame us. They blame *vampires*. The city, the GP, the mayor. We have to register with the city just to live here, like we're convicts on parole."

"What do you want me to say?"

That was a good question. What could she possibly say to erase the last few days?

"I don't know," I said honestly. "We have a lot of history together, you and I. And as glad as I am that you brought Ethan back, it will be a long time before you will make this up to the people you've hurt."

"The pain beat me," she quietly said. "The pain won. I know it's hard to understand . . ."

"It's hard to understand because you didn't talk to anyone about it. I found out you were involved when I discovered you betrayed me and my House. If you didn't think Simon got it, you should have talked to Catcher. Or my grandfather. Or someone. You should have done anything but what you did."

She was quiet for a moment. "Do you hate me?"

It didn't say much for either of us that I had to think about my answer. Honestly, I wasn't sure how I felt. Mallory and I had a history of friendship—more of a history than anybody else currently a part of my life. But she'd pushed forward regardless of whom else she hurt and regardless of the consequences. She'd nearly destroyed Chicago and she'd managed to unleash two Tates on the Midwest.

It was certainly hard for me to like her very much. And it would be a really long time before I could respect her again. But . . .

"No, I don't hate you. You brought him back to me."

"Not for the right reasons."

"No. But you still did it." It would have been all the better if Ethan hadn't been tied to her at all, but I wasn't about to clue her in to that. He may not be her familiar, but I didn't want her testing exactly how deep their connection ran. She wasn't ready for that yet. I wasn't ready for that yet.

"I hated him at first," she said. "And I think you did, too. He was overbearing, and he didn't sympathize with your situation. And then you let yourself be vulnerable, and then he invited another girl to your House. And then he took a stake for you, and he proved himself."

I nodded.

"Maybe he's not quite Darth Sullivan anymore," she said.

We were both silent. "I don't know if I can do this," she said after a couple of minutes.

"Do what?"

"Come back to this. Face up to what I did. I can take responsibility for it. I'm not stupid; I know it was my fault. But I'm . . . mortified, I guess. The shifters—I see how they look at me. There's disgust in their eyes, Merit. Catcher is so angry, so humiliated, and I know the Order's going to punish me. And I deserve the worst they can come up with."

She burst into long, sobbing tears, but I wasn't ready to go to her. I wasn't ready to comfort her—not when she'd hurt so many. Not while they were still grieving, while they still needed comforting.

"How do I go back into the world knowing what I've done?" She looked up at me, her eyes red and swollen, her face wet. "I hurt people, and you guys are in trouble. And Catcher . . . I don't know if I'll ever get him back."

"Did he say that?"

"He said he needed time." She covered her mouth with a hand but only barely managed to stifle her sobs.

"Then suck it up and give him time. God knows, he's earned it. We all have."

"I'm going to lose him. Oh, God, Merit, I'm going to lose him."

"Maybe you will," I agreed. "You betrayed his trust. You chose dark magic over your friends, your city, your boyfriend. I'm sure he isn't taking that well. I'm not taking it well."

"So much for sugarcoating it."

"I'm not here to sugarcoat it. There's no happy ending here, Mallory. No pot of gold. This isn't a TV show you can just turn off and the world goes back to normal. People were hurt. And since Tate's still out there, there's probably more pain on the way."

"I can't face that."

"Yes, you can. And you will."

She looked up at me.

"We all have days when we feel small. Really small. Completely inadequate, but saddled with all this responsibility. I have to keep my House safe, my city from destroying it. I have to do right by Ethan and the rest of my vampires. I have to fight battles against people who shouldn't be my enemies—especially when there are already plenty of enemies to go around. There are days when I would love to pull the cover over my head and say to hell with it.

"But I don't do that. And most people don't do that. Most people get up and do their jobs and work their asses off for no reward at all—but just so they can get up the next day and do the whole thing over again. The world isn't perfect, and some days it wears you down. You can either accept that, and face it, and be a help to others instead of a hindrance. Or you can decide the rules are too tough and they shouldn't apply to you, and you can ignore them and make things harder for everybody else. Sometimes life is about being sad and doing things anyway. Sometimes it's about being hurt and doing things anyway. The point isn't perfection. The point is doing it anyway."

Mallory nodded a little.

"You make a go of it," I said. "The hard way—one day at a time, and with patience. And you'll hope he has patience for you, as well."

She nodded again. The fire gone from both of us, we sat there for a little while—fifteen minutes, maybe—until there was a knock at the door.

We looked up. A shifter I didn't know pointed at Mallory. "You're needed downstairs," he said. He didn't wait for an answer, just disappeared again. I guessed he wasn't expecting disobedience.

She stood up. "I should go."

I nodded. "I should get back to the House. Good luck."

She tucked her hands into her pockets, hiding the physical evidence of her crimes. "Thanks. I guess I'll see you around."

I nodded and watched her walk downstairs to get to work. I hoped this time around something better would come of it.

CHAPTER TEN

JUSTICE LEAGUE

I drove back to Cadogan House and parked three blocks up the street. The road was packed with cars. A nearby home was well lit, with shadowed figures moving animatedly behind sheer window shades. Must have been a party. Vampires in their midst or not, life continued as usual for most folks.

I climbed out of the car and nodded at the two black-clad guards, both mercenary fairies the House paid to keep watch at the gate. Other than their queen, the rest of the fairies were tall, with narrow faces and similar features, long, dark, straight hair, and black uniforms. Most guards were men, although a female guard had watched the post on occasion.

My relationship with the fairies had been tense since my last encounter with Claudia, but since she'd promised our slate was clean, I thought it was worth checking in with them.

"Any sign of Seth Tate?" I asked. "Or someone who looks just like him?"

Both fairies shook their heads. "We're on alert," they said. "She is aware of his existence."

"She," I assumed, was Claudia. She'd once hinted that Tate was "old" magic. Maybe she knew more about him. That might be worth a visit. Or maybe a phone call, since her guards probably wouldn't let me anywhere near her again.

"Does she know what he is?" I asked.

The fairies looked at each other. "He is old," said the one on the right. "Older than the sky masters. That is all we need to know."

"Thanks," I told them. "Feel free to call me if you see him around."

They scoffed, probably at the implication they'd need my help, which was okay by me. Better that they consider me incompetent than dangerous.

I walked into the House and headed for Ethan's office. Our last visit had been weird, and I was hoping the intervening time he'd had to prepare for Darius's visit had calmed him down a bit.

His office door was open, so I peeked inside. He was at his desk, and I knocked lightly on the door to get his attention. He glanced up at the sound.

"I visited Mallory."

Ethan waved me in, and I took a seat at the desk in front of him like a good little Novitiate.

"She's staying at Little Red in Ukrainian Village."

"The bar?"

I nodded. "There's a bedroom above the kitchen, and she's working for Gabriel."

He sat back and crossed his arms. "Doing what?"

"Dishes, at the moment."

Ethan nodded thoughtfully. "Ah. Menial work, to remind her she's merely flesh and bone."

"That seems to be the theory. Berna was there, and I'm assum-

ing she's playing den mother, although Gabriel didn't give me a lot
of details."

"Did Paige or Catcher have anything to say about it?"

I shook my head. "They were going to visit Baumgartner, so
they didn't stay long. It also seems Catcher and Mallory are now
on a break."

Ethan grimaced. "Not entirely surprising given the circumstances, but still a difficult situation."

"She wasn't thrilled. I don't think she was surprised, but she
wasn't thrilled."

"How's her attitude generally?"

"The guilt and remorse are kicking in, which is a good step. I
assume she'll go through stages like any addict." I paused. "Can
you feel her?"

He nodded and looked away. "She's on the other side of town,
so the volume is lower, but the itch is still there. The vague sensation someone is hitchhiking in my brain."

That was a perfect segue to broach the topic of our relationship. But before I could do so, Malik walked in. His skin was the
color of rich caramel, and he wore an ensemble that mirrored
Ethan's. But there was worry in his pale green eyes.

"Liege," I said deferentially.

"She's more obsequious to you than she ever has been to me,"
Ethan observed with a tilted eyebrow.

"Better leadership skills," Malik said with a smile, but it faded
fast enough. "You got Mallory settled?"

"I did. She's with the shifters."

Malik nodded. "It's a good thing she's in hand. I just got a call
from your grandfather. He's been listening to the police scanners."

A handy way to get information when the mayor's office closed
your office and cut off your funding.

"What's happened?" Ethan asked.

"You remember Paulie, Seth Tate's former protégé? He's dead."

Paulie Cermak, a cigar stub of a man with an accent bigger than he was, had run Seth Tate's drug operation. They distributed V, a drug that enhanced the sensation of being a vampire and made users über-aggressive.

"Is that so surprising?" Ethan asked. "Mr. Cermak ran with a tough crowd."

Malik pulled out his cell phone and thumbed across the screen, then showed it to me. The image was in black and white, but its subject was clear enough: Paulie on his back on the ground, lying in a puddle of blood. It looked like his throat had been cut.

I grimaced. "I'm not saying I liked the guy, but I wouldn't wish that on him."

"No," Malik agreed. "It's not a pretty way to go."

"Time of death?" Ethan asked.

"About eight hours ago."

"Plenty of time for the Tates to make it back from Nebraska and do it."

"But why would they?" Ethan asked. "Paulie was old news. Why would he, or it, or they, or *whatever*, have any interest in taking him out?"

"Revenge?" Malik offered.

"But he worked for Tate," I said. "And Tate handed Paulie over to the cops. There's no revenge to be had."

Of course, there was also no theoretical revenge to be had against Paige, but that didn't stop the Tates from burning down her house.

Helen popped her tidy gray head into the doorway. "He's here."

Ethan stood up and nodded. "We have to assume this is the first of many pleasantries the Tates intend to visit on Chicago." He looked at me. "Talk to Luc and Kelley. Figure out what we don't know and what their agendas might be."

His words and tone were wholly professional; there wasn't even a hint in his manner that we had any connection to each other beyond our relationship as Sentinel and Master. Granted, we were discussing serious business and he had a meeting with Darius in the offing, but that didn't stop the gnawing in my stomach.

I nodded and walked into the hallway, closing the door behind me, then stood there for a moment, my head against the wall. Our relationship moved like an awkward and ill-timed dance—forever one step forward, two steps back. But for now, Paulie had to be my first and only concern. So I put Ethan out of my mind and headed for the stairs again.

Each of Chicago's three vampire Houses had a team of guards whose job was to keep the House—and its vampires—safe. As Sentinel, I wasn't technically a guard, but since our guards were shorthanded, I was helping out. Each set of guards had a captain and an HQ.

Our HQ was tucked into the basement of Cadogan House, appropriately near the training room and arsenal, and was outfitted with top-of-the-line electronic whoosits and goodies. Touch-screen panels, wall-mounted screens. Only the best technology for the keepers of Cadogan's safety.

Unfortunately, all the 'lectrics in the world wouldn't rid Luc, the former guard captain, or Kelley, the current guard captain, of their love of paper. They still stuffed our file folders with handouts every day—reports on House activities called the "Dailies," and any other bits of ephemera they thought we needed to know.

And Luc wasn't even our captain anymore. He was House Second and would presumably stay in that position until Ethan held the reins of the House again. Assuming Ethan would . . .

I walked into the Ops Room and found Luc and Kelley staring up at the image of poor deceased Paulie. Juliet sat at one of the computer monitors, her gaze on the closed-circuit cameras around the House and grounds. Lindsey must have been out on patrol.

"Pretty sight, isn't it?" I asked, taking a seat across from them at the conference table.

Luc made a snort and crossed his hands over his button-up chambray shirt. "So, you made it back from Nebraska in one piece."

There was a bowl of chocolates on the middle of the table. I leaned over and grabbed a piece. I'd earned it.

"I did," I agreed. "You would have liked it. There were farms and cows galore."

Luc still had the look of a cowboy just off the range, but at least he was dressed again. My retinas were still burning from my earlier interruption.

"My ranch days are over," Luc said.

"I thought your guard days were over, too."

Kelley snickered. "His excuse is that there are more than enough suits upstairs."

Luc grabbed his own piece of chocolate after carefully rummaging through the bowl for some select piece. "Ethan and Malik are both quite capable of serving as second of this House. They have plenty of years under their belts."

It was hard to imagine Ethan as anything other than head of the House, which made the current arrangement awkward at best.

"What was Ethan like as Peter Cadogan's second?" I wondered.

"Particular," Kelley said. "An avid learner, but usually convinced he was right. He respected Peter, but he chafed at the bit. He was eager for his own command."

"That was before my time," Luc said, "but it matches what I've heard." He sat up straight and pulled his chair closer to the table. "And now that we've reminisced, why don't we get down to business?"

"I presume Ethan filled you in about Tate?" I asked.

"He did. We have one more Tate and one fewer Tate accomplice." Luc tapped the screen and zeroed in on Paulie's injuries.

"Paulie was forty-two years old," he said. "He was killed while he was being transported from lockup to a med facility."

"How are the guards?" I wondered.

"Also dead, as were two med techs, although we haven't seen pictures yet. Information doesn't flow in like it did when your grandfather was official."

I nodded. "So it looks like a hit on Paulie by someone with a grudge."

"That could be Tate," Kelley said. "There could be facts we don't know."

"There could be," I said. "But let's play devil's advocate. What if this has nothing to do with Tate? Maybe somebody had a grudge against Paulie wholly unconnected to the mayor's office. That's not hard to imagine, since Paulie was running drugs."

"True," Luc said. "But I'm a fan of Occam's razor—the simplest explanation is usually the correct one. Two Tates explode onto the scene, and one of their comrades goes rather dead. It's not hard to imagine those two things are related."

"So for now, we work from the assumption that Tate killed Paulie," Kelley said. "And brutally. Why?"

"Cleaning up loose ends?" Luc suggested.

"I don't know," I said. "Ethan and I talked about this earlier. Tate had nothing to lose from Paulie being alive. He's the one who screwed Paulie, not the other way around."

"So what's his motive?" Luc asked. "Tate's all double-your-pleasure now, and the two of them are out there roaming the world." Luc pretended to hold a microphone. "Seth Tate, you've been touched by evil and split into two people! Where are you going next?"

He mimed extending the microphone to Kelley, who leaned solemnly over it. "To Disney World, Ron. I'm going to Disney World."

I looked up at the screen, the emptiness in Paulie's gaze, and the wound at his throat. "Cutting ties," I quietly said. "Maybe it's not about revenge. Maybe it's symbolic—Tate was cutting ties to his past. But why? And why cut him?"

"What are you thinking, Sentinel?"

I squinted at the screen. The wound was slick and clean, not unlike what happened when flesh met a sword. "The Tates literally flew out of the missile silo, and at least one of them has the power to control a vehicle. If Tate wanted Paulie dead, why not just wipe him out with magic? Why use a weapon? Why use a blade?"

Luc and Kelley tilted their heads at the screen. "Huh," Luc said. "Good catch, Sentinel."

"He had a sword in Nebraska," I explained. "I don't know if he created it or found it, but he was pretty good with it."

"If Tate was the perp," Kelley suggested, "maybe he wanted a tangible act. He didn't just snap his fingers and blow Paulie away. He wanted to participate in it, and he did so. Slowly—with purpose."

"So he's a man with a purpose," I said. "Or two men with a

purpose, who aren't afraid of murder. That doesn't make me feel any better."

"Especially since we don't know what the mission is," Luc said.

"It looks to be an angry mission," I said. "A brutal, angry mission."

"True that, Sentinel." Luc's phone beeped, so he pulled it out and checked the screen.

"Well, that is interesting," he said, then tapped his phone a little more. "I signed up for the Hyde Park neighborhood watch. They get crime alerts from the CPD."

"Sneaky," I complimented. "Not a bad way to stay in the loop."

"No, it is not," Luc said, then tapped the panel for the overhead screen. "Especially when it gets us a picture of our perp from the clinic's security camera."

Kelley and I both leaned forward, then watched as an image of a man who looked just like the former mayor of Chicago filled the screen.

"Looks like we can confirm Tate has an agenda," Luc said.

I sighed. "Yeah," I agreed. "Problem is, which Tate? And which agenda?"

We stared at Tate's picture in color and in black and white. We blew it up, then shrank it again, trying to discern any identifying feature that might tell us which Tate had done the deed. But there were no scars. No moles. No hair whorls or visible birthmarks. By all accounts, there was nothing distinguishable about this particular Tate.

So no dice.

That was problematic in two ways. First, it got us no closer to figuring out what the Tates were and where they were going. If we were to have any hope of closing these guys down, we needed to know what they were so we could plan our attack accordingly. Otherwise, we were severely outmatched against two magical something or others with no obvious weaknesses.

Wheaties couldn't even get me out of that jam.

Second, and more important, if one Tate was murdering former accomplices, where was the other Tate? Had they split up? Were they off satisfying their own agendas and wreaking twice as much havoc at once?

Sure, investigating murder wasn't exactly our job. But we had a history with Paulie and with Tate, which brought this under our relative jurisdiction. Besides, Diane Kowalcyzk had already let Tate off the hook once, and she certainly didn't seem to be doing supernaturals any favors.

We needed information. And I had a pretty good idea where we could get it. Well, three ideas, actually. If Tate could double up, I'd go one better; I'd triple up.

My first call was to my favorite shifter. Turns out, murder was also on his mind.

"You've seen the pic?" Jeff asked.

"I have seen the pic. I'm in the Ops Room, and you're on speakerphone. What do you know?"

"Not a lot," he said. "Four dead, one former mayor as suspect. Well, half a double former mayor, anyway. You got anything else?"

"Nope. We've been talking about the brutality, but that's about it."

"Yeah, Paulie definitely met a bad end. Or maybe a deserved end, depending on who you ask."

"Let's consider the deserved-end angle. Do you know anything about Paulie that would suggest Tate thought he had it coming?"

"Not that I'm aware of, but I'm not privy to the entire file. It's in the CPD servers, and I'd have to, you know, sneak around in there to take a look."

He paused silently for a moment, as if waiting for me to object to the possibility that he'd hack the servers to get information on a case. But if it weren't for Mayor Kowalcyzk, Tate wouldn't have escaped, so I didn't really feel that bad.

"Do what you need to do," I said at Luc's nod, absolving Jeff of any vampire-related trouble.

"Will do," he said. "I'll do some looking and get back in touch. In the meantime, be careful. Maybe I'm wrong, but it looks like Tate's clearing the slate. I'd advise anyone who's been in contact with him to keep an eye out."

Unfortunately, he was probably right. That made Gabriel (my second-favorite shifter, although I'd never confess it to him) my next phone call.

"Can you spare a moment?" I asked him, skipping the niceties.

"If it's a quick one. What's news, Kitten?"

"A former colleague of Tate's is dead. Murdered earlier today, as were four people who were around him at the time. It was a pretty gruesome scene, and we think Tate might have been involved."

"Why's that?"

"He's the only one who showed up on the security camera. He and the victim had a connection, so there's a theory Tate's visiting old friends. Mallory is one of those friends, at least theoretically, so you might want to consider doubling up on big guys with guns."

"Noted," Gabriel said.

Finally, since Paige hadn't yet made it back to the House, I gave her a quick call.

"You're a master researcher," I said. "Do you think you'd be able to try to figure out what Tate is and how we can stop him?"

"It's a nice idea," she said, "but as you know, I'm down a thousand books or so."

Oh, but I could solve that problem. "You leave that to me. Just get to the House when you can."

If there was one thing I had in full supply, it was books. And somewhere, in our stacks and stacks of them, had to be the answers we were looking for.

CHAPTER ELEVEN

LOST AND FOUND

If there was murder to be solved, might as well make the best of it. It was logical to presume that I'd be spending the remainder of the evening at work—either in the Ops Room or in the library. Calling in takeout for the crew was the least I could do.

Fortunately, the House's foxy chef, with tiger brown eyes and a bob of dark hair that curved into a point across her forehead, was a friend of mine. Margot was pinup curvy and a lot of fun, and as head of the House's culinary department, the one to ask for food-related favors.

She was also responsible for stocking the kitchens with Mallocakes. How could you not like a girl who did that?

The kitchen was located at the back of the House's first floor, just past Ethan's office. I found Margot leaning against a commercial-sized stainless-steel refrigerator, arms crossed over her white chef's jacket as she watched the activities in her kitchen with amusement.

The grill and prep areas were alight with activity, as the rest of the staff cheered on a man and woman who were sweating over sauté pans filled with what looked like asparagus.

I sidled up to Margot. "What's going on?"

She smiled. "We're having an entrée competition. T.J. and Alice get two ingredients, and they have to make an edible entrée we could actually serve in the cafeteria. *Edible,*" she repeated, slowly and loudly, so the staff and contestants could hear.

She glanced at me. "What can I do for you?"

"Darius is here. Are you making a big dinner for him and Ethan?"

Margot grinned at me. "Wouldn't you know better than anyone what Ethan's plans are?"

Not tonight, I thought. "Actually, I don't, but this isn't about Ethan. It's for the guard crew. I was thinking we might cater in, if you're not whipping up something exotic for Darius."

She snorted. "When it comes to food, he doesn't want exotic. He wants simple and very, very specific." She reached out and grabbed a clipboard that hung from a wall peg. "Charlie faxed this over last night. It's Darius's hospitality rider."

Charlie was Darius's majordomo, and a hospitality rider was a list of demands and snacks a band required at a concert venue.

"How long is Darius going to be here that he needs a hospitality rider?"

"Too long if you ask me." She handed over the clipboard and I scanned through the rider. Some of the stuff was innocuous—type A blood, bottled water, mint gum, Earl Grey tea. (He was British, after all.)

But the list was two single-spaced pages long. Darius was particular about everything from the thread count of his sheets (six hundred) to the content of his meals (preferring raw foods and green juices).

I handed back the clipboard. "Did he do this the last time he was here?"

"He did not," Margot said, hanging it up again. "It's no skin off my back—I can cook anything. It just doesn't bode well if he's setting up house, you know? Anyway, he's going to Navarre House tonight."

More power to Morgan Greer, the Master of Navarre House. Morgan threw tantrums that would impress a two-year-old, but I still wouldn't wish a GP dinner on him.

"In that case, how many favors would I need to owe you for a good Chicago-style meal for the Ops Room? Is that something you can whip up?"

"I can whip up anything," she said with a cocky expression. "I'll send it down when it's ready."

I thanked Margot and left her to her refereeing. I could admit dinner was a distraction, something to keep me occupied while I let my subconscious roll around the status of my relationship with Ethan and Tate's recent rampage. But I still had to function—including eating—even with Tates on the loose. Besides, it wasn't like I had any better idea where to look for them. I walked back through what we did know.

1. Seth Tate was a magical being of unknown origin. He was possibly an old creature and smelled like lemon and sugar.

2. He'd split into two "things" when he touched the *Maleficium* and Mallory triggered the spell.

3. One of those two "things" killed a former accomplice and those unfortunate enough to be around him, but not with magic.

I stopped. If the spell had triggered his split into two creatures, maybe learning more about the spell would give us some clue to his identity and how he could be stopped. I ducked into the back staircase and pulled out my cell phone. I wasn't sure if Mallory had even been allowed a phone or anything else from the outside, but I knew one person who had.

"Catcher Bell," he gruffly, but quietly, answered.

"It's Merit. You heard about Paulie?"

"I did. Jeff texted me."

"Listen, we're at a dead end. I need to know what kind of spell Mallory used to trigger the *Maleficium* this time. Can you find out?"

"She's actually not supposed to be talking about it. She's supposed to be focused on the here and now, not the magic that went down."

I took a seat on the stairs. "I get that. But Tate's already shown a willingness to kill, and I don't know who he'll go after next."

Silence, then, "I'll find out what I can."

"Thank you. Catcher, are you doing okay?"

That question took him longer to answer. "I'm coping. With her failures. With mine."

When he didn't elaborate, I assumed we were at the end of our conversation. "Okay. Call me when you know something."

He grunted, then hung up.

I put my phone away and rubbed my hands over my face, then sat in my self-made darkness for a few moments. Vamps didn't use the back stairwell often, so it was quiet and empty, a bit of solitude from the rest of the House. It wasn't much to look at—warm beige walls and neutral carpet—but I could take a moment to myself and just *be*. I didn't get a chance to do that very often.

With the place to myself, I gave myself another little break.

I let my guards down—the mental and emotional blocks I erected against all the random noise in the world. Sights. Smells. Sounds. My improved vampire senses made it all accessible to me, but the sheer volume of information became quickly overpowering.

But here, in the dark and silence, I could risk a bit of a slip.

Eyes closed, I blew out a slow breath and let the world envelop me. Smells from the kitchen—hot oil and acidic green vegetables. The feel of carpet fiber under my fingers, each discrete knot of yarn meticulously wound together.

And sounds . . . coming from Ethan's office next door.

My eyes flashed open. The back stairway bordered Ethan's office, and the wall separating the two was evidently fairly thin.

I heard Ethan, his tone clipped, and Darius, his careful words and British accent easily recognizable.

At first, I could hear only vague bits of noise, but the more I opened my mind to the sounds, the clearer the words became. And from the sound of it, they'd moved past the pleasantries and things weren't going well.

"I feel like I've been called to the principal's office like a child," Ethan said.

"I've flown to Chicago, if you recall, but I don't object to the analogy. My visit here was necessitated by acts of late in this House. There is the matter of the chain of succession, and the uproar that's been generated in the city more generally."

"My House did not generate that uproar."

"It's not your House," Darius reminded him. "You are not Master of it."

"That is a matter of circumstance, as you are aware, Sire." That was Malik. I guessed Darius wouldn't settle for berating only one Master of Cadogan House.

"Malik still holds this House. Ethan has not been reinvested by the GP."

"He acted in my stead while—"

"While you were *dead*," Darius finished. "You were dead and gone and a new Master was heralded in your place. That is the manner of such things." There was shifting in the room, and I imagined Darius crossing his legs. "While I appreciate your steadfast loyalty," Darius said, "the GP does not exist to satisfy the whims of Cadogan House. The GP exists to protect the interests of all vampires in the United States and Western Europe. Our territory is vast, and our concerns are numerous. They are not limited to a small square of ground in Hyde Park. This House isn't even our only concern in Chicago, much less the Western Hemisphere."

Darius paused. "Ethan, Malik, I will be frank. The GP is seriously concerned. We sent the receiver here to investigate this House, to assure ourselves that the House was stable and things were well in hand." He meant Cabot—the GP's receiver. "I understand his efforts were respected for a time. But ultimately those efforts were rejected and, in essence, so was our oversight."

"He limited the blood supply," Malik said. "He made our guards stand in the sun just to prove a point—and to see our Sentinel removed. He was patronizing on his best night, and abusive on his worst."

"So you assume," Darius said. "He was testing, as he is authorized to test, whether your vampires can withstand the sun and if they will obey the chain of command. One, Juliet, did both. Another did not."

He didn't say my name; he didn't need to. I forfeited the contest while I was still in the shade because Juliet was stuck in the sun, and she'd been too stubborn to give up her position. I wasn't willing to watch her burn to a crisp just to satisfy a GP rule.

"The GP should be their protector," Malik said, "not their torturer."

"And as for Merit," Ethan added, "he clearly wanted her out of the House. He set up the contest so she'd have to forfeit or risk Juliet's life."

"Perhaps. But that does not negate the validity of the test. If someone else, anyone else, had been in Merit's position, would you feel the same?"

"Yes," Ethan and Malik said simultaneously.

"Well, at any rate, the blood rations tested whether your vampires could sustain a shortage. It's not impossible to imagine that they may face something similar in the future, particularly if your politicians' opinions of vampires remain the same. They need to be prepared, and we needed to know how much assistance we'll be asked to provide."

I was probably the last person who wanted to agree with Darius. The problem was, I couldn't fault his logic. Things were bad in Chicago, and it wasn't impossible to believe they'd get worse before all was said and done. Were we spoiled vampires not afraid enough of what might happen? Had we become too soft?

I may have wondered, but Ethan definitely wasn't convinced.

"It can be dressed in pretty language," Ethan said, "but neither Chicago nor the Houses are to blame for Cabot's actions. He rationed blood in a time of crisis. He put an already stressed guard crew through brutal testing. I understand the need for testing—and make use of it when necessary. But I do not sanction exacerbating the crises already faced by this House's vampires. You test when the waters are smooth; you support when the waters are rough. The GP is adding to our problems, not helping fix them."

"The GP is aware of your position."

"And what do they propose to do about it?" Malik asked.

There was silence for a moment, and even when Darius answered, he didn't really answer. "The *shofet* had voted to remove Cadogan House's accreditation."

There was silence except for the sudden rush of blood in my ears.

"The GP cannot disband this House," Ethan quietly said.

"The GP can and will do what it deems appropriate. Tonight I need to speak with Morgan and Scott. I'll interview you two and Kelley tomorrow."

"For what purpose?" Malik asked.

Adding insult to injury was my best guess.

"Because I am head of the GP, and I'd like to see the data for myself." The sound of his voice changed, and I guessed he'd stood up. "Ultimately, the GP will make the decision that is best for all its vampires. The call is not yours to make. Is that understood, gentlemen?"

"Sire," they both said.

And that was apparently the end of that.

I heard the office door open and shut. I snapped my guards back into place and jumped to my feet, then peeked into the hallway. Darius—tall, rangy, and impeccably dressed in dress pants and a pin-striped shirt—walked down the hallway with Malik toward Malik's office.

When they were out of sight, I walked to Ethan's office. This was going to require serious damage control. Although I wasn't entirely sure I was up to the task, someone had to do something. It might as well be me.

I wished myself good luck and opened the door.

Ethan was behind his desk. The room vibrated with furious energy.

"Will they actually kick us out?" I asked, earning me a flash of green eyes.

"You spied on us?"

"I strategically gathered evidence."

"They've effectively done so," Ethan said. "We've been impeached. Now we see if they can make it stick." He rose from his desk, then walked across the room to the bar tucked into the built-in bookshelf. He opened a cabinet, pulled out a bottle, and twisted off the top, then poured two fingers into a short glass.

He took a sip, then glanced back at me. "Beverage?"

I walked toward the bar. "What are you drinking?"

"Forty-year-old Scotch."

I whistled. That couldn't have been cheap, and it probably didn't bode well for the House that he'd cracked it.

Ethan didn't show fear often. That he was worried now about what the GP might do made my stomach flutter with nerves. He was supposed to be the House's rock; the rock wasn't supposed to be nervous.

"No, thanks," I said, crossing my arms and leaning against the cabinets. "What now?"

"Contingency planning," he said darkly. "We have some backup plans in place, and if the House isn't long for GP membership, they'll need executing soon. Malik and I are going to finalize them."

"The GP hasn't done us any favors lately. Is it such a bad thing if we're gone?"

He didn't answer, and he wouldn't meet my gaze.

I guessed it was worse than I'd thought. "Tell me."

He took another sip. "The GP's general philosophy is that if we are not aligned with them, we are against them."

"That doesn't make any sense. There are Rogue vampires in

Chicago. I haven't heard Noah mention any kind of GP harassment."

Noah Beck was the unofficial leader of Chicago's un-Housed vampires; he was also a member of the Red Guard, like me and Jonah.

"For now, it's only a cold war," he said. "The GP believes Rogue vampires will sabotage the Houses; the Rogues believe the Houses exist solely to perpetuate the more fascist tendencies of the GP. The current peace isn't the usual state of affairs."

"So the GP might actually attack us?"

"Should circumstances call for it, yes. Both the GP and the Houses within it."

"Even Sheridan House? You made Lacey Sheridan a Master. She's from Cadogan House, and her alliance insignia is hanging over our front door." Also, Lacey Sheridan had a crush—or more—on Ethan, which made it unlikely she'd take up arms against him.

Glass in hand, Ethan walked to one of the club chairs in the seating area and leaned against it. "Haven't you ever wondered why we bear other Houses' alliance insignia if we're all members of the GP? It's a promise not to take up arms in the event worse comes to worst—or the GP orders them to act."

"Good grief," I said, moving to the chair beside him. No wonder Jonah had joined the RG.

Ethan finished his glass. "Vampires existed long before the GP was formed, and they will exist long after it's gone. We can survive. We just might need to remind our Housed brothers and sisters of that."

And some would take more convincing than others. "Morgan will be a terror."

"Quite possibly. Scott Grey, less so."

And Scott's crew, including the RG member masquerading as a

guard captain, even less than that. But that wasn't information Ethan needed right now.

"Maybe we should beat the GP at its own game," I suggested.

"How do we do that?"

"We could jump ship."

He laughed mirthlessly. "The vampires of Cadogan House do not 'jump ship.'"

"Not even if they get dumped?"

"Not even if," he said. "What's the phrase? You should dance with the one who brought you?"

"Not if you found out the one who brought you made out after third period with the head of the chess club, who was totally not as cute as you." I felt my cheeks warm. "But that's a personal issue we don't need to discuss here. The thing is, we can do better. If they don't want us, we find someone who does."

He chuckled a little, and I felt the wall of tense magic in the room crumble a bit.

"He said he wants to interview you. Do you think he can be convinced to back off?"

"I don't know. Darius would prefer an official House policy of 'shut the fuck up,' which we aren't particularly skilled at. I hardly think he'd waste time on interviews if they weren't for a purpose, but I can't imagine him standing down a decision of the *shofet*."

"Are you going to tell the House?"

"I doubt it. I'm not sure there's any point in raising a flag until the decision is firm and final."

Until then, we'd all have to wait and see what happened, which wasn't a comfortable position for anyone. And speaking of which, for the sake of my own sanity, it was time to discuss the thing we were steadfastly avoiding . . .

"Are we okay?" I asked.

Ethan brushed a lock of hair over my shoulder. I glanced at him, but when our eyes met, he froze and looked away.

My stomach twisted. Now he wouldn't touch me at all?

"I can't have you. Not now."

I could hardly form words. "What? Is this about the bruise?"

He stood up straight. "The mark I put on your body because I was upset? Yes, Sentinel, it is about that."

"That wasn't you," I insisted. "It only happened because of Mallory, because she was close and upset and her emotions were affecting you."

"And we're back in Chicago together," he said. "She's close enough. What if she's upset? What if she becomes angrier than she's been before? What if a bruise is the least harm I could do?"

I understood his point, understood well the risk he was trying to avoid. But he'd saved my life twice. I trusted him implicitly, and not because I feared him or what he might do. "I'm not afraid of you."

"You should be." Ethan walked back to the bar and put his glass on the counter, putting space—an obstacle—between us.

After a moment, he turned around, and his eyes had gone cold.

My stomach did the same.

"I've been thinking . . ."

"That's dangerous," I lightly said, but he didn't laugh.

"I think we should halt our personal relationship for the time being. Until we resolve things with Mallory."

My heart fell to my knees, and I found I couldn't speak a single word. This couldn't be happening. Not after all we'd been through. Not after I'd lost him and found him again.

"And if things aren't ever resolved with Mallory? If you can't ever be one hundred percent sure that you're free of her? What then?"

He looked up at me, and he didn't answer.

Apparently, four hundred years did a lot of damage to a man's psyche, and Ethan's defense mechanism was to throw up barriers to every emotion he didn't care to feel. A few months ago, I'd have walked away from this conversation, and from him. I'd have taken the emotional punch like a trouper and left the room without a parting shot. But he was facing down a demon of his own making, and I wasn't going to help him with the illusion.

I fought back tears. "You'd just give me up?"

"This isn't about giving you up. I can't—I'm not in *control* of myself, Merit."

"Then it's about not trusting me enough to help you when you're in a bad situation."

"It's about keeping you safe until this problem is resolved. I didn't save your life so that I could tear it down again, Merit. I will not put me or you in the position of hurting you again. God willing we can find a way to separate Mallory and me before our immortality has passed us by."

There were times I secretly enjoyed Ethan's alpha-male posturing. But this wasn't one of them. My anger began to rise, spurred by his irritating stubbornness and blind desire to control every situation.

"You're resolving this problem by pushing me away. You're a four-hundred-year-old vampire and avoidance is the best solution you've got?"

"Until you're at the mercy of someone else's thoughts and whims, I'm not looking to you for advice."

That bullet was aimed right at me, but I kept up my guard. "Ah," I said, nodding. "So you're going to take shots at me until I walk away? You know, we've been down this road before. It ended with your apologizing."

"This is different."

It wasn't. Not really. But if he believed it, what could I do? He thought he was protecting me; how was I supposed to convince him his instincts were wrong?

Tears threatening to spill over my lashes, I strode to the office door. I would not cry in front of him.

"We weren't done here," he called out.

I risked a glance back, and I could see the panic flaring in his eyes. Maybe the consequences of his ridiculous position were finally occurring to him. Good. Maybe he'd come to his senses. But I wasn't going to waste time arguing with someone who needed to be convinced I was an asset.

"According to you," I said, "we are done here."

Rarely had slamming a door felt so good.

CHAPTER TWELVE

HIS LIBRARY? WELL STOCKED

It was a good thing we weren't telepathically connected, because he wouldn't have enjoyed hearing my thoughts on the way back down to the Ops Room.

I decided my best option was to help the team with the investigation of Paulie Cermak's death, but with my mind absorbed by Ethan's stubbornness, I was pretty useless. Hoping to identify a specific motive for Paulie's death, I'd printed off as much information on Paulie Cermak as I could find on the Web. The stack of papers sat on the table in front of me, but I hadn't so much as glanced at them in half an hour.

All my brain cells were busy being furious at Ethan and wondering whether I could keep him from imploding our almost relationship. He was afraid he'd hurt me. It couldn't have been easy to feel trapped in someone else's neuroses, but that wasn't Ethan—the man who'd taken a stake for me.

But what was I supposed to do? What was the right thing to do? Respect his wishes and keep my distance? Play the sexy minx and use seduction to get him to change his mind? Or just ignore him until we got Mallory's mind meld squared away?

Getting her squared away was definitely the first thing on my revised agenda.

"Merit!"

I jolted to attention and found Lindsey, who was back from guard duty and sat across from me at the conference table, staring at me with amusement.

"What?"

"Your phone is ringing."

For the first time, I heard the phone ring from the pocket of my jacket, which I'd slung over the back of my chair. I managed to grab the phone just before it stopped ringing.

"Hello?"

"Too busy to answer the phone?"

It was Catcher. "Sorry. I didn't hear it ring. What's up?"

"I talked to Mallory. She used a conjuration spell."

"Which does what?"

"It conjures. Brings something into the space that hadn't been there before. The spell was also in the *Maleficium*, just like the familiar spell. She copied it before they took the book away so she'd remember the steps."

"Same magical theory as last time?" I wondered. "Use a bit of dark magic to upset the line between good and dark magic, and invoke the rest of the dark magic out of the *Maleficium*."

"That seems to be what she was trying to do. And that explains the second Tate. She conjured him into existence."

But had she? "I don't understand. If she was conjuring something, shouldn't something new have popped into the room? I mean, instead of Tate splitting in two?"

"That's possible, I guess, but it's hard to say. Tate *touched* the *Maleficium*. That's like being shot at point-blank range by magic. It could have affected the outcome of the spell."

"Okay," I said. "Thanks for the information."

"Sure," he said, and the line went dead.

I put the phone away, and when Luc rolled his office chair closer to the table for a report, I relayed what Catcher had said. But while I took Catcher's point about Tate having touched the *Maleficium*, the magical math still didn't make sense to me.

"He said conjuration is supposed to bring forth something new," I said, my gaze shifting between Lindsey and Luc. "Not duplicate something that already existed."

"The intricacies of conjuration aren't my specialty," Luc said. "There is, however, a library at your disposal. You should take full advantage."

I nodded. "Good idea. When Paige gets back, I'll stick her in the library and tag team with her. I'm hoping there's a logical explanation."

"As logical as a man asexually reproducing before your eyes."

"Precisely."

"And that's enough for me," Luc said, wheeling back to his desk.

As soon as he was gone, Lindsey leaned forward. "Where were you before the phone rang?"

My cheeks warmed. "I was just thinking."

"You were not just thinking," she whispered, frowning. "Do you want to talk? We can go outside."

There wasn't much point in trying to fool Lindsey. She was an empathic vampire and could read others' emotions.

"Not right now. Maybe later."

Lindsey straightened up again. "In that case, Sentinel, get back to work. We've got double trouble on the loose."

And double trouble in the House, even if no one knew it yet.

A few minutes—and no substantive work—later, the door opened and Margot walked in with an assistant and a rolling cart of fragrant food.

"What's this?" Luc asked, walking toward Margot.

"Your very thoughtful Sentinel ordered in dinner," Margot said. "She asked for a home-cooked meal, but I cheated a little bit."

Luc put a hand on my shoulder. "I knew you were worth keeping around."

I rolled my eyes. "What did you bring?" I asked, but the answer became clear quickly enough, and I smiled for the first time in a while.

"You made a trip to Maxwell Street," I said.

"It's cold out. I thought 'hearty' would do you good."

There were a number of foods in Chicago that were totally recognizable to tourists, like Chicago-style hot dogs and deep-dish pizza. But those of us who lived here knew some of the other secret delights: rainbow cones; Garrett's popcorn; and Maxwell Street Polishes. The latter were Polish dogs with grilled onions and mustard. They were hot, spicy, and crazy delicious. And there weren't just Polishes. She'd also provided cheese fries, ramekins of custard, and glasses of blood.

Cholesterol was no match for vampire immortality.

"This looks wonderful, Margot," Luc said as Juliet and Lindsey grabbed plates and Polishes. Pity Kelley was out on patrol.

"You're quite welcome." Margot finished up, then wheeled out the squeaky cart and closed the door behind her.

"You've outdone yourself, Merit."

"I didn't know she'd actually make a run for Polishes. She went above and beyond for that." I grabbed a Polish and took a bite, closing my eyes in sheer pleasure. I loved Chicago.

We ate quietly, four vampires with quick metabolisms and worry in our hearts, at least until Luc's pager buzzed. He unclipped it and checked the screen. "You might as well head upstairs. Paige is here."

I finished my dog and wiped my face with a napkin. "I'll get her settled in the library." The next words were out of my mouth before I thought better of it. "Could you tell Ethan about the conjuration spell?"

Luc and Lindsey exchanged a glance. "Why don't you tell him?" Lindsey asked.

Because he's being an ass, I silently thought, but played my cards diplomatically.

"I want to get Paige into the library, so I won't have time to drop by his office, and my phone doesn't work very well in the library. Because of the stairs. And such."

It was a crappy excuse, and I could tell neither one of them bought it, but they let it go.

"We'll tell him," Luc said. "You get to work."

I smiled with false cheer, then hightailed it to the door. Lindsey was going to have a field day with this one.

I found Paige in the first-floor foyer. She had shopping bags in hand, and she was wearing jeans and a long-sleeved White Sox T-shirt. She'd found some clothes of her own; pity she'd picked the wrong team. We did live on the South Side of the city, which made the White Sox a logical choice, but that didn't diminish my love for the Cubs.

"Welcome back," I said.

"Thanks. It's been a long night."

I guided her toward the stairs, and we headed to the second floor. "Where did you go?"

"Catcher gave me a lift to meet with Baumgartner. I talked to him. I talked to Simon."

"What did Baumgartner have to say?"

"Not a lot." She sounded saddened by the answer.

We rounded the second-floor landing. Paige paused and tapped her fingers against the banister. "I had this idea—that I was part of something good. Something important."

"And you don't think so now?"

She looked away. "I don't know. I asked him about Mallory, about Simon, about Catcher. About what they all missed."

"What did he say?"

"He shrugged. Just kind of"—she imitated a beefy, shoulder shrug—"shrugged, and said we do the best we can."

"That's pretty lame. I mean, the Order failed this city—and Mallory—in a pretty spectacular way."

"Yeah," Paige said. "And I asked him about Tate. He said it was interesting, and that was that. He went back to polishing his bowling ball."

"He was not polishing his bowling ball."

"Hand to God. The Order is a union, and I guess not in the workers-rights-and-fair-labor-standards way. More like the let's-sit-around-and-blame-Jimmy-Hoffa way. I've only talked to Baumgartner on the phone, and I guess I never got how truly lame they are. And there's so much talk about the majesty of our magic, how powerful we are, how special. And how do we use that power? We talk a lot and completely ignore what's going on around us."

"Too much talky, too little walky?"

"Exactly!"

"That is a bummer."

"How's Mallory doing?" I felt weird asking the question, like I was checking in with my best friend's new best friend.

"You'd know better than me. I didn't know her before, so it's hard to compare what she's like now. The shifters still have her doing manual labor, and I don't think they're going to change that plan anytime soon."

"A little more of that walking we were referring to," I thought aloud. "They're very particular about the things they get involved in, but when they're in, they're in all the way."

Paige nodded. "That was my impression."

"Catcher told you about the spell she tried to work?"

"Conjuration?" Paige nodded. "Yeah. That's another advanced spell, impressive for her to work."

"I still don't buy that a conjuration spell made one Tate split into two Tates. That doesn't make any sense to me. That should be the result of a duplication spell or something."

She nodded. "Duplication's not the way the conjuration spell is supposed to work; it's not the predicted outcome. Hey, about Catcher, and what I said earlier. I'm not trying to bash him. He's a legend in Order circles. Famous—or infamous, as the case may be. I know he's got the goods, or the Order wouldn't care so much. But when I called him out yesterday, I really felt like I had to lay down the law, you know?"

"You definitely put him in his place."

She grimaced. "I wasn't trying to humiliate him, but somebody has to step up."

I couldn't argue with that. "What's the story about the prophecy?"

"He made a prediction—you know we can do that, right?"

I nodded.

"The prediction was about really bad things going down in Chicago. He warned the Order, but the Order was afraid that because he'd made the prediction, he'd be involved in those really bad things. They banned him from coming to Chicago."

"He came anyway."

"He came anyway," Paige agreed, "and they kicked him out of the Order because of it. I asked him about it."

"What did he say?"

"He said the world would continue to turn and the prophecy would fulfill itself, and he wanted to be here when it did. He said he worked to stop all the natural disasters when they were going on and tried to help you figure out what was going on. The irony was that the trouble was boiling in front of his eyes, but he was so focused on the city, he completely ignored it."

"And so here we are," I said.

"Here we are," she agreed.

"Actually, I meant that literally." I pointed Paige to the double doors in front of us, then opened them with a *whoosh* of air.

It was an impressive reveal, if I do say so myself. The Cadogan House library was pretty spectacular. Two floors of books linked by a red wrought-iron staircase. The library held volumes on all sorts of vampire and supernatural topics, from history and food to a complete set of the *Canon of the North American Vampire Houses*, the codified law for American vampires.

Paige's reaction was pretty similar to what mine had been a few months ago. She walked inside, mouth agape, and stared up at the shelves and stacks and balcony of books. I figured it was an important room for an archivist.

"Welcome to the Cadogan House library."

"Shut the front door," she said. She walked toward the closest row and began to scan the books' spines. "*Morphology of Vampirus Americanus. Pixies and Their Parts. The Horn of the Unicorn, and Other Important Features.*"

She trailed her fingertips across more of the spines, then looked back at me, eyes wide in amazement. "Your anatomy section is crazy impressive."

Not that I'd looked, but I didn't have the supernatural literature chops to disagree with her. "Yeah. It's pretty good."

She rubbed her hands together like a plotting evil stepmother. "So I need to research the secondary and tertiary effects of conjuration spells. Where might I find—"

"Quiet down, could you?"

We turned around. The House librarian, whom I knew only by his title, stood at the end of the row. He was a little shorter than average, and his arms were crossed over a black short-sleeved polo shirt. His shortish brown hair stood up in little whorls, like he'd been running his hands through it.

"Sorry," I said with an apologetic smile. "She got a little excited. Your library is pretty phenomenal."

"She?" he asked, turning his gaze on Paige. He cast a long, lingering look at her boots-clad legs before meeting her gaze. "You're tall, aren't you?"

"I am . . . yes . . . tall. So, yeah. Tall."

The room went silent as they stared at each other. There must have been something in the water today.

"This is Paige," I said. "She's the Order's archivist. She's stationed at the silo in Nebraska where the you-know-what is sometimes kept. She's staying with us for a bit. Do you have any literature about conjuration?"

He ignored me, probably because he was still staring at Paige. I knew she'd like the books; it hadn't occurred to me that the librarian would like her.

I cleared my throat to get his attention. "Conjuration," I said, more loudly, when he finally looked my way. "Got any books on that?"

His expression was flat. "Of course we do. Follow me."

He disappeared into a row. We didn't dare disobey.

An hour later, the books had piled up. There were four stacks, each two feet tall, on our library table, and there was a pile of open volumes around us.

The evidence of our failure to find anything useful.

I closed one more and rubbed my eyes, which were beginning to blur from scanning tiny print. The library doors opened, and Ethan stepped inside. My stomach lit with nerves, and I darkly wondered if that was going to happen every time I saw him for the rest of our immortal lives. I did not look forward to that possibility.

But it was what it was, and until I figured out a way to end his connection to Mallory or change his mind, I still had work to do, and I wasn't going to let an irritating man get in the way of that.

He strode to our table and surveyed the mess with his hands on his hips.

"No luck?"

"Not even a little. We've found plenty of descriptions of conjuration. But not a single mention of anything remotely like what we saw. Nothing about one creature splitting into two identical creatures. I like books, but I don't like it when they fail me. And tonight, they have failed me."

Ethan glanced around. "Where's Paige?"

"With the librarian. They seem to be getting along well."

He looked impressed. "Our librarian and the Order's archivist. I suppose that's fitting."

Clearly, Ethan was trying to act like everything was okay between us. And in a sense, it had to be—we had to work together, regardless of our personal drama. But if that's what we were doing—pretending all was well—then two could play at that game.

"They do have books in common. But then, I love books, and I'm not exactly hitting on him. We'll see how it goes. How are the transition plans coming along?"

"Slowly. Our ties to the GP are complex and contractual. Tentacular."

I looked up at him. "Tentacular. Nice word."

"I aim to impress." He glanced at his watch.

"Busy night?" I hated that I had to ask him, that I had no idea what his schedule held.

"On occasion it feels as though I exist to move from one meeting to the next."

"You could let Malik handle those meetings."

He gave me a flat look, the look of a Master vampire who couldn't believe the Novitiate before him had said something so ridiculously naive.

"I am not officially the Master of this House," he admitted, "but nor will I relinquish my responsibilities."

"I wouldn't dare suggest otherwise. What's the next meeting about?"

"The vampire registration laws. One of Mayor Kowalcyzk's aides has requested a meeting. There's talk of stationing a booth in the foyer."

"Intrusive, but convenient."

"My thoughts exactly."

Paige stepped out of a row, a couple more books in her hands and a frown on her face.

"No luck so far?" Ethan asked.

"Nothing at all." She pulled out a chair and took a seat. "But you can't fault the resources."

"I shelve a nice library," Ethan agreed. "Well, I'll be off. Good luck, and let me know if you find anything."

"Of course," I promised. I wasn't going to miss a chance to tweak him a little more. On the other hand, I was the one who took in the view as he crossed back to the library door.

I'm pretty sure I sighed.

"Have you been together long?" Paige asked when I turned around again.

"We're not together now."

She looked decidedly skeptical.

"It's a long story." I leaned forward. "Listen, about this connection between him and Mallory—do you know anything that would stop it?"

Paige frowned. "To tell you the truth, I'm not sure why he still has the connection, especially since the book was destroyed. But there could be methods or work-arounds I'm not familiar with."

I nodded. "Okay."

"Maybe he could learn to control it? He does seem to have a lot of willpower."

"That is an understatement," I agreed. "Tall, blond, and stubborn."

Paige laughed. "Tall, blond, and stubborn is usually right in my wheelhouse. I'm actually kind of surprised I'm interested in the librarian." Her cheeks went a little pink. "Put two guys side by side—a fair one and a dark one—and I am usually tuned in to the tall, blond, and handsome type."

Something she said rang familiar in a deep part of my brain. "What did you say?"

"What? Oh, I was just saying I normally prefer blonds."

But it wasn't her taste in men that interested me—it was the phrase she'd used. "Dark one," I repeated, my gaze shifting back and forth as I searched my memory. "Why does that sound familiar?"

"Like, as a phrase?" Paige frowned. "I don't know it. When did you hear it?"

"When we were in Nebraska," I realized, and the memories clicked into place. "Todd, the gnome, called Tate a 'dark one.' I thought he was referring to the color of Tate's hair—because it's dark brown. But maybe that's not what he meant. Maybe it's not a description. Maybe it's a name, or a species."

"I'm not familiar with the term, but I can look it up." She pulled a giant book closer to her. "I'll check the sorcerer's omnibus."

"Sorcerer's omnibus?"

"It's like a giant magical dictionary," she absently said, and she was already thumbing through the entries. "If it's not in here, it doesn't exist."

She flipped the book open to a page, then skimmed a finger down the page she'd found. But when her shoulders slumped, I knew she hadn't found it.

"Nothing?"

"It doesn't exist." She looked up at me. "If that was really a term of magical art—and not just a description—it would be in here. This thing is super-thorough."

Maybe, but I wasn't willing to give up so easily.

"Dark one" was an odd phrase. It wasn't the kind of thing someone would just randomly say. On the other hand, Todd was an unusual guy.

"'Sorcerers just don't get us,'" I remembered him saying, and I began to smile. Maybe we weren't coming at this from the right direction. Maybe "dark one" was a magical term of art . . . but not for sorcerers.

I jumped up, ignored Paige's question about where I was going, and ran down the aisles until I found the librarian.

"Are you running in my library?"

"Only because I need you. Do we have any books written by gnomes?"

He frowned but nodded. "Yes. Why? I thought you were looking for conjuration spells."

"Been there, done that." I smiled and thought of Todd. "I need gnome books. You know, because sorcerers just don't get them."

He didn't get the joke. "They're in cultural studies. About four rows to the left. Your *other* left!" he corrected, when I dodged right.

A few minutes later, Paige found me on the floor pulling books into my lap. "Bright idea?"

"I think it's a gnome's phrase."

"Damn," she said. "I wish I'd thought of that." She sat down on the floor beside me, and I handed over *A Gnome's Guide to Names*.

"Come on in," I said. "The water's fine."

It wasn't in *A Gnome's Guide to Names*. It wasn't in *Life from the Ground Up*. It wasn't in *Better Underground Gardening*, *Home Sweet Hillock*, or *Homes for Gnomes*. (I couldn't make this stuff up.)

We did learn that gnomes are especially careful about the layout of their underground dwellings. We learned they preferred plaid to gingham in their decor and often used a dozen or more false entrances and baffles to thwart unwelcome visitors.

When we could map out their favorite color palettes, we called the librarian back into it.

Well, *Paige* called the librarian into it. After flouncing up her hair.

Maybe she had been lonely in Nebraska.

"What exactly are you looking for?" he asked.

"Todd, one of the gnomes who fought with us in Nebraska, called Tate a 'dark one.' We're wondering if there's anything to that."

The librarian rolled his eyes and walked down the row. "Sometimes I wonder why you don't just ask me the questions in the first place. Follow me."

We shoved our books back on the shelves and traced his path to a bureau of long, flat drawers. He opened a long drawer and rifled through it, then pulled out a dark blue paperboard box with brass corners, which he carefully carried to the closest table. He walked slowly, as if the materials in the box were delicate enough to disintegrate if he rattled them too much.

He placed the box on the table and lifted the lid. Scents of old paper and herbs—rosemary and thyme—filled the air, along with the damp scent of earth.

"Gnomes," I said.

The librarian nodded and pulled a pair of thin cotton gloves from the pocket of his jeans. He slipped them on and carefully removed a sheet from the box.

The sheet was thick and yellowed, the warp and weave of fibers from some ancient plant visible like a watermark through the page.

Across the surface were tidy rows of neat Latin words, and the lines were illuminated with drawings and fanciful letters in red, blue, and gold paint. It wasn't unlike medieval manuscripts I'd seen while in graduate school.

"It's beautiful," I said. "What's it from?"

"It's a hand-copied page from a document called the *Kantor Scroll*. Kantor was a gnome, a scrivener who put together an impressive library of texts."

Paige walked around the table to give the document a closer look. "About what?"

"The usual. Love. Religion. Politics. War was a particular specialty. Gnomes are close to the ground, so people tend to forget they're there. They do a great job of war reporting because they can get in and around so easily."

The librarian set the first sheet aside and pulled another from the box. This one had a drawing. The images weren't very sophisticated, but their subject was clear—a mud and stone city under attack by a storm of blue sparks as big as a cloud. The cloud had already consumed some of the buildings, leaving them in shambles.

"I've seen that before," I said, thinking of the wall of magic Tate had sent after us in Iowa. "Where was this?"

"Carthage," the librarian said. "The city was completely decimated by the Roman army, and they salted the earth afterward so nothing could grow."

"They destroyed the city with magic?" Paige asked.

"That wasn't the human version of the story," I said, but looked at the librarian.

"Do the Romans strike you as folks willing to credit someone else for a victory?"

He had a point.

"According to Kantor," he said, "the Roman armies claimed the victory, but they didn't exactly fight the battle."

I pointed at the document but was careful not to touch. My heart began to race as we moved closer to an answer. "Whoever did the fighting here, Tate can do the same kind of magic. What does Kantor have to say about it?"

"He says the magic was made by a 'Dark One.'" The librarian smiled smugly, but he'd earned it. He was good.

"So what is a 'Dark One'? Genies? Demigods? Are they related to fairies? Claudia, the queen, seemed to know who Tate was."

The librarian didn't look impressed by my magical auction. "You'd hardly believe me if I told you."

"Try me."

"They're called 'messengers.' They were tall. Winged. Their magic allowed them to serve the world."

"Are you talking about angels?" Paige had leaned forward a little, like she was afraid we'd think the question was crazy.

"Yeah, but without the religious baggage," the librarian said. He pulled out another document. This one showed a fight between two creatures—one with the white wings of a traditional angel, one with wings as dark and slick as a bat's. They were both tall and sinewy with muscle, their bodies draped in flowing cloth, their wings slicing the air like blades. They were locked in battle with each other.

"There were two kinds of messengers," the librarian said. "Those who carried peace and bounty, and those who carried out justice."

"I assume this story does not have a happy ending?" I asked.

"You would be correct," the librarian said. "The messengers of peace did their jobs. They rewarded the good. The messengers of justice did their parts, too. They punished the evil. Together, they kept the world in balance.

"But the messengers of justice enjoyed the violence a little too much. They decided small missteps by humans were worthy of severe punishment. It wasn't about justice anymore. It was about ego, about their conceptions of right and wrong. They lost their moral compass."

"The Dark Ones?" I guessed.

"The Dark Ones," he confirmed. "Angels with brutal swords of righteousness. Humans fought back against them; the Dark Ones went nuclear. They took out entire cities they thought didn't measure up to their standards. Carthage was just one example. The conflict goes back much, much further."

"How far?" Paige asked.

"Sodom and Gomorrah far."

"Why call them 'Dark Ones'?" Paige asked.

"According to Kantor, the darker their souls became, the darker their wings became." He flipped a page again. This drawing showed only a caricature of a creature with dark wings, their size dwarfing the rest of the image. "Because of that, some sups, including your gnomes, referred to them as 'Dark Ones.'"

"And other sups?" I wondered.

He glanced at me. "Humans think of them as demons, although to be a 'demon' doesn't really mean anything. 'Demon' is a quality, not a species. *To be demonic*—those who abandon good and give themselves wholly to the darkness."

"So Todd thinks Seth Tate was a Dark One," Paige said. "Theory or fact?"

"Tate fought Ethan with a sword, and Paulie was killed with a blade," I said. "Paulie's definitely guilty of some transgressions. Manufacturing *V*, for one. If Seth is a Dark One, he could have had a justice motive. Harsh justice, but still."

"Ironic he doesn't consider himself worthy of that kind of justice," Paige muttered. "But even if that explains Seth," Paige said, "what about the *other* Seth?"

"I have no idea. So, to summarize, Seth was an angry angel, Mallory tried to conjure evil, and Seth touched the book at the same time she triggered the spell. That somehow doubled him up, so now we have two identical angry angels flying around Chicago."

The very idea made me want to run away screaming . . . or hide under my bed for a few weeks.

"That would appear to be the case," Paige said.

I glanced back at the librarian. "Were there a lot of messengers? If he's one of them, can we narrow down which one?"

"There aren't many. Some you've heard of: Michael, Gabriel, Raphael."

"The archangels," I said.

"An angel by any other name," the librarian said. He flipped back to the first page he'd showed us, the one with the Latin text. "There are three Dark Ones listed: Uriel, Dominic, and Azrael."

"Are there any drawings that show their faces in any detail?"

"Not that I'm aware of."

Every question we managed to answer about Tate seemed only to spawn four or five more.

But the real question was how much time we'd have to figure it all out.

The sun was nearly up before I returned to Ethan's apartments. I'd have much rather returned to my room, but we'd made too much progress not to give him a report. Trouble didn't care if he was being an ass; in fact, the Tates probably would have been thrilled to hear it.

I found him in a leather armchair in his sitting room, one leg crossed over the other, his head on the back of the chair, his eyes closed.

He looked exhausted, and I could sympathize. It had been a long night—too full by half of magic books, pretentious Brits, and murder, and not nearly full enough of satisfying answers. But we had at least one more than we'd had a few hours ago, so I stood in front of him at attention and gave him a precise report.

"So Tate is a Dark One. An angel of retribution who couldn't control his more violent urges."

"That seems to be the case. Do you know anything else about the 'Dark Ones' myth? Does it sound familiar to you?"

"You mean because of my age?"

Angry or not, I wasn't going to pass up an opportunity to tease him. "Well, you were alive during the big bang, weren't you?"

He rolled his eyes. "I know the myths of the fallen angels. Those who didn't support the right camp and ended up cast aside at a decidedly downward angle. I wasn't aware they were alleged to have caused the destruction at Carthage. It hardly seems possible the Romans would have been able to destroy all the evidence they weren't the true victors."

"You came back from the dead," I pointed out. "You really aren't in a position to argue what is and isn't possible."

"A fair point."

"How are you feeling?" I asked him.

"She's there," he said, rubbing his temples. "There's a dull buzzing. But I've pushed it back into the corner of my brain dedicated to football and video games."

"In other words, rarely used."

"Just so."

"Is it wrong of me to say this could have been avoided if only the Order had paid better attention to Mallory?"

"Not wrong at all," he murmured. "Unfortunate that it's come to this, but not wrong. They have failed all of us, and Mallory, in a multitude of ways. And they appear to be offering no assistance in cleaning up the mess they so tidily made."

We were quiet for a moment, watching each other. Ethan seemed to be at peace, but it seemed likely his mind was roiling with possibilities, probabilities, strategies, outcomes. I just wasn't sure how many of those involved me.

I decided to save myself the rejection, even if it was only

temporary. "Well, I should get back to my room. Dawn will be here soon."

"I want to pretend all is well in the world," he said. "I want to pretend our House will be safe tomorrow and secure in the bosom of the GP. But that's not the world around us."

I think he meant it as an apology, but I wasn't in the mood. I wanted sleep and a warm body to curl against, and I wasn't going to get it.

"The world is what it is," I said. "We can only battle it back."

As dawn approached, I slipped back into my room and my own bed, the sheets cool and undisturbed. I tried to quiet my mind, and I tried not to worry about what tomorrow might bring, or the fact that the Tates were still out there, undoubtedly planning their next attack. The sun was rising, and there was nothing I could do about it now.

I hoped Chicago wasn't Carthage. I hoped we could all find some peace. I hoped the sunrise wouldn't bring more problems than it solved.

CHAPTER THIRTEEN

EVERY TIME A BELL RINGS . . .

I jolted awake nine hours later, still alone in my chilly bedroom. My phone was ringing, so I grabbed it from the nightstand and checked the screen. It was Jeff.

"Hey," I said, checking the time. It was barely after sunset; Jeff must have been aching to call me.

"We have news," Jeff said, "and it's not looking good."

Not exactly the way I wanted to start the night, but then not terribly surprising, either. "What's happened?"

"Not what has happened, but what *might* happen. Turns out, the crime scene folks found something at the scene of Paulie's murder. They thought it was just a random bit of paper at the scene but, when they checked the blood patterns, discovered it was put there after Paulie's throat was cut."

I sat up and pulled my hair from my face. "What was it?"

"A newspaper article. Remember I told you about those four cops who got busted for beating up those vamps?"

"The ones you told us about in Nebraska? Yeah. Why?"

"The evidence at the crime scene? It was an article about them."

"Why would Tate be interested in something like that?"

"The article was about the cops being released. I guess they had to do some processing, or waiting for the bail money to go through, I don't know. Their release is scheduled for tonight—there's a big to-do at a CPD lockup on the South Side. Plenty of people are pissed about it."

That made more sense than I'd wanted it to. "Crap," I muttered.

"What?"

"As it turns out, we're hypothesizing Tate's an old-school messenger—an avenging angel with a revenge problem whose halo fell off many, many centuries ago."

"A fallen angel?"

"That's the one. And if he thinks the cops didn't get the justice they deserved, he might be hoping to wield his sword against them."

"Tate the supernatural avenger," Jeff muttered. "In what universe does that make sense?"

"This one, unfortunately," I said. "First things first. Can you make contact with the cops or their attorneys? Let them know he's a threat?"

"Already tried that route. Chuck called one of the attorneys—apparently he'd had some relationship with him when he was on the force—and tried to get him to cancel the conference."

Chuck was my grandfather. "The attorney didn't buy it?"

"He did not. He said his client was a cop and he could take care of himself, especially against, and I'm quoting here, a 'desk-riding politician.' He said he wouldn't cancel the press conference because the city of Chicago needed to know how poorly his client had been treated. He supposedly went on for ten minutes about the injustice of being a cop behind bars."

I rolled my eyes. "Then maybe the cop shouldn't have helped beat the crap out of four people."

"I believe that was Chuck's point. But I'm sure he said it more diplomatically."

"Probably so. I guess the lawyers will find out soon enough about Tate's 'desk riding.' If you'll send me the article, we'll see what we can do from this end."

"Will do," he said.

"Thanks, Jeff. We appreciate it."

"No prob, Merit. I'm sure we'll talk later."

The e-mail came almost immediately. The article was lengthy; someone had done an in-depth review of the cops involved and their attorneys' unsurprising friendships with Mayor Kowalcyzk. That certainly explained the early release, and it might very well have been enough to trigger another burst of angelic retribution.

I hung up, grabbed a shower, got dressed, and ran upstairs to Ethan's bedroom.

He opened the door in nothing but silk pajama bottoms, and I nearly wept at the sight. Long, flat abdomen, ridges of muscle at his hips, his hair loose around his shoulders. It was almost cruel to see and not be able to touch.

"Is everything okay?"

I told him about the article Jeff had found. "This could always be a trap," I warned. "Maybe one of the Tates wants another run at us and left the article at the crime scene so we'd find it. But we have to take the chance. The attorneys aren't listening, the mayor has dismissed the Ombud's office, and there could be hundreds of people at the press conference."

Ethan nodded. "If we're the only ones who see the threat, I suppose we'll be the ones to handle it. And I agree—the risk of collateral damage is too high to ignore. I'll get dressed. Get your sword and meet me in the office."

This time, I did as I was told.

Luc, Malik, and Ethan were already in Ethan's office when I arrived, the blade of my katana impeccable, my body clad in head-to-toe leather for the impending fight.

I'd finally remembered to grab the worry wood from my room. It was a small ridge in my jacket pocket, a comforting reminder that magic wasn't all bad, that it could even be helpful. That was a lesson I was fighting hard to remember lately.

They were seated around the conference table. I joined them.

"The officers are scheduled to be released within the hour," Ethan said. "I contacted Nicholas Breckenridge." Nick was an old family friend and a former flame; he was also a Pulitzer Prize–winning journalist. "He said the cops are planning to make a statement, and the lawyers have invited the media to cover it."

"There will definitely be a crowd, then," Malik said. "Everyone will be fighting for sound bites—those who think vampires are evil, those who think cops aren't limited by rules and regulations, the family members of the humans assaulted."

"Collateral damage," Ethan murmured, as Luc spread a satellite image of the lockup onto the table. The building wasn't huge, but there was a span of long concrete steps across the front bounded by a couple of columns on each side.

"Perfect place for a *Law and Order*–style shooting," Luc said.

Malik nodded. "And there's more poetic justice if Tate takes them out on the steps. What's the plan?"

"Merit and I will take positions here and here," Ethan said, pointing at the columns. "Our goal is to keep Tate away from the cops and limit the amount of damage he causes."

"How are you going to do that?" Malik asked.

"I'm still working on it," Ethan said, eyes scanning the map.

"I do have one small objection to the plan," I said.

"Which is?" Ethan asked.

"Your participation. You aren't going."

Luc and Malik instantly froze, and Ethan's eyebrow perked upward. "I'm not going?"

There was no denying I was afraid of the coming fight—Tate was a monster beyond all I'd had to fight before, and I didn't even know of a way to fight him now—but fear wasn't going to help me, and it certainly wasn't going to help Ethan. I opted for logic, instead.

"Protecting these cops might mean throwing ourselves in front of them. You can't do that. And as Sentinel, I can't let you do that. We've already lost you once, and the House is in too much political chaos for you to be at risk again. The House needs stability. They don't need a Sentinel."

"And if I say no?"

"My job is to protect this House, even if that means disagreeing with you."

Ethan sat back in his chair and pursed his lips.

"Darius is on his way back for our interviews," Malik added. "You can't blow him off. Not right now."

Ethan kept his gaze on me. "Luc will join you."

I shook my head. "Luc needs to stay here in case this is a ploy so the Tates can get to the House."

"I'm not going to let you go out there on your own."

"I have backup."

His expression flattened. "Who?"

This is business, I reminded myself, *nothing else.* "Jonah. He can meet me there. He's skilled and strong. He's not as good with a katana as you are, but he also doesn't have a history with Tate."

Jonah did, of course, have a history with me . . . or he'd wanted to. That might make things more than a little awkward between us, but he was still my best option.

My only option.

Ethan looked at me for a moment, the tension in the room building as the interlude of silence grew longer.

"Gentlemen, give us the room."

Malik moved to Ethan and whispered in his ear, but my senses were so tautly strung it was easy enough to discern the words.

"What she says makes sense," he whispered.

Ethan nodded, and Malik followed Luc to the door.

"There will be no heroics," Ethan said when the room was empty again. "Do what you can to protect the officers and keep the public clear of Tate's shenanigans. No heroics," he repeated. "That is an order."

"I have no plans to the contrary." That was half a lie. I didn't want to be a hero, but I wanted to keep our people safe.

"I don't approve of this plan."

"Your disapproval is noted. But you know there's no better way."

His lip curled in distaste, but finally he nodded. "And you're sure Jonah is trustworthy?"

I found him trustworthy, but by Ethan's estimation? Probably not, especially since he was a member of the RG.

"He is. He was a great help when Mallory was trying to destroy the city. Malik and Catcher can testify to that."

Ethan tilted his head and watched me for a moment. "Is he in love with you?"

My cheeks turned flame hot. I wouldn't call it love, but Jonah had definitely professed interest. He'd gotten as far as a kiss before backing off. But perhaps, given our current situation, that wasn't information Ethan needed to know . . .

"I'm not sure," I said. "And as long as our relationship is on halt, I'm not sure it's any of your business, *Liege*."

Ethan's jaw tightened, but he still wouldn't abandon his position, even if the ship was sinking around him. "I see," he said.

I nodded. "As long as we're clear. I'll update you as soon as I have news."

This time, when I left his office, I was smiling a little.

Jonah, as I suspected, was up for the meet. He also called out a handful of other RG members to take spots in the crowd in case things got completely out of hand, which I fully expected them to.

Tate and his clone were maybe, possibly, planning to kill four Chicago police officers in a public space populated with attorneys, judges, protestors, and reporters. How could this *not* get fully out of hand?

It did make me feel a little better that Ethan was locked safely away in Cadogan House under Luc's and Malik's watchful eyes. He'd worry about me from there, but Luc had plenty of Ops Room toys—satellite surveillance, feed from traffic and CCTV cameras, and scanners covering a full range of frequencies. Ethan could keep eyes and ears on us from Hyde Park.

Jonah met me half a block away from the CPD building, standing on the sidewalk in jeans and an open long wool coat. Easier to hide the sword beneath, I assumed.

Jonah was tall and lean, with broad shoulders and shoulder-length auburn hair that waved around his face. His mouth was wide, his nose long and straight, his jaw square. He was wearing a little stubble tonight, along with a Midnight High School T-shirt that marked him as a member of the Red Guard . . . at least to other members of the Red Guard.

His gaze was on the CPD lockup building.

I looked back at the building—a typical government shop built in white stone to look Greek or Roman, with the spill of steps in front of it. A portico covered the top half of the steps, that half roof held up by the two columns.

There was a podium about halfway up the steps—the perfect post for a few enterprising criminal defense attorneys to claim a little credit.

An area had been roped off at the front of the stairs for reporters and photographers. Men with cameras and impressive lenses stood behind it, waiting for the cops and their attorneys to emerge from the building. And on the edges of the knot of reporters stood two groups of protestors. One group protested the cops' release. Their signs read JUSTICE FOR VAMPIRES AND KEEP CRIMINALS BEHIND BARS! The other group's signs weren't nearly so pleasant. They congratulated the cops—and rued they hadn't managed to wipe us out altogether.

The steps were already lined by people waiting for the cops to emerge from the building. There were plenty of CPD officers on the perimeters, and I was momentarily nervous they'd ask for the registration papers I didn't yet have.

On the other hand, if we were right about what was about to go down, my paperwork would hardly matter.

"Hey," Jonah said, glancing at me.

"Hey."

"How's Ethan?"

"Alive, so far. I kept him at the House so he'd stay that way."

"Good call." He looked at me with obvious curiosity.

"What?" I asked.

Jonah shrugged. "I'm surprised you called. Since he's back."

"I made a promise to the Red Guard," I said. "I intend to keep it. And my feelings for Ethan aside, the GP's on my shit list. Now more than ever."

Jonah nodded. "Darius came by the House last night. I wasn't privy to his discussions, but Scott was in a foul mood when he left."

That news made my stomach curl. Had Darius confessed to Scott the *shofet*'s plan to close down Cadogan House? Was that why Scott was upset? I wanted to interrogate Jonah for details, but if Scott wasn't ready to tell Jonah, his guard captain, what they'd talked about, it probably wasn't news I wanted to know.

"Do you know what's up?" Jonah asked.

"Not that I'm free to say. Suffice it to say, the GP is up to something."

"They usually are," Jonah said with a grin. "We try to stay under the radar. It's a strategy Cadogan might want to consider."

"*Har-har.* You know, we can't all afford to keep our heads in the sand. Especially not when crazies keep targeting us."

"You do have an awful track record. And I don't want to dwell on this or make things awkward, but since your boyfriends have a tendency to wind up deceased, it's probably better nothing happened between us."

I gave him an arch look. "That only happened once." My tone was dry, but I was secretly glad he'd brought it up and put it out there. Better to make a joke out of it than to have something weird and awkward between us.

"I guess that's true," Jonah said. "I mean, Morgan got promoted."

"You are just hilarious. Are we the only ones here?"

"On the sides of good and righteousness? No. There are two more Red Guards in the crowd. They'll stay quiet unless something pops."

"Like an angel of justice taking them down with his giant sword of righteousness?"

"That sounds like the tagline for a bad porn flick."

"It does, doesn't it? And yet, it's true. Or so we suspect. We haven't exactly had a chance to ask Tate if he's a dispenser of wrath."

He smiled down at me. "You know, every time I hang out with you, things get weirder."

I nodded. It was hard to argue with that. "It's a personal flaw. I'm making a resolution for next year to become much more average. Ordinary, even."

"I'm not sure that's possible. Any known weaknesses for our angelic friend?"

"None that I'm aware of. And it could be friends, plural. Only one showed up to Paulie's party, but who knows what they're thinking right now. We can't even differentiate between them."

Jonah linked his fingers together and stretched out his arms, limbering up for the fight. "I do like to play for the underdog."

He might have been bluffing; he might have meant it. Either way, it was good to have a partner who kept his sense of humor in the face of pretty bad odds.

"So how are we playing this?" he asked.

I offered up the plan Ethan had suggested. "Let's each take a column. When the cops come out, keep an eye out for the Tates, or one of them. I can't imagine he'll wait around and risk missing his chance. And the cops know he was involved in Paulie's murder, so he'll either have to be in disguise—"

"Or he'll have to come in with a bang and not give them time to wrestle him down," Jonah said.

"Exactly. A quick strike either way. I'm sure he could take out a cop or two pretty easily, but there are a lot of people here, and a lot of cops. Unless he wants to be riddled with bullet holes, he'll have to get in, get it done, and get out. So if we can throw him off, slow down his schedule, anything, we might have a chance to keep him from killing anyone."

"Even if we stop him—or them—tonight, he might take another run at it."

"He might," I agreed. "The cops' attorneys have already been warned Tate was coming, but they didn't believe it. Maybe if he shows himself tonight, they'll take the threat seriously. Maybe they can be put into protective custody or something."

"Any chance this ends well?"

"I can't imagine that it will," I said. "But we fight the good fight anyway."

"Spoken just like an RG member. I'm so proud." He gave me a supportive clap on the back. "I'll take the west column. You take the east."

"Sounds good. Good luck."

"You, too."

Jonah disappeared into the crowd, and within seconds the building's doors opened. The protestors began screaming and chanting en masse, their signs bobbing up and down with the new burst of energy.

The attorneys came out first—four men in expensive suits and probably equally high-maintenance egos. They were followed by the officers—four men of various ages and races, still in uniforms, despite how much they'd tarnished them.

They walked down the steps and grouped together at the podium. The first attorney adjusted the microphone.

"Ladies and gentlemen. Members of the press. We are thrilled tonight that justice has been done in Chicago."

There was no sign of Tate, but he couldn't be far behind a statement like that.

Someone tapped my shoulder. "Hey, you can't have that here."

At the same time, I caught sight of a tall, dark-haired man moving through the crowd. My heart quickened.

"Hey, did you hear what I said? Hand over the sword or we're taking a little trip into the lockup."

I glanced behind me. A uniformed CPD cop—a barrel-chested man with a thick mustache—tapped my sword with his stick. A second cop moved in closer, probably thinking I was the threat they were supposed to be watching for.

"Sir, the guy who killed Paulie—the drug lord?—he might be in the crowd."

"Yeah, I'm sure." He stuck the stick back into his utility belt but put a hand on the butt of his service weapon. "Give me the sword, ma'am, or we're going to have some trouble. And there are a lot of uniforms here tonight. You don't want to start something you can't finish."

I glanced back at the crowd. Just as the attorney finished his remarks and the cops stepped up to the podium, the dark-haired man had wedged his way through the crowd to the front of the rope line. Now that he was clear of the crowd, I could see his face.

It was Tate. One of them, anyway.

I looked back and appealed to the cops. "It's definitely him—Seth Tate. Do you see him? He's standing at the front of the crowd. Dark hair?"

The second cop, a little savvier than his friend, frowned and looked over, but the first cop wasn't buying it.

"All right, I'm taking that weapon, and you're coming with me." He put a hand on the sheath of my sword and pulled hard to dislodge it from my belt.

"I'm really sorry about this," I said, chopping his hand away with a swipe of my arm and whipping out my sword.

Tate picked that moment to act—ripping the rope away and stepping into the gap between the crowd and the cops. He screamed out—that same primordial noise we'd heard in the silo. He wore a trench coat. He whipped it off to reveal a naked torso, and summoned the giant broadsword back into his hands.

And that wasn't all he was carrying.

Tate arched his back and held out his sword. As the horrified crowd looked on, great black wings sprouted from his shoulder blades. The purple-black membranes of his wings were marked by veins and tendons, stretched taut by long, thin bones that ended in needle-sharp claws. His wingspan must have been twenty feet. Twenty terrifying feet. They flapped once, then twice, filling the air with the scents of sulfur and smoke.

A shock of base fear ran through me. It was easy to think of Tate as a storybook creature, but this was no storybook. He was something old and fundamental to the earth, created not to protect men, but to *judge* them. He would see into your heart of hearts, and if he found you lacking, you had only yourself to blame for your suffering.

My worry wood was so *not* going to help with this.

The crowd screamed. I was distracted by the sights and sounds before me, and the second cop managed to pull the sword from my hand.

I could have fought him for it, but I really didn't want to assault a cop if I didn't have to. I opted for pleading instead and held out my hand. "Please, someone has to stop him. I can try, but only with my sword."

Tate probably had no idea I was in the crowd and most certainly didn't care if I was being handled by the cops. Tate was busy fighting a battle of his own. He pushed away a uniformed cop from the crowd who tried to stop him and swiped his sword at one of the released cops. The cop stumbled backward to get away, but the sword caught him on the chin, and he screamed out.

While everyone else ran away from the monster and his

weapon, Jonah jumped right into the fray, unsheathing his own sword. Before Tate noticed he was there, Jonah struck out and gashed the thin webbing of one of Tate's wings.

Tate screamed out and turned, his giant wing pivoting through the air and throwing Jonah backward.

"Jonah!" I yelled out, then looked back at the second cop, pleading in my eyes. "Please, for God's sake, give me back my sword."

He looked nervously between me and the drama that was playing out a few dozen feet in front of him. "What the hell is that?"

Cops trained for a lot of things, but likely nothing had prepared this poor guy for what he was seeing.

I picked an easy answer; this wasn't the time for complicated honesty. "He's a monster. He's something that doesn't belong here, but he's going to do a lot of damage until he's gone. I'm a vampire, and I think I can stop him, but I need my sword."

Still nothing. The guy was stuck in a paralyzing panic, so I broke out the big gun.

"I'm Caroline Merit," I said. "Chuck Merit's granddaughter."

His eyes cleared, understanding blossoming in his expression. Not for me, most likely, but for my grandfather, who'd walked a beat in Chicago for years before he'd become Seth Tate's Ombudsman.

The officer Tate had nicked on the chin screamed as Tate cut him down with the sword. Other cops in the crowd fired, but their bullets had no effect on him.

So he had magical weapons, giant wings, and a sword, and he was immune to bullets. This was getting better and better.

"I need to go now!" I told the cop.

It took him a second, but he finally nodded and handed back my sword. "Go! Go!"

I nodded and took it, savoring the bite of leather cording

against my palm. I yelled out over the barrage of bullets, "Please try to stop them from firing at me, if you can. It won't kill me, but it will hurt like a son of a bitch."

The cop nodded back, and I watched his eyes flatten as his instincts took over. He'd be fine.

"Hold your fire!" he yelled out, arms flapping the air to get the others' attention. "Hold your fire!"

The shots trailed off and finally stopped. The attorneys had abandoned their clients, leaving three of the released cops frozen in fear on the stairs. The fourth lay arms and legs akimbo on the step below them.

I said a silent prayer, gripped my sword, and moved forward.

"Tate!" I called out when I reached the bottom step.

He stopped and froze, and I suddenly knew how every movie heroine who'd tried to save someone by diverting the monster's attention felt. The obvious problem with that approach? It put the monster's attention squarely on you.

Slowly, Tate turned toward me. His face so handsome but so deadly. His eyes burned like blue fire, fed by zealotry and a power that eclipsed anything else I'd seen before.

It seemed the rest of the city fell quiet to hear him speak. "This isn't your fight, Ballerina."

He recognized me—but did that mean he was Tate Part One or Tate Part Two?

I took another step. "You've attacked my city, Tate. That makes it my fight. Walk away and leave them be."

"You think you can take me?"

In the corner of my eye, I saw Jonah nearing Tate again, back on his feet with his sword in hand.

"Whether I can or not is irrelevant. I will try because you don't have the right to attack these men."

"Justice is not being served," he said.

"That's an issue for humans. It's not your concern."

"And yet here you are," he said, reaching out to grab one of the other three released cops by the neck. The cop screamed and kicked, but Tate was unmoved. He held him in the crook of his arm like the cop was nothing more than a game animal, caught for sport.

Or in this case, to prove a point.

"This city is corrupt!" Tate yelled out, thrusting the sword into the air with his free hand, the fervor of a zealot in his voice. "It must be cleansed, and mine is the sword that will see it purified."

It was time to bring him down a peg. I took another step forward. "You know, Tate, if I had a quarter for every time a politician promised to clean up this city, I'd be a millionaire by now."

I heard an appreciative chuckle in the crowd, as Jonah stepped slowly toward Tate from behind as I moved closer in front.

"Justice will be done," Tate said, then threw the cop to the ground and raised his sword to strike.

Neither Jonah nor I wasted any time. Jonah struck Tate from the back, and I launched toward him, katana in the air, from the front. I aimed for his sword and managed to knock him off target. Our swords clanged together with body-shaking force, and I hit the ground in a roll before popping up again.

"Run!" I told the cop, and he squirmed away.

Tate roared out his displeasure, turning to swipe at Jonah, which sent his wings flying in my direction. I jumped back, but the tip of a claw grazed my stomach, sending a sharp spike of pain across my belly.

I cursed but hopped to my feet again. Jonah and Tate began sparring, Jonah's thin, sleek katana an odd foil against Tate's massive sword—like a samurai fighting a medieval knight.

They battled in a circle, Jonah moving spritely up and down the stairs as Tate moved after him.

The cop who'd given me my sword back was moving toward the released cop, who still lay motionless on the ground.

It was my turn to tap in. "Tate!"

He stopped and glanced back at me, eyes narrowed like a predator. Or a crazed angel.

I crooked a finger at him, then loosened my knees and positioned my sword. "Come and get me."

Tate took a step forward, but it wasn't to get to me. Instead, he launched toward the cop who'd given me my sword back and lofted his sword in the air.

There was no way I was going to reach him in time. I said the only thing that occurred to me . . . and did the very thing Ethan had forbidden me to do.

"Tate!"

He looked at me, ferocity in his eyes.

"Let him go," I said. "Take me instead."

I'd hoped to throw Tate off his mark or at least gain a little time. But he didn't pause to think.

"Very well," he said. Before I could move away, Tate lunged forward and grabbed my wrist.

My skin flamed beneath his touch, and everything went black.

CHAPTER FOURTEEN

YOU LIGHT UP MY LIFE

I woke to searing pain and blinding light. My leather jacket was gone, and sunlight poured over my bare arms. I pulled them back into the shadow that covered the rest of my body.

Tears sprang to my eyes as blisters lifted down my arms, but the pain was the least of my worries. My mind fuzzy, I squinted against the glare and looked around.

I was in a square concrete room with a window on one wall. The window was uncovered, and sunlight spilled across the room. I was tucked into the only shaded corner, a little ball of vampire . . . and my phone had been in my missing jacket.

"Handy, isn't it?"

I also shouldn't have been awake at this hour. Slowly and groggily, I looked toward the sound of Tate's voice. He stood in an open doorway that was twenty feet of sun-drenched concrete away from me.

The doorway led directly outside. Even if I managed to cross the room, there was nowhere to go.

Tate had imprisoned me with sunlight. He'd even left me my

sword, because what could I possibly do with it? I had no room to wield it, unless I hoped to spare myself the pain of death by sunshine.

"You're a sadist," I said.

"Hardly. I'm a realist," he said. "The world could be better than it is. I intend to prove that."

My mind was dull and slow. "Where are we?"

"That's not important," he said. "The more important question is *why* we're here."

"Because you're a vindictive son of a bitch?"

Tate laughed and walked into the room. He wore dark pants and a T-shirt. His wings had disappeared, but his T-shirt was mottled with blood. I guessed Jonah had gotten in a few shots.

He chuckled and moved closer. It was disturbing to watch him move. So handsome . . . and so deadly. I looked him over, scanning his face and body for any detail that would help me differentiate between the two of them. But I saw nothing.

"I prefer messenger of justice, thank you."

I guessed the librarian had been right. "Prefer it all you want. Playing judge, jury, and executioner doesn't make you just. It makes you arrogant."

"I'm not the arrogant one, Sentinel of Cadogan House."

"You're a fallen angel, aren't you? A Dark One? That's arrogance by definition. You thought you knew better than everyone else."

"I know right from wrong."

"Is this right? Punishing me because I tried to help save four police officers? Putting me in this room, where I'll burn to ashes in a couple of hours?"

"Those men were corrupt," he said. "Their souls were corrupt."

"Those men have families. They have wives and children."

"They hurt others. They deserved punishing," he insisted.

"That's not your call to make."

He stilled, and it was almost scarier than arguing with him, like I was staring back at a furious man suddenly frozen in marble.

"Those who say we cannot tell right from wrong have no courage. They have no will to make the decisions that must be made. Justice should be meted out by those who have the willpower to act, the stomach for punishment. No one forced those men to their actions. They chose their own paths. They should bear the burden of the consequences."

"They would have. That's why they'd been imprisoned."

"And they were released. The human justice system has no backbone."

"You don't get to make that decision. Isn't that what got you in trouble millennia ago?"

My hands began to shake with exhaustion, my body rebelling against the fact that I was awake. I squeezed them into fists and forced myself to concentrate.

"You are weak creatures with no stomach for justice."

"What you call justice, we call war. Destruction. Havoc." I swallowed down a scream of pain. Ethan was probably frantic, but Jonah would have seen me disappear. They'd have to work to find me, but they would. God willing, they would.

"Why did you bring me here?" I asked.

"To make an example of you."

"For what?"

"You stopped me from completing my work, just as the scarlet witch tried to do. You asked for this, remember?"

Paige must have been the scarlet witch. "You burned her house down because she tried to stop you?"

"Justice does not veer for cowards."

"And killing people doesn't make you brave. It just makes you a killer."

"I can see that you're regretting your decision to stand in for the corrupt cops. You'll have a little while yet to regret that decision, won't you?"

He pointed at the line of sunlight, which had shifted a few more degrees. Soon my bit of shadow would shrink to nothing, and I would be completely exposed to sunlight.

"I'll admit," he said, surveying the room, "this is my first time using this particular mechanism. A single slice with a sword wouldn't quite have the same effect on you, would it? You'd too easily survive that."

For the first time, I actually regretted having fast healing powers. But I wasn't going to let Tate get the emotional upper hand.

"You've already lost once today," I said. "We stopped you. They'll find me, and you'll lose again."

But with each second that passed, it seemed more and more unlikely that they'd find me in time. The press conference had taken place in the early evening. An entire night had come and gone, and the sun had risen again. No one had found me yet. And now the sun was up, and neither Jonah nor Ethan could look for me.

Soon I'd be out of time.

Tate pulled something from his pocket, then held it up. It was shiny and reflected the light, and I looked away again, blinking back the glare.

"You still have my Cadogan medal," I said. "That's not news."

"It is, actually." I heard the clink of the chain and assumed he'd tucked it away again. No point in waving it in my face if I wasn't going to look.

"I find it interestingly symbolic. A girl, a graduate student, changed into a vampire one night against her will. Reborn into a vampire House right here in Chicago. She fashions herself a savior of lost souls and decides to battle me for supremacy. She loses, and here she dies."

"So you won't be needing that anymore."

"*Au contraire,*" he said. "It is a prize. A remembrance."

He meant when the sun finished its journey, I'd be gone. Reduced to ash, but he'd still have a trophy of having beaten me. (Either he didn't notice I was wearing a replacement medal, or he wasn't going to let a bit of inconvenient fact get in the way of the victory he was already imagining.)

I knew I couldn't hear Ethan anymore, but I still imagined his voice in my head, giving me a speech similar to the one I'd given him on the field in Nebraska. Reminding me I was a Cadogan vampire, that I was stronger than Tate believed, that I would survive until he found me.

And he would find me. *He would.* I only had to hang on until he arrived. I only had to survive.

Move! I told myself. I shifted a centimeter to the right, and I forced myself to keep talking. I might as well use the time alone with Tate for a good purpose.

"There are two of you now."

"In a fashion," he enigmatically said.

I frowned at him. "I saw you. You touched the *Maleficium* and you split in half."

He clucked his tongue. "I am not split in half, Ballerina. I am whole. My name is Dominic."

He was one of the three Dark Ones the librarian had identified—Uriel, Azrael, and Dominic. "You destroyed Carthage?"

He laughed heartily. "I did not. That was not my particular

handiwork. It belonged to my brothers in arms. But at least you better appreciate what we're about."

"Destruction and revenge?"

"Only if deserved," he said, clearly having no qualms about appointing himself the man to decide what someone did or didn't deserve.

"The world is a cruel place," he said. "Often unfair." Dominic moved to the window and looked outside, then back at me.

"I'll be back in a moment," he said. "Don't move."

He strode from the room. For a moment, I hoped he might have seen someone outside—a rescuer intent on saving me. But the world remained quiet.

I shuddered with exhaustion, the edge of my arm grazing a band of sunlight. Pain shot through me, and I pulled my knees to my chest and wrapped my arms around them. If things got worse, I could stand up, squeezing myself into the tiny sliver of space. But then I'd be out of room, without even my jacket to protect me.

That he'd taken away my jacket just to bare my arms and expose me to even more sunlight was disgustingly thorough. I guessed I should have been thankful he hadn't stripped me naked and left me entirely vulnerable, not that the clothes would help much when my bit of shade was gone.

And it was disappearing fast.

Please, someone, find me, I thought.

Merit?

My name echoed in my head. I thought a panicky response. *Ethan?*

It's Morgan. I'm with Ethan. He's here. He asked me to talk to you. Do you know where you are?

I closed my eyes in relief. I'd all but forgotten about my connection with Morgan Greer. Thank God someone had remembered.

I looked around the room, the images blurry, my head swimming with exhaustion. *I don't know. I'm in a room; there's a lot of sunlight. I'm trying to stay in the shade. But there's not much left.*

Can you see anything? Does anything look familiar?

I squeezed my eyes closed to clear my vision, then opened them again. I squinted against the sunlight and caught a glance of red outside the window. My retinas burned viciously.

Red, I told him, closing my eyes again and weeping in relief. *There's red outside.*

For a moment, there was only silence. Panic stabbed through me. *Morgan? Are you there? Don't leave me. Please don't leave me.*

I'm here, Merit. Jeff and Catcher and Ethan are here. We're talking about where you might be. Can you tell me what kind of red you can see? Bright red? Dark red?

I swallowed thickly and made myself look again. *Dark red. Orange-red.*

Anything else?

Tears slipped from my eyes. *I don't know. I'm so tired.*

I know you are. But you must concentrate. What else is around you?

I can't see anything else.

That's okay, Merit. Use your other senses. What do you smell? What do you hear?

I closed my eyes and loosened the barriers against the sights and smells of the room. I heard the scuffle and *coos* of pigeons roosting in the ceiling above me and felt the damp breeze in the air.

I think we're near the lake, I told Morgan.

That's good, Merit. What else?

He meant it wasn't enough to know I was near the lake. Lake Michigan was enormous, and they might never find me.

No, I told myself. *Focus. If you want to live through this, focus!*

I tried again, letting my senses explore the world around me. More pigeons. Gravel. Damp and dying grass.

And beneath all of those smells, a sharp, dry scent. Something powdery. Something dusty.

Something familiar.

I searched my mind for the memory, but my brain was sluggish.

Merit? Are you still there? Ethan is asking about you.

Morgan meant it encouragingly, but I could tell it was hard for him to mention Ethan's name, to reference our relationship.

He was hurting himself to help me, I thought, and that realization was enough to focus my mind and send the memory back into sharp focus: I was standing in a room, and Seth Tate was seated at a table before me. The smells of lemon and sugar filled the air. But beneath that scent, there was something more . . . the same scent of chalk that I smelled now.

I knew where I was.

The ceramics factory, I said.

It was an abandoned compound where Seth Tate had been held before he'd sought out the *Maleficium*. I'd visited him there—*here*—twice. Both times at night, but both times for a good long while as Tate taught me about the *Maleficium* and magic.

There are pigeons above me.

They know where you are, Merit. They're coming for you. Hang on.

Please don't leave me. I skittered an inch deeper into the corner. If they didn't find me in time, I didn't want to be alone. Not here. Not in this place with Tate.

I won't, he said. *I'm right here.*

I don't know how many minutes or hours passed, but I was standing in the corner, my back pressed to the wall, mere inches of space between me and the moving sunlight, when a sound as loud as a gunshot split the air, and I clapped my hands over my ears.

Voices burst out. Yelling, the roar of an engine, the sound of rocks and gravel.

Unaware of the danger it posed, immune to my tears, the sunlight crept closer. I was running out of time. "Please be help. Please be help."

Morgan's voice popped into my head again, as exhausted as mine must have sounded. *Merit, they're coming to get you. Hold on, okay?*

I dropped my head back to the wall behind me, tensing every muscle to keep myself upright and poised in the tiny bit of shade. *You can do this*, I told myself over and over again. *You can do this. You can do this.*

Paige burst into the room. "I found her!" she called out.

I sobbed in relief.

Jeff rushed in behind her, a shiny silver blanket in his hands. Immune to the sunlight, he ran to me. "I'm getting you out of here, okay?"

I managed a nod before he threw the cloth over my head and whipped me into his arms like I weighed nothing. I wrapped an arm weakly around his neck. "Tate?"

"Temporarily incapacitated," Paige said, hustling Jeff out the door. "So we don't have much time."

Jeff carried me outside, where I heard the sound of an engine revving and a door opening. I was gently placed on something soft, and then we were moving again.

Jeff pulled away the blanket. My heart skipped at the sudden darkness. I reached out, and he squeezed my hand.

"I can't see anything."

"It's temporary," said another voice. Catcher, in front of us. "It's because you were exposed to sunlight for so long; it's too dim in here for your receptors. It will pass."

I nodded but couldn't stop the tears that slid down my face. A minute more, and I'd have been a pile of ash.

I sobbed, and Jeff pulled me into his chest.

"Shhh," he said, as I breathed in the spicy scent of his cologne and gripped a fistful of his shirt. "You're okay. Rest for a few minutes, and we'll get you home. Oh, and I think Catcher found your jacket."

"Thank you," I said, crying in relief until my eyes closed again.

I didn't wake up again until midnight the next evening.

I sat up in my bed, the room lit by a golden light that filtered in from the open hallway door. My eyes took a moment to adjust, but I could finally see again.

"Water?" I touched my throat. I was parched, my voice harsh and gravelly.

Ethan walked into the room, relief on his face. He wore a suit, but the top of his shirt was unbuttoned and his tie was loose around his neck. He strode to the bed and handed me a cup of water from the nightstand.

I drank it greedily.

"How are you feeling?" Ethan asked.

He looked down at the bed but didn't touch me. Even after the night we'd faced, he was keeping his distance.

"I feel miserable," I said, and I didn't just mean the Tate situation. "Like I haven't slept in twenty-four hours." I handed the empty glass back to him. "More, please."

He refilled it. "Blood would also be a good idea. Keep drinking that, and I'll get you some."

I didn't argue and kept drinking. I drank so much so quickly I nearly didn't keep it all down. Nausea overwhelming me, my stomach suddenly swollen, I sat back and closed my eyes.

"Is Jonah all right?" I asked.

"He's fine. He's the one who called us. He waited here until just before the sun rose, then returned to Grey House. Catcher and Jeff looked for you for some hours. Apparently, you led them on quite a chase."

"How's that?"

"You don't remember?"

I shook my head. "He touched me at the lockup and knocked me out somehow. I didn't remember anything until I woke up in that room." I looked up at Ethan. "I know what he is. His name is Dominic. He's a fallen angel, just like the librarian said. He has great black wings, Ethan. Bat's wings."

"If he's Dominic, what's Seth?"

I shook my head. "I don't know. Dominic was the only one there. At least, I think he was. How did Paige stop him?"

"Magical flash bang," he said. That explained the loud noise. "It disorients someone sensitive to magic, but the effect is only temporary."

"I should thank her, too."

"She's out tonight. She said she needed to talk to Baumgartner. She said she had some things on her mind."

I smiled. "Good for her. She seems like the type to take her magic seriously—unlike everyone else in the Order."

I flipped back the covers. I was dressed in a slinky nightgown. I gave him a look. "Seriously?"

"That was Lindsey's doing," he said. "She said it was the first thing she found, and time was of the essence. We weren't sure how badly you'd been burned, and we wanted you out of your clothes." We both checked out my arms. They were still pink from the burns, but they were clearly healing.

"They may be tender for a bit," he said, "but you'll heal." He paused. "I was afraid it was going to be too late." True anguish crossed his features.

"They cut it close."

"They found you," he corrected, "and that's what counts."

"Morgan was the key. If we hadn't been able to communicate..." I trailed off as tears threatened to breach my lashes again.

Ethan nodded. "He called after you were home to ensure you were okay."

"He did good. Comforting, but with just enough push to make sure I stayed awake."

We'd been concerned Morgan had been too immature to handle his position as House Master. Maybe he could grow into it. Maybe he *already* was growing into it.

"I need to thank him," I said. It was the right thing to do and might help clear the air between us.

"You may do so in one hundred years when I let you leave the House again."

"Ha."

"I'm only slightly joking, Merit. I have a nearly irresistible urge to lock you away and keep you out of trouble."

"Locking me away wouldn't keep me safe or out of trouble. And if you locked me away, I couldn't keep you safe." Of course, there were some things from which I couldn't protect him. "How did your interview with Darius go?"

He shook his head. "Let me navigate the political streams. I am the captain of this ship, after all."

"Wow. You usually go for naughty. Tonight it's nautical. It's bad, isn't it?"

"It's not good."

"What happened? Is he going to remove our accreditation?"

Ethan stood up and walked to the window and didn't say a thing. My chest tightened uncomfortably.

"You aren't going to tell me?"

"I'm not avoiding the conversation because I don't trust you," he said, glancing back at me, that line of worry between his eyes. "But because there's nothing to tell. The *shofet* ruled; you know that. Darius will decide what he decides. He hasn't verbalized that decision, and until he does so, we have to wait."

With that enigmatic statement, he went silent on the issue. I decided he'd been through enough tonight and didn't press him further.

"What about the fallout from the press conference? I can't imagine the new mayor is thrilled someone who looks like the former mayor, except with bat wings, tried to take out four of her cops."

"She wasn't thrilled," Ethan agreed. "But she also didn't try to blame it on vampires. Of course, that's pretty easy, since you were there with a sword trying to defend the cops. The human-interest reporters loved that."

"Ironic," I said.

"There has, however, been a bit of a change in the status quo." Ethan reached over and grabbed a folded newspaper from the nightstand and handed it to me.

The top half of the front page was devoted to a photograph of Dominic, his black wings spreading ominously across the newsprint. Beneath the photo was the headline: WINGED MAYOR AT-TEMPTS COP HIT; CITY HOME TO OTHER SUPS.

It hadn't actually been the mayor, of course, but I could forgive them the error. The city didn't know two Tates were on the loose, and they were hard to tell apart, anyway.

"Read the first paragraph," Ethan said.

I read aloud: "'Chicago reels today after Mayor Seth Tate, bearing a pair of batlike wings, attacked the so-called South Side Four outside the police precinct where they were released. In response, three new species of supernaturals—so-called nymphs, sirens, and trolls—were outed in a press release sent to news outlets across Chicago. Mayor Diane Kowalcyzk says she was shocked to learn Mr. Tate was 'one of the monsters.' A source close to the mayor's office says Kowalcyzk is aware the city harbors dozens of supernatural species but kept that information from the public.'"

I glanced up at Ethan, nervous about his reaction. But he was smiling.

"Someone just outed more supernaturals to the mayor and everyone else." I pointed to the paper. "You're okay with this? How are you not freaking out?"

"Because your grandfather was the source."

I could only blink. "What? Why in God's name would he do that?"

"Because they told him to. It makes strategic sense. One, it makes Kowalcyzk look as incompetent as she really is. That's a fun bonus. Two, we're fighting a losing battle. The information has spilled out, a bit at a time, since Celina announced our existence, and not usually on our terms."

He was right about that. Celina outed vampires, and Gabriel had to out the shifters after his brother launched a full-out attack on Cadogan House.

"You said he had permission?" That was as big a surprise as any. There were all sorts of supernatural creatures the general public didn't know about, and I hadn't heard any of them express any strong desire to mingle with humans.

"In light of Tate's—*Dominic's*—behavior, your grandfather thought it best to revisit the issue with the city's supernatural communities. Chicagoans have already seen two supernatural reveals.

You add yet another reveal—Dominic's wings—and the public starts to believe there's more out there than they've seen, assuming they don't believe that already. If they were going to be outed, they wanted to do it on their terms.

"And frankly," he added, "I think your grandfather stressed the fact that vampires have been taking the supernatural heat in this town for a while now, and it was time to share the burden. He says it helped considerably that you've been meeting the groups and conducting yourself honorably. Attempting to solve problems that weren't yours in order to keep the peace for everyone."

I blushed at the praise. It meant a lot that they'd said those things to my grandfather. He'd all but raised me, and I was glad to have done good by him.

"This could change a lot of things in Chicago," I said.

"It could."

He had a little smile on his face, and I figured out the reason for that fast enough. "And with that much change, Darius would be hard-pressed to dump one of his Chicago Houses."

"That is an unintended side effect."

It might not, of course, have any bearing on what the GP ultimately did. After all, they tended to ignore the cold, hard realities of what went on in Chicago. But it would certainly make them think twice before disbanding us.

"How's the public reacting?" I asked.

"The usual mix. Some are celebrating; some are afraid. Some are convinced we are the harbingers of the apocalypse."

"Dominic's wings can't be much help with that." They looked exactly like something you'd have seen at the end of the world as the four horsemen rode down upon you . . .

"I don't imagine they did. On the upside, with so many other options, the protestors have completely abandoned us."

"No kidding?" That I had to see. I climbed out of bed and joined Ethan at the window. I could see only a corner of the front yard, but no signs bobbed above the Cadogan House gate.

On the other hand . . . "There's a hatred vacuum," I said, crossing my arms and turning back to him. "If humans aren't out there protesting vampires because there are so many other things to protest, it leaves a gap for McKetrick to fill. Kowalcyzk's still in office, and as far as we know, he'll still have her ear. He's going to be pissed if folks are lovey-dovey in our direction. And he'll fire things up again."

"That does seem possible. Likely, even. He is motivated."

We were quiet for a moment, probably both considering the likelihood of another enemy raising the stakes around the House.

But when I looked back at him, his gaze was on the silk slip that barely covered me. Magic rose around us, swirling as desire deepened.

Ethan caressed my bare shoulder with a fingertip, and I shivered. I closed my eyes, my body warming as his hand splayed across my bare back.

"Ethan," I said, the word an invitation, but instead of bringing him closer, it broke the spell.

Frustration poured through me.

"There are plenty of things in the world to be afraid of," I said. "But you are not one of them. Nothing but fear is holding us back from each other," I quietly said, then walked toward the shower.

"Where are you going?"

"To take a shower and get dressed."

"You are sun drunk if you think you're going anywhere," Ethan said. "You need to recuperate."

My hand on the doorjamb, I looked back at him, my gaze as flat as his had become. "I don't have time to recuperate. Dominic is still out there, and God only knows who he's going after next. I need to figure out how to stop him."

Ethan pointed to the bed. "Get back over there."

"I will not."

He arched an imperious eyebrow. "It wasn't a request, Sentinel."

"Great, since I wasn't asking for permission."

"You could have been killed."

"Unfortunately, that's true every day of the week. Danger is part of my job, Ethan. The one you assigned me to."

His lip curled. "I'm trying to remember my reasons for appointing you Sentinel. Was I attempting to teach you a lesson?"

"And who has learned the lesson now, Professor?"

He growled, so I didn't push him further.

"We can't argue every time I have to go to work. That's not going to be productive for the House. Besides, you would have been proud of me out there last night, notwithstanding the fact that I nearly became ash. I managed to move a fallen angel off his target and sweet-talk a cop into giving me back my sword."

"That is impressive."

"It is. And we both know I'm going anyway."

He fumed silently for a moment. "You are as stubborn as they come."

"We are well matched, Mr. Sullivan."

Ethan humphed but relented. He turned to the side and held out a regal hand. "Go have a shower and report to the Ops Room."

"As you please, Liege," I said, then closed the bathroom door.

Why did all of our interactions have to end with a closing door?

CHAPTER FIFTEEN

PERFORMANCE EVALUATION

I found my leathers in my closet when I emerged from the shower, including the jacket Catcher had picked up during my rescue. The leather was clean and shiny, in perfect condition after a hard night's work.

I got dressed and checked my phone and found a message waiting from Jonah. Not surprisingly, he was checking in, making sure I'd gotten the rest and blood I needed to recuperate. I messaged him back to let him know that I was still alive, even if I could have used a few more hours' sleep.

I also thanked Morgan with a message. I didn't get a reply.

My grandfather was a little more loquacious. "Baby girl! You're okay? Catcher and Jeff said they got you home safe."

The relief in his voice brought tears to my eyes. "They did great. Jeff was a hero—and he carried me out just like one."

He chuckled. "I'd tell him you said that, but you calling him your hero may cause more trouble than it's worth. I'll call your father and let him know you're okay, although I'm sure he'd like to hear it from you."

I doubted he cared much either way, but I wasn't going to argue with my grandfather about it. "Thank you, Grandpa. And speaking of trouble, I understand Mayor Kowalcyzk's city got a lot more diverse than she'd imagined."

"Let's just say her knowledge is now a little closer to reality. In all seriousness, that woman was in some pretty heavy denial. I may not have many pleasant things to say about Seth Tate right now, but the man appointed me to office and usually gave a fair shake to sups."

"Seth Tate is still the unanswered question," I said. "It's Dominic—the fallen angel with the bat wings—who's causing all the trouble."

He whistled. "I wouldn't have imagined this world was possible if I hadn't seen it with my own eyes."

"I understand the feeling."

"At any rate, I believe everyone realized their secrets had very limited life spans. Better to come out on your own terms than be forced out by registration laws and black helicopters."

"That makes sense to me. It was a brave thing to do—especially now, when the hatred's a lot louder than the love. I'm proud of them for taking that step."

"I don't know that everyone's thrilled about it," he said, "and there were certainly some dissenters, but it was time to do the right thing. Vampires have hoisted up the weight for long enough; it was time for others to do their fair share. I think they realized that."

We'd certainly tried to do our fair share, but it was our failures that stood out in my mind, not our victories. Chicago had nearly burned because I hadn't seen that Mallory was behind the chaos. Ethan had taken a stake because he'd come looking for me, and I'd nearly died for a punishment I'd basically volunteered to take.

Maybe Ethan was right. Maybe I would have been better off in the library.

But there was no time for self-pity. Not with Dominic and Seth still out there. Not when others had work to do, as well. This was the time for graciousness and gratitude.

"Thanks, Grandpa," I said. "I try to do my best."

"I know you do. We all know it. Stay safe, baby girl."

"I will. You, too."

We said our good-byes and I put the phone back into my pocket, glad that I had family to count on and turn to, even if it wasn't the family I'd expected.

My phone calls made, I left my room and made my way to the basement. I kept my fingers crossed that everyone would be dressed and in an upright position when I opened the door. But I still braced myself for horror, especially when I heard loud thumping coming from behind the double doors—music, something of the techno or electronica sort, with a solid bass line and a strange, high-pitched melody.

Since musical thumping could easily be accompanied by physical thumping, I opened the door carefully and peeked inside.

Success! There were no chaps in sight.

Kelley and Juliet sat at the conference table. The computers and CCTV monitors were all staffed. Although their faces looked familiar—they were Cadogan vamps I'd seen around the House—I'd never seen them in the Ops Room.

Curiosity piqued, I walked inside, pointed at the newcomers, and looked at Kelley. "What's going on?" I yelled over the music.

I hadn't exactly been shy about the question, and all of them turned to look at me.

I waved a little.

"Helpers," Juliet said. "New probationary guards."

"You actually hired someone? How long was I out?" I looked over the guards, who all wore the Cadogan uniform (black suits) and small earpieces tucked around their earlobes. They typed quickly and scanned their screens intently, and generally looked pretty competent.

"They're temps," Kelley said, her head bobbing with the music. "We gave up on interviews."

That was understandable, especially if the few interviews I'd seen were any indication of the whole. The applicants weren't big on social skills. Or physical skills. Or really any skills that would have made them decent candidates for House guards.

"Glad to hear it. That you have temps, I mean, not that the interviews were awful. And the music?"

"Vamps and shifters are no longer the only sups in town!" Juliet said, raising her hands in the air.

Luc and Lindsey appeared in the doorway, and Lindsey squealed when she saw me. She pulled me into a hug that nearly rebroke my rib. After a moment she released me but still pressed a big kiss to my forehead.

"We were so freaking worried about you!"

"I'm glad to be back."

Luc pulled the door shut, then directed one of the newbies to turn down the music. "The big man's in the House," he said, "so let's keep the celebration quiet and simple. As far as we are concerned, this office is more efficient and under budget than any other in the House. We keep our little corner of things quiet, and we keep the GP out of it." Luc sat down at the conference table and kicked his feet atop it. "Although we are celebrating because of a very important tenet. One of my key rules for House success, actually."

Lindsey and I rolled our eyes. Luc had a lot of "key rules," as well as "tenets," "scenarios," and "protocols." And he liked to share them regularly.

He pointed at me. "A vampire's best ally, Sentinel, is the guy that makes your enemy more nervous than you do."

I assumed he was referring to the other sups' announcement that they existed, and he was probably right.

"And I'll tell you what else I know," he said, punching his fingertip into the top of the conference table. "We have our Master back, our Sentinel is alive, and I have four new probies to harass. Life hardly gets better than that."

Lindsey cleared her throat. Loudly.

Luc's ears turned crimson red. "Well, it gets a little better."

Lindsey sent him an arch look. "A little?"

"*Hugely* better," he said. "Fundamentally better. Tremendously better."

"Thank you."

"Sure thing, Sugar Lips. But that's not even the best part. Now that we have staff to cover House security, our Sentinel can focus on her job instead of slumming around here."

I sat down at the table and pouted a little. "I like hanging out down here. I don't have a staff."

Lindsey cleared her throat again.

"Or a Lindsey."

"You're welcome here anytime you like. But you don't have to worry about taking patrol shifts when you should be out there mixing it up with the bad guys. Deal?"

"Deal," I said.

"And speaking of deals, let's figure out why the hell we've got a man-sized bat picking off our city's fine, uniformed police officers." His expression changed—from silly-in-love vampire to master tactician. He reached over to the console in the middle of the table and pressed some buttons. The sound of a ringing phone filled the air.

"Yo?" Jeff answered.

"Jeffrey, it's Luc. I'm here with Kelley, Lindsey, Juliet, a very healthy Merit, and the rest of our now fully staffed office. You may refer to them as 'Probies.'"

"Hello, everyone and Probies," Jeff said. "Especially a very healthy Merit."

"Hello, my knight in shining armor," I said, taking a seat. "Or at least my knight with a very shiny reflective blanket."

"It was nothing. Just doing my duty. What's up?"

Luc leaned over the speakerphone gadget. "We're just about to get an update from Merit. If you've got time, we'd love for you to join us."

"God, yes," Jeff said, a little quieter. "I've been fielding calls from nervous sups all day."

"I thought they agreed to reveal themselves?" I asked with a frown.

"Only the big four," Jeff said. "The rest are now extra-nervous and they apparently want to vent about their concerns. Loudly. And there's nothing I can do for them right now."

"I feel their pain," Luc said. "Now, Sentinel, tell us about the angel in our midst. What is he, and how can we take him out?"

"His name is Dominic. He's a messenger—a fallen angel—from way back in the day, and he split off from Tate when Mallory tried to conjure something and Tate touched the *Maleficium*. Dominic has black wings, as I'm sure you've seen. And he looks exactly like Seth. There's no physical differences, as far as I could tell."

"And he's a sadist," Kelley said, taking notes on an electronic tablet.

I smiled grimly. "I told him the same thing."

"I don't suppose he gave you his master plan while you two were chatting it up à la sunlight?" Luc asked.

"Not expressly, but his motivation's pretty easy to figure out. Back in the day, he thought punishment wasn't severe enough. He's big on justice and retribution, Hammurabic Code–style. He wanted to take out the four cops because they'd done wrong, and he wanted to take me out because I interrupted his work. That's the same reason he burned Paige's house down after he and Seth escaped the silo. As far as he's concerned, he's conducting business as usual."

"Fallen angel. Sword of justice," Jeff said.

"Exactly," I said. "From that perspective, Paulie's murder makes sense. Dominic seems to be completely blind to his own flaws— the murder and whatnot. Paulie did wrong for this city—he sold drugs. That's enough to trigger Dominic's justice reflex, even though Paulie was actually working for him at the time."

"That explains Dominic," Luc said. "But what about Seth? Any sign of him? Any word at all?"

"Nothing at all, as far as we know," Jeff said. "And there's no sign of him or talk online or among the other sups."

"So he's lying low," Luc said. "And even if one of them popped up, it's not like we could tell them apart. But at least we know what they are."

"At least," I agreed. "But that doesn't solve our larger problem."

"Which is?" Luc asked.

"We don't know how to stop them."

That's when we got to work.

There's at least one common thread linking detective stories and cop shows—the board that shows a victim's picture, the potential suspects, and the witnesses. We opted for something similar, except instead of victims and suspects, we had a demonic angel and a something or other we weren't quite sure about.

Well, we had pictures of Seth Tate and a movie still from *Hellboy* Jeff had e-mailed us, red skin and all.

I glanced over at Luc, who stood beside me, studying the whiteboard.

"Sometimes, we need a little humor," Luc said.

"I guess I can't argue with that." I drew a simple image of a book on the board between Seth and Dominic.

"Seth touched the *Maleficium*. He split into Seth and Dominic. But why were they linked together in the first place? And if Dominic is a fallen angel, what's Seth?"

"And most important," Luc said, "how can we use that against them?"

We stared silently at the board for five minutes. Unfortunately, we still didn't have an answer for either question.

"Angel, man, or monkey," Lindsey said, "it makes no difference to me. I will kill him all the same." She put an arm around me. "He hurts you, he goes down."

I put an arm around her waist. "I appreciate the support."

There was a knock at the door. Malik peeked his head in.

"Liege?" Luc asked.

"Darius would like to speak with Merit."

I was half stunned, half confused, and one hundred percent nervous. "He wants to talk to me?"

"You are, and I quote, 'a lynchpin in my review of the House.'"

Lindsey winced on my behalf.

I stood up and walked for the door, wondering if I should have just stayed with Dominic.

———

I followed Malik to the first floor of the House, then the second, and the third. Since there weren't any public rooms up there, I was admittedly confused. "Where are we going?"

"The roof," Malik said, following the hallway toward Ethan's apartments.

"I'm sorry, the roof?"

"The roof," he dryly confirmed, as if he was equally confused by the location. "Just follow me."

Without a reason to argue, I followed him to the end of the hallway. He opened the last door on the right, then flipped on the light in an empty, vampire-sized bedroom. But unlike the others, a folding pair of simple stairs offered access into the ceiling.

"Attic?" I wondered aloud.

"Yep," Malik said, then hopped up the stairs.

I grabbed the railing and followed Malik into the ceiling and then the space above. This was clearly an older part of the house. The beams were still exposed, showing antique square-headed nails and insulation that looked like horsehair. Kowalcyzk would have loved to send some building code inspectors in here.

"Watch your head," Malik said, and I followed as he half walked, hunched over a bit to accommodate the low ceiling, across the room.

The air was chilly. An open window let moonlight and a stiff fall breeze spill into the room. The breeze carried the scent of clove cigarettes.

Darius was the only man I knew who smoked cloves.

Malik stopped a few feet from the open window and motioned me toward it. At my nervous expression, he smiled, then leaned in.

"Remember who you are, and who you were appointed to be," he whispered. "We all believe in you."

I smiled appreciatively, then climbed out the dormer window

and outside onto the thin widow's walk that capped the edge of the roof.

It was cold, and I zipped up my jacket as soon as I stepped outside and stuffed my hands into my pockets. I found my bit of worry wood still lodged there, and I rubbed its surface for luck. As if that would help me.

Darius leaned against the thin wrought-iron banister that outlined the widow's walk. He wore a button-up shirt and trousers that couldn't have been much protection against the chill, but he didn't look cold. He looked well at home up here in the dark.

A dark cigarette between his fingers, Darius cast me a glance. "Sentinel," he said, blowing out a stream of smoke.

"Sire."

He looked out over the city, the moon milky beneath a haze of clouds.

"It's quiet out here," I said, not sure of the etiquette. Was I supposed to start talking? Or wait for him to do it?

"It is," he said. "Although I suspect the city bustles considerably more in the daytime."

I looked toward downtown Chicago, where skyscrapers blinked at us. Lights in condos and offices twinkled, and bright red beacons on the roofs rotated to warn passing planes. The view wasn't unlike the postcard I'd stuck in the car for my trip to Nebraska, and I realized I hadn't thought to check if that little bit of paper had survived the crash.

"The Loop definitely bustles," I finally agreed. "A lot more than Hyde Park."

"London has its quiet parts, as well."

I nodded, and for a moment we stared out at the quiet city. But it was time to get this show on the road. I had a monster to hunt.

"You asked to see me?"

"I'd like your opinion."

"My opinion?"

"On the state of affairs of your House, Sentinel. You've been here some months. You must have a sense of the House and its goings-on."

I "sensed" a lot of things, but that didn't mean I wanted to raise them with Darius West. "I think the House is operating as well as it can in troubled times."

"Troubled times?"

Did he really need me to recite the list? They were the same grievances we'd been leveling against the GP for months now.

"Our existence was announced to the public without our consent. Celina made attempts on our lives. Mallory threw dark magic across the city. A supernatural mayor, or two of them, are out there somewhere. All problems that we have to solve."

"And why you, Merit? Why must you solve them?"

I didn't really have an answer for that, except the obvious: *If not us, then who?* The GP seemed to be stuck in a mode of refusing to make decisions. Who refused to act, even when the choices were clear and present before them? Were they afraid they'd be judged? Afraid they might be wrong? We had allies, unofficial or otherwise— a select few Houses, shifters, nymphs, a few fairies, a rebellious sorcerer or three. Together, we seemed to be the only ones willing to actually do anything.

It was easy to judge Ethan—or me, Malik, or Luc—when you could stand on the sidelines or quarterback from the couch. It was harder to be in the trenches, to do the best you could . . . and it hurt more when others didn't believe you were acting for good.

Darius took a puff on the cigarette, then blew the smoke from his mouth in a slow, steady stream. "I have been alive a long time," he said. "Not as long as Ethan, but a long time. I have seen much in my life, but I must disagree that these times are troubled. I have seen world wars, Sentinel. I have seen vampires staked in public with no investigation, no remorse."

I nodded. "With all due respect, that you've seen *more* troubled times doesn't mean ours *aren't* troubled. It doesn't take a world war to make a situation precarious. Or dangerous. Before Celina outed us, I had no idea vampires existed. Nor, I would bet, did most people. Perhaps the Houses had troubles then that I'm not aware of. But if they did, they weren't the kind of issues that face us now."

"That's very poetic." He tapped the cigarette's ashes against the wrought iron, and a thousand tiny sparks fell through the sky. "But ultimately, irrelevant."

He took a final puff of his cigarette, then smudged the butt against the dark rock of the wall behind us and put the remainder in his pocket.

"You are young," he said. "And I don't doubt your intentions are noble. But those intentions are directed toward this House, its vampires, and its Master. My intentions are necessarily much larger in scale."

"We are not trying to make your job more difficult, but we can't just ignore these problems."

"That, Merit, precisely *is* the problem. You take arms against the sea of troubles, to quote the bard, but you don't end them. You make them worse." He held up a hand before I could argue. "The evidence is incontrovertible. Things in Chicago have deteriorated over the last few months, and not just because there are enemies in your midst. Consider Grey House. They keep their heads down and they focus on survival, and we have no arguments with their Novitiates or their leadership."

Yeah, but that was only because he didn't know the truth. He didn't know the captain of the Grey House guards was a member of the Red Guard and that he was out there mixing it up with the rest of us.

Maybe that's precisely why Jonah had joined the Red Guard—to keep his efforts hidden from the GP and out of Darius's sight. It wasn't a bad idea. Nevertheless, "Celina didn't target anyone from Grey House, nor did Tate. Or McKetrick. The shifters didn't ask Grey House to act as security for their convocation. What would you have us do? Stick our heads in the sand?"

"I am suggesting," he said firmly, "that there is a skill inherent in handling a crisis and not making it worse. And I am suggesting the current leaders of this House do not have that particular skill."

I was too pissed at the insult to Ethan and Malik to respond. This man sat in a cushy chair in England and complained about what went on here, in *Chicago*, on the ground. He didn't have to make the types of decisions we did; he didn't have to investigate and solve the kinds of problems we did. What right did he have to complain about how we reacted?

"Compose yourself, Sentinel. I can feel your irritation from here. You need to learn to better guard your emotions. Stealth is difficult when you're broadcasting your position."

I didn't respond to the constructive criticism.

"There's no point denying relations between humans and vampires in Chicago are on a rather unfortunate course. Perhaps that course could have been avoided; perhaps not." He looked over at me. "It is crucial that the Master of this House be capable of handling that course, whatever it may be."

"Meaning?"

"Is Ethan Sullivan capable of leading this house?"

My heart began to pound. He wasn't here to evaluate me. This meeting wasn't about my role in the House, or the manner in which I'd been made a vampire.

Darius hadn't come to Chicago to take a long, last look at Cadogan House before enforcing the *shofet*'s decision.

He'd come to Chicago to take a long, last look at Ethan.

Unfortunately, I was long ago tired of politics and strategies and games. "What are you afraid of?" I asked.

Darius looked startled. "Excuse me?"

"Are you afraid of what he'll do if you disown the House . . . or if you don't?"

He looked at me for a moment, and I felt a bolt of panic that I'd thoroughly overstepped my bounds.

But then he called my bluff. He leaned forward, his face only inches away from mine, and his voice dropped. "You tell me, Sentinel. You tell me about the man Ethan has become. He was raised from the dead by a witch who wanted to control him, to make him a thing to be used in the effectuation of her magic. That woman would destroy the world if allowed to do so. Can you tell me, with one hundred percent certainty, that Ethan bears no scars from his experience with her? That he is one hundred percent free of her influence?"

I'd never been a good liar. I'd always believed in a truth—the unassailable facts that either were or were not.

But what could I tell Darius? That Ethan and Mallory still had a connection? That she had the ability to drive him to his knees and assault him with pain?

That the Master of one of the country's twelve Houses—the fourth-oldest House in the United States—was at a witch's mercy?

My heart pounded in my chest, but I forced myself to meet his eyes, to fight through the fear, and to say the words that needed to be said, even if they weren't the absolute truth.

"Ethan Sullivan is the man he always was. A better man, perhaps, because of what he's been through."

"A very strategic answer. I don't approve of relations between Master and Novitiate. I didn't approve when Lacey and Ethan were involved, and I don't approve now. I find such relationships to be essentially incestuous. Regardless, you are his confidante. You have his ear, Merit. Steer him straight, Sentinel. Steer him straight . . . or his future will be considerably darker than it is tonight. I'm going to speak with the dueling Masters now. I'll not mention we had this discussion."

With that, he moved past me and climbed inside again.

I closed my eyes and blew out a breath, then stood there for a moment on the roof, the world dark and quiet, the breeze cold. A light rain began to fall. With my heart heavier than it had been when I'd arrived, I climbed back inside and closed the window behind me.

It was gonna be a long night.

I'd just opened my door when Margot came rushing down the hallway, a worried expression on her face. She still wore chef's whites stained with vegetal green, and a vibrant scarf covered her hair. Whatever brought her up to the third floor, she'd left in a hurry.

"What's wrong?"

"Ethan and Malik just went in to talk to Darius, but someone is here. You need to come downstairs."

"Who is it?"

"I'm . . . not entirely sure."

Without waiting for me to agree, she turned and headed toward the stairs. I followed her, and I was just panicked enough that the trip seemed to take twice as long as usual. Wasn't that always the way? Maybe it was anticipation that stretched out the seconds, much in the same way that a trip to some exotic destination seemed to take twice as long as the return voyage.

We took the stairs at a trot and found a protective net of vampires between the stairs and the front door. They split to make room for me, and I stepped between them, my eyes widening at the dark-haired figure at the door.

"See?" Margot whispered.

I nodded, my brain reeling as I tried to figure out what to do.

"Hello, Ballerina," he said, and I whipped my sword from its sheath.

CHAPTER SIXTEEN

YOU TAKE THE GOOD,
YOU TAKE THE BAD

He looked tired. Tall, handsome, and exhausted. And he'd traded in the Armani suit for a long black cassock, the dresslike garment worn by priests. He was a Tate, to be sure. But I didn't know whether he was Dominic or Seth, or what Seth was in any event, so I wasn't going to take chances.

"Can we talk?" he asked, gaze on me.

Lindsey and Juliet stepped beside me, swords bared.

"You have three seconds to turn around and leave this House or meet the business end of my steel," Lindsey said.

"Wait," I said, putting out a hand, my gaze tracing the lines of guilt carved into Tate's face. Guilt wasn't exactly Dominic's type of emotion.

"Identify yourself," I said.

"I'm Seth Tate," he said. "The former mayor. An angel, in your parlance."

The foyer went silent.

I was stunned and confused . . . and then a little more stunned. If Dominic was essentially a demon, how could Seth be an angel?

They'd split apart from the same person—from Seth when he touched the *Maleficium*.

How were things getting even more confusing?

"You're a messenger?" I asked.

He visibly relaxed, perhaps relieved that someone had figured out the truth. "Yes, Merit. A messenger. That's why the fairies let me in."

It hadn't even occurred to me that he'd gotten past the fairies.

"We don't know that," Lindsey said. "This could be a ruse."

It could have been, but as we stood there, I came to realize an important difference between Seth and Dominic.

"I can tell them apart," I said. Everyone looked at me. "They smell different," I sheepishly added.

Seth smiled a little, but the vampires' reactions weren't encouraging.

"They *smell* different?" Lindsey asked. "You want us to trust him because he smells different?"

"Seth smells like lemon and sugar. He always has. When Dominic unfurled his wings, he smelled like sulfur. Sulfur and smoke." I looked at Seth. "Right?"

"It's the wings. They darkened, much like his aura. His soul."

"He could be making this up," Lindsey said, her sword still tipped at Seth's neck, but I shook my head and pulled my little secret weapon from my pocket—the worry wood.

I held it up for all to see. "This is worry wood. It works against old magic. The powerful stuff. Add it to my natural resistance to glamour, and there's not much chance he could put something over on me."

The crowd's murmurs were a little more supportive but still not convinced. I had one more weapon in the arsenal. I looked at Lindsey. "You're the empath. What's he feeling right now?"

She shook her head. "He's a blank canvas to me. I have no idea."

That might have been true psychically, but not physically. There was no doubting the grief and guilt etched into his face. He was still handsome, but he looked like he'd aged a few years in the last few days.

"I swear on all the deep dish, red hots, and rib-eyes in Chicago that this isn't Dominic. And believe me, I would know better than anyone."

No need to get into the gory deets of what he'd put me through, but having been around both of them, I now had a pretty good sense I could pick them out.

Lindsey slowly lowered her sword again. "Okay, Sentinel. You feel okay about this, I'm going to trust you. But one false move, and he gets it."

And now Lindsey was stealing lines from movies. Maybe she and Luc dating wasn't such a great idea.

I looked back at Seth and gave it to him frankly. "By 'it,' she means thirty-two inches of honed steel. And she's no slouch with a weapon. I'd believe her."

Seth nodded. "I'm here to talk. Not make trouble. There's been far enough of that."

I was fine with talking, but—given the curious and worried looks around us—it seemed we should do it somewhere else. I glanced at Lindsey. "We need a room. Any thoughts? I assume the bigwigs are in Ethan's office."

She frowned. "Training room? Ballroom?"

I didn't like the training room idea. There were too few exits in the basement in the event I was wrong about Seth. I didn't think that was likely, but they didn't pay me fancy Sentinel wages to take those kinds of chances.

The ballroom was on the second floor. Closer to our living quarters than I would have liked, but it was a big, mostly empty room, and it was right beside the stairs.

I glanced around, looking for Luc or Malik or Ethan or anyone actually in charge of the House. But it was just us. Me and Lindsey and the other Novitiates in the foyer. I was the highest-ranking person in the room, and I was going to have to make the call.

God willing I'd make the right one.

"Ballroom," I decided.

Lindsey nodded, then looked around the room. "Show's over, everyone. Get back to business."

But they didn't move, either too curious or too worried to simply turn around and walk away.

"Okay, let me try this another way," Lindsey said, her voice firmer now. "Get back to work before Darius feels the magic, comes out here, sees this one lounging around our foyer, and strokes out."

It still took a moment—they seemed loath to leave Seth here with us or me here with him—but they finally got moving and filed back down the hall and up the stairs.

Lindsey, Juliet, Seth, and I were left in the foyer.

Lindsey pointed at Seth. "You, follow me. Cause any trouble and you'll be wearing steel in very uncomfortable places."

"Duly noted," Seth said.

She looked at me and Juliet. "You heard him. Any funny business and you have his consent to skewer him like a kebab."

I wanted to laugh, but this didn't seem like the time. "I'll take the rear," I told her, then looked at Juliet. "Can you find Ethan?"

Juliet nodded gravely and disappeared, and Lindsey started for the stairs. His hands crossed before him obsequiously, piously, Seth followed her, the rough fabric of the cassock *thrush*ing as he walked. It didn't sound especially comfortable. I imagined stiff, starched fabric rubbing raw skin, and the thought gave me cold sweats.

Had he found religion? Did he feel guilty for what he'd done, or for what Dominic had done? Was the garment, as itchy as it sounded, some kind of personal punishment?

We rounded the stairs at the second floor. Lindsey opened the double doors to the Cadogan ballroom, watching suspiciously as we filed in. When we were well inside, she shut the door behind us.

The room was large, with oak floors, golden walls gilded with framed mirrors. Chandeliers hung from the high ceiling above us. They'd once held hundreds of candles, but those had been replaced with lightbulbs after an attack by a group of rebel shifters. The bulbs didn't offer as much ambience, but one less fire hazard in a building reviled by people who'd once carried torches to flush out monsters seemed like a good precaution.

Seth walked into the room. He stopped beneath the chandelier, then turned a half circle as he looked up at it. "This is a beautiful space," he said.

"Your approval is appreciated," Lindsey said. "Start talking."

Seth looked at me, and I nodded. He began to talk, less a discussion than a monologue. A sermon.

"Millennia ago, the world was a different place. The divisions between humans and others were . . . less rigid. Humans were aware of supernaturals. We, the messengers, bridged the gap between them. Messengers like me arbitrated for peace. Messengers like Dominic administered judgment. At first, humans called us angels and deemed us virtuous."

"And then what happened?" I asked.

"The angels of judgment, the *others*, grew to love violence," Seth said. "They satisfied their lust for it, their compulsion for it, by meting it out for any perceived slight. Humans, so often the victims of that compulsion, didn't appreciate it. They called them the Dark Ones, and they deemed them fallen. Demonic. Devilish. The source of evil."

"And so humans began to distinguish between good and evil."

Seth looked at me thoughtfully. "You remembered what we talked about when I was incarcerated."

I nodded.

"Humans wanted the violence to stop, but the fallen angels were arrogant and refused to believe their actions were wrong. And so a war was waged between humans and messengers. Incensed by the humans' conceit, the justice givers delivered redemption on their own terms, destroying human cities and salting the earth so nothing could grow again."

"Carthage," I quietly murmured.

"You said messengers, plural," Lindsey said. "There are others of you?"

"There are many, although our roles are diminished. Our magic is old, and our ways are old. We aren't part of this world, not in the way we once were."

"And the *Maleficium?*" I asked.

"When humans grew sick of the destruction, they called their magicians, who separated evil from good and placed it into a vessel that would contain it. The *Maleficium*, the book, was created to hold the evil they'd separated out. But it wasn't just a thing. A power."

"What was it?" Lindsey quietly asked, transfixed by the story.

Suddenly, it all made sense. Well, most of it.

"It was *them*," I said. "The fallen angels. The *Maleficium* was created to separate good and evil—they thought the fallen angels were evil. Which means the *Maleficium* was created to hold the fallen angels. Dominic and the others."

"The magicians didn't know how to kill them," Seth said, "so they thought to lock them away for eternity. At least until Mallory came along. Mallory's spell at the silo—what was she trying to do?"

"It was a conjuring spell," Lindsey said. "It does seem like she conjured someone."

But I shook my head. "The *Maleficium* didn't release Dominic. He didn't pop out of the book. He split off from Seth."

"Is that why you look alike?" Lindsey asked.

Seth's expression was sad. "No," he said. "I'm afraid the answer is much simpler. Messengers of justice and of peace were always born to earth in pairs. It was an innate way of keeping the world in balance."

The magical world was big on balance. Good and evil. Dark and light. The reason Mallory's first attempt to unleash the *Maleficium* on the world caused so much havoc in Chicago was precisely because dark and light magic were thrown out of whack.

And humans thought magic was all about fairy tales and simple stories. Little did they know.

"You are twins," Lindsey said. "Real-life twins."

"We were. *Are*," he corrected, his expression slinking toward despair. "Although he and I are very different creatures. We always have been."

Before any of us could react to that, the door burst open. Ethan stood there, Juliet and Luc behind him. A perk of magic filled the air, and Ethan had the fire of a devil in his eyes.

He moved toward Seth, his strides long and determined. His hair had come loose from its tie, and it streamed around his face as he moved like he was a warrior moving into battle.

"Ethan," I said, but he threw me a silencing look. The look of a Master vampire whose irritation at me was matched only by his irritation at the party crasher in his House.

He grabbed Seth's cassock by the shoulders and pushed him backward. Seth stumbled but stayed on his feet, and stared back at Ethan with equal intensity, but much less hatred.

"Are you looking for a fight, Tate? Because I will show you a fight."

Oh, God. Ethan didn't know this wasn't Dominic—the man who'd tried to kill me—and he was ready for war.

"You would have killed her, goddamn it. Do you understand that?"

Seth's eyes went wide, and his gaze snapped to me. "Merit?"

"I'm fine," I said, eyes shifting between him and Ethan. "Ethan, this is Seth. Not Dominic."

"Merit can tell the difference between them," Lindsey said.

But neither Ethan nor Seth was willing to listen; they were both too wrapped up in their own emotions. Ethan thought the man who'd tried to kill me was here again. Seth, who'd known me since I was a child, had only just learned his twin brother had tried to kill me.

"This will not stand," Ethan said.

"He hurt you?" Seth asked.

"Dominic decided I'd interrupted his work. He put me in the sun. But I'm fine now."

Seth looked horrified but turned back to Ethan. "I am sorry," he said, and there was no mistaking the sincerity in his voice. "I am so sorry. I didn't know. I wouldn't have come here if I'd known."

The words finally seemed to shake Ethan out of his fury. Chest heaving, he ran his hands through his hair, then linked them atop his head and walked away from us. Just a few feet away, but enough to gain distance. Enough room for him to think.

He didn't walk toward me. He wouldn't even make eye contact.

My stomach tightened with worry.

"Lindsey?" Ethan asked. "You allowed this man to enter our House?"

She looked nervously at me, and I nodded. "This is Seth," she said. "Merit believes she can tell the difference."

Ethan looked back at me, expression flat. "Can she?"

"I can. But he can prove it better than me," I said. After all, I'd seen the pictures in the *Kantor Scroll*. There was at least one difference between demon and angel, even if it wasn't normally visible.

Even if *they* weren't normally visible.

I looked at Seth. "Show them."

Seth looked at me for a moment, debating the request, then looked at Ethan. "I can prove what I am."

He unclasped the top button of his cassock, then continued down the row until each was unclipped. He wore simple dark pants and a shirt beneath. He dropped the cassock onto the floor, then pulled the T-shirt over his head. His chest was well carved with planks of muscle, but that wasn't the feature attraction here.

"Back up," he said, and we did, stepping farther away from him. He closed his eyes and rolled his shoulders.

I knew what was coming, but that didn't diminish the effect of actually watching it happen.

With a *whoosh* of air, he unfolded his wings. Like Dominic's, they were at least twenty feet from tip to tip. But unlike Dominic's, Seth's wings were still feathery and white. The top ridgeline was iridescent and downy, while the long, straight feathers below were sharp and crisp. His feathers arced along the top and bottom to points at each end that gleamed like opals.

The smell of lemon and sugar filled the room—the sugar-cookie smell of a millennia-old angel in twenty-first-century Chicago.

"They're beautiful," I said. But neither the extension of his wings nor the sentiment lifted the veil of sadness from his face. Seth looked, in a word, tortured. As if embarrassed by what he'd done, he whipped his wings into hiding again.

"I'm sorry," Ethan said, but Seth shook his head.

"He is Dominic's twin brother," I explained. "Seth, the angel. Dominic, the demon. Born together but with different roles in the world. The *Maleficium* was created, in part, as a prison for Dominic and the others like him."

"So Dominic was inside the *Maleficium*?" Ethan asked. "How did he split apart from you?"

Seth shook his head. "I don't know." He turned to pull his T-shirt back over his head. His wings, apparently magical in nature, had completely disappeared. But there in the middle of his back between his shoulder blades was a gruesome scar, a vaguely star-shaped burst of raw pink.

"Your back," I began. "What happened?"

"Magical burn. It happened when I touched the book."

I'm not sure how I knew, but I knew. That wasn't a magical burn.

"I was right. Mallory didn't conjure Dominic from the *Maleficium*," I said.

Ethan frowned at me. "What do you mean?"

"Dominic popped into being, sure, but not from thin air, or even from the *Maleficium*." I looked at Seth. "We watched you split apart. But she didn't divide you in half, not really. She pulled Dominic *out of you*—and you have the scar to prove it."

"How is that even possible?" Ethan asked. "How could Dominic exist within Seth?"

"I don't know," I said. "That's what we have to figure out." And once again, every question we managed to answer led to six or seven more.

Seth pulled his T-shirt down.

"You came to our House," Ethan told him. His posture and tone had changed—back to calm, cool, and collected Master. "Why are you here?"

"Atonement," Seth said without hesitation. "I should have come sooner, but I was, well, mortified. Horrified at what we've done. Dominic has killed again. He was created as a being of justice, but he misapplies the rules. Very rarely is murder just, and certainly not when humans have already adjudicated the guilt of those he seeks to punish again."

Seth was right—and that was a similarity between Paulie and the cops. Paulie had already been convicted; the cops had been acquitted. Humans had already done their justice making, but Dominic wasn't satisfied with their results.

"He's not the only guilty party." He walked toward the ballroom wall and looked into one of the mirrors, staring back at his visage as if it were unfamiliar.

"I have done things." He shook his head. "Throughout my life, I have worked to build communities, to strengthen individuals. I ran for mayor here, in this time and this city, to help those efforts. But somewhere I fell off course. I endangered people who trusted me. I promoted the sale of drugs to vampires." He put a hand to his temple. "It made sense at the time?"

He met my gaze in the mirror. "I owe you a specific apology, Ballerina. Particularly for the things that happened in my office. For putting you through hell. I had information. About your father." Seth glanced at the others in the room. "About the manner in which you were made a vampire," he carefully said. "I thought you had the right to know."

"At the fund-raiser," I said. "You said you wanted to talk to me. That's what you wanted to talk to me about?"

Seth nodded. "There was never time to say the words, and when the confession finally came out, it came out in violence. It caused violence." He looked away. "Whatever her faults, Celina did not deserve to die at my hand. Or yours."

Something clenched in my gut, the monumental regret that I'd taken a life, even one as wasted as Celina's. She hadn't been the first I'd killed, but she was undoubtedly the most memorable.

"And there's nothing we can do now to change what happened," I added.

"Not to change it," Seth said, "but perhaps to atone for it."

"Those actions may not have been yours," Ethan said. "If Dominic was somehow inside you, leading you astray . . ."

"Maybe it was Dominic. Maybe it was the slow, creeping influence of the *Maleficium*. Maybe it was just me. But I have never killed. And I would never do so. He must be stopped. I'll help however I can. I will make my atonement in that fashion. I will stand here, and I will help you face him."

There was strength in his eyes, but I knew it was going to take a lot of time before he was truly healed again. And even if his scar faded, he would be tortured for a very long time.

"What did you have in mind?" Luc asked. "Do you know how to stop him?"

"I do not. I'd hoped your magical friend might have some idea. Her people bound Dominic and the others into the *Maleficium* in the first place. Perhaps we could bind him there again?"

I broke the bad news. "The *Maleficium* was destroyed when you split apart. But surely there's something else we can do. If he was born, he can die, just like the rest of us."

"We saw the footage from his attack at the lockup," Luc said. "He's powerful. Strong. Bullets don't affect him."

"Bullets don't affect us, either," I pointed out. "He may be strong, but we already know he's susceptible to magic—that's why the conjuring spell worked. What magic could we work now to bring him down again? Could we create another *Maleficium*?"

"The *Maleficium* was the work of hundreds of sorcerers over decades," Seth said, raining on my parade. "That wouldn't be possible. Not in the near term."

And not before he killed more people. Dozens? Hundreds? Thousands?

"There must be a way," I said. "There will be a way. There were battles against demons—Carthage, Sodom, Gomorrah. There must have been some fatalities on the demons' side."

Ethan nodded. "We have to try something. We are immortal. Better we take a chance on putting him away than humans he could so easily injure. Or worse." Ethan looked at Luc. "Find Paige and get her and Seth in a room together to discuss the magical underpinnings."

Luc nodded, then held out an arm to guide Seth back to the door. Seth walked back to us and picked up his cassock from the ground. He stopped when he reached me.

"I am sorry."

I wasn't sure I owed him honesty, but I decided I needed it. "I killed someone there, I watched my lover staked through the heart, and you made me believe my father paid him to make me a vampire. Forgiveness will take time."

He nodded. "Then I accept the challenge of my contrition." He put a hand on my shoulder, then walked past me toward the door, lemons and sugar in his wake.

Lindsey leaned toward me. "Is it wrong that I really want to eat a cookie right now?"

"Not at all," I said.

"Let's go, Lindsey," Luc said, ushering her and Juliet outside again. Linds gave me a small smile, then left Ethan and me in the ballroom together.

He'd come into the room fighting, and he'd been sullen for most of the conversation with Seth. I had a pretty good sense a fight was looming, so I bucked up my courage and made myself meet Ethan's gaze.

His eyes flashed silver. "You invited him into this House."

"Only after I was sure it was him."

"You believed he wasn't Dominic. But as you know nothing else about Seth or who he is, that may not have mattered at all. Did you stop to consider what anyone in a position of authority in this House would have decided?"

I didn't appreciate the insinuation that I hadn't thought through the considerable consequences of bringing Seth into the House. My own temper rising, I crossed my arms and glared back at him.

"There was no one else in authority," I said. "Because all the men in this House are too busy whipping theirs out for comparison with Darius West and the *shofet*. And, more important, I stand Sentinel; it's my job to protect this House. I did so."

"By bringing its enemy *here*?"

"Seth Tate is not our enemy. Dominic is."

"And Seth will lure him right into Cadogan House."

"There's no evidence Dominic is looking for Seth. And we aren't exactly kicking Dominic's ass on our own. We need help. I'll admit it was a risky move, but I evaluated that risk and made the best decision I could. Hearing him out was the only play I had, and I took it. Besides, you just invited him to make himself at home and you handed him a sorceress."

Ethan put his hands on his hips and looked away. My answer was perfectly rational, but that hadn't mitigated his barely contained anger.

"Tell me I'm wrong," I quietly said. "If I made the wrong call, tell me I did."

He looked back at me, and there was something much worse than anger in his eyes. There was *disappointment*.

"The rightness or wrongness of the call isn't the point, Merit. It's far beyond your authority as Sentinel."

"I did what I was called upon to do. *There was nobody else to decide*."

He blew out a breath. "He almost killed you. How can you be so lackadaisical about your life?"

So that's what this was about. Not about the decision—because he had to agree I was the only one available to make it—but because I'd put myself at risk. Once again, his desire to protect me was overwhelming his ability to make a good decision.

"Seth isn't Dominic!" I yelled, goose bumps lifting on my arms from the prickle of magic I'd sent through the room. I imagined my eyes were silver, too, and guessed that every other vampire in the House would be able to feel our argument as the magic permeated the building.

If that bothered them, too bad. I'd put my ass on the line, and I'd been right. I wasn't going to apologize for making the decision—not when I was cleaning up the messes of so many other people who'd flat-out refused to act.

"I was in that room with Dominic, Ethan. I've seen that shine of justice in his eyes. Dominic nearly killed me, and he was excited by it. He reveled in it. But that was yesterday. I can't sit in a locked room for the rest of my life because he *almost* managed to kill me. Celina's Rogue almost managed to kill me. Celina almost managed to kill me. Mallory almost managed to kill me. McKetrick almost managed to kill me. I've been a vampire less than a year and I've topped any number of hit lists. I can't help that, and

I'm not going to sit here waiting for it to happen again. Not when I can do something about it.

"Seth isn't Dominic," I said. "And we need Seth. That makes the math easy for me. If you don't think I'm making the right kinds of decisions as Sentinel, then you know what to do."

A thought occurred to me. Not one that he'd want to hear, certainly, but something that needed to be said. "Are you really mad at me, or is this because of Mallory?"

"Does it matter?"

I took a step closer to him. "Ethan, for God's sake, if you're angry at me, then be angry at me. But if this is Mallory, don't push me away. Let me *help* you. We are partners—we have proved time and again that we are better together than we were apart. We have battled back angry shifters and crazy Masters and vampire saboteurs. We can manage a skinny little sorceress."

I saw the flicker of hope in his eyes, and I waited for him to grab on to it, but fear got the better of him, and he turned away again.

"I need to get back to Darius," he said. And as he walked out of the ballroom, I put my hands on my hips and stared up at the ceiling and wished for patience.

—✠—

CHAPTER SEVENTEEN

SHE'S GOT A WAY

I stormed up the stairs to the third floor, fueled by my own indignation.

Why did everything have to be his way? Why did he have to control every situation, even when that very control threatened to tear everything apart?

Fear loomed in the back of my mind. Fear that I'd changed, and Ethan had changed, and who we'd become in the months he'd been gone was too different for us to find each other again.

But I put it aside. I was Sentinel of the House, and since Kelley and Luc now had plenty of House guards, I was officially a full-time Sentinel again. I was going Sentineling, and my first stop was Mallory. Paige and Seth could investigate the Dominic-Seth link from here; I'd use my original source. She still may not have been trustworthy, but I doubted anyone else in Chicago had as much knowledge about the *Maleficium* and the evil stuck into it.

I zipped up my leather jacket, pulled my hair into a ponytail, and grabbed my sword. I still gave Kelley a heads-up before I left, but Ethan was in time-out as far as I was concerned. If he needed me, he could call. I had work to do.

I trotted down the sidewalk to the gate, and both mercenary fairies stared at me as I passed them by. I stopped short, glancing back at them in turn.

"Is everything okay?"

They looked at each other. Since they were nearly identical, it was like watching one of them look into a mirror. A strange effect in the middle of an already strange city.

My instincts triggered, I walked back to them. "What is it?"

They looked at me simultaneously. "Your Dark One," said the one on the left. "It is possible he will contact her."

"Her? You mean Claudia?"

He nodded. "They are acquaintances, of a sort."

So Dominic and Claudia knew each other. She certainly hadn't confessed that to me. On the other hand, I hadn't asked her outright, either, and Claudia wasn't exactly free with information.

"Did they know each other before his wings turned black?"

"Before, during, and after," said the other fairy, not with approval, but earning a narrow-eyed look from his partner. He must have spilled too much.

I looked back at the apparent team leader and decided to skip the political wrangling. "Why are you telling me this?"

They both look flummoxed by the question. Since we paid them to stand guard outside our House—and, admittedly, I'd been baited into going for one's jugular while visiting Claudia—the confusion was understandable.

"He is dangerous. She is our queen, but she is . . . vulnerable to his suggestion. The sooner he is gone, the better for all of us."

Not that I needed the incentive to nab Dominic, but I'd heard Claudia's threats before. "Nuclear" was her first and only option.

Whatever had been between them, love or business, it wasn't a complication I needed right now.

I nodded at both of them. "Thank you for the heads-up."

I climbed into my orange, boxy Volvo, which was admittedly a downgrade from Ethan's shiny new Aston Martin. But until I got a promotion or a stiff pay raise, the Volvo would have to do.

My phone rang nearly as soon as I buckled my seat belt. I propped it on the dashboard and turned on the speakerphone.

"Merit," I answered, pulling onto the street.

"Hey, it's Jeff."

"What's new?"

"Absolutely nothing. Catcher went to see Mallory, and it's dead quiet over here. I mean, I racked a new server, and the cabling was a bitch, but that's about it. I thought I'd call and see if you had any news."

"Well, Seth Tate showed up at Cadogan House, if that counts."

"Oh, shiz. That totally counts. How do you know it was him?"

"Long story short, about twenty linear feet of white, fluffy wingspan."

"That's a pretty good indication."

"Yes. It was. We did manage to get a little more background. It's no coincidence that they look alike. Dominic and Seth are twin angels, although Dominic turned to the dark side after his mythological hissy fit. We think Dominic has somehow been inside Seth for centuries, and they got split apart when the *Maleficium* was triggered. Seth has the scar to prove it."

"And he had no idea?"

"Not as far as we can tell. Personally, it sounds like Dominic may have been the little red devil that sat on his shoulder and told him to do naughty things, but Seth's accepting responsibility for now. Which is kind of a nice change."

"No kidding. It's definitely usually the other way around. What did Seth have to say?"

"He wants to help us deal with Dominic as part of his atonement. Unfortunately, he doesn't have any idea how to go about doing that. What about you? Might there be anything in your shifter encyclopedia about that?"

"We don't have an encyclopedia. We're more of a storytelling people. But I'm not aware of a fable on bat-winged, parasitic dudes who feed off mayors. Although that would have explained a lot of Chicago's political history."

"Sad but true. I'm heading out to see Mallory. I'll ask if she has any information. Oh—and another weird one. The mercenary fairies at the gate think Dominic and Claudia, their queen, are going to have a meet and greet. While you're researching him, look for any connection with the fairies."

"Will do."

"I appreciate it. And Jeff, how's Fallon?" I felt like I hadn't heard anything about Gabriel's sister—and Jeff's newish flame—in a while. I wasn't sure if that was because things were going well, or because they weren't.

"She's good. She's . . ." He sighed. "I think she has things to figure out."

That didn't sound good. "What kinds of things?"

"What she wants in life and in a man. There's a lot of pressure growing up in the Apex's family. I think she's still sorting out who she thinks she is versus who she thinks her family expects her to be."

"That's tough. Anything I can do?"

"Just stay in play as my backup."

I nearly swerved the car off the road. "I'm sorry—your backup?"

"You know, in case it doesn't work out with Fallon."

"And what about Ethan?"

Jeff chuckled. "I just figured he was your backup for me."

Of course he did. "Good night, Jeff," I said, and hung up the phone.

Boys.

Traffic was horrible, and the drive to Ukrainian Village took exponentially longer than it should have. Even as late as it was, and with a clear sky above us, traffic on Lake Shore Drive had slowed to a crawl, and the freeway wasn't any better.

Even Little Red was packed, every spot outside the bar filled with a motorcycle, and a cadre of shifters stood just outside the door, smoking and chatting one another up. Sure, there was a deadly angel on the loose, but there were cigarettes to be rolled and whiskey to be drunk.

Supernatural man drama was making me grouchy.

I parked two blocks away and thought about leaving my sword in the car. But since Dominic was on the prowl, I decided not to take chances. My next visit to the sunlight prison might not have such a happy ending.

I dodged drunken revelers as I headed back toward the bar, and I was full-on ready to argue about whether the guys outside the bar would let me in with a sword at my side. But no one paid me any mind.

The bar was overflowing with shifters. Berna was back at the bar, helped by a young woman with deep-set eyes, dark hair, and a very snug T-shirt. I pushed through bodies and mildly intoxicated magic to reach them.

"Upstairs," Berna said, without looking up.

She was busy, and I was smart enough to stay out of the way. I walked through the back room, the table again empty of shifters and card players, and up the stairs.

The door to Mallory's small bedroom-slash-prison-cell was open, and I could hear people chatting. Since I already had one black mark for snooping this week, I decided to actually announce myself.

I knocked on the doorjamb and peeked inside.

Mallory sat cross-legged on the bed. She looked thin and tired and still oddly blond, but she looked more like Mallory than she had in a long time. Her eyes were clearer, somehow. The knot of worry around my heart unclenched a bit.

She wasn't alone. Catcher stood nearby, arms crossed and a frown on his face as he stared at the third person in the room, who was new to me. He was older, probably in his late fifties or early sixties. Average height, round belly, and a thick head of silvery white hair. He wore a thick green Packers jacket, jeans, and shiny white tennis shoes with thick soles. Grandpa-style tennis shoes.

They all turned to look at me.

I waved a little, suddenly self-conscious, the uninvited vampire. "Hi."

Catcher waved me in.

"Merit, this is Al Baumgartner, head of the Order."

You could have knocked me over with a feather.

This guy was Al Baumgartner? This guy who looked like someone my grandfather bowled with was in charge of all the sorcerers in North America? I'd expected someone a little more Darius, maybe. A little more polished. A little more professional. A little slicker.

Al Baumgartner smiled politely, then stretched out a hand. "Merit, it's very nice to meet you."

"It's nice to meet you, as well."

"We appreciate your help in getting all this sorted out," he said. "It's good to know who your friends are."

I didn't say it aloud, but we weren't friends, and Mallory wasn't a problem to be "sorted out," like he'd simply forgotten to pay the electric bill on time.

But from what I'd heard from Catcher and Paige, there was no point in arguing with him.

"We did what needed to be done," I said politely. "Am I interrupting?"

"Not at all. I'm just here to check in. The world is changing, and we're just trying to keep up."

I slid Catcher a surreptitious glance and enjoyed his dramatic eye roll.

"I see," I said, although there was no doubt he was telling us only part of the story.

"Well," Baumgartner said, "I should probably be off. I've got some things to attend to while I'm in town." He looked at Mallory, and his features changed. From grandfather caricature to magical overlord. That expression looked a bit more honest on his face, I thought.

"We'll talk" was all he said to her, then smiled politely at me, zipped up his Packers coat, and walked out the door.

I waited for the sound of footsteps on the stairs before I spoke. "Why is he really here?"

"Punishment," Catcher said.

It didn't say a lot that the answer didn't surprise me—because the Order rarely seemed to pay that much attention. "What's he proposing?"

"Nothing yet," Catcher said. "Could be rendition—a mix of isolation and indoctrination. Could be nullification."

"What's nullification?"

Mallory uncrossed her legs. "That's where they take away my magic for a specified period of time."

"That doesn't sound as bad as rendition."

"It's not," Catcher said, "but it's worse than it sounds. She's had the magic for a long time, even before she was aware of it. It's integrated into her body, which makes nullification akin to a magical lobotomy."

Put that way, it sounded pretty horrible. "And when will they make a decision?"

Catcher shrugged. "They're mulling things over."

It was clear the "mulling" was getting to Mallory. Even though she looked better, she picked nervously at the edge of the blanket.

"How are you feeling?" I asked Mallory.

"Like I'm trying to quit smoking again. If the smoking killed everybody else but me, turned me into a she-bitch, and made me screw over all of my friends."

That about said it.

"It takes time," Catcher said.

"I know," she said, then squeezed her eyes closed. "I'm sorry. I know this is an addiction and I know it will take time to really feel better, and I am trying my damndest not to fuck up my life any more than I already have. But in the meantime, it sucks. I feel like crap." She laughed hoarsely. "And it doesn't help that I have a Packers fan deciding my fate. I mean, seriously? You're going to wear that jacket in Chicago?"

The words were sarcastic, but I could tell she was walking a knife's edge of fear and anger. That would certainly explain Ethan's irritability.

"What brings you by?" Catcher asked.

I gave them the same overview I'd given Jeff, and I wasn't thrilled when they looked as surprised as he'd sounded. I was hoping for a little more familiarity with the problem—and through that, a solution.

"How did they end up together?" Catcher asked.

"That's the part we aren't sure about. I was hoping you might have an idea."

Mallory shook her head. "It doesn't ring any bells for me. You, Catcher?"

It saddened me that Mallory was back to calling him Catcher. She had a million nicknames for him and used them more often than not. But they were on a break that Catcher deserved, so there wasn't much I could do about it.

"I don't know," Catcher said. "I can ask Jeff."

"He's already on it, as are Seth and Paige. I'm sure someone will come up with something."

Catcher nodded, then glanced at his watch, then up at Mallory again. "I need to get back."

She nodded a couple of times. "Okay."

"I'll let you know if we find anything," he said, then walked out the door.

No hug, no kiss good-bye for Mallory. No good-bye at all, really.

I looked back at her, but she wouldn't meet my gaze. She just kept picking at that spot on the blanket.

"Do you want to talk about it?"

She laughed mirthlessly. "I have flushed my entire life down the toilet. That's really all there is to say right now." She put both hands over her face, then pressed her palms against her eyes.

I nodded, my heart aching for her, even though I could completely sympathize with Catcher.

"You and Ethan?" she asked, trying to smile a little. Somehow, that made her seem even sadder.

"We're . . . working on it. Things are complicated right now."

She nodded, then chewed the edge of her lip.

"This is so awkward," I said.

"It really is." She seemed relieved to say it.

"Like we're strangers to each other."

Mallory nodded. "We are. I am a stranger to you. You didn't know I was capable of all these things—of the things I've done. Horrible things. Turns out, I am." She looked up at me. "I'm the kind of person who hurts others to get what they want. I shouldn't be here right now, Merit. I should be in prison."

Her sadness was palpable, but at least she was beginning to see reality.

"Have you talked to Gabriel?"

"He thinks I'm redeemable."

That simple statement made me feel better than I had in a long, long time. Gabriel wasn't an easy one to impress, and he had insight—magical or otherwise—into the future. If he thought Mallory was redeemable, that meant something. And it wasn't like he was prone to overcomplimenting.

"That's something," I said.

"It's something," she agreed. "I'm working at the bar. This is my lunch break, I guess, although I'm not hungry much. I'm not much of anything right now. Numb, I guess. I know the things I did. They replay in my head over and over and over again. But they feel removed, like it wasn't me. Like I'm just watching a video playback or something."

"Those things happened. They were real."

She nodded. "Gabriel says—he thinks I have a sensitivity to the imbalance the *Maleficium* created. He thinks that's why I was so drawn to it."

I nodded. "Paige said all sorcerers felt that a little."

"Some more than others, I guess. And I'm not trying to make an excuse. I'm just—I'm trying to understand why—" She began sobbing again.

I sat down on the bed beside her. Not touching—I wasn't ready for that—but acknowledging what she was going through, and that she was finally facing her demons.

"God, I am so sick of myself," she said after a few minutes.

"A lot of us are," I said with a smirk, and she choked out a laugh and nodded.

"I needed that," she said, knuckling away tears. "I can't use my magic here. He arranged it or something."

"I know."

"It will be a long time before they let me use it again. But Gabriel thinks I have talent, but I have to be trained how to use it for the right causes."

"Gabriel said that?" It was an unusually hands-on position for a shifter, who was usually more concerned with carousing than counseling.

"He says there's work I can do. Hard work, but fulfilling."

"Did he say what?"

She shook her head. "I'm not sure it matters. I'm not sure I'll ever make this up to anyone, no matter what I do."

She and Seth were a pair right now. Both facing guilt and the specter of never being able to atone for what they'd done, both suffering because of a book intended—ironically—to make life better for everyone.

The moral of the story? Don't fuck with the magical order.

"There's one thing you can do to help," I said.

She looked up at me, and I trusted her with my secret.

"You may not have completed the familiar spell, but you and Ethan are linked together somehow."

Mallory blanched. "What?"

"I think when you feel strong emotions, he does, too. You're connected to each other because of the spell you attempted."

She looked horrified, which actually made me feel better. "Oh my God, Merit, I didn't know."

"I didn't want to tell you," I confessed. "Not until I was sure you were in control of yourself." I wasn't entirely sure she was in control of herself now, but she was aware of her weaknesses and of what she'd done, which was more maturity than I'd seen from her in a while.

I'd expected more tears from my confession, but she steeled her expression and looked up at me.

"I will fix this," she said.

"Then do it," I said. "Make this your first act of contrition. Give him back to me."

The small black alarm clock on her bedside table buzzed, and she tapped it with a hand. "I should get back to work."

I nodded. "What do you have to do?"

"Dishes again. The bar serves some food, and shifters eat. A lot."

She'd gone from high-profile ad executive to high-powered witch . . . and now she was cleaning up for drunken shifters in the back of a run-down bar.

"Does it bother you? That you're doing dishes?"

"It's not the best job. Hot. Swampy. Kind of gross—all those little bits of wet bread and crust." She made a gagging sound. "But it's something to do that's not magical. And there's a kind of security, I guess, with all of them around me. Like I can't backslide while they're watching. And that they really believe I could do something worthwhile someday."

"How long is someday?"

She shrugged. "How long does it take to make up for what I've done?" She stood up. "I need to get downstairs."

I didn't want to go back to the House. I didn't want to face

Dominic on the way or Darius or Ethan when I arrived. I got her point about security. Here, I was behind a wall of dozens of shifters and lots of firearms. It might not have been safe from Dominic, not really, but it felt safer. It felt removed from the world, and I could use that right now.

"I could help you?"

She looked at me, tentative hope in her face, and nodded.

So I stayed with her. We walked downstairs again and I hung my leather jacket on the back of the door. She dumped food while I rinsed, and in the rising heat and steam, under the watchful eye of a very big shifter with a very large gun, we did our work in silence.

It wasn't an act of forgiveness, but it was a step forward. And right now, I needed one of those.

CHAPTER EIGHTEEN

DEEP DISHING

I left Ukrainian Village with the radio on and the windows up. I baked in the sauna of a full-blast heater but only marginally enjoyed the warmth on the way back to the House.

I nearly popped a fist on the dashboard when the radio was interrupted with a staticky beep, but it wasn't a problem with my radio.

It was a warning.

"Folks, we're sorry for the interruption," said the announcer, "but we're going live to the home of Dan O'Brian, who you may remember was one of the South Side Four—the four Chicago Police Department officers recently released in connection with the alleged attack on vampires and humans."

Sirens wailed in the background. Knowing this message wasn't going to be good, I pulled the car over onto the side of the road, turned down the heat, and turned up the radio.

"Officer O'Brian, along with Officer Owen Moore and Officer Thomas Hill, were found dead outside O'Brian's home just moments ago, and parents, this will be graphic if you have any young ones listening, it appears all three died of severe wounds to their throats. Officer Coy Daniels had been killed in the attack at the officers' release. We have learned the remaining officers refused protection details offered by the city—"

I switched off the radio, closed my eyes, and put my head back on the headrest.

All that work to save the rest of them, and it had been for naught. Dominic had found them and killed them anyway. What was the moral of *that* story supposed to be? That evil would always win? That fighting the battle was pointless?

This night needed a happy ending, and soon.

There were few places in Chicago where I was all but guaranteed an unhappy ending. One of them was the home of the city's sky-masters, the tower in Potter Park where Claudia, the queen of the fairies, lived.

As I'd told Ethan and Paige, my last visit to the fairies hadn't exactly been promising. But Claudia said we left with a clean slate, so I was hoping against hope that she'd remember that promise today and not kill me on sight.

I was desperate for information, and if she and Dominic had a connection, I was going to ferret it out.

The park was empty and quiet, and I parked along the street and walked through dying grass to the tower. It was made of stone and barely managing to stand, but Claudia had made it her home. I carefully took the spiral stone staircase to the door at the top, stopping at the ornate tower door.

Steeling myself, I knocked twice.

It opened, and a mercenary fairy stared out. "Yes?"

The last time I'd done this, Jonah had spoken in Gaelic to request admission to see Claudia. I didn't have any such skills, so English would have to do.

"I would like to speak with Claudia, if she'd allow it."

The door thumped closed, pushing a puff of dust and wood rot into my face. I brushed off my cheeks just as it opened again.

"Briefly," the fairy said with a snarl, stepping back to allow me in.

The room in which Claudia lived was round and magically enhanced, filling a space significantly larger than the tower's appearance outside would have let on. It was simply furnished and smelled of a garden's worth of flowers.

Claudia, her long, strawberry blond hair in a loose braid down her back, sat at a round table on one side of the room. She wore a dress of pale pink and a leafy crown, and she glanced over her shoulder as I walked inside.

"Bloodletter," she said, as much a hiss as a greeting.

"Madam," I said.

She rose from her table and walked toward me, her blue eyes tilted in curiosity. "You visit our abode again. Why?"

"I understand you know Dominic, the messenger, and I wondered if you'd tell me about him."

She laughed, the sound simultaneously whimsical and ancient. "Who are you to inquire about such things? You are a child, and a bloodletter at that."

"He is hurting people," I said. "I'm trying to find a way to stop him."

That was precisely the wrong thing to say. Her smile faded, and the Queen of the Fae strode toward me with grim determination on her face. Before I could move out of the way, she slapped me.

"Who are you, that you believe you have the right to control the destiny of a messenger?"

My cheek burning, I forced myself to look back at her—and not to push her away. She was too testy, and she'd lured me toward violence before.

"I am Sentinel of my House and a protector of this city," I said. "He threatens those within it. That gives me the right to question and, if necessary, to act."

"You know nothing," she spat out, turning on her heel and pacing a few feet away. She turned back again, shoulders back and breasts arched forward, as if proving her femininity to me.

"Dominic is under my protection, and so he will stay. If you seek to harm him, you seek to harm me and mine. No such thing will be allowed." She gave me a disdainful look. "You are no protector. You are a poppet with a pointy stick and the arrogance to match. Leave this place. If you deserve justice, he will find you, and you will find no more voice for your threats."

The sword's point suddenly at my lower back punctuated her dismissal. I was escorted back to the door and into the stairwell, and the door was slammed shut behind me again.

Not exactly the most productive meeting I'd ever attended, but one thing was for sure—Claudia knew Dominic. Had they been lovers? That seemed likely. Partners? Also possible. Details were thin on the ground, but I had a sinking feeling this wasn't the last time I'd spend quality time with the fairy queen.

My mood not even slightly improved, I parked the car and nodded at the fairies before heading into Cadogan House. I found Lindsey on her way upstairs from the basement.

"Hey, you. You all right?" She frowned. "You look weird."

"I'm okay. Tough night."

She nodded. "Have you heard about the cops?"

I nodded. "On the radio."

"Rough thing to hear."

"I wasn't thrilled," I agreed. "It makes me feel pretty useless."

"What could you have done? If they weren't smart enough to

get protection, there's nothing that could keep Dominic from them."

I shrugged. I understood the argument; it just didn't make me feel any better. I still felt like I'd let the city down, and that was a tough burden to bear.

"Did you learn anything helpful at Mallory's?"

"Not really. Catcher and Jeff are going to look into Tate's history." I told her what I'd learned from Claudia, which wasn't much. "What are you up to?"

"It's end of shift. The girls are waiting upstairs with a pizza. Are you hungry? You look like you could use a bite."

When *didn't* I look like that? In all seriousness, I wasn't sure I was ready to talk to Ethan, and I certainly wasn't up for another argument tonight. Not with sorcerers and cops and fallen angels on my mind. On the other hand, Lindsey and I had a pretty good history of late-night pizza-and-movie relaxation.

"Yeah," I said. "That sounds good."

"Okay," she said, slipping her arm through mine. "Are you sure you're okay?"

"I'm not," I said. "But I will be."

A crowd was already gathered in her small room. Margot was there, along with a few male vampires I vaguely recognized but hadn't really spoken to. Notwithstanding the fact that we were vampires, the air smelled of cheese, tomato sauce, and lots of garlic. Three of my favorite food groups, baked into one deep-dish pizza amalgamation so thick and saucy you had to eat it with a spoon.

I was greeted by cheers (always better than jeers) and tiptoed my way across vampires toward an empty spot on the floor.

"We were just deciding what to watch," Margot said as she

served up a slice of deep dish onto a paper plate and handed it over. "As social chair, I think you should get to pick which one."

Ethan had named me House social chair as a half joke and half punishment. He thought I needed to become better acquainted with my fellow vampires. It was undoubtedly a good call, although I hadn't done much at all in the position. I'd thought about hosting a mixer for Navarre, Grey, and Cadogan vampires, but magical drama always seemed to get in the way.

"What are our options?" I asked.

Lindsey flipped through some movies. "Animated with a good moral. Three ladies being saucy about their jobs and boys. And, my personal favorite, poor kid proves she's the best dancer at Dance-Off High and wins the lead role in a Broadway musical." She slid me a glance. "The guys won't appreciate this, but there is singing. Much singing, and you can make the lyrics scroll across the bottom of the screen."

She knew me as well as anyone. I loved to dance, and in high school I'd had plenty of ambition—but sadly, no talent—to become a musical theater songstress. Thank God I'd had good grades to fall back on.

"I can't possibly say no to sing-along lyrics," I said, diving into the pizza. It was ridiculously good.

I caught a pretty bad habit in graduate school of obsessing about my work to the point of ignoring anything and everything else. I rarely visited friends. I rarely did *anything* that wasn't related to getting the job done. I became a hermit, not because I didn't like people, but because I wasn't very good at balancing work and play. "All work" was a lot easier to manage.

Times like this made me remember that I could do both. I could be busy, productive even, while having a social life. While interacting with people. While being out in the world instead of sequestering myself away from it. Times like this I felt like a normal person, not just a solver of problems for a House of vampires.

Friendship, I thought, quickly downing my wedge of pizza, wasn't a burden. It was a gift. It allowed us to remember what all the fighting was about in the first place. Why we struggled to protect the House—and what we were protecting.

So I sat back with Lindsey and the others, and I sang horribly to lyrics that were wincingly bad, and I remembered why we went to all the trouble of fighting in the first place.

When the movie was over, I helped the crew clean up and was happy to take the last piece of pizza for myself back to my room.

But when I made a move to leave, Lindsey stopped me.

"Oh, no," she said. "We have words for you." She looked around the room. "All boys out of the room, please."

There were only a couple of male vampires left, but they shuffled out after whistles and catcalls about what they joked was going to take place with me, Margot, and Lindsey after they left.

Lindsey closed the door behind them, then looked back at me. "Spill."

"I don't know what you're talking about," I said, but Margot and Lindsey exchanged a glance that said they knew better.

"You and Ethan should be doing the nasty with aplomb and frequency," Lindsey said. "And instead, you're barely talking to each other and you're having me and Luc relay messages between you. If the sexual tension in this House gets any thicker, we'll have to paddle through it. What the hell is going on?"

I closed my eyes. Part of that was completely humiliating, and I really didn't want to get into the rest of it.

On the other hand, I needed help. And unlike a certain pretentious Master vampire, I knew when to ask for it.

I sat down on the floor again. "He's driving me crazy."

Lindsey and Margot joined me. "What happened?"

"It started in Nebraska. We realized he and Mallory have some kind of connection because of the spell she tried to work. He's not her familiar or anything, but if she gets emotionally freaked-out, he does, too."

"That's scary," Margot said.

"It is," I agreed. "But he can control it—he controlled it in Nebraska. Anyway, during one of these spells he grabbed my arm, and now he's convinced he's going to hurt me if we keep seeing each other while Mallory's in his head. So we're 'halting' our relationship." Yes, I used air quotes.

Lindsey gave me a flat stare. "He's an idiot."

"Oh, I know."

"After all the shit you two have been through—all those months of fighting and driving the rest of us crazy—this is the thing he gets freaked-out about? Because he grabbed your arm?"

"That's it."

Lindsey fell back onto the carpet with much drama. "I knew he was stubborn, but this truly takes the cake." She leaned up on her elbows. "He knows you're immortal, right? And that you've broken ribs before? And been shot?"

"He might know those things," Margot said, "but consider it from his perspective—the man is Master of this House, or was anyway. His life is about control and order and combating chaos. And now he's got someone else shacking up in his head who can affect his behavior—and cause him to hurt one of his vampires? That's not a comfortable place for him."

"I get that," I said. "But that's exactly my point—Ethan didn't suddenly turn into a jerk. He has a sorceress living in his head, creating his moods, and causing his emotions to go magically wonky. I'm not one to excuse people for their bad behavior, but in this case, *it really isn't his fault*. And, more important, it's *me*. He knows I can take care of myself. And instead of letting me help him, we have, as you put it, the giant wall of tension that is driving me *crazy*."

"You know what the problem is?" Lindsey asked. "You two are stuck in a prelationship."

"What's a prelationship?" Margot and I simultaneously asked.

"That stage when you clearly have the hots for each other, but you haven't yet agreed that you're actually *in* a relationship. It's the pre-relationship stage. He has convinced himself he's not really breaking up with you for an idiotic reason, because you're in a prelationship, so this 'halting' business doesn't seem as bad to him."

I sighed. "That makes sense. But what do I do about it? I want Mallory to disappear from his head, but that could take time. What if it takes years? Am I supposed to stand around and wait? I mean, he answered his apartment door half-naked."

"He wants you," Lindsey said. "Physically and otherwise. Maybe you only need to remind him that you can handle yourself."

"How?"

"Girl, you're the Sentinel of this House, and you've been trained by Catcher and Luc *and Ethan*. He's in the training room right now. Get down there and *kick his ass*."

I smiled slyly. Now, that was a plan that made sense.

I was a woman with a plan, and it wasn't a plan I was going to half ass. I was bringing every skill I had to bear on the problem—and taking off most of my clothes to do it. The official Cadogan House training ensemble was pretty tame—a top that looked like a black sports bra and yoga pants. It was an outfit geared for movement and comfort.

By contrast, Catcher Bell's training uniform was designed to allow me to watch my body move—and because of that, there was a lot less to it. Short black shorts and a bandeau-style bra.

I wiggled into the ensemble, straightened my ponytail, and made my way to the basement training room. Ethan must have needed a break from meetings and politics; he wore a white martial arts ensemble and was coaching a handful of Novitiates through a *kata*, one of the building blocks of vampire combat.

But when he saw me—and my ensemble—he stilled and his eyes went hot. Without a word to the Novitiates, he walked to me.

"Yes?"

"We weren't finished with our discussion earlier."

"And you intend to go another round?"

"I intend to bring you to your senses."

"Watch your tone, Sentinel."

I took a step forward, bringing me nose to nose with him. He'd taken a stake for me; I wasn't afraid of him. One way or the other, I'd prove that tonight.

"You've seen me in action," I quietly said, "and you know I can protect myself. You know I wouldn't let you hurt me. I am not human. I am an immortal, practically indestructible, highly trained Novitiate vampire *and* Sentinel of this House. But if you think you can do it, I *dare* you to try."

Shock filled his face. "Excuse me?"

"Me and you, right now. You try your best to hurt me." I gave him the cockiest expression I could muster. "I guarantee you can't."

My words were softly but intently spoken, and they seemed to finally get through to him.

He marched to the center of the room, interrupting a cadre of half a dozen vampires who were sparring on the tatami mats that covered the floor.

"Out," he bellowed, and no one stopped to ask for clarification. Without a word, they gathered up their things and headed for the door.

"Lock it," Ethan directed, and I closed and locked the door behind us, my heart thudding in anticipation.

When I turned around again, he beckoned me forward. "Ready when you are, Sentinel."

Oh, I was ready. He'd been obnoxious enough that I had no compunction about trying to hit him now, and I didn't wait for him to make the first move. I ran toward him and executed a scissor kick, but he was fast enough to deflect it.

I prodded the back of his knee and sent him stumbling forward. But he caught himself and managed to use his momentum to spin the stumble into a backward kick.

I yelped in surprise but jumped over his foot. We were up and facing each other in less than a second.

First round: a tie.

"You aren't trying very hard," I said.

"I'm not actually going to hurt you."

I chuckled. "That presupposes you *could* hurt me. You can't. Try again."

Ethan halfheartedly aimed a couple of jabs at me. In response, I offered a jab, an uppercut, and a double jab again. He dodged the shots, managed a side kick that grazed my right kidney. His eyes widened, but I made a sarcastic sound.

"It's going to take more than that, Sullivan. As Morpheus would say, quit trying to hit me and *hit* me."

I must have pricked his ego, as he spun backward and went

for a crescent kick, which was one of his better moves. He had the lean strength of a soccer player and the fluidity of a dancer. The edge of his heel just grazed the outside of my thigh, and I quickly executed a side kick that tapped his butt just as he turned around.

But Ethan didn't give up on the crescent kick. He spun again and caught the back of my knee with his heel. My leg bobbled and I went down, landing on my back. Before I could hop to my feet again, he pounced, flattening me to the mat and pinning down my arms.

My eyes silvered immediately, the speed of the transition almost embarrassing. It was unnerving that he had the power to affect me so immediately—that the sensation of his body atop mine immediately turned me into a needy mess.

"Point to me," he said.

I considered my options—a scissor kick that switched our positions and put him on the floor, or a surrender that would keep him exactly where he was, his body warm and long above mine.

"Point to you," I said, "but I'm still perfectly healthy."

"It might not always be so simple," he said, his eyes still dark with worry.

I understood his point, understood well the risk he was trying to avoid. But he'd saved my life twice. I trusted him implicitly, and not because I feared him or what he might do. "I'm not afraid of you."

His eyes silvered. "You should be."

"Never. You took a stake for me."

"I was a different man then."

"Bullshit. You are the same man now that you were before. A little ballsier maybe, and a little more moody because of Mallory's intervention. But the same man." I trailed a finger over the spot that bore the stake's scar. "You took a stake for me. You bear a scar for me because of what you sacrificed. Would you do it again?"

"In a heartbeat."

And that, I thought, was answer enough. He might have been afraid he'd hurt me, but he knew what he was willing to do to protect me.

"You told me in Nebraska that you'd choose me over Mallory." I brushed a lock of hair from his face. "That's what I'm asking you to do now, Ethan. Choose me over Mallory. Give up some control and let me help you."

When he rolled over and sat up beside me, my heart sank. Tears suddenly bloomed at my lashes as I thought hope was lost.

"I haven't told you how Malik and I came to be on campus that night."

He meant that night he'd saved my life the first time and made me a vampire. My heart stuttered a bit, anticipating information that would either make me swoon—or make me furious. "No, you didn't," I carefully said.

"After your father came to me and I refused him, Malik and I were nervous he might, shall we say, shop around."

He was quiet, watching me as I decided how to take his confession. Honestly, I wasn't really sure how to take it. "You followed me?"

"We weren't privy to your discussions with your father, but Malik thought it best to keep an eye on you, and I concurred." He cleared his throat. "I'd decided you deserved the truth."

"You were going to tell me what he did?"

"We knew you were enrolled at U of C, and we'd learned you were at school that night. We'd just gotten out of the car to find you when you were attacked."

Of all the nights for him to attempt to speak to me.

And I'd hated him—loathed him—when I'd first been changed. I'd been so angry to have been denied the choice to become a vampire, and I'd taken that out on him. Of course, he'd been terrifically arrogant about it, and he hadn't exactly handled my withdrawal from school very well. But still—he'd saved my life. And not just because he'd randomly happened upon me that night on campus, but because he'd made a decision to enter my life that night, and for the right reasons.

My father had offered him thirty pieces of silver, and Ethan had declined, and he'd tried to rectify what my father had sought to do.

My eyes filled with tears, and I said a silent thank-you to the universe for sending him to me. "I told you that you saved my life."

He gave me no warning before his mouth sought mine, and he kissed me greedily, hungrily, and with obvious intention. His fingers pulled at my hair, drawing me closer, his arousal leaving an indelible mark on my body.

His free hand found my breast, and I moaned against his kiss, passion igniting and leaving my body on fire.

After only a moment, when my chest was heaving and my body pliant and ready, he pulled back.

"If you use the word 'halt,' I will hit you."

"Not halt," he breathlessly said. "Upstairs. Now."

I thanked whatever strength he'd found to utter those words. And I was not going to argue with him.

CHAPTER NINETEEN

UNCHANGING

We barely made it back upstairs without ripping each other's clothes off. As it was, we probably left a trail of telltale energy through the House that made our mutual agenda clear to everyone.

When we made it to his apartments, he slammed and locked the door, then found my mouth again. His hands were possessive, insistent, knotting into my hair and drawing me closer, challenging me to believe in who he was and what he'd promised.

"I missed you," I confessed, as he pressed me down into the bed.

"I wouldn't have it any other way," he murmured. For a moment, he hovered over me, his body scant centimeters away from mine . . . but still far away.

"What is it?"

"It seems forever since we've done this."

"It's been at least two months," I said with a small smile, then placed my hand over the scar above his heart.

His expression went serious, his eyes changing to the green of ancient Celt forests. "You are mine, Merit."

I smiled and put a hand on his face, running my thumb along the soft bow of his lips. "I am yours until you ban bacon, or otherwise as long as I can put up with you."

He grinned wickedly, but his eyes were on my body as he did it. "Let's see just how long you can put up with me."

I should have taken that for the warning it was.

His eyes were molten silver, and there was no mistaking his intent in his gaze. The *desire* in his gaze. I shivered from the ferocity of it.

"I thought you weren't afraid, Sentinel." His eyes and his body were an invitation . . . and I wasn't about to refuse.

"Never afraid," I promised, even as I squeezed my hands into fists in nervous anticipation. I'd watched him die, but here he was, lust in his eyes and wickedness in his smile.

He wasted no time stripping me of clothing, but each bit of fabric was slipped off and away with such slow and careful consideration my skin was on fire by the end of it.

And soon enough, as promised, I was wearing only my Cadogan medal and a smile.

Clad only in his pants, revealing those lines of muscle at his hips and the flat of his abdomen, his golden blond hair falling across his face, he stretched beside me and caressed the tips of his fingers across my stomach until my entire body was awash in goose bumps. His long fingers roamed my abdomen, barely touching, trickling across my skin, a promising hint of things to come, until my entire body was tinder, waiting for a spark.

With steady hands and deft fingers, he stripped me of my final barriers; I lay naked before him, a halo of dark hair around my head, my body adorned with the fading scars of battle.

"You are a universe," he reverentially whispered, and then his game began. A game of pushing me to the brink, of building the anticipation . . . and leaving me stranded in the midst of it.

His mouth and hands found my breasts, and he tortured me with nips and kisses and quicksilver eyes that never looked away.

I made a sound of pleasure but immediately remembered my surroundings. His fingers splayed and contracted in time with my heartbeat until my body was liquid, but he wouldn't stop . . . and he wouldn't move closer.

I made a sound of displeasure when he evaded my own searching hands. But he popped up an eyebrow. "You're putting up with me just fine, Sentinel."

I growled and decided I'd been teased enough.

I stood Sentinel of Cadogan House, by God. He was mine, and we knew it, and I would claim what was mine.

With a twist of my leg I reversed our positions, straddling his waist, the evidence of his own arousal undeniable beneath me.

"Satisfied?" he asked, masculine satisfaction in his expression.

"Getting there," I said. I stretched out along his body and kissed him, and switched the tenor of the game. From a duel to a mutual journey of pleasure. From lust to passion.

Ethan wrapped his arms around me and didn't resist when I stripped him of the rest of his clothes. And then we were both naked and bare of all pretentions—except for the Cadogan medals around our necks. Him, the blond Master, four hundred years old, and yet newly born. Me, the dark-haired Sentinel. New to vampiredom although it felt like I'd aged years in the span of the last two months.

He'd pushed me to the brink, but he wasn't done. In a flash I was on my back again, and the weight of his body was finally atop mine. I gripped him fiercely, determined not to let him go again. Willing God that I wouldn't have to let him go again, and tomorrow wouldn't be the end of both of us.

His long, nimble fingers found my core, and he took bare seconds before my body ignited. His name flew from my lips with abandon, as if my body were unable to contain its pleasure.

But we weren't alone in the House, and he muffled the sound with a sudden, fierce, and hungry kiss. I struggled for breath, shocked by the suddenness of my reaction, and—if possible— even needier than I'd been before.

He smiled, eyes still closed, his expression changing to that thin line between pleasure and pain as I sought out his arousal. I let my hands explore his chest, his thighs, those diagonal muscles at the edges of his hips. I claimed him with hands and mouth, and watched his eyes flutter and body arch as he neared his own pleasure.

But he suddenly stilled me with a hand.

"It's your turn," he groaned, regret obvious in his voice.

"My turn?" Admittedly, my brain was still fuzzy, but I was pretty sure I'd had my turn.

"You have been bitten," Ethan said. "But never like this."

"Does it matter?"

"You are a vampire," he growled out. "It matters as much as anything else, more than anything else."

Ethan climbed above me again, and I wrapped my legs around him, our bodies intertwined. He looked down at me, his eyes swirling silver, his needle-sharp fangs fully descended.

His breath hot at my neck, my vampiric instincts kicking into overdrive. Images flashed through my mind. A harvest moon. Gleaming fangs. The beating of wings. Footsteps in the dense undergrowth of an ancient forest. An animal's call.

My instincts urged me forward, but this was still new territory, for me undiscovered. He'd bitten me before, but not like this. Would there be pain? Pleasure? Consequences? I was vampire, but still recently human, and I was afraid.

"Ethan?"

But he wouldn't be swayed. He put a hand on my chest, across my heart. "This is for you," he whispered, "as vampire, as woman, and for us, and for me."

With two simultaneous thrusts, he bit—and thrust his body into mine.

I'm sure I screamed; I must have. The pain was immediate and intense, the sharp bite of needles piercing skin. But the pain was gone as quickly as it came, and then there was only pleasure. A euphoric spill unlike anything I'd ever experienced before. It burned like flame had been poured directly into my bloodstream, warming me from the inside out. Desire and heat raced through every artery and vein, forcing the sudden awareness of every molecule in my body.

But he was also there. I was simultaneously aware of every inch of him, and I wondered if he'd had the same experience when I'd bitten him, and how he didn't spend every waking moment of every night with his fangs in someone.

I'd long ago made my oaths to Cadogan House, sworn my fealty and promised my allegiance. But this was vampire. Truly, honestly vampire. *Dasein* vampire, as he'd once said.

Ethan suckled at my neck, his fingers digging into my hips, his body plunging into mine over and over and over again. Suddenly he pulled back his fangs, his lips at my ear, and groaned out his pleasure. The sound was enough to push me over the edge. Fire contracted through my body, and I clawed at him as the sensation overtook me.

And then the world stilled again.

We lay there for a moment panting, my body suddenly heavy as the sun breached the horizon. And before consciousness left me, I smiled a little, thinking it was little wonder he'd wanted me to bite him twice before.

An hour later, the sun on the rise, he stroked a hand down my back.

"You've grown, while I was gone. Into your skin. Into your position. You'll forgive me if I'm not used to it."

"I couldn't be clumsy forever," I agreed. I had grown while he was gone, as much out of necessity as because of my own loyalties to the House. They needed me when he was gone, and I owed them my best. Besides, it was a lot more fun to be the capable vampire than the awkward one. I'd already had my stint as a weird, geeky teenager, thank you very much.

"I'm sorry I had to miss it. Granted, the reason I had to miss it was incredibly daring. Incredibly brave."

"Daring? Really?"

"I saved your life, Sentinel. Even you said so."

I rolled my eyes. "The statute of limitations is quickly expiring, Sullivan."

"The larger point stands." He touched my cheek, green eyes boring into me. "A moment of anger doesn't affect the feelings that I have for you, nor does the unrequested involvement of an immature witch. They are constant. They are immovable. But that's not to say that I don't have fear. That I don't worry I cannot protect that which is mine. My House. My vampires."

I put a hand on his cheek, my heart bursting at the sentiment, but my own emotions in check by the sudden rush of memories . . . and fear.

"What's wrong?" he asked.

"We've had so many stops and starts. For two months, you were gone. I soldiered on, Ethan. I battled Mallory back, and McKetrick, and Cabot, and I dreamt of you, and I cried, but I soldiered on." I looked back at him and let show the fear in my heart. "You came back, and you rejected me again. What if you change your mind again?"

"You were right," he said. "You were right and I was wrong. I reacted badly to her presence, and I pushed away the one person who understood, who fought beside me and challenged me to fight her. I don't know what she can do to me. But one way or the other, we will find a way to fix it together. I will not leave you again, Merit. Not now, not ever. Granted, there will come a time in which you're disappointed in me," he said. "Or angry."

"Or furious?"

He grinned wickedly. "I'm not sure I'm possible of infuriating you, Sentinel."

"Liar," I boldly said.

"The point is, I hardly think your feelings for me will suddenly evaporate because you're angry." He wrapped his arms around me. "Fear, on occasion, rises up. As does anger. By me and by you. But they are the enemies. And as you might say, love battles them back."

How could a girl not succumb to words like that? So I basked in the warmth of him, in the crisp smell of his cologne.

"Stay the day," he said. "Stay with me today, and let me be still."

How could I possibly refuse that request?

We prepared for bed. Brushing our teeth side by side in the bathroom seemed strangely intimate, and not just because I was spitting in front of him.

I gave him an update on what I'd learned from Mallory and the issues I'd asked Catcher and Jeff to investigate. I also told him that I'd visited Claudia again. He clearly wasn't thrilled, but he managed to hold in his irritation that I'd put myself in danger.

"Going alone isn't the best course of action," he gently chastised. I could work with that.

"I know. I should have taken a partner, but time was of the essence. I thought I had a string to pull, so I took a chance. I got lucky, and next time I'll use a partner."

He looked amazed that I'd answered so logically.

"I really do like being alive and in one piece."

"All evidence to the contrary," he muttered, and I punched him—deservedly—in the arm.

Since we seemed to be on relatively solid footing again, I delved into the other crisis.

"How were your meetings with Darius?"

"Full of numbers," he said. "Ours is the second-strongest House in the country. Navarre is first, possibly because Celina wasn't entirely conscionable in her selection of investments. Our funds are well diversified, our debt-to-income ratio is low, and our credit rating is high."

He splashed water on his face, then tamped it dry with a towel. "We are in good financial shape."

I leaned against the doorjamb. "Why do I have a sense Darius couldn't care less about our financial shape?"

Ethan pushed his hair behind his ears and gestured toward the bedroom. He followed me out, then turned off the light behind us.

"Because the majority of the American Houses are superbly good at managing their finances. If he wishes to rearrange the American system, that's not the best point of contention."

I sat down on the bed and pulled a pillow to my chest.

Ethan flipped off the bedroom lights, leaving us in momentary darkness until our eyes adjusted. I slung the pillow behind me and pressed into his body.

"Darius talked to me," I said.

"Did he now? What did he have to say?"

"He's confident any and all crises in Chicago are our fault."

"So par for the course, then."

"In that respect." I hesitated to add more, but Ethan pressed on.

"Tell me the rest, Sentinel."

"He isn't sure who you are. I think his meeting with me was just to get dirt on you. He's not thrilled with our relationship, halted or otherwise, but he wanted to know more about you. About your weaknesses. About whether you'd changed after Mallory brought you back."

"What did you tell him?"

"That you are who you are . . . and you're too stubborn to be anyone different. I think he's afraid of you. Not for who you are, but for what you might do if the House is excommunicated."

"We will find out soon enough."

"That sounds ominous."

Ethan nodded. "He's called a House meeting: tomorrow at midnight. If you'd stayed in your room, you'd find a note to that effect on your door tomorrow evening."

"You wouldn't let me stay in my room."

"No, Sentinel, I would not. For now, let us sleep. We will undoubtedly face new dangers tomorrow."

That seemed undeniable, but for now, I had his body to protect me.

Some hours later, we woke to a pounding on the door.

"That better be breakfast," I said.

"Margot is rarely so loud, and I am hardly dressed. Perhaps you better answer the door."

I flipped off the blankets and sheets and, as the knocking sounded louder, jogged to the door and pulled it open.

Juliet stood at the door, a furious expression on her face, and I could hear yelling downstairs. "It's a raid—the cops think Dominic is here."

Dominic wasn't, but I'd have bet his twin brother still was, and I didn't think Mayor Kowalcyzk or her storm troopers would much care about the difference.

Think fast, I told myself.

"Seth has wings," I said, "and I know he can fly. Get him to the widow's walk. We'll be down in a minute."

When I shut the door, Ethan was already up and behind me. "What is it?"

"If you had any plans to vote for Mayor Kowalcyzk, you might want to rethink those."

CHAPTER TWENTY

THE FAIRY TALE

We hurried into clothes and ran down the stairs. Cops in black shirts and cargo pants with yellow SPECIAL UNIT designations on their backs were tearing through the first floor of the House. The yard was littered with paper and other objects, as the cops had already overturned furniture and flipped open drawers, as if the secrets of the city's sups were hidden away in a notebook in a foyer drawer.

The leader appeared to be a woman in a black pantsuit. She was tall and slender, with dark skin and darker hair pulled into a bun so tight it stretched the corners of her eyes. She might have been attractive if her face hadn't been pinched into an "Aha, I caught you!" expression.

"Lieutenant Tamara Hays," she said, flipping out a wallet-style badge for Ethan's inspection and then shoving it back into her pocket.

"We have reason to believe you are harboring a fugitive," she said. "Mayor Seth Tate. He's wanted in connection with a series of murders."

The city might have known supernaturals were out of the closet, but they really had no clue what was going on behind the scenes.

"Mayor Tate is not here," Ethan said, and I hoped he was right and Juliet had gotten Seth out in time. I doubted the cops would check the skies to see if a white-winged Seth Tate was flying by overhead. On the other hand, they had seen Dominic.

Hays gestured toward one of her cops, who passed a couple of folded sheets of paper to Ethan. He looked them over, then handed them to Malik. "Call Fitzhugh and Meyers," he said. I assumed they were our attorneys. Hays blanched at the name, so the firm must have meant something to her.

"High-profile lawyers won't help you here, Mr. Sullivan. We have the authority to search the premises."

Ethan held out a hand. "Then do so."

There were probably a dozen cops in all. While suited Cadogan vampires looked on, they stormed up the stairs, eager to find evidence that would implicate us all, whatever that might have been.

"Keep the vampires calm," Ethan told Luc. "Have the guards get as many as possible onto the first floor in the event we need to make an exit. Tell them not to lock their bedroom doors—there's no point in giving them an excuse to break the hardware, too."

Ethan stood beside the open door, hands on his hips, watching as strangers ripped apart his home and terrorized his family. But his gaze was calculating, recording each wrong move they made, no doubt for recollection to the House's attorneys later on.

One way or the other, the city would pay for this.

Magic erupted in nervous bursts as vampires began to funnel toward the first floor. I pasted on a smile and directed them into the front room.

"Everything's under control," I said, watching to ensure they were settled and wouldn't—given the rising tensions—make everything worse.

An hour later, Lieutenant Hays came storming out the front door.

Ethan followed her but stopped on the threshold. "As I was saying, my attorney looks forward to your call and your explanation about your apparent lack of probable cause."

"This isn't over," Hays said. "We know you're behind this, and one way or the other, we'll prove it."

"'We,' as in Mayor Kowalcyzk's misguided administration, or 'we,' as in you and whoever else in your office believes harassing citizens is the way to a promotion?"

She growled. "Just watch yourself," she said, then marched down the sidewalk again, her cabal of officers behind her.

We all released a collective breath.

"It seems we have made another enemy," Ethan dryly said.

"We'll add her to the list," Malik said, stepping behind Ethan. "But first, let's get this place cleaned up."

I volunteered to help clean up the yard, raking bits of the hacked-away shrubbery into piles and moving furniture back into the House again. It wasn't glamorous work, and the night air was chilly, but the manual labor was a nice change from the usual. I could lose myself in the rhythm of the work, instead of fretting over the problems I couldn't solve.

I'd just raked up the final pile of branches when one of the fairies at the gate approached. I stopped working but kept a hand on my rake just in case.

"What do you want?"

His gaze was narrowed, his expression fierce. "Come with me."

I gave him an Ethan-esque eyebrow arching. "You may ask me,

and I will accept or decline. But you do not dictate where I do or do not go."

His lip curled. "She wishes to see you again."

Claudia wanted to talk to me? "Why?"

"She does not share her motivations with us," he said. "Nevertheless, we understand there has been a falling out of sorts."

"Between her and Dominic?"

He nodded. "You will see her. I believe you will find it . . . enlightening."

He gestured toward a black SUV that pulled up to the curb in front of the House. Two fairies already filled the front seats. It was odd to see a mercenary fairy driving a car, probably because I imagined them in different times, perhaps standing in an ancient keep, bow and arrows at the ready.

"I know where she lives. I can drive myself."

"She is not there."

"What? I thought she couldn't leave the tower."

"She cannot—not without cost," he said. "She wanted fresh air and believed the matter worth the risk."

I looked back at him. "What's your name?"

He looked confused. "My name?"

"You want me to go with you. I'd like to know your name."

He looked vaguely uncomfortable. "My name is Aeren."

"I'm Merit."

"The car, please, Merit."

But I shook my head. I'd well learned my lesson about running off alone with supernaturals. "I appreciate your invitation, but you have your procedures, and I have mine. Give me a moment?"

He didn't look happy about the request, but he acceded. I ran back to the House but found Ethan's office empty. Malik, however, was in his, straightening files disturbed by the police. He looked up when I darkened his door. "Are you okay?"

"I'm fine. Claudia, the fairy queen, wants to talk to me about Dominic. Apparently they had a falling out. I think I need to go. There's a connection between her and Tate that I need to figure out, and they aren't going to wait around."

"As per usual, this could be a trap," he said.

"Par for the course," I agreed. "That's why I'm telling you."

"Your instinct says to follow this through?"

I appreciated the question. "It does. But let everyone know. You can plan a rescue mission if necessary."

"You have your phone?"

I assured him I did. My due diligence addressed, I ran back to the car again and cast a final glance at the House behind me.

The car smelled of flowers and grass, and I wondered if Claudia had ridden in it. We didn't drive toward the park, but toward the lake. The driver steered the car into a public parking lot, and the man in the passenger seat hopped out of the car and opened my door.

"Take that path," he said, pointing to a sidewalk that led closer to the lake. "She awaits you there. Alone."

Claudia was waiting for me, and without guards. Dangerous or not, this certainly bore investigating.

I walked closer to the lake, huddling into my jacket as the wind picked up, icier as I neared the water. The lake was bounded by a long sidewalk. It was usually filled with runners and bikers on pleasant days. But tonight, in the dark and chill, it was empty. A lone figure stood in one of the low stone circles that offered seating along the path.

It was Claudia, in a long brocade dress with pointed sleeves, and a voluminous velvet cape long enough to pool on the ground. The hem was dirty, and the hood was pulled over her head, but tendrils of strawberry blond escaped.

"You wanted to meet me?" I asked, stepping inside the circle as a hundred Irish and Scots women might have done in older days to seek an audience with the fairy queen.

She lowered her hood, her hair gleaming in the moonlight. "It is time to tell the truth," she said.

I thanked God my instincts had been right.

"He was strong," she said, and I assumed she meant Dominic. "A messenger. A man of right and justice and willpower. I was a queen, with legions at my command. The union between us was powerful. It was righteous."

"You were in love?"

"Fae care not for love," she defensively said. "We understand desire." Her expression darkened. "We are not cowards, but nor do we involve ourselves in the adjudication of others. We are brave, but we do not fight battles for the sake of the fight. Dominic began killing more often. Fighting more often. Humans were angered. The magicians believed they could simply lock the messengers away. The messengers, of course, had no desire to be confined for eternity."

"So what happened?"

"We had not spoken in many moons, but he came to me one night. We shared our bodies and he asked for a boon. He did not trust the magic makers, and he feared he and the others weren't strong enough to avoid their magic."

"He wanted you to keep him out. To protect him from being sent into the *Maleficium*."

She nodded. "This I would do for him, although he was not fae."

I was so close; I could feel it. "How did you help him?"

"I offered him the only boon I had to give. We cannot make magic; it is part of us. We are beings of magic that connects us to this world and the next. You know he is a twin?"

I nodded. "Seth and Dominic. The messenger of peace and the messenger of justice."

"In your parlance, yes. They were conceived into this world as one but split apart from each other at birth. He believed, *he hoped*, that he might make use of that bond again. That magic, if powerful enough, could reconnect him to the brother of his birth and bind him to this world instead of the *Maleficium*."

A memory sharpened into focus—a memory of Celina and Ethan in a park beside the lake, Celina insisting things were changing in Chicago. That was before Mallory had begun her quest to reunite good and evil magic. She'd said the bonds were breaking between angels and demons.

She'd been ahead of her time, but she'd been right.

"And you offered to help him rebond to Seth?"

"I offered, and I helped. There was a mage who believed in his cause. His name was Endayel. The only magic I could barter was that which connected me to the green land, but Endayel took it and used it to save Dominic, to rebind him to his brother so that he might have a chance to live again. And so I was relegated to my tower, apart from time, apart from green meadows, apart from the immeasurable sky."

"A prison," I muttered. "Did other messengers try the same method?"

"I know not, but messengers were powerful things; I doubt they went willingly into confinement."

"Why are you telling me this now?"

"At the break of day, I summoned him to the tower. Centuries have passed since last I have seen his face, or him mine. He is so handsome. So powerful. Even his wings—defiled as they are—sway me not. I offered my body to him." She looked back at me, her expression fierce, and magic lifted. "I gave him everything. And now, finally, he has escaped his bondage, and how has he repaid my boon? He has rejected my sacrifice. He has rejected me."

She may have been a centuries-old fairy queen, but the despondence on her face was the same as that of any other woman who'd been rejected. No matter the species, human or supernatural, we all had emotions in common.

"How do we stop him?"

Her expression went fierce, and I imagined her a modern-day Boadicea, leading her troops into war. "You control the terms of the battle. It is the only way to fight his ilk."

"How do I do that?"

"Summon him. Each demon has a sigil—a symbol—a secret name assigned to him. If you draw his sigil correctly, Dominic must appear." She reached into the pocket of her cape and pulled something out, then handed it to me.

It was a circular disk of wood about two inches across. A symbol had been burned into it—a triangle containing smaller figures. "This is his sigil?"

She nodded. "His brother will know how to use it for the summoning. When he appears, you'll only need a sword."

I definitely had one of those. I tucked the sigil into my pocket. "Thank you, Claudia."

She nodded and took a step forward but nearly stumbled. I reached out to grab her arm before she could fall and caught a whisper of her flowery perfume. But beneath it, a subtle smell, cloyingly sweet. *Decay*, I thought. She was dying even as she stood here because she'd left her lair.

That's why she wanted to meet me here. She wanted me to know—to understand—what she'd given up for him. The entire world outside, all for the chance that he might survive the making of the *Maleficium* and escape his bonds.

He had, and although that victory could be laid entirely at Claudia's feet, he'd rejected her.

"I will see him punished," I said, using words she might have. "I will see your boon collected."

"So it is done," she said, walking to one of the stone ridges and taking a seat, the fabric of her dress and cape spreading out around her, the moon on the rise behind her.

I walked silently back to the car, and the fairies drove me silently back to the House again.

As soon as the door opened, I dropped to the ground and ran into the House. I found Ethan and Malik in Ethan's office.

He jumped up as soon as I entered. "Thank God."

"I'm fine. They were telling the truth, and I think I know how to stop Dominic."

Eyes wide, Ethan sat down again. "I'm listening."

I made him wait until Seth, Luc, and Paige had joined us in person, and Jeff and Catcher had joined us on the phone. If we were going to discuss battle plans, we needed the entire team.

Everyone was too nervous to sit, so they stood around Ethan's desk, awaiting the rest of the fairy tale. I sat on the edge of his desk, and I wove my tale.

"Dominic and Claudia, the fairy queen, had an affair. Things went south when he got violent, but that wasn't enough to shake her affection. When he found out what the sorcerers were trying to do, he went to Claudia for help." I looked at Seth. "Claudia realized Dominic could use his bond with you to keep him in the world. So Claudia used her limited power—her connection to the fairy world—to power the spell that linked Dominic and Seth back together."

"That's why she can't leave her tower," Ethan said.

I nodded. "And Seth was the anchor that kept Dominic out of the *Maleficium*. That's why it hurt. He was, quite literally, ripped away."

"It makes a kind of perverse sense," Luc said. "You'd been twins before. It probably wasn't difficult to reimagine the magic that made you twins again."

"Did you feel anything when it happened?" Paige asked. "When the *Maleficium* was completed and Dominic would have tried to rebond himself?"

"There was pain," Seth admitted. "Weakness. But we all thought that was the result of the separation of magic. Of good and evil. That division was artificial, and all supernatural beings felt the sting."

"Dominic undoubtedly wanted to lie low," I said. "If he popped up too often or tried to control you outright, you'd have known what was up."

Seth nodded. "And I would have immediately found a sorcerer to rip him out again and force him into the *Maleficium*."

"And that would have put Dominic back at square one," I said. "He had no incentive to make himself known." It also explained why Dominic was so eager to let Mallory do her thing. She was his first real chance in centuries to get out.

"But Dominic is the only one who split when the book was finally triggered. Why only him?" Paige asked. "Surely others tried the same thing. Why didn't the *Maleficium* release all of them?"

"There may have been others," I agreed. "But Dominic is the only one who actually touched the book when it happened."

Seth nodded. "Any other demons who didn't bond would have been pulled into the *Maleficium* in the first place and were destroyed when it was. Or they were bonded to their twins and weren't able to escape as Dominic was because they didn't have contact with the *Maleficium*."

"So what do we do?" Jeff asked.

"We fight him," I said. "It's the only thing we can do."

I pulled out the wooden token Claudia had given me and handed it to Seth. "This is his sigil. We can use it to summon him to a battlefield of our choosing. When we call him, he must appear."

"Correct," Seth said, looking over the sigil. "But we'll need supplies."

"I'll get help with that," Paige said. "I know a bit about summoning, and the tools you use can make a big difference in the operation of the magic."

Seth nodded. "We can certainly make him appear, but then what?"

"I will fight him."

We all looked at Ethan.

"I owe him one," he said. But before I could object, he held up a hand. "I know the arguments you will make, Sentinel, and while I'm sure you would have made them well, this fight is mine. There will be no discussion. There will be no debate." His eyes narrowed. "He has brought this battle on himself, and I mean to see it through."

"All due respect, Liege," Luc said, "but Jonah and Merit together couldn't take him out with two swords. A few nicks and cuts aren't going to do it. Hell, a few slices and stabs aren't going to do it. The man can fly, and he made Merit disappear just by touching her. I'm not objecting to your doing the deed, but we have to even up the odds."

Ethan and I looked at each other. I had a duty to object, but he seemed to understand my objection even if I didn't voice it to him or the rest of them. That said, it was easy to see that he needed the battle. And if that's what he needed, far be it from me to stand in his way.

But I'd certainly stand by his side.

I looked at Ethan. "If the odds are bad, we even the odds."

He gave me a smile that curled my toes. "And how do you propose we do that, Sentinel?"

"He'd be easier to fight as a toy poodle. Or a dire badger," I jokingly added, then looked at Paige. "Got any spells for that?"

"Yes, we do," she said.

I frowned. "Seriously? You can make him a toy poodle?"

"No, I meant more generally. If we can't fight him the way he is because he's too strong, let's make him less strong. Let's take away his magic. Let's make him human. Or more human, anyway."

Ethan's expression lifted. "Can that be done?"

Before Paige could answer, the clock in Ethan's office suddenly chimed, striking twelve.

It was midnight—the witching hour and the time for Darius's meeting.

"Time is short for all of us," Ethan said, rising from his chair. "Paige, Seth, Catcher, talk to Mallory and see if there's anything to this idea. We'll meet back here in two hours. And God willing, we'll have a plan."

We might have a plan. But would we have a House?

CHAPTER TWENTY-ONE

TWELVE COLONIES

I was last into the ballroom, which was already full of vampires and nervous, agitated magic. Darius stood at the platform at the front of the room, Ethan and Malik beside him. The vampires whispered and shuffled as they waited for whatever was about to begin.

I moved quietly through the crowd to the front, stopping only when I was close enough to make eye contact with Ethan, to let him know that I was there. Ready to assist if necessary . . . or be there to soothe him once it was over.

"We live in strange times," Darius said, his accent seeming extra-clipped as he prepared to lecture this room of Chicago vampires.

"The public is aware of us and other of our supernatural brethren. By registration, they have demanded we warn them of our very existence. The Order is in the midst of a crisis of its own, and the city's leadership is in chaos. There are many in the world who revile us, who would have us destroyed en masse if authority permitted."

The magic in the room stirred nervously.

"In such times, the stability of the Houses is even more crucial. Financially, managerially, procedurally. The Houses exist to protect vampires from the whims of humans. Without them, chaos. Wandering without homes, without support, without leadership."

I wasn't sure about all that, as Noah and the other Rogue vampires in Chicago seemed plenty well fed and happy.

"The GP exists to support and guide the Houses. The GP has existed, in one form or another, for a very long time, and although some do not believe it, we do have experience and knowledge to offer."

The crowd snickered appreciatively. Whatever Darius's faults, and I'm sure they were legion, he knew how to work a crowd. On the other hand, a captive audience of vampires who feared for their survival wasn't exactly going to boo its purported "king" off the stage.

"Franklin Cabot is not a perfect man," Darius announced. "And his work as receiver of this House may not have been perfect. Nevertheless, his job was to review, analyze, stabilize, and report. Despite his premature evacuation from this House, he has done so."

The vampires around me stiffened. They knew something was coming, and they weren't convinced the news would be good. By the look on Ethan's face—and the line of worry between his eyes—he wasn't, either.

"Cabot perused the financial and other records gathered in this House through the nearly one hundred years of its existence. Financially, the House is in superb shape. Its investments are adequately diversified, its assets are substantially larger than its debts, and there are sufficient funds for emergency purposes in a number of international accounts. The House has sufficient contingency planning, and its resident vampires seem well satisfied with their lot. However . . ."

I steeled myself for bad news.

"The official position of the GP and its Houses respecting human affairs is avoidance. Vampires keep to themselves. Human civilizations have risen and fallen over the course of history, and they will continue to do so. It is in our best interest to let them do so and, simply put, stay out of it. The actions of Cadogan House are not consistent with that position. That, of course, raises some obvious concerns about how well Cadogan House fits within the parameters of the Greenwich Presidium—if at all."

I froze. Around me, nerves churned as vampires considered the possibility at which Darius hinted—that Cadogan House wouldn't be a member of the GP much longer. Instead, we'd be its enemies.

"Cadogan House rejected the efforts of the GP to review and stabilize this House. If Cadogan House does not wish to support the GP's efforts, the GP must inquire whether Cadogan House should remain within the GP."

Darius looked out across the sea of vampires before him, and then back at Ethan.

"The Presidium called a *shofet*," he said. "And that *shofet* has voted to excommunicate Cadogan House from membership in the GP."

The magic went panicky, vampires whispering about the possibility that they'd be Houseless in less than a month. I heard their whispers, and while many felt the House was being betrayed by the GP, they weren't all favorable to Ethan.

"The GP has no right to do this."

"Ethan will fix this—he has to."

"Is this Ethan's fault?"

For the first time, I was glad Ethan couldn't mentally hear what his vampires were saying about him.

"I am not convinced that excommunication is the right decision. Although I have serious doubts about decisions made by this House, I do not doubt they were made with good intentions. But those decisions were made, and they were made in full awareness of their consequences by experienced vampires.

"Therefore, tomorrow I will call the full GP for a vote on this issue. And whatever decision is made, I wish you all happy and productive futures."

Darius looked over the crowd and gave a final nod, then stepped down from the podium and into the crowd. It split as he walked through the vampires, all turning to watch his procession to the door. He walked out of the ballroom, and for a moment we all stood there silently, wondering what was going to happen and what was going to become of us.

Could Cadogan House survive on its own? Did the protections of the GP really matter? I wasn't sure. And from the expressions on the faces around me, I wasn't the only one.

Needing reassurance, we turned and looked back at Ethan.

"Shut the door," he said, gesturing to the vampires in the back of the room. It closed with a *thush* behind us.

Ethan stood on the podium, gaze still on the door, his hands on his hips. The line of worry between his eyes was gone, and there was a new determination in his eyes.

"The GP has existed for many years," he said. "Vampires formed Houses within its control because it was in their best interest to do so, because the protections afforded by the GP—financial, political, military—were worth it."

He looked down at us. "But the world has changed. The British

Empire no longer rules the world, and the United States are no longer colonies in need of protection. If the GP decides Cadogan House's membership must be revoked . . . then perhaps it is time we ask ourselves if the GP should be our concern."

"They can't just kick us out!" A male vampire—dark hair, worried expression—stepped forward from the crowd, his eyes moving frantically between Ethan and Malik. "Our immortality has never been more precarious."

"We aren't Rogue vampires!" someone else called out. "We are better than that."

There were murmurs of agreement in the crowd.

"We can't just defect," someone yelled out. "We can't just give up."

The murmurs grew to a cacophonous roar. However strongly these vampires felt about Ethan—and however many doubts they may have had about the GP—their fear of being Houseless was apparently stronger.

"Silence," Ethan roared out, and the room went quiet. His gaze went green and steely—the gaze of a Master vampire, not a man standing by while Darius West set forth his destiny.

"Remember who you are, and who we are together. Do not let your fear lead you—that's what the GP has done. We have survived for more than a century as Cadogan vampires, and whatever else happens in Chicago or the world beyond, we will remain *Cadogan vampires*."

Ethan's eyes softened, and he took a step forward on the platform, his body visibly relaxing as he changed from Master vampire to friend and confidant.

"There is no doubt this situation is serious," he said. He spoke more softly now, and the room was silent to catch every word that fell from his lips. It was an effective technique.

"But consider what we have seen over the past year. We were

outed without our consent by a Master who killed three human girls that we know of. Our vampires were recruited and hunted by her and her minions, and we have become the targets of militia apparently intent on eliminating Chicago's 'vampire problem.'"

The crowd got a kick out of his air quotes. Riding the good humor, Ethan pushed his hands into his pockets and stepped down into the crowd. "Sit down," he said. "All of you."

Vampires looked at one another nervously before sitting down on the hardwood floor.

"Good," Ethan said, and then did the same, sitting down on the edge of the platform to face them. It was a remarkably casual move for Ethan—maybe another bit of his postmortem transformation.

With nearly one hundred vampires at his feet, Ethan linked his hands and put his elbows on his knees. He leaned forward.

"They sent a man to this House who rationed blood, who sent our vampires into the sun, who stripped us of our protections. Are those the acts of an entity that supports us? That protects us? Or are those the actions of an entity that tests us and provokes us? The world is different than it was a hundred years ago, and it is worthwhile to seriously consider whether membership is, as they say, worth the privilege."

He looked across the sea of vampires. "To excommunicate a House is a profound action. Not being affiliated with the GP would not be an easy course. There is a stigma, of course, and the concern we lack protection if we are not affiliated. But this House is financially secure and would be able to maintain itself without the GP. It has connections throughout this city, including Merit's grandfather, the Apex of the North American Central Pack, water nymphs, fairies, the Lake Michigan siren, and potentially the Queen of the Fae. My friends, my brothers, my sisters, *I am not afraid*."

He stood up again, walked to the edge of the platform, and

lifted up a small box that had been placed there. There was a slit in the top, just wide enough for a piece of paper or two.

It was a ballot box.

"We are not colonials of the British Empire. We are citizens of these United States, and our ways are different. I say we make our own decision. We can wait for a formal excommunication to be handed down tomorrow. Or we can act tonight. We can leave the GP on our own terms. We can establish a new kind of vampire organization which recognizes our contemporary needs."

He put the box down again and slipped his hands into his pockets. He must have had doubts about leaving the GP, but you'd never have known it to look at him.

"All I ask is that you vote your consciences," he said. "If you do that, whatever the outcome, I will support it. I will be proud of it." He nodded once. "You are dismissed."

The vampires filed out of the room again, and the chatter started immediately.

"What are you going to do?"

"Is this completely crazy?"

Their doubts were loud, but at the same time there was a bit of nervously hopeful energy. I guessed these weren't the types of decisions Novitiates were usually allowed to make.

When the room was mostly clear, Ethan stepped down from the platform and walked to me, hand extended. I took it.

"What do you think they'll do?" I asked.

"It hardly matters," he said. "The decision isn't important. The action is. Either we recommit to the GP and beg for their forgiveness, or we reject their authority on terms of our own. These are exciting times, Sentinel."

Hand in hand, we walked to the ballroom door. "By exciting, do you mean moderately terrifying?"

"I wasn't going to use those words, but if the shoe fits . . ."

"*Que será, será*," I said. "Now, let's go kill an angel."

Okay, that had sounded a lot better in my head.

We assembled in the Ops Room: the messenger, the sorceress, the vampires. And on the phone, a sorcerer, another sorceress, and a shifter.

We hardly fit around the conference table, but that wasn't the important part. We were a team, working together to solve a problem, even if Darius would have preferred we simply let the world spin around us.

We were also working the low-tech way. Instead of whiteboards or touch screens, we'd placed giant sheets of white paper in the middle of the table, and everyone had a permanent marker.

"So," Luc said, "we know the actual battle goes down with a sword. That's Ethan's job." He pointed at Ethan with his marker, then wrote SWORD on one end of the page.

"And on the other end," Lindsey said, "is actually getting Dominic to the battle spot. That's where the summoning comes in." She wrote SUMMONING on the other end of the page.

"That process is relatively straightforward," Seth said, putting the sigil on the table. "The sigil is like a phone number for an angel of justice. We draw the sigil, and Dominic must appear."

"Does that work for you, too?" I asked.

Seth shook his head. "In fact, it's entirely new to me. According to our research, only angels of justice were assigned sigils. It was a check on their power, created by archangels who apparently believed there was a risk the angels of justice would act beyond their authority."

"Which is precisely what they did," Ethan darkly said.

Seth nodded.

"Okay, then," Luc said. "We have summoning magic to get him here. We have a sword bearer to fight him." He drew a circle in the middle of the page. "Now, we just need a way to make him vulnerable." He looked at Paige. "Thoughts?"

Paige grimaced. "Not yet. I mean, technically, we've got some ideas. We think nullification would work on him. If it can work on sorcerers, there's no reason it can't work on messengers. They're both creatures of magic. But there is a bit of a logistical problem."

"Which is?" Ethan asked.

"Nullification is what's called a wicking spell. The person working the magic has to actually touch the other one to wick their power away. It doesn't take long, and there are things we can do to expedite the spell, but there's no way Dominic is going to let me, Catcher, or Mallory touch him. He knows what we are, and he won't let us get near him."

"That's a problem," Luc said.

"Actually, maybe not," I said. "There may be a way to manage it."

"What's that?" Paige asked.

I blew out a breath, steeled my courage, and looked at Ethan. "You can get closer to Dominic than anyone else. He won't think you're a threat—not like they are. He's let you close enough to punch him before. But we already know Ethan and Mallory have a connection to each other. I was thinking we could use that."

"No," Catcher and Ethan simultaneously said.

"There is no way in hell I will let someone control me," Ethan said. "Besides, I'm supposed to be fighting him. I can't concentrate on anything when she's in there, much less fighting him."

"We're not talking about control," I quietly said. "Mallory can't do that anyway, because the spell wasn't completed. But maybe she could work the wicking spell through you."

"No," Catcher repeated. "She's not putting herself at that kind of risk. He's an *angel*, for Christ's sake. Do you know how much magic he has? And how much she'd have to funnel through both of them? That could kill her."

Magic peaked in the room as tensions rose—from Ethan and the rest.

"I'll do it," Mallory quietly said.

We stared at the phone.

"This is my fault," she said. "There's no argument about that, and no way around it. If this is the way it has to be, then so be it."

"Mallory—" Catcher interrupted, and I imagined her shaking her head.

"I have to do this," she said. "If Ethan will allow it."

The room was quiet as he silently fumed. And after a moment, I watched the anger fade into something else—savvy.

"How would it work?" he asked.

I leaned toward the phone. "Mallory, as I understand it, the point of a familiar is to give you an extra bit of capacity for controlling the universe, right?"

"That's the basic idea," she said. "The familiar's like a battery. Kind of. But he's not a familiar."

"Not enough that you could actually make him do something," I agreed. "But you have a connection, certainly. And if your emotions are connected, maybe the magic could be, too? And maybe, if you can use Ethan to funnel power, couldn't he also be used to take it away from Dominic? You don't need to control him for that—he just needs to act as a conduit. A magical conduit between you and Dominic."

Silence.

Ethan ran his hands through his hair, then looked back at me. "He wouldn't expect me."

"Not to use magic. To punch him in the face, though? Yes. He would probably expect that. But that's the key—it fits with who he thinks you are. He'd suspect you were getting close enough to hit him. Not to wick his magic away."

"So I'm to become a utility. A functionality of magic?"

"A tool," I said. "And a handsome one."

"And only a temporary one," Mallory assured.

"Mallory, you want me to trust you," Ethan told her. "To allow you to use me as that tool. As a puppet on a string. You ask much of me. Much that no vampire gives willingly."

"You give it willingly to a vampire," she said. "Each time a new one is made. You communicate with them, don't you? Call and control them, in a fashion?"

Ethan looked sharply away.

"He can't communicate with anyone anymore," I confessed, not that the vampires in the room would have been surprised. "The spell seems to have knocked that out of him."

"I'm sorry," she quietly said. "I know that's not good enough, but I'm sorry."

There was silence for a moment.

"I am glad I'm alive, Mallory. I thank you for that. But you have put me and mine in danger, and those acts may ultimately prove unforgiveable." He looked over at me, love shining in his eyes. "And for all that, Merit still seems to believe in you. I don't trust you," he said after a moment, "but I trust Merit. And I have seen her fight. And if you do anything to hurt me, she will come after you with all that she has."

"I understand," Mallory said.

"Wonderful. But if I'm doing the nullifying, who battles Dominic?"

Courage, I reminded myself. "I will."

All eyes turned to me.

"No," Ethan said.

"*Yes,*" I countered. "I'm the only one close to your level. You can argue," I said, parroting back his words, "and I'm sure that argument will be well reasoned, but you know I'm right."

We looked at each other again, the risk of losing ourselves again between us. But this wasn't the first time, nor would it be the last, that we were faced with choices like these.

Ethan nodded. "You will fight him."

There was a collective heave of relief in the room.

"There is one more issue," Paige said. We all looked at her.

"I'm fairly confident this counts as black magic. If so, it seems unlikely the shifters or the Order will allow her to do it."

That was a bit of a sticking point.

"There's risk," Mallory said. "Even if Gabriel said it was okay, I'd be nervous about backtracking. About getting worse instead of getting better. But for the first time, I'd have the chance to help someone else, not just myself."

"I'll be there," Catcher said. "I'll keep an eye on you."

The decision made, Luc uncapped his marker again and filled in the empty space in the middle of our plan. WICKING, he wrote.

"When he appears," Seth said, "you'll only have seconds to strip his magic. The summoning only calls him to appear—it won't hold him forever."

"And if he's summoned, he'll already have his guard up," Ethan said.

"Quite probably. You'll need to act fast."

Another reason for Ethan to work the mojo instead of Mallory. Dominic would instantaneously react if Mallory appeared at his side, but if Ethan was there, he might just be curious enough to wait a moment, just long enough for Ethan to get the job done.

"We'll set things up before he arrives," Paige said, "so you only need to touch him to trigger the magic."

Ethan nodded, but the worry was clear in his face.

"And when his magic is gone, he won't be able to leave again. He'll be stuck here, and in human form." Seth looked at me. "That will be your cue."

I nodded.

"Then we know the plan," Seth said. "I will summon him. Ethan and Mallory will neutralize him. Merit will fight him."

His list left out an item: *Merit will kill him*. However unpleasant, that result seemed inevitable and would be required regardless of whether step number two worked. Dominic had to be eliminated, or even more people would die. And he had no right to play judge, jury, and executioner. Although I wasn't looking forward to playing that role myself—playing a game that would end only with a death by my hand and sword—I didn't think we had a lot of other options.

"It's not a bad plan," Luc said. "I mean, in my opinion. Lots of parts."

"Lots of places for things to go wrong," Catcher agreed.

"Where can we do this?" Ethan asked.

"Hallowed ground," Seth said. "It has to be."

Paige nodded. "If you're messing with dark magic, you want to stick to hallowed ground. The goal is to make this better—not worse."

"We'd need a church?" Ethan asked.

"Not necessarily," Paige said. "Any land that's been blessed or purified would work."

"How do we locate suitable property?" Ethan asked.

"I can ask Gabriel," Jeff suggested.

"Gabriel?" Ethan asked.

"We have bonds with the land," he said. "If anyone would know it, he would."

"Gabe may not want us summoning Dominic on ground he's decided is blessed," I pointed out.

"Yeah, but I don't think you'll find a pastor in Chicago who's crazy about it, either."

Jeff had a point.

Ethan nodded. "Shifters it is. Jeff, please make the call and see if he has time to talk or survey or whatever else it will take." He looked at Seth and Paige. "Make sure we have what we need to make the magic work. If you need materials, have Helen order them, and get double sets of anything we might need."

"Eye of newt and toe of frog?" Mallory asked.

"'Double double toil and trouble,'" Ethan said, quoting Shakespeare's *Macbeth*. "Just get it done. Let's meet back here in an hour."

I murmured the rest of the witches' song. "'Fire burn, and caldron bubble. Cool it with a baboon's blood—'"

Mallory's voice echoed through the phone. "'And then the charm is firm and good.'"

An ominous chill ran through me. But it was too late to turn back now.

CHAPTER TWENTY-TWO

THE FIRM AND GOOD CHARM

I spent the first bit of the hour in my room, oiling and cleaning my blade, ensuring it was as well prepared as I could make it, and then in the training room, slinging and slicing the katana around to limber up my body and my mind.

Maybe the fight would come tonight. Maybe it would come tomorrow. Crises didn't work on predictable timetables. If you had most of your pieces in place when the need arose, you were doing well, by my account.

I tried to clear my mind of the importance of what I had to do, the battle I had to wage. Worrying about the impact of the outcome wasn't going to do anything but make me more afraid. More nervous.

I tried to focus on my body, my movements, the dance of the fight and the rhythm of it, just as Catcher and Ethan had taught me.

It was hard.

A knock at the door threw me off balance, and I landed a move in an ungainly position. I righted myself just as the door opened.

Malik walked in.

"Hi," I said.

"Hello." He closed the door behind him and walked inside. "You're practicing?"

"I guess. More like working off nerves."

"You can do this," he said.

I nodded. There was much to be said for Malik's quiet confidence, but my crisis of confidence was bigger than any one vampire.

"I know Catcher and Ethan focus on technique," he said. "But don't be afraid to trust your instincts. Let the sword be an extension of you, not just something you wield."

I nodded. "I appreciate that. Got anything else?"

Malik chuckled and looked over the walls of the training room. "Most of these weapons were his, you know."

I assumed he meant Ethan. "I didn't," I said, following his gaze. The paneled walls were periodically decorated with antique weapons: pikes, shields, swords, and the like.

"They are symbols of his victories. Of the battles he won and lost. Not always perfectly. Not always with rigorous technique. But always with heart."

He looked back at me. "There are few things in the world that he loves more than this House, Merit. Possibly only one."

At the knowing gaze in his eyes, my cheeks flushed.

"And in all the world, he entrusted one girl, one scholar, with the right to defend it."

I knew he meant it as a compliment, but it felt like a burden. "That's a lot of pressure."

"Not pressure to win," he said. "Pressure to *try*. Pressure to push through pain and fear and to do the thing even if you don't want to do it. He did not trust you with this task because you guarantee him a victory; he trusts you with this task because he believes you will give everything you have to the effort. It is the heart, Merit, not the sword, that rules the day. Remember that, and good luck."

With that, he walked out of the training room again, leaving me dumbfounded in the middle of the room, the katana still in my hand.

Maybe Malik would hold Cadogan House for years to come; maybe he would hold it only for days more. Either way, there was little doubt he was a Master among men.

When our hour was up, we gathered together again in the Ops Room to report our progress, the advance team on the phone.

Jeff went first.

It turned out the requirements for consecrated ground weren't as specific as you'd think. We didn't necessarily need a church or graveyard. Although both would have been consecrated or blessed, all sorts of religions blessed all sorts of places. Community gardens were blessed by neighborhood pastors; parks with strong magnetic currents were blessed by those who believed in the power of that kind of thing.

We needed a nice, clear area for Seth to create the sigil and call Dominic. We wanted to be close enough to the House that we could retreat, if necessary, but not so close that we risked anyone who might be living or working around us.

Gabriel had recommended a spot. "Proskauer Park," Jeff said, and we all looked down at the map he'd transmitted. "It's about one mile from the House."

"That looks like it's in the middle of a neighborhood," Ethan said.

"It was going to be, until the developers lost funding. Now it's empty lots and empty buildings."

"If they didn't finish the subdivision, how does a future park do us any good?" Luc asked.

"They didn't finish the *houses*," Jeff said. "But they finished the park. They decided the best way to sell the lots was to create the park first. They had a priest bless it. They were pretty optimistic they'd sell the lots quickly. Fortunately for us, they didn't, and the park is sitting there, all blessed and whatnot, but completely empty."

"Good find," Ethan said.

"Yeah," Jeff agreed. "It's pretty awesome. Like finding the Higgs boson."

Silence.

"Aw, no physics fans here? Learn things you must," Jeff said in his best Yoda voice.

I rolled my eyes. "So we have a place," I said. "What's next?"

"Goods," Seth said, putting a canvas tote bag on the table.

"Helen was very helpful in gathering the materials," Paige said. "There are a few extras she's looking for now, although it might take a little more time to find them."

"Which we don't have a lot of," Ethan said. "Mallory?"

"Gabriel gave me permission," she said, "as did Baumgartner. Not that he had a lot of choice."

"Oh?" Ethan asked.

"Gabriel made it clear the problem was ours to solve. And if we didn't solve it, Gabriel would solve it for us. In a much messier fashion."

Ethan grinned slyly. That was the kind of bravado he appreciated.

"Do you know what to do?" Catcher asked.

"Yes. I've finagled a bit of the familiar spell and tweaked the recipe. This will be a much less minor intrusion. I also wrote down some counterspells for Catcher, just in case something goes wrong. Which it won't. But I only have a ten-minute window. That's how much time Gabriel's giving me to use magic again."

"Is that enough?" Catcher asked.

"It will be enough," Mallory said. "I will make it enough."

Ethan looked at me. "Are you ready?"

"As I will ever be." I looked at Seth. "Does he have any particular weaknesses? Things I can exploit?"

"His wings are vulnerable. They're sensitive to pain, and they're a major source of his balance. But an injury there will likely make him even testier, and possibly harder to predict. Otherwise, his anatomy is similar to yours."

I nodded, *katas* running through my head, when the door burst open. Malik rushed in.

Ethan stood up. "What's wrong?"

"The radio is reporting that Dominic is terrorizing a building on the South Side. He's set it on fire, and there are still people inside. Cops and fire squads are on their way, but they won't be able to do much against him."

I stood up, too, my heart pounding. "Why that building?"

"It's a way station for crack in the area."

"He's playing avenger again," Ethan said.

"Avenger without conscience," Seth said. "And if he thinks the responders are hindering his progress, he'll cut them down, too."

"How do they know it's Dominic?" I wondered.

"I am quoting here: 'He has giant bat wings.'"

"That does narrow it down." I looked at Ethan. "There's no time for practice. If we can move quickly enough, we can get him away from the building and let the CPD calm things down."

He nodded his agreement. "Luc, assemble the guards and have them circle the House. If this goes bad, I don't want it rebounding back on Cadogan. Malik, you're in charge, although I suppose that doesn't really need to be said since you are still Master."

Malik and Luc nodded.

"We don't have all the supplies we need," Paige interjected, "not enough to guarantee accuracy."

"We don't have the luxury of a guarantee," Ethan said. "Figure out a way to make do with what you have."

She looked up at Seth, who nodded. "We'll make it work. Summon, nullify, eradicate. That's our plan."

But when did such plans ever go smoothly?

We got dressed quietly. I pulled on my entire suit of leather—pants, bandeau top, jacket. It would help a bit against the night's chill, but more important, it would also protect me against errant sword slices better than jeans or cotton could.

I pulled my hair into a ponytail and made sure the bit of worry wood was still in my pocket. It might not be necessary, but it certainly wouldn't hurt.

I touched my fingers to the Cadogan medal at my neck and took a moment of silence to remind myself why we were doing this, and the things Malik had said. That I only had to try my best.

We met downstairs, Ethan and I both quiet, greeting each other with a nod and a check to ensure the other had the right equipment. Clothing. Swords. And just in case, medals.

"You're ready?"

I nodded, incapable of speech. Too nervous for words.

"Let's go."

We walked past the ballot box, and outside to the portico. The House's front yard was full of fairies—all black clad, with the same severe features and long, dark hair.

One fairy stepped forward; I put a hand on the hilt of my sword just in case.

"There is no need for that, vampire," he said, looking between me and Ethan. "We are not here for battle."

"Respectfully," Ethan said, "why are you here?"

"Tonight, you battle the one who rejected her?"

I nodded.

The fairy looked me over. Evaluating. "You will beat him?"

"I will do my best," I promised.

The fairy nodded. "So it shall be. Tonight, if you will have us, we will guard your home. You help to rid this city of a pestilence; we help protect you and yours against any who would seek to cause harm in your absence." He scowled. "Such acts are not honorable, but humans so rarely are."

Ethan seemed dumbfounded by the offer. We usually had to pay the fairies to guard the House while we slept. And yet, here they were, offering to defend us gratuitously? The city was changing, but maybe not for the worse. Even if humans gathered to revile us, perhaps the supernaturals might find new friendships.

Ethan dropped his head. "We acknowledge your offer and are honored by it."

"It is done," the fairy said, then stepped back into line with his colleagues. Half of them marched outside the gate. The other half dispersed inside the fence, a fairy every few feet, creating a shield against whomever—or whatever—might seek to injure the House while we were gone.

I drove Ethan, Seth, and Paige to the park. Catcher arranged to meet us there with Mallory and Jeff.

My grandfather—at my demand—stayed home to keep an ear on the scanner and coordinate what he could with the CPD.

Along the way, Ethan told Malik of the fairies' offer. A good idea, lest Malik should suddenly think the House was under attack by a completely new enemy. The ride was otherwise silent. I was nervous, my hands gripping the steering wheel like the car might suddenly dive off the road if I didn't.

Of course, with Dominic on the loose, I suppose stranger things had happened.

Jeff's description of the neighborhood had been right on. It looked not unlike other run-down areas in Chicago. Empty lots, strewn with trash. Boarded buildings. There were few signs of life. FOR SALE markers offering the development's lots appeared at the edges of the street, and abandoned equipment stood near unfinished concrete foundations.

And just as Jeff had found, a metal arch announced that Proskauer Park was open for play. Tonight, it simply looked abandoned. Brightly colored equipment sat empty. Swings, their chains tangled together, creaked ominously in the dark. The cherry red paint on picnic tables that had probably never held lunches was beginning to peel. A carved wooden sign that held the park's rules seemed pointedly irrelevant with no children to mind them.

"Is it just me," Paige asked, "or is this place creepy?"

"It's not just you," Seth said.

Car doors opened and closed. Catcher, Jeff, and Mallory walked toward us.

"There's an overgrown baseball diamond over there," Jeff said. "Good spot. Empty, flat ground."

Ethan nodded. "Then let's get this started and done."

We moved to the diamond at a quick jog. Catcher flipped on the lights at a pole on the edge of the field.

As they began to glow, Seth, Paige, and Jeff walked into center field and wasted no time preparing the sigil. Seth pulled a bottle of black granules from the pocket of his cassock. The bottle was clear, and the contents looked like ground charcoal.

"What is that?" I asked.

He uncapped the top and walked in a straight line, sprinkling the powder on the ground as he moved. "They call it witch's flame."

Paige leaned toward me. "They call it that, but it's actually household cleaners in granular form. Margot helped me mix it."

"That woman is a wonder with a spoon," I said.

Apparently satisfied with the line he'd drawn, Seth stopped, turned thirty degrees, and started walking and pouring again, then joined the first two lines with a third, making a triangle, ten feet across at the base.

Seth stepped outside the triangle. "Witch's flame combusts, creates a nice little long-lasting flame that won't burn the grass below it. It will give us a little time to work."

He looked at all of us. "Dominic's sigil contains four symbols. This was the first. When I finish drawing the next two, I will stop and give you a warning. When the last sigil is drawn, I'll formally call him, and Dominic should appear almost instantaneously. You'll want to be ready to go."

I nodded. "Thank you, Seth."

He nodded, then began to draw.

Ethan slid an arm around my waist. "You know what to do?"

"Yes. As much as anyone does."

"You'll be careful?"

I smiled a little. "Would you allow otherwise?"

"No."

I couldn't help it. The conviction in those two simple letters made me laugh aloud.

Ethan leaned in, his lips at my ear. "Unstoppable force," he said. "Immovable object. Choose the one you want to be, and do it. You are a vampire of great power, Merit. Prove it to us, to the city of Chicago, to the Houses. Prove it now."

I swallowed down fear and let the rush of adrenaline fill me with something closer to courage. Not quite bravery, but something that would suffice.

I looked back at him with silvered eyes.

"Well," he said, a bit amused. "That was even more effective than I thought it would be."

I humphed, and followed his glance to Mallory and Catcher, who stood chatting quietly a few feet away.

"You can do your part, as well," I said.

"I know I can. It's her I wonder about."

I looked back at Ethan. "She's asked for a chance to redeem herself. She only gets one. If this goes bad, if there's any threat to you at all, I will take her out."

Neither the words nor the sentiment scared me. I'd given Mallory chances she hadn't earned; Ethan had earned chances to spare.

"God willing that it won't come to that," he muttered.

"But be prepared if it does," I said. "That's a lesson I learned from a certain Master vampire."

Their conversation apparently done, Mallory and Catcher walked toward us. Her hands were balled into fists, and I wondered if they were shaking.

"Are you ready?"

Ethan nodded warily. "As ready as I'll ever be to turn control over my body to someone else."

"It will only last a few minutes," Mallory said. "And then he'll be Merit's problem."

"How does this work?"

"I'll establish a full connection with you. Once he appears in the sigil, you only need to touch him. It doesn't matter where. Hand. Shoulder. Wing."

"How long do I have to maintain my grip?"

"Until you feel the magic recede. You'll know it when you feel it. It shouldn't take more than a few seconds."

"He's probably going to realize what's happening during those few seconds," I pointed out.

"You have your sword," Catcher said. "I have magic. Our job is to distract him. Ethan's job is to hang on."

"And, hey," Mallory said, with a little too much cheerfulness. "There is an upside to this."

"What's that?" Ethan asked.

"I'm going to pull Dominic's magic through you, and with it, my own connection. You should come out the other side with no connection to me at all."

I squeezed Ethan's hand and hoped to God she was right.

"As long as you can stay out of Dominic's grasp while we're triggering the spell, you'll be fine."

Ethan nodded.

I walked a few feet away, unsheathed my sword, and tossed the scabbard away. The steel rang like a clear bell through the darkness as it freed the scabbard, and I gripped my hands around the ray skin and felt it bite comfortably into my skin. I held the sword; it held me.

"I'm ready for the last sigil," Seth announced.

I looked at Ethan and smiled a little.

"I love you," he mouthed.

It was the first time he'd spoken those words to me, and I wished I had time to scream out my excitement and share the news with my girlfriends. But this was neither the time nor the place, so I gave him the only response I could.

"I love you, too," I mouthed back.

"And I'm nauseous," Catcher grumbled. "Let's get on with this. I am seriously in need of a beer and a Lifetime movie."

"Drinks on me if we survive this," I said, then winked at Ethan, blew out a breath, and let my eyes silver again.

Catcher, Jeff, and Paige backed away from the circle. I took point in front of it, body bladed, sword at the ready. Ethan and Mallory stood at my right.

"I'm starting now," she said, then extended a hand toward him.

Ethan clutched his head, then screamed out and went down to his knees.

"Ethan!"

"Hold your position, Merit!" Seth called out. "Do not move!"

"What did you do?" I screamed at her.

Eyes wide, she shook her head. "Nothing. I'm just trying to get it to work. I can stop."

Weakly, Ethan put his weight on one foot, then the other, and struggled to his feet. "Do not stop. This ends tonight. Now. *Finish it.*"

Mallory looked, in a panic, between me and Ethan. "But I—"

"Finish it!" he demanded.

She didn't stop to think about it. With the kind of determination I'd seen on her face before only when she was trying to hurt me and mine, she closed her eyes and chanted something to herself. Her body began to shake, and the ground began to rumble beneath us.

"Jesus," Jeff said, arms out to keep his balance.

Sweat popped across Ethan's forehead, even in the chill. His teeth were gritted together against the pain, but he wouldn't let her stop. "We are nearly there; I can feel it. Keep going, Mallory."

Her lips curled wickedly. "As if you could stop me."

"Oh, crap," Paige muttered, no doubt seeing the same thing in her eyes that I did.

The enjoyment of this bit of dark magic.

"Mallory, hold it together!" I called out, nearly yelling over the suddenly rising wind. A light rain began to fall, clouds suddenly swirling overhead.

The four elements reacting to this disturbance in the balance between good and evil.

"Almost there," Ethan said.

"The sigil is nearly drawn," Seth called out.

I regripped my fingers around the sword.

Mallory wet her lips, her nails cutting into her palm, trails of blood beginning to trickle down her forearm.

"One bit left," Seth warned. "Finishing it . . . now!"

CHAPTER TWENTY-THREE

SOLDIERS WISELY LED

The sigil burst into blue flames, pushing all of us backward except Ethan and Mallory, who maintained their positions at the edge of it.

Jeff and Paige hit the ground a few feet away. Falls like that were going to take time to recover from.

"Mallory!" Catcher called out. "Stay strong!"

If she heard him, she didn't react. Mallory still looked oblivious to everything but the connection between her and Ethan . . . and the pain it was putting her through. She hit her knees, too, tears streaming down her face as she held open the connection.

With the sigil alight, Seth looked at me. I nodded, and it began.

"Dominic!" he called out. "I will and summon you to appear!"

The sigil brightened, the flame rising, but no angel appeared in the middle of it.

"Seth?"

"Low-grade materials," he said. "We had to make do. We're trying."

I blinked rain from my eyes, my breath steaming in the chill.

"Try harder! Mallory can't keep this up much longer!" She was already, I figured, seconds away from writhing on the ground and taking Ethan back to dark magic town with her.

Seth pulled off his shirt, flexed, and unhinged his wings. They released into the night, sending that sugar cookie smell through the park. My stomach picked the wrong time to grumble.

"Dominic! I will and summon you to appear! Bear witness to my command!"

The sigil flashed and flickered again, and then completely extinguished.

"Is it the rain?" Jeff called out from the other side of the sigil. "Do we have to start over?"

For a moment, there was silence. As if fearful of what we'd wrought, the earth trembled beneath us.

And then, suddenly, the earth inside the smoking circle burst open, and Dominic shot through the air, wings extended.

He roared with impressive gusto, then locked eyes with Seth and flapped his wings back to earth again, stalking toward him with obviously malicious intent.

"You dare call me? You, who cower behind the words and deeds of humans?"

With what little strength he had, Ethan reached out to grab him, but Dominic stepped beyond the bounds of the sigil and out of Ethan's grasp.

Seth caught the miss and rotated around, luring Dominic back toward the sigil and Ethan.

"Unlike you, I have been working, dear brother. Trying to rid the world of the pestilence you and yours seem so eager to forget."

Seth's lip curled. "Humans are not a pestilence on the world. Protecting them is our sole obligation. Our sole responsibility."

"They are a plague!" Dominic leapt toward Seth, who maneuvered away from him but didn't manage to get him any closer to Ethan.

Who had said this part was going to be easy? Just grab the monster, she'd said, and pull away his power. I muttered a curse. And tried my own tactic. If Seth couldn't lure him closer, maybe I could.

"Dominic!" I called out, spinning the sword in my hand, hoping a distraction might be enough. "Fight like a man!"

"I am *more* than man." But he was too preoccupied with Seth to bother with me. He pushed Seth like a school bully and, when Seth jumped into the air, followed suit, his wings flapping slowly behind him.

"Every being with power has its purpose," Dominic said. "I have served mine, and I was punished regardless. My wings bear witness to that."

His voice was exactly like and unlike Seth's. The timbre was the same, but the cant of the words was different. Seth spoke plainly; Dominic pronounced.

"You weren't punished," Seth said. "You did dark things and your body changed as a result of it."

They wrestled in the air, the twins of light and darkness, just as in the picture the librarian had showed me. It occurred to me that I was seeing a battle that was primeval, fundamental in nature. Creatures of the beginning of the human world, fighting over whether humans should be allowed to rule themselves.

"Catcher!" I called out. "Throw some magic!"

"I might hit Seth!" he called back. I guess, given what we were battling against, I had to appreciate his concern for the collateral victims of his magic.

They pushed each other away, separating midair before battling again. "I made decisions no one else would make!"

"You destroyed people and cities."

"They deserved it."

"It wasn't your call to make!" Seth raised his voice, his words booming across the park. I expected CPD patrol cars and picture-snapping residents any minute, so I acted.

I got a running start, held my sword upright, and leapt into the air toward the flying dervishes. The edge of my blade caught the webbing of Dominic's left wing. He screamed out his pain and the wing flapped backward with enough force to propel me through the air, just as he'd done with Jonah.

I hit the ground with a dull thud that pushed the air from my lungs.

The rain had soaked the ground and made the playground muddy, washing away the remnants of the sigil. But Ethan and Mallory waited, magic at the ready, both of them all but humming with the energy of it.

Seth and Dominic rolled through the mud, which put the top of Dominic's wing within a hand's length of Ethan.

"Ethan, Mallory, now!" I yelled out.

Ethan grabbed the edge of Dominic's wing. It took a second, and then Mallory screamed out as the connection burst open between them. There was no pleasure in her scream.

Dominic roared out again, flipping his wing in an effort to dislodge Ethan. He put his palms together, and with a crackle of light, the giant broadsword appeared in his hands. He swiped at Ethan, but Ethan, helped by his vampire strength, dodged the blade and wouldn't let go, and Mallory wouldn't break the connection between them.

"Nearly there," Mallory said, pain in her expression.

Dominic arched back, roaring again like an injured lion. Catcher didn't miss this opportunity. He wound up two bright blue orbs and tossed them in Dominic's direction.

They exploded against his chest in a burst of blue sparks. Dominic fell back, hitting the ground with a thud.

But so did Ethan and Mallory.

The dark magic had stopped, and so did the rain.

I knew any reprieve would be temporary. Body aching, I pulled myself off the ground and limped toward them again.

"Mallory! Ethan!"

Ethan's grip was still on Dominic, but the magic seemed to have knocked him out, too. Catcher dragged Mallory away, her palms red and chafed from the magic she'd pulled out of Dominic. I did the same with Ethan, ignoring the bleeding gash on his arm and the intoxicating scent of blood.

"Watch him!" I demanded of Seth, but Dominic was up and roaring again before I could even pull my sword. Seth took point this time.

I patted Ethan's face. "Ethan! Wake up."

He suddenly sat up, coughing and sputtering for breath as if Mallory had sucked out the rest of his oxygen. "I'm okay. I'm fine."

Tears bloomed at my lashes. "Thank God. Did it work?"

"I think so. I felt so much magic. If he's not cleaned out, he has a hella large tank."

I couldn't help the sarcasm. "Who says 'hella large'?"

But Ethan's focus was better than mine. "Sentinel," he weakly said, pointing back to the fray.

Dominic had Seth pinned in the mud and was whaling, older brother–style, on his twin. I made it to my feet again, my sword now filthy with mud, and wiped it on my leather pants.

I was just about to launch my attack, hopeful Ethan was right about Dominic, when I caught a new trouble blooming.

Mallory was standing again, her hair spread out around her like a static halo, and a gleam of dark magic in her eyes.

I sighed, my stomach curling with the fear that she'd never be able to come back from her addiction. Not if a little demonic filtering took her out.

But she looked at me, and I saw the fight in her eyes.

She wasn't succumbing to the dark magic. She was just trying to hold it in.

"Paige, Catcher. Help her. She needs to let the magic go!"

When they rushed to her aid, I turned back to Dominic and Seth. I blew out a breath.

"Now or never," I muttered, and called out his name. "Dominic!" I twirled the sword in my hand once, then twice.

Dominic glanced back at me, grinned maniacally, then stood up. Seth was still in the mud, and he didn't move. There were bleeding gaps in his wings, and a deep red gash across his shoulder.

If this was going to happen, I was going to be the one to do it.

"Hello, Ballerina."

"You don't have the right to call me that." I backed up a bit, moving the fight away from everyone else.

"Don't I?" he said. "I was there for all of it. I saw everything that he did, all of your interactions."

One of his wings shot out, and I rolled across the ground to get away, popping up muddy and bruised again.

"You weren't invited," I pointed out. "You were a spy." His other wing whipped out. The claws at the edge of this wing grazed the ground, and I jumped into the air to avoid it, popping down in a crouch on his other side.

"You're all flair," he said, turning to face me.

He thrust out with his sword, and I silently apologized to my katana for any nicks I was about to create, and met his thrust directly.

The jolt sent a wave of pain down my arm.

Dominic laughed and thrust down. I parried, pushing his sword to the side, and used the momentum to swing myself into a butterfly kick. I managed a punch to his kidney, but his wing dipped forward. I still caught the tip of a claw, and it ripped a gash in my calf. The pain was sudden and intense and carried a nauseating sharpness that had to be magical in nature.

I stumbled away, regripping my sword, and turned to face him.

"Hurts, doesn't it?"

Water dripped into my eyes from my ratty, muddy bangs. "It doesn't feel like purring kittens," I admitted. The pain be damned, I ran forward, slicing down with a shot that put a four-inch gash in the top of his left wing.

He screamed out and tossed me away like a doll. I landed on my back again in a puddle of cold water, promising myself a hot bath if I'd only get back on my feet.

One hand behind me, I arced my body and popped up again.

His wing gashed and bleeding, and obviously in pain, Dominic limped toward me. "You don't know when to quit, do you?"

"I'd say the same for you." I regripped my sword.

He was tired and injured, and his next shot was sloppy but still powerful. A forward thrust I had to drop down under. I rolled across the ground, clenching my sword to keep from losing my muddy grip, and kicked his leg out from under him, knocking him onto the ground. I scrambled away, but he caught the hem of my pants.

"We weren't done," he said, dragging me backward again.

"We were totally done," I assured him, kicking his brick-solid chest until he reflexively let me go again.

Now breathing a little harder than I did in my practice sessions, go figure, I made it to my feet again. I could keep fighting for a while, but he was going to nail me in terms of brute strength and endurance. I would lose a war of attrition against him.

I remembered what I'd said earlier. *Change the odds.*

While Dominic got to his feet again, I looked around . . . and spied something useful.

Sword in front of me, I faked a limp and hobbled backward.

Dominic, the gleam of success in his eyes, stalked me like prey. I called on my musical theater background and made some pretty convincing noises of pain.

He grinned devilishly, then lifted his sword, and, when I faked a backward stumble, ran forward into the tangled skein of swing-set chains.

That was my chance.

Dominic may have been back in human form, but I wasn't. I still had vampire speed and strength, and I was sure as shit going to use them now. I dropped my sword.

With speed so quick my motion was blurred, I ripped the chains from their moorings. The links were still solid, but as I'd hoped, their connections to the swing set had rusted through. I ran around Dominic, and as he tried to stumble back to his feet, his wings caught in the side supports. I wove the chains around him until he was good and caught and roaring with the indignity of it all.

He was really big on the roaring.

I picked up my sword and stood in front of him, arms raised, sword pointed down, ready to finish this.

"Then do it," Dominic said. "Suffer your witch to live, and put an end to me."

"I don't take joy in it," I told him. "That's the difference between us."

"Are we so different, Sentinel? You kill because you believe it's right. As do I."

"I kill to save the lives of others. Unlike you, I have no illusions it makes me a better person." My hands trembling, I prepared to strike.

"No!"

I froze and glanced back. Seth limped toward us, still holding his wounded arm, one wing dragging on the ground pathetically. "Stop, Merit. This is not your task."

Wincing, he held out his good hand. "I'll do it," Seth said. "I will end his life."

I looked back at him. "You've never killed before. Are you sure you want to start now?"

"He was part of me for centuries. He is, for better or worse, my brother. His blood shouldn't be on your hands, but mine."

I wasn't sure how to argue with him. I wasn't keen on the idea of killing a man already down, but there was no question he'd keep killing if the opportunity arose. On the other hand, Seth was already racked by grief, and I didn't want to add to his burdens.

"It would bring me peace," he said, "to know that you weren't forced to take another life at my expense. It would help me atone for the trouble I have already caused. For the pain. For the suffering."

There was no doubting the earnestness in his gaze. He was a grown man—well grown, as it turned out—so I handed over the sword.

He nodded, and as he closed his fingers around the handle and his eyes slipped shut, I'd have sworn he shivered. "The blade was tempered with *your* blood."

I nodded.

Seth bowed, his shoulders dipping forward over the gleaming steel of the blade. "I am honored, Merit of Cadogan, to use a blade you have so honorably prepared."

I blinked back surprise and, when Ethan slipped his fingers into mine, squeezed hard.

Seth walked to Dominic, his wings still pinned, and stood over him. "Messenger, you have failed in your mission, and you have darkened the name of justice. You refused to leave this world when your name was called into the book. Tonight, justice shall be done."

Dominic swallowed hard, but then he nodded. "Justice shall be done."

Seth lifted the katana, held it horizontal to the ground. And with a single slice, ripped through Dominic's chest. Dominic and Seth screamed simultaneously, and light burst forth from the wound Seth had made, angry and red, rays of it shooting across the night like furious lasers. The burst of light opened farther, and then Dominic's entire body was engulfed in light. The light pulsed, then again, then faster and faster like a beating heart until it exploded into a trillion red sparks.

They rushed across the sky, fading as they moved, and then the light was extinguished, and Dominic was gone. The only trace of him was the bit of blood that still stained my sword.

Without a word, Seth wiped the sword upon his pants, then placed it carefully on the ground. "It is done."

It became D-Day all over again. The only things missing were soldiers and nurses locked in exuberant embraces. Instead, we had vampires and sorcerers.

Jeff and Paige hugged each other. On their knees in the mud, Catcher hugged Mallory to him, his arms around her. "It's over. It's over."

I looked up at Ethan, whose eyes were closed in relief.

"She's gone," he said. "Oh, thank God, she's gone."

Thank God, I thought, a silent prayer to whoever might be listening, and wrapped my arms around him. He embraced me.

"She's gone," he said again.

"So I heard. Congratulations." *For both of us,* I thought.

"You were amazing. A sight to behold. And the swing set was inspired."

"I had a good teacher."

"And don't you forget it," he whispered, pressing a kiss to my temple.

"She meant me," Catcher said. "Vampires are so arrogant."

I couldn't help but smile. Maybe things could finally get back to normal around here. Whatever that might be.

CHAPTER TWENTY-FOUR

EXODUS

While the ballot box was being filled below us, we cele-
brated the end of drama with SuperDawgs, fries, and
the chocolate-covered cherries Margot brought me as
congratulations for felling an evil foe.

Ethan growled happily as I sat across his lower back, rubbing
his shoulders. He'd decided he needed a shoulder rub after dinner
to erase away all that he'd been through. Since "all he'd been
through" had been my idea, I didn't think I had much room to
argue.

I kneaded his shoulders carefully, then trailed my fingertips
down his back and up his spine again.

Oh, Merit.

I froze. "You just called my name."

"No, I didn't. You're hearing things."

"No, not aloud. In your mind. I heard you."

I crawled off him, and he flipped over again.

You can really hear me?

I smiled at him. *I can indeed.* "Maybe you didn't lose the ability to speak silently. Maybe Mallory's magic just interfered with the frequency or something."

Ethan's smile blossomed. It clearly meant a lot to him to be able to converse with his Novitiates—and more that the power he'd had for so long hadn't been lost to him forever. *I believe this calls for a celebration.*

We have chocolate-covered cherries, I reminded him.

I was thinking something a bit more physically taxing, he silently intoned, and then he pounced, his fingers trailing the sensitive skin at my hips until I was wiggling and squealing in a really un-flattering way.

I *hated* being tickled.

But I'd power through it.

I dreamt of Ethan, but the dream wasn't a harbinger of grief . . . it was ecstasy. He found me on a boardwalk beside a vast blue sea and we danced until the sun lifted above the sky, my skirt of liquid black silk flowing around us. Boats with huge white sails bobbed upon the water, dancing around our island retreat as we spun to the melody of a song I couldn't hear.

I woke to the sound of a light tap on the door with a smile on my face. Ethan was still asleep; the automatic shutters still covered the windows.

I unlocked the door and peeked into the hallway. It was quiet and empty, but a silver tray sat on the floor just outside the door.

"What is this?" I quietly asked, holding the door open with a foot while I picked up the tray and brought it inside. I sat it down on a table near the door and looked it over. Two pastries. A cup of coffee and a cup of hot chocolate, both still steaming. Orange juice, cutlery, and a tidily folded newspaper.

"This, I could get used to," I murmured, picking up the paper.

"Talking to yourself, Sentinel?"

"Just ruminating on how much Margot spoils you. Pastries and coffee, delivered nightly?"

"A man cannot live on meat and potatoes alone. What's in the news?"

I glanced down at the paper. "Sex. Violence. Rock and roll."

Ethan was already out of bed and on his way over. That he was half-naked—clad only in thigh-hugging boxer briefs—was even more distracting than you'd expect.

He grabbed a pastry and took a bite.

"I'm going to take a shower," he said, then turned and walked away. I appreciated the view and also got a pretty good look at the dark tattoo that marked the back of his calf.

"Hey, what does the tattoo mean?"

"I don't know what you're talking about," he said, then stepped into the bathroom and closed the door behind him.

It was worth a shot.

It wasn't until I'd dressed and rebelted my katana that I saw the small burgundy box that sat on the bed. It was bound in a white silken ribbon and topped with a perfect bow.

"Ethan Sullivan," I murmured. "What did you do?" My heart thudded in anticipation.

I picked it up and shook it gently. Something moved around in there, and I didn't hear any obvious ticking. I pulled off the ribbon and dropped it on the bed, then lifted off the top.

A small white card was tucked inside, bearing only the letter *E*. I lifted the card.

Beneath it, on a small pillow of white satin, was a silver key.

I didn't need to bother asking what door it opened; its small white tag was inscribed: MASTER'S SUITE.

Ethan had given me a key to his apartments.

For a moment, I stared down at the unfamiliar weight in my hand and considered the access it offered me. It wasn't the key to a consort suite, where Ethan could stash me as a lover. It was a key to his room—his *home*—allowing me access whenever I liked, whenever I chose.

However awkwardly we might have started, and however many stops and starts we might have had along the way, there was really no denying it now: Ethan Sullivan and I were in a relationship.

My, how things had changed.

He stood in the House foyer, back in his cassock again. But while the clothing was the same, there was something different about him. Something I hadn't seen in a long time. He looked peaceful. And maybe even hopeful.

"You're leaving?" Ethan asked.

"I think it's best. They believe I committed the murders here, and now that Dominic is gone, there's no evidence it wasn't me. Besides that, there's work I need to do. Apologies I need to make."

"Good deeds?" Ethan thoughtfully asked, but Seth's expression remained serious.

"Ensuring justice is done, that those who deserve blessings receive what they ought. We have both been fortunate, you and I. We've had multiple lifetimes to make decisions, face consequences, right our wrongs. I'll go forward with that motive in mind, and I will try to rebalance the lives I disrupted. And speaking of which . . . ," he said, then pulled a glint of gold from his pocket.

He extended his hand. My gold Cadogan medal dangled from his fingers. "I believe this is yours."

I took it from him and clenched it in my fist. "Thank you. How did you get it back?"

"He wore it in the battle last night, and I snatched it. I thought you'd prefer to have it. I'm sorry it was taken from you in the first place, and glad I can return it."

Ethan stretched out a hand. "Good luck on your journey. If you need shelter, you'll find a home in this House."

Seth took Ethan's hand with obvious gratitude. "Your friendship is appreciated." He smiled at me. "And yours, Ballerina."

I smiled at him. "Good luck. And Godspeed."

"To you as well, Merit. Ethan, I hope our paths will cross again, but under more favorable circumstances." With that, he disappeared down the sidewalk, through the gate, and into the night.

Ethan looked at me. "Are you ready?"

"As I'll ever be. Are you?"

"As you said. These are exciting and terrifying times."

We walked upstairs to the ballroom. It was full of vampires again, the atmosphere as tense as it had been when Darius had taken the stage. But this tension was different. There was less fear in the anticipation. The vampires shuffled nervously, a low buzz of excitement in the room. Would we defect from the GP, or would we wait for the GP to once and finally deem us unworthy?

Malik and Ethan made their way to the stage, the ballot box on the platform between them. I searched their expressions for any hint of what was to come but found nothing there.

Ethan raised his hands, and the crowd went silent. "Your ballots have been cast," he said, "both by you and by your brethren outside the House. The final vote was close. Only eighteen votes separated the sides. It is clear you are divided on this issue, on the future of this House. I take that as an indication of your thoughtfulness, your attention to the weight of this decision."

The crowd murmured nervously.

"By a majority vote of this House," Ethan said, "its vampires have determined to defect from the Greenwich Presidium."

The vampires erupted into noise. Some cheers, some jeers, some tears. I stood still in the midst of the chaos and kept my eyes on Ethan's.

For a long moment I held his gaze. I thought about how far I'd come and where we might be going next. I thought about Ethan and the life he was intent on giving me, even if that life existed in the midst of a new kind of chaos. A new reality for Cadogan House and its vampires.

For now, with his emerald eyes locked on mine, where I was going didn't seem so scary.

Photo by Jeremy Dixon

Chloe Neill was born and raised in the South but now makes her home in the Midwest—just close enough to Cadogan House and St. Sophia's to keep an eye on things. When not transcribing Merit's and Lily's adventures, she bakes, works, and scours the Internet for good recipes and great graphic design. Chloe also maintains her sanity by spending time with her boys—her favorite landscape photographer (her husband) and their dogs, Baxter and Scout. (Both she and the photographer understand the dogs are in charge.)